THE IDENTITY FACTOR

JAMES HOUSTON TURNER

THE IDENTITY FACTOR

For information, address Comfort Publishing, 296 Church St. N., Concord, NC 28025. The views expressed in this book are not necessarily those of the publisher.

First U.S. printing

Book cover design
by Reed Karriker

Author photo by Bill Rich
www.therichimage.com

ISBN: 978-1-936695-52-2
Published by Comfort Publishing, LLC
www.comfortpublishing.com

Printed in the United States of America

For Alexandria Elizabeth Turner

and

Jacob Houston Turner

ACKNOWLEDGMENTS

Books are team projects and I am grateful to everyone who helped make this novel become a reality. Topping the list is the most talented and beautiful woman I have ever known: my wife, Wendy. You light up my life. Huge thanks also to Pamilla Tolen and the wonderful people at Comfort Publishing: Jason and Kristy Huddle; Reed Karriker, for working his cover art magic yet again; and marketing coordinator, Rob Hamilton, for doing what it takes to make a book tour happen. and to Kristin Overn, editor extraordinaire and screenwriting guru, with whom I spent one of the most arduous and exhilarating years writing the screenplay adaptation of this book. Mate, I will never forget the quicksand! Special thanks also go to Wally Mariani and Mandy Bluett of Qantas Airways. I would not be doing what I'm doing if it weren't for you. You've enabled me to write about some of those cities that never close down.; to my old friend and Country Music wizard, Garth Fundis; to the Broken Spoke and the Hula Hut restaurant in Austin, Texas; to Mick and George O'Rourke; to Jerry and Melanie Rhodeback, for helping me stay true to the heart of this story; to Pam Lewko, for opening your heart and home to us time and again; to promotional analyst Michael Ziviani; to Kay Scott Marone-Hansen, Dale Louise Odom, Rhonda Davis, Chris Attwood, and Chris Tafft, for years of friendship, encouragement, and faithful prayer support; to Rose Wilkinson, our superstar model; to Max Popenker, for technical assistance with various makes and models of weapons; to Mark and Judy Thomas, my embedded reporters in Cairo; to Ed Erwin, of the National Geophysical Data Center; to Joyce Irvine, for her eagle eye; a huge thanks to Charity Ellis, for a spectacular book launch at the University of Houston - Clear Lake. Mate, you are a true warrior! Special thanks to Los Angeles photographer and good friend, Bill Rich, for taking my author photo. Mate, you know how to work wonders! And to Walker Hanson, an awesome friend whose words I'll never forget: "You will never walk on water, Jim, if you don't get out of the boat."

For Alexandria Elizabeth Turner

and

Jacob Houston Turner

ACKNOWLEDGMENTS

Books are team projects and I am grateful to everyone who helped make this novel become a reality. Topping the list is the most talented and beautiful woman I have ever known: my wife, Wendy. You light up my life. Huge thanks also to Pamilla Tolen and the wonderful people at Comfort Publishing: Jason and Kristy Huddle; Reed Karriker, for working his cover art magic yet again; and marketing coordinator, Rob Hamilton, for doing what it takes to make a book tour happen. and to Kristin Overn, editor extraordinaire and screenwriting guru, with whom I spent one of the most arduous and exhilarating years writing the screenplay adaptation of this book. Mate, I will never forget the quicksand! Special thanks also go to Wally Mariani and Mandy Bluett of Qantas Airways. I would not be doing what I'm doing if it weren't for you. You've enabled me to write about some of those cities that never close down.; to my old friend and Country Music wizard, Garth Fundis; to the Broken Spoke and the Hula Hut restaurant in Austin, Texas; to Mick and George O'Rourke; to Jerry and Melanie Rhodeback, for helping me stay true to the heart of this story; to Pam Lewko, for opening your heart and home to us time and again; to promotional analyst Michael Ziviani; to Kay Scott Marone-Hansen, Dale Louise Odom, Rhonda Davis, Chris Attwood, and Chris Tafft, for years of friendship, encouragement, and faithful prayer support; to Rose Wilkinson, our superstar model; to Max Popenker, for technical assistance with various makes and models of weapons; to Mark and Judy Thomas, my embedded reporters in Cairo; to Ed Erwin, of the National Geophysical Data Center; to Joyce Irvine, for her eagle eye; a huge thanks to Charity Ellis, for a spectacular book launch at the University of Houston - Clear Lake. Mate, you are a true warrior! Special thanks to Los Angeles photographer and good friend, Bill Rich, for taking my author photo. Mate, you know how to work wonders! And to Walker Hanson, an awesome friend whose words I'll never forget: "You will never walk on water, Jim, if you don't get out of the boat."

PROLOGUE

Within twenty-four hours, Sir Edmund George Clayton would be dead, his murder but another in the dustbin of inconsequential memories, were it not for the legacy of his discovery.

The year was 1919, and for three days Clayton and his Bedouin porters had been searching the rugged slopes of *Gebel Shama'un*, a small mountain in the northern heart of the Sinai Peninsula. For centuries this sun-baked terrain had been gouged by wind and rain, its topsoil having long ago been stripped away. All that remained now were mountainous shoulders of rock protruding out of the desert like petrified bones.

The subject of these expeditions was Ishmael. The object: find where he lived.

From previous trips to the Sinai, Clayton regarded the local Bedouins to be unreliable and difficult. But strong backs and extra hands were what he needed and those belonging to the Bedouins were the only ones around.

However, a youngster named Mulazim showed such enthusiasm and ability that by the end of the second day Clayton had rewarded him with the title of First Officer. It was an appointment to which Mulazim proudly devoted himself to the degree of saluting Clayton each time instructions were given.

It was mid-morning of the fourth day when Clayton paused to lean against a boulder.

"What does Clayton hope to find?" Mulazim asked from a squatting position near his feet. Like most Bedouins, he wore a loose cotton garment – a *jellaba* – and wide leather belt into which was stuck a curved dagger.

Clayton glanced down at his young First Officer while soaking his handkerchief with water from his canteen.

"If my theory proves correct," he said, rubbing the wet cloth over his face, "this mountain may well provide the final piece of the puzzle about Ishmael."

A thoughtful wrinkle appeared on Mulazim's brow.

1

Clayton pushed himself away from the boulder. "Come, we have work to do."

The young Bedouin sprang to his feet. "You write now?"

Clayton chuckled at Mulazim's zeal. He knew the boy wanted to practice his English, which he did each time Clayton wrote in his journal. And because the journal described the wildlife, topography and geology of the mountain, it was like a storybook to Mulazim, who constantly asked questions about words he did not understand.

"Not now," Clayton replied. "It's time to get back on the camels. Go and gather the others."

Mulazim looked anxiously toward the others.

"What's wrong, lad?" asked Clayton.

"I hear others say it is too hot, you make them work too hard, not pay enough."

"A price was agreed for what was required."

"I think they want go back."

"I'll not have it! Tell them it's time to move on."

"Clayton must speak with them. They not listen to Mulazim."

With an annoyed huff, Clayton checked his pistol and approached the three Bedouins sitting together in a group on the ground. They, too, carried daggers and wore loose robes with wide leather belts.

"Is there a problem?" Clayton asked.

The three Bedouins looked up at him but said nothing.

"Then snap to it. We've work to do."

The Bedouins did not move.

"I said, we have work to do."

"We hear what Clayton say," the oldest of the three replied.

"Then what's the problem?"

The old Bedouin shrugged. "There is no wood to make fire on this mountain. And you said we are to get coffee."

"Not every time we stop! Blast it, man, you laid around the entire day drinking coffee while I made my initial survey. Let's go. You'll get coffee tonight back in camp."

"Work is harder than you tell us in Suez," the old one said in a whining, high-pitched voice. "Clayton must pay more money."

"If you want your wages *at all* you'll get to your bloody feet! I have the remainder of this mountain to investigate; and the sooner we resume, the sooner we'll finish, and the sooner you'll get your pay. Now *get up!*"

Climbing timidly to one knee, the old Bedouin put out his hand as if he were a beggar. "Clayton pay more?" With his other hand, he fidgeted with his moustache, his dark eyes greedy and anxious.

Clayton was reliant on their help and they knew it. If they ran off, it would set him back weeks. Yet he could not give into their extortionist demands without inviting repeated attempts in the future. Standing firm was imperative.

Along with a little incentive.

"You'll not get another *piastre* out of me and that's that," he said. "However, if we discover any unusual artifacts – and I mean *unusual* – I'll see to it that you're handsomely rewarded." He then hardened his expression for emphasis. "But not if you persist in challenging our agreement, my authority or the instructions I tell Mulazim to give you. Now, either you work under these conditions or the lot of you can clear out and I'll hire some men who will."

Clayton walked back to where he'd left his canteen and waited while the three Bedouins discussed the matter among themselves.

With a troubled expression, Mulazim looked up at Clayton. "What Clayton mean about mountain?" he asked.

"You mean about it being a missing piece of the puzzle?"

Mulazim nodded.

Clayton uncorked his canteen and took a drink of the tepid water. "How much do you know about Ishmael?" he asked.

"I know long ago Abraham send Ishmael away into desert. He and his mother, Hagar, wander until water skin empty, and Ishmael grow very weak. Twice Hagar run after water she see in distance. But it only desert playing tricks. Hagar cry to see Ishmael so weak, so she go away. She not want watch him die. But she look back and see him raise foot and bring down and hit earth. And water go *whoosh* from earth! They drink and were saved, and this well we call Zamzam. It in our holy city of Mecca!"

"You know a great deal," remarked Clayton with a nod of approval.

"Yes!" said Mulazim proudly. "I have learned much about our great father, Ishmael."

"Are you ready to learn more?" asked Clayton.

"Learn more? What does Clayton mean?"

"I'm not sure, Mulazim, but I'm hoping this mountain will tell us."

The young Bedouin stared at the Englishman. "I do not understand. What can mountain tell us?"

Before Clayton could answer, the three Bedouins approached.

"We accept because Clayton pay more," the old one said. "You pay us now."

"You conniving *jackals!*" Clayton shouted, throwing down his canteen and starting toward them. With one hand he pulled out his pistol.

The three Bedouins scurried away.

Clayton charged after them until they fell to their knees at the edge of a cliff, their hands up, begging for mercy.

"I've agreed to pay more *only* if we find any unusual evidence!" Clayton yelled. "Bedouin campfire sites do not qualify, nor do any rock carvings you may decide to create with your knives."

The cowering Bedouins nodded.

"Furthermore, I want you to spread out. No more dawdling along as a group, or dismounting to discuss every step before you take it. Am I *clear*?"

The Bedouins nodded again, their hands still raised for protection.

"All right, get going," Clayton said, shaking his head at the pitiful, almost comical sight. "Stay within sight of one another, and if you find anything, call out. I'll be there as soon as I can."

The Bedouins jumped up and ran to their camels.

After the group had departed, Clayton directed his camel along a ridge on the eastern face of the mountain. Hours passed, and the temperature climbed steadily. By midday, the heat was oppressive.

Clayton paused for a drink. To his right, the precipice dropped five hundred feet. Erosion had gouged the cliff face into deep gullies that eventually fed into the famous *Wadi el Arish,* or the Biblical "River of Egypt."

With the brim of his hat pulled low, Clayton cupped his hands and surveyed the faded horizon. Dry mountains stood in the distance, their hazy peaks a reminder of how desolate this wilderness now was. After a final swallow of water, he put the cork back in his canteen and goaded his camel.

The animal lurched toward the edge. Clayton yanked on the

reigns and kicked the animal in the shanks. The camel growled its protest and lumbered away from the cliff.

They soon reached the crest of a small rise. On the other side lay a shallow basin, and on the far side of that basin was what looked like a deteriorated section of an old wall.

Clayton surveyed the site, then climbed down off his camel, skidded his way into the basin and crossed to the other side. Most of the wall – if that's what it was – had long since collapsed, although clusters of stones were still standing.

This is definitely an old structure of some sort, he thought. *But what? Ishmael's house? A corral?*

Or was he so desperate to find evidence of Ishmael that he was losing objectivity? The stones could well be nothing more than an old windbreak for a family of local Bedouins.

His eye caught a glint of something black. He stared at it for a moment before kicking it with his boot. When it didn't budge, he knelt to inspect.

Brushing away the loose gravel, Clayton saw what looked to be a chunk of cut stone buried in the earth.

Cut stone out here? he wondered.

He brushed away more of the gravel.

It is cut stone! Diorite, perhaps? Or basalt?

He returned to his camel, removed his excavation kit from behind the saddle, and returned to the site, where he knelt and began scraping at the hardened earth. After a few minutes' work, he stood, unable to believe his eyes. Staring up at him was an exposed portion of a smooth black monument.

Clayton fired his pistol once into the air. He then grabbed his journal and made a sketch of the site. Taking a reading with his compass, he unfolded a map of the region and listed the coordinates in his journal before writing a brief geological description.

Mulazim and the others soon approached.

"Clayton has found something?" Mulazim asked, jumping off his camel.

"A rather spectacular something," said Clayton, brushing away more of the dirt.

Mulazim looked into the shallow hole.

"This stone, is it piece of puzzle?" he asked as the others gathered around.

"We'll know once I've dislodged it. Tell the others to set up camp."

The other three Bedouins were looking curiously over Clayton's shoulder when Mulazim issued the order. But instead of moving, they began pointing at the black stone and whispering excitedly. When Mulazim saw that his command was not being obeyed, he repeated it in a louder voice. Their response was a tirade of coarse gestures and insults.

Clayton turned to face the three men. "You heard him," he said.

"What has Clayton found?" the oldest of the three asked.

"I'll know once I've finished."

"It is important, yes?"

"That will be up to the experts."

"The black stone – it is worth money?"

Clayton could see where this line of questioning was headed.

"You needn't worry that I'll not reward you, despite the fact that it was I who made the discovery."

"But you say it is valuable?"

Clayton sighed impatiently. "Yes, it could be quite valuable. Which we'll never know so long as we stand here yapping. Go and set up the tents!"

Rubbing his chin thoughtfully, the old Bedouin motioned to the others.

"Wretched thieves," muttered Clayton, using his spade to chop carefully at the hardened earth surrounding the monument.

Nearly an hour later, Sir Edmund George Clayton stood back. The black monument had been freed from its tomb.

After making another sketch, Clayton and Mulazim carefully flipped the stone.

To Clayton's astonishment, he saw that it was covered with hundreds of proto-Sinaitic hieroglyphs, the numerous rows of small characters still legible because the stone had originally toppled face down, which in turn had been shielded from the abrasion of the elements.

Clayton brushed away the remaining clumps of dirt, then splashed water from his canteen across the surface and wiped it with a rag before making a series of charcoal rubbings in his journal. When finished, he began translating the text.

Within minutes, however, Clayton's excitement had turned to

shock when he found himself staring at an exact copy of the twelfth chapter of Genesis. Linguistically primitive, to be sure, but definitely a copy.

Except that this rendition, which was written on stone and in proto-Sinaitic, had to be some five hundred years older than Genesis.

Clayton was speechless.

"What is wrong?" asked Mulazim.

Clayton did not answer.

Mulazim asked again, but Clayton continued staring silently at the stone.

The chilly nighttime breezes were blowing when Clayton finally joined Mulazim in their tent. Wearing a troubled frown, Clayton sighed wearily and sat.

"Why is Clayton not pleased?" Mulazim asked, handing him a strip of dried meat.

The other Bedouins were in their own tent a short distance away, the occasional sound of their laughter punctuating the night.

"I'm terrified," Clayton replied, taking a bite.

"I not understand. Clayton has made an important discovery."

"Yes, Mulazim, I have. But what I've found is going to make a lot of people very unhappy. In fact, it could destroy the church."

"How can stone do such a thing?"

"Remember how I told you this mountain may reveal the final piece of the puzzle about Ishmael?"

Mulazim nodded.

"What I discovered is an Egyptian account of what Genesis says about Abraham, the father of both our religions."

"What words say?" asked Mulazim.

"They tell the same stories about Abraham that are found in Genesis. Which implies that Genesis was *not* written by Moses, but was copied from much older Egyptian records."

"Why this worry Clayton?"

"Because it could well mean that Abraham is nothing but an Egyptian legend," Clayton answered, his dejected eyes staring into the dim flame of a kerosene lantern. "So, tomorrow, I must transport off this mountain something I'd like to destroy."

"Destroy?"

"I won't, of course," he said, and with a sigh handed Mulazim his journal. "What I need you to do is leave before daybreak and take this to Suez. Make sure that it gets sent to England. The address is in the back."

"Why does Clayton not carry journal himself?"

"Because the monument must be tied carefully on the back of a camel, and progress will be slow. Plus – and I do not wish to dwell on this point – accidents can occur. So either the journal or the tablet must reach London. Separating the two is prudent."

Mulazim nodded. "I will do as Clayton asks. Still, why is Clayton frightened of words on black stone? You not even know who wrote them."

Clayton was about to repeat his explanation when the impact of Mulazim's statement hit him like a thunderbolt.

"My God, how could I have overlooked it?" he exclaimed, jumping to his feet.

"Overlooked what?"

"The colophon!" shouted Clayton, grabbing his journal and the lantern and racing out of the tent.

"What is colophon?" asked Mulazim.

But Clayton was gone.

With the tent now in darkness, there was little Mulazim could do but curl up beneath his blanket and go to sleep.

As instructed, he rose before dawn and found Clayton's journal on top of his canteen. Sticking it in his belt, he tiptoed out of the tent. Within minutes, he had climbed up onto his camel and was gone.

Having been awakened by Mulazim's departure, the old Bedouin roused the others.

"Quick, follow me!" he whispered. He led them silently toward Clayton's tent. They paused briefly to pick up heavy rocks they had placed there the night before.

Pulling back the flap, the three Bedouins crept in.

The old Bedouin heaved first. His large stone crushed the side of Clayton's skull as he slept peacefully on his side. Then came the next stone, then the third. Each rock made a dull crunch as it shattered bone.

The Bedouins dragged Clayton's body out of the tent and over to the cliff, where they rolled it over the edge. The body tumbled away with barely a sound.

Once it was daylight, the three Bedouins hoisted the black tablet onto a camel and lashed it securely with rope.

"We are rich," the old Bedouin said, leading his companions to the fire, where a long-handled pot of coffee was gently boiling.

"But the body?" asked one of the others. "Surely Clayton will be missed."

"And a search party sent to find him," added the other.

"By then, scavengers will have picked clean his bones," replied the old Bedouin, "with the sun then turning them into dust."

He picked up the copper pot and poured each of them some of the coffee.

"And Mulazim? What about him?" asked one of the others.

Raising the small cup to his lips, the old Bedouin tapped his dagger.

CHAPTER 1

"Kill the tower lights in sector one," commanded Jackson Teague, Deputy Director of Operations for the CIA.

"Yes, sir," a communications officer replied while Teague continued to scrutinize each of the fourteen television monitors in the mobile command center while the communications officer relayed the order into the filament microphone curving out of her headset. Seconds later, the order was carried out, and two halogen floodlights were extinguished over a section of pipes and hissing flow valves.

"Now, move sniper five into that pocket of shadow," instructed Teague, a forty-one year-old African American. His bald head and stern features reflected tension in the greenish glow from the screens.

"Yes, sir," responded the communications officer.

Camouflaged to look like a utility shed complete with oil drums and discarded forklift pallets, the command center was in fact a customized semi-trailer full of enough computers and communications equipment to coordinate a full-scale military invasion. But the command center had a different purpose tonight. Tonight it was the brains of an operation designed to capture or kill the terrorist, Abu Nazer, when he attempted to assassinate Rolf Gerhard, CEO of the San Gabriel Industrial Fuel Depot.

With his snipers in place, Teague had just walked to the front of the trailer for a sandwich when his cell phone rang. He checked the caller ID and lifted the phone to his ear.

"You there yet?" he asked.

"Almost…I think," analyst Zoe Gustaves answered from an SUV eighty miles to the south. With spiked raven hair, half a dozen earrings and three tattoos, Zoe enjoyed being anachronistic to her starched and pleated mother, Congresswoman Diane Gustaves. Piercings, tattoos, and resentments aside, she had walked the straight-and-narrow as a straight-A psychology major at Columbia who spoke four languages and topped her class in marksmanship.

With the headlights on high, Zoe slowed her vehicle and squinted at an address marker beside a stretch of winding highway in the forested hills of Rancho Santa Fe, California. On the seat beside her was a laptop computer.

"I still think you're wasting your time," said Teague, unwrapping a sandwich.

"I know he's involved. I can feel it," said Zoe.

"You'd better have something more than feelings for the FBI, I can tell you that right now."

"You did clear me to see the Senator though, right?"

Teague did not reply.

"Sir, you did clear me to see the Senator, didn't you?" Zoe asked again.

"Not exactly."

"What do you mean, not exactly?"

"It means I tried but was reminded in no uncertain terms that kidnapping is not our turf."

"Did you tell them about Abu Nazer?"

"Tell them what, exactly? Look Zoe, as much as I respect your instincts, the FBI does not want us snooping around. Not without some kind of hard evidence linking Abu Nazer to the disappearance of the Ashford kid."

"Her name's Amy."

"And she's thirteen years old, five-two, last seen wearing a plaid skirt and dark green blouse – yeah, I got it. Point is, without some kind of hard evidence linking Abu Nazer to Amy's disappearance, they're not going to let you through the door."

"Isn't that why I'm making this trip? To ask questions? To look around?"

"I'm not the one you need to convince. The Fibbies are. And they pretty much said what I've been telling you all along: we just paid Abu Nazer a million dollars to assassinate Gerhard, so that's where his focus will be. In their minds, any attempt to connect him with the kidnapping is a waste of time."

"I think he's playing us. I think his real aim in accepting the assassination assignment was to get close to Amy."

"And you've got nothing to back that up."

"Then why didn't Abu Nazer carry out the assignment last month when Gerhard was at their refinery in Venezuela? Security down there's a joke. But no – he insists on carrying it out up here, in the heart of Homeland Security, where people like us can surround the place and wait for him. Why would he do that?"

Teague started to reply but Zoe cut him off.

"I'll tell you why!" she said. "To get even with the Senator for locating and freezing a big chunk of his financial assets. Think about it. Nancy Ashford's estate is just ninety miles from the fuel depot. Amy goes missing the day before Abu Nazer's supposed to assassinate Gerhard. He's behind the kidnapping, I can feel it!"

"How many times do I have to say this? You've got no proof. In fact, nothing in Abu Nazer's profile even remotely suggests that he would be involved in a kidnapping. You, of all people, should know that. You wrote the thing!"

"Like I said, Senator Ashford has been hitting him where it hurts – in the wallet. She got the Swiss to close down several of his accounts. She located his Asian assets and had them confiscated. Abu Nazer's got to be feeling the pinch. Which gives him motive for kidnapping Amy."

"It also gives him motive for wanting our million dollars. So I repeat, with Gerhard arriving here soon, this is where his focus will be."

"Then why hasn't he accepted our payment?" asked Zoe, sliding her laptop toward her. "I'm online now and I can see the money still sitting there in the account."

"Obviously because he hasn't completed the job yet. And you sure as hell better not be driving a moving vehicle while reading a laptop!"

"I think he knows it's a trap. That we set the whole thing up."

"There's no way Abu Nazer could know anything other than that a group of leftwing environmentalists hired him to assassinate an industrial polluter."

"He's behind the kidnapping. I know it!"

Teague noticed his assistant, April Delgado, waving a phone at him.

"That possibility – however remote – is why you're down there," Teague told Zoe. "But you sure as hell better come up with something more than what you've been telling me. Wayne Hall's in charge and he's not exactly the warm-and-fuzzy type."

"How can I give them evidence before I've had a chance to look for it?"

"I'm just telling you the way it is." To April: "Who is it?"

"Congresswoman Gustaves. She wants to know how Zoe is doing."

"Tell her we're in the middle of an operation!" To Zoe: "Like I said—"

"Come on, sir! We both know Abu Nazer doesn't leave bread-crumbs lying around. He's like a phantom, a ghost. Sure, I've compiled the only profile anyone has on him; but all we have are patterns of behavior. That's why I need to be making this trip – to sniff around, ask questions, look for clues."

"And I'll say it again, the Fibbies are not going to let you through the door without proof of Abu Nazer's involvement."

"Which I can't give them without knowing what happened!"

Three workstations away from Teague, a technician named Tony Cooke noticed a triangular blinking dot on the right side of his radar screen. His eyes locked onto the flight number: XXX-00. In other words, the aircraft had no registered flight number and Air Traffic Control did not know who it was. Tony angled his microphone closer to his mouth.

"COMRAD to Team Leader," he said quietly.

"Go ahead, COMRAD," Team Leader replied.

"We have an unidentified airspace intrusion at forty-two degrees east. Can you get me a visual?"

High on a darkened catwalk rimming one of the depot's massive LPG tanks, Team Leader trained his electronic binoculars on the eastern horizon. A numerical reading along the bottom indicated the directional bearing, based on the user's global position.

"I see a low-altitude point of light at forty-one-point-seven degrees east," he replied. "It appears stationary, so it's heading toward us, but is still too far away to tell whether it's fixed wing or rotor."

"Stand by," Tony answered.

Knowing that military, commercial, and private aircraft were being diverted around the depot's airspace, Tony entered some commands that accessed the Air Traffic Control database, where he saw flight XXX-00 blinking in relative position to all other flights in and around Los Angeles. He beckoned to Teague.

"What is it?" asked Teague.

"We've got an unidentified aircraft moving toward us from the east," Cooke replied.

"Did you check with Air Traffic Control?"

"Yes, sir. Their database confirmed everything's being diverted. Nothing should be entering our airspace."

"ETA?" asked Teague.

Tony clicked an icon that calculated the craft's air speed.

"Eleven minutes," he answered.

Teague glanced at the clock on the wall. Gerhard was due here in twelve.

"Sir, if Abu Nazer's launching an air strike," said Tony, "one missile is all it would take to detonate the depot's fuel tanks."

When Tony made that statement, all breathing in the command center seemed to stop. Anxious eyes focused on Teague, whose attention was on XXX-00 moving slowly across the screen.

"April, get General Ramsey on the line," Teague said, tossing his sandwich in the trash. He lifted his cell phone to his ear. "We're in crisis, I gotta go."

"An air strike by Abu Nazer?" Zoe asked, having overheard the conversation.

"Possibly. Our airspace has been penetrated, but it's too early to tell who it is."

"Want me to head back? If I push it, I can be there in an hour."

"Aren't you nearly at the estate?"

"Five minutes, give or take."

"Follow that through and find out what you can. I can't ignore the possibility that Abu Nazer may be involved."

Teague ended the call and looked again at XXX-00 blinking on the monitor.

Nine minutes and counting.

"Sir, General Ramsey's on the line," April said from the other end of the command center.

"Okay, people, we are taking this to active status!" Teague called out. He approached April's desk and she handed him the receiver.

"General Ramsey, this is Jackson Teague."

Teague's conversation with the general took fifteen seconds. Twelve seconds later, claxons were sounding at Edwards Air Force Base, seventy-five miles to the north.

"*Go, go, go!* This is not a drill!" shouted Colonel Cheryl Chapman, wing commander of the 95th Tactical Air Defense Squadron. Eight pilots sprinted past her, flight helmets in hand.

Crossing the darkened tarmac toward their waiting F-15 Eagles, several of the pilots glanced toward the galactic glow of Los Angeles illuminating the western horizon.

This is not a drill, the colonel had said. Did that mean one of them would be shooting Abu Nazer out of the sky? Who *wouldn't* like the honor of vaporizing that bastard? Dar es Salaam, Nairobi, the U.S.S. Cole – Abu Nazer had been linked with those and a host of other atrocities requiring the bomb-making skills he both possessed and offered for hire.

But to shoot him down over Los Angeles? The thought made each of them shudder.

And yet there may be no other choice. For Abu Nazer could, at this very moment, be flying a plane directly toward the San Gabriel Industrial Fuel Depot.

Because their squadron had been placed on standby alert earlier that day, the F-15s were already fueled and armed with Sparrow, Sidewinder, and Python air-to-air missiles.

The pilots climbed into the cockpits, strapped themselves in and began flipping switches, bringing an array of instruments to life. Ninety seconds later, the high desert reverberated as the squadron of Eagles pulled onto the taxiway in a staggered single file column, their powerful twin engines lighting the night with ferocious, fiery eyes.

"Sir, we are ready and holding," Chapman told Ramsey over the phone.

"Your green light is confirmed, Colonel. Get 'em in the air!"

The order was relayed and the first jet pulled onto the runway, the point of its nose aimed between the parallel rows of white lights stretching into the darkness.

Suddenly, two cones of fire thundered out of the F-15's engines, and 47,000 pounds of thrust catapulted the jet forward, vibrating the concrete beneath it. The Eagle lifted off and climbed steeply upward and banked to the west, just as the next jet pulled onto the runway.

In the Rancho Santa Fe hills to the south, Zoe slowed her vehicle. Up ahead loomed the adobe wall of Senator Ashford's estate.

At the gate, Zoe was stopped by a team of agents. One of them inspected her ID and waved her through.

Zoe steered her SUV along a manicured gravel lane that curved its way through a grove of well-tended orange trees.

"Probably writes the whole thing off as an agricultural enterprise," she muttered.

Fifteen seconds later, the lights of a house came into view.

Senator Ashford's lavish hacienda was alive with activity and Zoe had trouble finding a place to park among the marked and unmarked police cars and government Suburbans. Teams of agents wearing FBI jackets patrolled the grassy lawns. Near the front walk, several uniformed officers chatted quietly.

Zoe squeezed her SUV between two of the Suburbans, then climbed out and made her way toward the house.

"Man, the Feds get all the hot ones," one of the policemen remarked, eliciting grunts of agreement from the others.

They watched her climb the flagstone steps onto the covered verandah. Subdued lights complimented lanky trails of magenta bougainvillea that gave the home a welcoming feel. Special agent Wayne Hall then pulled open the front door and truncated that feeling.

"So you're Gustaves," he stated rather than asked, his akimbo stance filling the doorway.

"You must be Hall."

Zoe and Hall exchanged unflinching stares.

"What can I do for you?" asked Hall.

"I'm here about the Senator's daughter," replied Zoe.

"Why is that? Kidnapping isn't your turf."

"It is if Abu Nazer's involved."

Hall's eyes narrowed. "Are you saying he's responsible?"

"That's what I'm here to find out."

An agent named Bill suddenly touched Hall on the shoulder.

"A tactical defense squadron's been scrambled out of Edwards," the agent murmured.

"What for?" asked Hall.

"An unidentified aircraft just entered restricted airspace around the San Gabriel Industrial Fuel Depot."

"The alarm's ours," said Zoe. "We've got an operation going on."

"I know," said Hall. "Which makes me question why you think Abu Nazer's involved in a kidnapping when he's supposed to be assassinating your target."

"Proximity, timing, and the fact that Senator Ashford has been after him like a bloodhound."

"In other words, you've got no evidence."

"I just gave you evidence."

"You gave me conjecture."

"It's evidence when it comes to Abu Nazer. I should know. I wrote his profile."

"Spare me the infomercial. Without some kind of proof that he's responsible, I'm not letting you upset the Senator any more than she already is."

"I can't give you proof if I don't know what happened. Five minutes, that's all I ask."

"No way."

"Then at least allow me to read your reports."

"Like I said, this isn't your turf."

"Who cares about turf? We're talking about Abu Nazer!"

"Bill, please escort Agent Gustaves to her car."

With a roar of frustration, Zoe whirled away just as a FedEx delivery truck skidded to a stop in the parking lot. The driver jumped out and passed Zoe on the steps.

"What have you got?" asked Hall, meeting the driver.

"A package for Senator Ashford."

"I'll take it."

"Not without a signature."

Hall grabbed the clipboard, scribbled a signature, then exchanged it for the package, which he handed to Bill.

Zoe watched Bill take the package to a black van. Meanwhile, the FedEx driver dashed back to his truck, jumped in, and sped back down the lane.

Climbing into her SUV, Zoe opened her laptop and accessed the Agency intranet. She checked her inbox and saw an e-mail from an informant named Toy Soldier. She read the message, then dialed Teague.

"Gerhard's limo just pulled off the 710," the communications officer was saying when Teague's cell phone rang.

"Is our blackout still in effect?" asked Teague.

"Yes, sir, but I don't know how long it'll hold. Sooner or later we're going to have to start answering questions."

Teague put the phone to his ear. "What's up?"

"Have you seen the latest e-mail from Toy Soldier?" asked Zoe.

"I'm kind of busy right now."

"He says Abu Nazer wants information on an ancient Egyptian tablet, and that someone named Tariq Yassin will be delivering it to him tomorrow in Saudi Arabia."

"Saudi Arabia? Abu Nazer can't be in two places at once!"

"No kidding."

"Maybe the meeting's with one of Abu Nazer's confederates. Toy Soldier didn't say the meeting was actually with Abu Nazer, did he? Only that information on this tablet will be delivered to him there."

"I guess you could take it either way."

Teague stopped and looked again at XXX-00 blinking its way across the screen. "Hang on a sec," he said, lowering his cell phone. He picked up the red receiver that was the live connection with the wing commander at Edwards. "Colonel, how soon 'til your squadron gets a visual on that inbound?"

The Eagles were thundering across greater Los Angeles when the question was radioed to the squadron leader. Sitting in the glow of his cockpit instrument panels, he checked the digital map on his screen and saw XXX-00 in relation to their rapidly approaching formation.

"Thirty-five seconds," he replied.

Chapman relayed the information to Teague.

High on his darkened catwalk, the CIA sniper team had their binoculars trained on the inbound blinking light.

"No wing lights; must be a chopper," Team Leader said to the others.

"I've got him in my sights," one of the snipers replied, his black cap on backwards as he peered through the powerful scope on his rifle.

"Keep him there," Team Leader replied.

He notified Teague, whose eyes were darting from the radar screen to the various other monitors.

"I need to go," said Teague.

"One more thing," said Zoe. "Toy Soldier said Abu Nazer's been collecting information on a journalist named Rutherford Tyler. Isn't he the guy who interviews celebrities?"

"He interviews a lot of people."

"Why would Abu Nazer want information on Tyler?"

The communications officer waved to Teague.

"Later, I gotta go," said Teague. He ended the call and stepped over to the communication officer's desk. "What have you got?" he asked.

"Team Leader reports a visual on a helicopter," she said.

"Get Colonel Chapman on the line."

At that moment, the pilot of the helicopter pointed toward the giant LPG tanks up ahead. Most were illuminated. A few were not.

"Everything looks peaceful," he said into his microphone. "I'll circle around and come in from the rear."

Back at the Ashford estate, Zoe heard a door slam. She turned and saw Bill step away from the van and meet Hall on the gravel, near the steps.

"Everything looks normal," Bill said, handing a cell phone to Hall. "There's also a note."

"What's it say?" asked Hall.

"It's from the kidnappers. They've instructed the Senator to wait for their call. They promise that if she does exactly what they say, her daughter will not be harmed."

"What time are they going to call?"

"Ten-twenty."

Hall checked his watch. "It's ten-fifteen right now!"

Eighty miles to the north, Rolf Gerhard's limousine slowed as it approached the candy-striped boom lowered across the entrance to the fuel depot. In case approaching drivers didn't quite get the message, an oversized stop sign had been bolted to the boom. Less obvious were two rows of retractable metal teeth angling out of the concrete below.

Teague knew that attention to the smallest detail could make or break an operation. Hence, although he preferred to have one of his agents manning the guardhouse, he decided against it in case Abu Nazer had been studying the depot's operational patterns. Thus, when Gerhard's limousine stopped in front of the boom, it was the regular security officer who ambled out of the small cubicle and over to the driver's window, clipboard in hand, cap hiked back on his head. The only difference was the thin Kevlar vest he was wearing beneath his uniform.

In the distance, the thumping of a helicopter rotor was becoming audible.

"I see…Holy *shit!*" the helicopter pilot exclaimed as four jets boomed past. "I knew we shouldn't be doing this."

"Maintain current heading," crackled the radio.

"Are you *crazy?* Those jets were fully loaded, and I can see them circling back around. Get on the phone! Tell them who we are!"

"They won't do anything. Get down there and do your job."

"In about fifteen seconds, those Sidewinders will be pointed at my ass, not yours, so get on the goddamn *phone!*"

Inside the fenced compound below, Gerhard's limousine passed beneath a bridge of pipes, then followed the access road between two of the earthen dikes surrounding the massive tanks. The limo entered a small parking area, made a slow, wide circle on the oily gravel, and stopped near the command center.

"Eagle One to Base," the squadron leader reported into his microphone. "I have a visual on what appears to be a news crew."

"Come again?" asked Chapman.

"A news crew," repeated the squadron leader. "We'll circle around and make another pass."

"Copy that," answered Chapman.

High on the catwalk, Team Leader watched the helicopter circle wide.

"You see what I see?" one of the snipers asked, lifting her head away from the scope.

"It's a news crew!" Team Leader replied, spotting the station's logo painted clearly on the side of the aircraft. He lowered his binoculars and relayed the information to Teague.

"*News crew?*" shouted Teague. "I thought we threw a blackout over this!"

"We did," replied the communications officer.

"Get them on the phone!"

Overhead, the jets thundered past.

Seconds later, the station manager was on the line.

Teague grabbed the phone and demanded answers.

"Of course the chopper's ours," bleated the station manager. "We've been trying to get hold of the military to let them know who we are!"

"You're violating restricted air space!"

"Hey, we understood this to be a general re-routing for commercial and private aircraft. No one said Tactical Air Defense was involved."

"That's need-to-know. Why are you here?"

"We got an anonymous e-mail informing us that the CIA was trying to cover up what happened at tank seven."

"Tank seven?" repeated Teague, motioning for someone to follow that up. "Did your informant say what he meant?"

"Only that we should be there with a camera crew at ten-twenty. The e-mail arrived just minutes ago, which is why we sent a chopper."

"Get it out of here!"

"Not with a story like this."

Teague responded with a threat of legal action should the news crew persist. The station manager answered that he would see Teague in court, adding how a string of editorials about the illegality of CIA operations on U.S. soil was sure to make interesting viewing.

Teague slammed down the phone and cursed.

"Call Chapman!" he barked. "Have those jets return to base."

"Do you want Gerhard's stand-in to get out of the limo?" asked the communications officer.

"No! Keep him there until we find out what's going on at tank seven."

"Unit four is investigating now."

Rubbing his forehead, Teague paced back and forth.

"Awaiting your orders," Team Leader said.

"Maintain positions," answered Teague.

A news blackout and yet someone tips them off. But who?

A bizarre thought popped into his mind.

Could Abu Nazer have alerted the media?

"What's the status of our million dollars?" he asked.

"Still there," said Cooke.

Above tank seven, the helicopter circled in close.

The cameraman flipped a switch and a powerful flood-light illuminated the weedless brown earth surrounding the tank.

"My *God*," the pilot exclaimed as the camera began to roll.

Below, a team of six snipers advanced into the wash of light, sweeping their weapons back and forth as they secured the area.

Walking slowly over to the tank, Team Leader lowered his rifle. On the oily ground in front of him was the twisted body of a girl. She had been shot once in the forehead. Her clothing was soaked with blood.

He looked up. Spray-painted on the side of tank seven were these words:

Nice try. Don't fuck with me again.

"Chief!" one of the agents called out. "There's a hole cut here in the fence."

Team Leader nodded absently. With the TV helicopter hovering overhead, he brought his wrist mike to his mouth.

Teague listened to the report, then closed his eyes. How in the hell did Abu Nazer manage to penetrate the compound with the body of a girl?

"What do you want us to do?" Team Leader asked.

"Maintain perimeter until—"

Teague's eyes suddenly flew open.

"Give me a description of the girl," he said.

"Dishwater blond. Thirteen or fourteen."

"What's she got on?"

"Looks like a school uniform of some kind. Plaid skirt, dark green blouse..."

"Son of a bitch!" exclaimed Teague, pulling out his cell phone.

Zoe was nearly to the main road when her cell phone rang.

"Gustaves," she answered.

"Where are you?" asked Teague.

"Just leaving."

"I need to know what you found out."

"Zip," said Zoe, hitting the brakes. "They wouldn't let me in."

"I think you were right," said Teague.

"About what?"

"About Abu Nazer being behind the kidnapping. We discovered the body of a girl near one of the tanks. Age thirteen or fourteen, plaid skirt, dark green blouse."

Zoe stared out the windshield as gravel dust floated through the vehicle's high beams.

"Abu Nazer must have found out about our trap and alerted the media," Teague continued. "He killed the girl to taunt us, and wanted the media to see her body. Especially with the message he painted on the tank."

"What message?"

"'Nice try. Don't fuck with me again.' He told the news crew to be here at ten-twenty with a camera."

"Ten-twenty?" asked Zoe, her eyes on the glowing numbers of the dashboard clock.

"That's what the station manager said."

"FedEx just delivered a package to the Senator. I overheard the FBI saying it contained a cell phone and a note instructing her to wait for a call at ten-twenty."

"Obviously he wanted to telephone her and gloat," said Teague.

"And allow the FBI to record his voice? Abu Nazer would never do that."

With the engine idling, Zoe stared intently off into the darkness.

"My God, that's *it!*" she exclaimed, jamming the gear stick into reverse and hitting the gas. Her tires sprayed gravel as the vehicle careered backward up the lane.

"What?" said Teague.

"The kidnapping was his way of drawing Senator Ashford into the open."

"She's hardly in the open," said Teague. "The FBI must have turned her estate into a fortress."

"Which Abu Nazer just penetrated with a cell phone. That means at ten-twenty, Senator Ashford will be waiting for what she thinks is the kidnapper's call."

Inside the house, a titian-haired Senator Ashford was nervously wringing her hands as she stared at the cell phone on the coffee table. If *only* she had not allowed Amy to remain in California to attend school. If *only* she had taken her back to Washington.

"It's ten-twenty," one of the agents said quietly.

Senator Ashford watched Hall and half a dozen agents gather around the phone. Plugged into one of the instrument's tiny sockets was a wire that ran to a portable console and recorder.

"We're ready for the trace," said a technician.

Outside, Zoe's SUV skidded to a stop. She jumped out and sprinted toward the hacienda.

"Everybody out, it's a *bomb!*" she shouted.

"Isn't that the Agency chick who was just here?" one of the agents by the front door asked.

"What's she yelling?" the other agent asked, his hand drifting instinctively toward his pistol.

Racing between two of the parked Suburbans, Zoe shouted her warning again.

24

"Did she say *bomb?*" asked the agents, spinning toward the door.

The white flash occurred milliseconds later, followed by a massive detonation that shook the hacienda. Windows shattered. The front door splintered. Roof tiles exploded high into the sky as a thunderous fireball billowed out into the night. Then came a blizzard of ash.

Teague waited anxiously, phone to his ear, hearing Zoe's shouts as she ran toward the house.

He heard the blast. Then the static.

Then silence.

"Zoe?" shouted Teague. "Are you okay?"

No answer.

"Zoe? *Zoe!*"

CHAPTER 2

"Haven't we met somewhere before?" the co-ed asked. She peeked around Tyler's shoulder and smiled, cleavage bursting from her blouse. Her streaked blonde curls were gathered up and fastened with a pink alligator clip.

Seated at the Hula Hut's outdoor bar on the shore of Lake Austin, Texas, Tyler glanced at the blonde, then across the table at Johnny Bill Sandborn, who simply grinned and finished his beer. Johnny Bill was a big man with a ponytail and a full beard.

"Don't think so," Tyler replied, looking toward the bar.

"Tammy Carter?" she asked, looking Tyler over and liking what she saw. *Muscular shoulders, chaotic blond hair. Definitely a nice hunk of beef.*

"Sorry," answered Tyler. He waved a hand, got the bartender's attention, and pointed to Johnny Bill. Behind the bar, Mary Lou nodded, grabbed a mug, and began filling it with beer.

A long moment of silence passed.

"I am, like, *so* busted!" Tammy confessed, touching her chest with an embarrassed sigh. She pulled out a barstool and sat. "Truth is, we haven't met. But I know I've seen you around." She stirred her margarita, puckered her lips around the straw, and drained the contents of her glass.

It was Friday afternoon at the Hula Hut and the bar was packed with students and locals ready to accelerate their way into the weekend. Having arrived ahead of the crowd, Tyler had managed to secure a spot by the railing. Below, several ducks swam eagerly after bits of tortilla chips tossed into the water by some girls at a neighboring table.

"Here you go," Mary Lou said, sliding the mug of beer in front of Johnny Bill. She snatched up Tyler's empty bottle. "Another swamp water for you, I suppose?"

"Yes, I do believe I'll have another one of your New England gourmet lagers," answered Tyler with a grin.

"I'll have another margarita," said Tammy. "But no salt. I hate it with salt."

Mary Lou arched an eyebrow before returning to the bar.

26

"You look like that guy on TV," remarked Tammy.

Tyler did not respond.

"You gotta know who I'm talkin' about!" Tammy said. "C'mon, what's his name? That guy who interviews celebrities. I mean, he's like, famous, and you kind of look like him. But not exactly. I mean, no one looks like someone exactly. He's got, maybe, longer hair or something. Maybe it's shorter, I don't know. But you do kind of look like him. But not exactly. Know what I mean?"

Tyler stared at Tammy for a moment, then pulled out his wallet.

"I best be headin' back to the garage," he said, dropping some cash on the table.

"Garage?" asked Tammy.

"Sandborn's. Down on Maple."

"You're a *mechanic?*"

"Some people might argue the point," said Tyler, pointing to an orange sixty-three Ford pick-up in the parking lot. "Ain't she a beauty? Found her rustin' outside o' Tucumcari a few years back. Brought her back on a buddy's flatbed, gave the body a good sanding and some paint, then dropped in a small V-8. The interior's not finished but she runs like a top."

Tammy's interest took a visible nosedive. "I really do need to be goin'," she said as she burped and stood.

But just as Tammy turned away, a discreet warble sounded. Glancing around, she saw Tyler put his cell phone to his ear.

"Tyler," he spoke into the instrument.

A wrinkle of doubt creased Tammy's forehead as she sidled between several tables full of laughing students.

"May I buy the lady a drink?" asked a man in a blue polyester suit. He stood and tipped his hat.

"Sure, why not?" answered Tammy absently, her eyes still on Tyler. "Say, who's the grease monkey?" she asked, nodding toward Tyler.

The man laughed. "Is that what he told you? Hell, that's Rutherford Tyler, the journalist. He interviews celebrities on TV. Now, what's your name? Mine's Ted. I'm the service manager down at Red Rock Motors."

Tammy's mouth dropped open.

"I'm sorry, what did you say?" asked Tyler, one hand over his ear in an effort to block out the clamor.

27

"I said, is this Dr. Rutherford Tyler?" a woman's voice asked.

"Yes, it is. Who's this?"

"Sharifa al Rashid."

Tyler glanced at his watch. "Didn't we have an appointment earlier for lunch?"

"We did, and I apologize for not phoning until now. I missed my connecting flight in New York and just got in. I'm at the Austin airport, and I can meet with you now, if you're free."

"Now, as in right now?" he asked.

"Unless it's not a good time?"

"Now's fine, I guess," he said. "Come on down to the Hula Hut. The cab drivers all know where it is. When you get here, ask at the reception desk and they'll point you to my table."

"I'm on my way."

At precisely six o'clock, a taxi pulled into the parking lot. The door opened and Tyler saw an elegant woman in a tailored black business suit climb gracefully out. She looked to be in her late thirties, with light brown skin and shoulder-length hair. He watched her pay the driver, glance in the direction of the Hula Hut, then start down the sidewalk toward the entrance.

The woman's stride was noble and aloof, and Tyler found it impossible not to stare. She seemed pleased, almost smiling, and yet it wasn't really a smile. It was an attitude of confidence wrapped in an air of detachment, and by the way she carried herself, Tyler sensed she did not smile indiscriminately.

He watched her descend the front steps, her hair bouncing lightly with each stride. He saw her pull open the front door and enter the restaurant, his eyes remaining fixed on the door long after it had cushioned closed.

An alarm sounded in a distant part of his brain but Tyler didn't care. This woman had him in a spell and Tyler did not want it broken.

"*Tyler!*"

"Huh?"

Johnny Bill sighed with exasperation. "You ain't heard a word I been sayin', have you?"

"I, uh…"

"I *knew* it! Dang it, Tyler, you're zonin' out on me again!" He rotated on his barstool and scanned the parking lot. "What is it – some chick?"

"What were you saying?" asked Tyler.

"I was *sayin'* we got to finish that interior. You got any time this weekend?"

"Sorry, no, I don't."

"Hell, don't be sorry. It's your truck. If you don't mind ridin' around in a dump, it don't bother me."

Lifting his mug of beer, Johnny Bill opened his throat like a drainpipe and poured the remainder down in a gulp. He then wiped his mouth with the back of his hand.

"Now, you're comin' tonight, ain't ya?" he asked. "Ben 'n' Jenny are countin' on you bein' there."

"Wouldn't miss it," said Tyler.

"Say, when you gonna get yourself some young-uns o' your own? You're headin' toward the big four-o, and the stud clock's tickin' away."

Tyler shrugged.

"You could have any number of chicks if you'd quit being so dang picky. Hell, Gloria's sister's still single and is so ripe she's just oozing with motherhood. She ain't bad looking, either."

"Tempting," said Tyler, looking toward the restaurant. "What time's the party again?"

"Seven. Gloria's makin' one of them chocolate-pecan fudge cakes with the gooey icing. Them kids really go for that cake."

"Say, look, you know that business appointment I thought stood me up? Well, she's here and she's headed this way."

Johnny Bill looked around. "Which one?"

"In black. With the cocoa complexion."

"No *way!*"

"No lie. She's here on behalf of her boss. A collector from Cairo I've been wanting to interview." He looked again at Sharifa, who was parting the crowd without trying. "So, if I happen to be running a little late…"

"Hey! I ain't acceptin' no excuses! You gonna be late, you bring her along."

"I'm not bringing a stranger to Ben's birthday party."

"Why not? The kids'd like meetin' a real Egyptian."

"She's not a zoo animal, Johnny Bill."

"But she's an *Egyptian.* Queen of the Nile and all that."

"I don't think so."

"Come on! I'll throw on some extra ribs."

"I really don't think I should—"

"Dang it, Tyler, quit arguin'!"

"I'll think about it," said Tyler just as Sharifa reached the table.

"I'm so sorry for this inconvenience," she said, her hand extended. "Sharifa al Rashid."

"Johnny Bill Sandborn, nice to meet ya," Johnny Bill said, springing to his feet and intercepting her hand.

Sharifa stared dumbfounded at Johnny Bill.

"Think nothing of it," he continued, gesturing her to the barstool on which he'd been sitting. "I often leave women speechless. This here's the man you want."

Sharifa looked at Tyler, then at Johnny Bill, then back at Tyler, uncertain about what to say.

"If you'll excuse me, I'd best be goin'," Johnny Bill said. He winked at Tyler, a mischievous grin hidden beneath his thick tangle of beard. "Seven o'clock. Ya both gotta eat!"

With a wave, he made his way through the crowd toward the exit.

"Sorry about that," said Tyler. "He pulls that stunt whenever he can."

With a flustered sigh, Sharifa sat.

"Something to drink?" asked Tyler.

"A glass of white wine sounds heavenly."

Tyler waved a hand, caught Mary Lou's attention and flashed three fingers twice for "w-w".

"How was your flight?" he asked.

"Long. And very late. I'm so sorry…"

"You're here now. You can relax."

Sharifa smiled and nodded.

"I must admit, I'm surprised to get a personal visit," said Tyler.

"Mr. Qaderi is thrilled that you wish to interview him. Your television specials are very popular in Cairo."

Tyler acknowledged the compliment with a nod.

"But why Mr. Qaderi, if you don't mind my asking? He's not a celebrity of the caliber that you are used to interviewing."

"If that tablet of his is genuine, he soon will be."

"Did you have a date in mind?"

"How about next week?" answered Tyler.

"Next *week?*"

"Unless it's not a good time?"

Sharifa caught the quip and realized that Tyler was playing with her.

"Well, let's have a look," she said, pulling an electronic diary out of her purse. She brought up Qaderi's calendar onto its tiny screen. "How about next Wednesday? Soon enough?"

"I'll be there," he said.

"Then it's arranged," she said, entering the information with her fingernail. "Naturally, Mr. Qaderi would like to extend you his hospitality."

"Thank you. That's very kind."

"It will be his pleasure. Do you have any dietary restrictions?"

"I prefer to keep my distance from *molokhiyya.*"

Tyler's reference to Egypt's notorious green soup, famous for its look and viscosity of phlegm, caused Sharifa to lean back and openly stare.

"You are certainly full of surprises," she declared.

Tyler shrugged.

"How in the world do you know about *molokhiyya?*" she asked. "Most people have never even heard of it, much less been able to pronounce it – accurately – as you just did."

"Discovery Channel," answered Tyler.

This time Sharifa laughed outright.

"Getting back to Clayton's tablet," he said. "The underlying issue, as I'm sure you know, is whether or not it's genuine."

"A team of scholars is being assembled to make that determination. If it is genuine, Youssef plans to send the tablet on a world tour before placing it on permanent display in the Cairo Museum."

"Who's directing the study?" asked Tyler.

"Dr. Philippa Eaton, of King's College, London. She's an expert on ancient Near Eastern literature."

"A successful world tour would earn your boss a lot of money."

"Youssef hasn't bought himself an expert, if that's what you're implying," Sharifa responded coolly.

"Don't be offended," said Tyler. "My job is to ask those kinds of questions. With such an obvious benefit to be gained, well, let's just say I won't be the only one asking."

31

"Dr. Eaton and her team are world-class scholars, and neither they nor their institutions will be receiving any monetary benefit from this whatsoever."

Mary Lou served Sharifa's wine and Tyler nodded his thanks. He then leaned forward and placed his elbows on the table.

"If the tablet is found to be genuine," he said, "there could be other more serious ramifications. Are you prepared for that?"

"I'm afraid it's already begun," Sharifa replied.

"How so?" asked Tyler.

Sharifa leaned forward and placed her elbows on the table just as Tyler had done.

"Death threats," she said. "Which means, if you become involved, the same threats being directed at Youssef may soon be directed at you. Are you prepared for that?"

"We all die sooner or later."

Sharifa scrutinized Tyler's features – his untamed hair, blue eyes and friendly squint lines.

"Are you merely trying to impress me or do you actually believe that?"

"Are you impressed?"

"Not by machismo, no."

"That doesn't answer my question."

"I'm impressed if that's how you live."

"Like I said, we all die sooner or later."

"And that doesn't answer my question."

"Touché," said Tyler, taking a sip of his beer.

"Well?" Sharifa asked.

Tyler grinned. "That's how I live."

Sharifa smiled thoughtfully then took a sip of her wine.

You are definitely the man for this job.

CHAPTER 3

Teague felt like roadkill after his meeting – make that *grilling* – with Director of Operations, Philip Trent. It was never pleasant when an operation went south, and this one had gone off the map. Worse yet, Teague could not explain why.

And Trent was demanding a reason.

"I'm riding you because the DCI's made Abu Nazer my number one headache. So, I'm making him yours. I want the bastard *stopped!*"

"Yes, sir," answered Teague.

"If that means adding extra people, then do it. There's all kinds of shit coming down on me because of this. He made us look like *fools.*"

Thankfully, it was after hours and no one was in the elevator to ask how things went. Not that they would have needed to ask by the look on his face.

The doors parted and Teague stepped out. He glanced across the labyrinth of work stations and saw the tops of several heads visible above the chest-high panels. One in particular caught his eye.

Zoe was reading an e-mail when Teague appeared at her desk.

"What are you doing here?" he asked.

"Have a look at this," Zoe replied.

"I said, what are you *doing* here? I told you to go to the doctor."

"I did."

"You were in a *bomb blast.* People were killed!"

Zoe rotated in her chair and looked up at Teague. "And I was not among them, thanks to those big Suburbans the Fibbies like to drive. The doctor fixed me up and said I could return to work, so here I am. Now will you *please* have a look at this?"

"It's after hours."

"There's no such thing."

With an exasperated sigh Teague looked at the monitor. "What am I looking at?" he asked.

"Remember how I told you Tariq Yassin was delivering information on an ancient tablet to Abu Nazer? Well, in this follow-up, Toy Soldier says Tariq went to Kings College in London and copied the journal of

33

Sir Edmund George Clayton, the archaeologist who found the tablet back in 1919. The librarian said Tariq copied everything he could find, which amounted to several articles from the nineteen-twenties, plus a master's thesis from the seventies. Most were skeptical of the alleged discovery, since no one's ever seen the tablet. But the master's thesis argued that the Book of Genesis had been copied from Egyptian documents, since the tablet was an exact copy of what's found in Genesis."

"Why would Abu Nazer be interested in this?"

"Toy Soldier must have wondered the same thing because he sent us an article by Dr. Philippa Eaton, a Kings College faculty member who's an expert on ancient Near Eastern literature. She claims the tablet could ignite Armageddon."

"Ignite Armageddon? Come on!"

"That's what she claims. According to Dr. Eaton, both the tablet and the corresponding passages in Genesis were written by Ishmael, who was the founding father of the Arab nations and eldest son of the patriarch Abraham."

"And this is important because…"

"In both the tablet and Genesis, Ishmael declares Palestine to be the inheritance of Israel."

Teague let out a low whistle. "No wonder Abu Nazer would love to get his mitts on it. Thank God it's never been found."

"Apparently, it has."

"*What?*"

"Toy Soldier says a collector named Youssef Qaderi found the tablet in an Italian junk shop. Bought it for peanuts. Apparently, the owner had no idea what it was. An expert from the Cairo Museum has already made a preliminary declaration of authenticity, but Qaderi has commissioned Dr. Eaton to conduct an independent study."

"When and where?"

"San Francisco. Not sure when."

"Find out. I want to know everything Abu Nazer knows, including backgrounds on all the players."

"On it," answered Zoe, closing Toy Soldier's e-mail and opening another.

"Don't tell me there's more."

"From our man in London. He said Tariq makes regular donations to the extremist group *Qamat*. Tariq also received the equivalent of ten thousand dollars last week from a numbered account in Switzerland."

"What for?"

"No idea. Though the timing of the deposit and his trip to Saudi Arabia suggest a connection. Maybe travel money, or some kind of payment. Our man tried getting the Swiss to identify the owner of the account on the basis that Tariq's contributions to *Qamat* demonstrated a link between him and a quasi-terrorist group. The Swiss didn't go for it. They said Tariq's activities in no way implicated the owner of the account, and we'd need a lot more than insinuations to violate the sanctity of a numbered account."

"Figures," said Teague.

"He e-mailed us a photo of Tariq, describing him as quiet and polite. The model businessman."

"As terrorists frequently are. Where is he now?"

Zoe glanced at a clock on the wall. "Just landing in Saudi Arabia. The airline confirmed him as a passenger."

"Who do we have on the ground there?"

"Omar. I e-mailed him Tariq's photo and told him to find out what Tariq's up to."

"You ordered a tail? On whose authority?"

"Yours. You were in one of your do-not-disturb meetings with the D-O and I had to act fast."

Teague paced the floor of Zoe's cubicle for several seconds, his features like hardened walnut.

"All right," he finally said. "But don't make a habit of this. I don't like my people circumventing protocol."

"Yes, sir."

Trent waved a hand from the doorway of Teague's office. Teague nodded then turned back to Zoe.

"Good work. Now go on, get out of here. You can pick this up in the morning."

"I'll leave as soon as I'm done."

"Go home, Gustaves. That's an order."

Teague started for his office, then glanced back and saw Zoe still at her desk. He stopped and pointed toward the door.

With a sigh, Zoe stood and began shuffling papers. When she looked up again, she spotted Teague eyeing her sternly.

"O-*kay!*" she said, switching off her monitor. She opened her purse, took out her keys, and jingled them for Teague to see. With a shake of his head, Teague disappeared into his office with Trent.

Zoe put her keys away and sat back down.

CHAPTER 4

The young flight attendant welcomed the passengers of Flight 133 to Saudi Arabia's Jiddah airport. She reminded everyone of the local time and told them where luggage could be collected.

Wearing a loose white *jellaba,* the bearded Tariq descended the stairs with the other passengers. A thin briefcase was in his hand. In his mid-twenties, Tariq's features were sharp, his eyes intense. He walked briskly through the bustling airport and out to the waiting sedan.

Sitting in his taxi a short distance away, Omar started the engine when he saw Tariq climb into the sedan. Nearly sixty years of age, the balding Omar was a Muslim informant who sometimes helped the CIA.

Other than a name and a photo, the CIA had provided Omar with only one other piece of information: *Tariq Yassin had come to Saudi Arabia to meet with Abu Nazer.*

Abu Nazer. The phantom. Death's demon. The CIA, of course, wanted a description, and hoped Omar could provide them with one.

The task seemed simple enough – follow Tariq and either photograph or describe the man he met with. If Omar could overhear portions of a conversation, so much the better.

But tasks involving Abu Nazer were never that simple.

It was no accident that Abu Nazer had never been identified. If a person got too close, that person became his next victim. That's why no one knew for certain whether Abu Nazer was even of Middle Eastern origin. A few claimed he was Norwegian. Others said he was South African. Many believed him to be a Western diplomat, while still others said he lived the life of a common peasant somewhere north of the Sahara.

In the final analysis, however, it was always the same: Abu Nazer could be anyone, in any location, at any time, and the authorities – or a potential victim – would never know.

Four cars ahead, Tariq's sedan made a turn onto a two-lane highway and headed east into the desert.

Toward Mecca, Omar realized as he negotiated the turn with half a dozen other cars.

The thought of Tariq meeting Abu Nazer in the Holy City made Omar furious. And yet, strangely, he understood. For by making it appear he was Muslim, Abu Nazer preserved the bubble of deception, confusion, and mystery that surrounded his identity.

But Omar could see another reason why he would choose Mecca. It was a city virtually impregnable by Western agents.

The line of cars reached Mecca with the setting of a vibrant orange sun. Omar followed Tariq's sedan through the angled streets into the heart of a monotonous jungle of concrete nestled among low desert peaks. By now traffic had slowed to a virtual crawl and Omar drummed his fingers impatiently while he waited.

Up ahead, the sedan pulled over and Tariq climbed out. Cranking his steering wheel to the left, Omar swung his taxi into a narrow lane. He jumped out, locked the door, ran across the street, and followed Tariq into a spacious plaza filled with hundreds of people.

Omar knew the plaza well for he had been here many times. He paused, as he always did at the sight of Islam's holiest mosque, the beautiful al-Masjid al-Haram.

Aglow in brilliant floodlights, the mosque's entrance was constructed of three great arches framed by a majestic stone facade. Rising above the entrance were two stone towers – minarets – each of which was encircled by a small balcony topped with an Arabic dome. The mosque was a breathtaking sight, and Omar gazed at it in reverent silence before reminding himself of his purpose.

He watched Tariq bypass the mosque, cross the plaza, and continue along a street of drab storefronts.

Omar followed Tariq for several minutes. Up ahead, Tariq turned a corner and disappeared.

Hurrying to the corner, Omar peered into a narrow alley that widened into a small brick courtyard. A single tree occupied a low planter in the center of the courtyard. Several benches were positioned around the tree. Framing the courtyard were small shops and several residences. Interior shades had been drawn over their lighted windows.

Omar ventured cautiously forward.

Where was he?

He paused to listen for footsteps but could only hear murmurs of conversation and a faint drift of music.

Suddenly, from behind, came a chorus of voices. Omar turned just in time to avoid a collision with two laughing couples. Passing him with barely a glance, they crossed the courtyard and disappeared through an arched doorway.

Above the doorway was an illuminated sign: *Wahah Caliph¬ –* The Caliph's Oasis.

Following the sound of clinking dishes, Omar climbed a flight of steps and turned into a corridor that led to another arched doorway – this one surrounded by geometric arabesque designs.

The Caliph's Oasis was a restaurant that specialized in lamb and fish. Omar approached the reception desk and was greeted by a smiling young woman in a dark green head cloth and long sapphire dress. Her white teeth and diamond nose stud contrasted beautifully with her caramel skin.

"Table for one, sir?" she asked.

"I'm to meet a friend," Omar replied. "May I stroll through and see if he's here?"

"Of course," the young woman said.

The restaurant was a maze of aisles. Booths with ornate lattice panels were positioned between columns supporting thick arches. Each of the booths had decorative curtains tied back on each side. Fairy lights and candles created intimacy.

The restaurant was packed full, and Omar did not know which of the aisles to choose first. He stood trying to decide while waiters hurried by him.

Glancing back, Omar saw the hostess staring at him. Forcing a smile, he took the aisle to the right.

Slowly and casually, Omar told himself as he strolled along the aisle, discreetly scanning the faces in each of the booths. But the very act of his walking by a booth attracted attention. Eyes turned and conversations paused until Omar moved on.

A pair of waiters approached with large platters balanced overhead. Omar stepped aside and allowed them to pass. Next came the hostess with a group of businessmen.

He turned a corner and saw Tariq. He was sitting alone in a booth. And the booths on each side of him were vacant.

What luck, Omar thought. *I'll ask to be seated in one of those booths.*

On his way back to the receptionist's counter, Omar paused. Who was he trying to fool? Abu Nazer would never talk freely with a stranger sitting in the next booth. For all he knew, the booths on each side had been reserved as buffer zones.

Another idea came to mind. Whenever he was on an assignment, he carried a satellite phone in case he had to phone Langley. But he also carried a cell phone for use in all other calls. Using the satellite phone, he would call his cell phone. Then, leaving the connection open, he would conceal the cell phone in a strategic position so that he could overhear Tariq's conversation with Abu Nazer. It just might work!

He stepped into a corner and made the call. Once the connection was made, he followed the aisle back to where Tariq was seated and quietly slid into the next booth. He allowed a moment to pass before discreetly inserting his cell phone beneath a string of fairy lights beside the lattice panel dividing the booths. To further hide the phone, he dislodged one of the bulbs, causing a small section of the fairy lights to go dark.

Omar had just rotated back around when the hostess appeared with three men. Two of the men looked like everyday businessmen, wearing suits and head cloths and carrying briefcases. The third man, however, was different. He was tall and sinewy and wore a brown *jellaba*. He had suspicious eyes and a gaunt, almost skeletal look to his olive-skinned face. The severity of the man was accentuated even more by a black moustache and pointed chin beard.

"I'm sorry, but this table is reserved," the hostess said.

"My mistake," Omar replied, avoiding the glare of the men as he slid out. He bowed politely and melted away.

At the first corner, he turned and put the phone to his ear.

"This is everything I could find on the tablet," a voice said. "It duplicates what I sent you before."

Omar heard the flipping of pages. Nearly a minute of silence ticked by.

"It is everything you claimed it would be," a baritone voice replied. "And the stone itself?"

"With Qaderi, in Cairo."

"Excellent. I'll wire the remainder of your funds."

"If you require anything else, you know how to contact me."

"One more thing," said the baritone voice.

"Yes?"

"Do you know how to use a gun?"

"Majli, please. Don't insult me."

Omar nearly dropped his phone when he heard Majli's name. He was one of the most feared terrorists in this part of the world.

And he was here, right now, in this restaurant!

Majli laughed. "I needed to know. It concerns an assignment in San Francisco."

A hand touched Omar on the shoulder and with a gasp Omar whirled around.

"Would you care to be seated?" asked the hostess.

Omar covered his phone with a hand. "Thank you, but my friend has been delayed. He's not sure when he will arrive."

"Would you care to wait out front?"

"Of course," Omar said with a pleasant smile. "I will be there in a moment."

The hostess eyed him curiously and left.

Omar put the phone back to his ear.

"…your plans to kill Rutherford Tyler and Youssef Qaderi," Majli said.

"I'll phone you once I reach Cairo," Tariq replied.

A waiter rounded a corner carrying a large platter of kebabs overhead. He saw Omar at the last minute and veered to avoid hitting him, nearly losing his balance. He gave Omar a dirty look as Omar jumped to the side.

Omar caught his breath. He needed to phone Langley!

He refocused. *What were those names again? Someone named Tyler…Rutherford Tyler. And a second man — Youssef Qaderi. Where was it they were they going to be killed? Was it San Francisco?*

He spun to go.

And collided with another waiter.

In what seemed like horrifying slow motion, Omar watched the waiter's platter of dirty dishes began to topple. He saw the waiter's desperate attempt to catch them. Saw the panic in his eyes when he knew it was no use. Saw plates, bowls, glasses, and silverware slide off the platter and cascade toward the floor.

The sound of the crash tore through the restaurant. Glasses smashing. Plates splintering. Silverware clattering across the floor.

The restaurant fell instantly quiet.

Omar and the waiter locked eyes. No one breathed.

Suddenly, from the kitchen, excited voices.

"Sir, I'm so sorry!" said the waiter. "Are you all right?"

Omar stared in shock at the phone in his hand.

The connection was still open.

"Sir?" the waiter asked again.

Omar saw people looking at him. Aproned kitchen staff hurried toward him.

Dazed, Omar staggered back, motioning that he was not hurt before retreating to a quiet corner.

Regaining his composure, Omar considered his next course of action. With Tariq and Majli on the other side of the restaurant, it was unlikely either of them had actually seen him. And there was a fair chance the sound of the crash filling the restaurant had drowned out the sound over the phone. Still, he needed to get his phone back, not that it could easily be traced back to him. Assuming, therefore, that he had not been recognized, and with restaurant activity returning to normal, he should be able to stroll past Tariq's booth unnoticed. If it was empty, he would grab his phone. If it was not, he would call Langley and return for the phone later.

With a steadying breath, Omar lowered his head and made his way casually along the aisle. When he passed Tariq's booth, he saw that it was empty.

With a sigh of relief, Omar slid into the adjacent booth.

But when he reached behind the darkened section of fairy lights, a bolt of fear shot up his spine.

His cell phone was gone.

CHAPTER 5

The telephone rang, and Zoe answered it.

"Put him through," she said, slamming down the receiver and running down the corridor to Teague's office. She threw open the door and rushed in.

"I told you to go home," said Teague.

"It's Omar, line one!" Zoe replied just as the phone on Teague's desk rang.

Teague growled then punched the speakerphone button.

It took Omar a little over two minutes to relate what he had seen and heard about Tariq's meeting with Majli, about the tablet, about Tariq going to Cairo, and about Tyler and Qaderi being targeted, possibly in San Francisco.

"Are you certain it was Majli?" asked Teague.

"I am certain," Omar replied. "But when I went back for my phone, it was gone. If Majli traces that phone to me, I'm dead. My entire family is dead."

"Don't worry, the phone's untraceable."

"You don't know Majli."

"Did you actually see him take it?" asked Trent.

"Who else would have taken it?" asked Omar.

"Maybe a waiter? A busboy?"

"It was Majli, I tell you!"

"I think you're overreacting."

"I'm not! It was *Majli!*"

"Omar, calm down, we'll protect you," said Teague.

"I can't do this anymore!"

"We'll set you up in a different city."

"I want out. I want to come to America, like you promised."

"I told you, those things take time."

"I haven't got time! You said I had to earn the right to come to America, that I couldn't be silent in the face of terrorism any more than you could be silent when fundamentalists murdered doctors and blew up abortion clinics. You told me that! Well, I have not been silent! And I helped you because I hate terrorism. But it is dangerous here for me now. I need to get my family out of this country right away!"

Teague looked at Trent and got the nod.

"Hang with me a moment," said Teague.

He brought up a list of U.S. warships and their current positions on his computer screen. He pointed to the USS George Washington. It was pushing north toward the Arabian Sea.

"Do it," said Trent.

"You there, Omar?" asked Teague, calling a map of Saudi Arabia onto the screen.

"I'm here."

Teague zoomed in on a particular area of the map.

"Do you know the coastal road south from Al Lith?" he asked.

"Of course."

"Hamdanah's the next town, and about twenty kilometers south of there is a small cove on the Red Sea coast. Be there tonight – at midnight – on the beach. Dark clothing, no pets, no more than one suitcase each. That's one each, Omar, for you, your wife, and your two daughters – a total of four. If it can't fit in those suitcases, it doesn't come. Drive down close to the water and stay in your car. A team of Marines will come ashore and ask you to identify yourselves. Tell them who you are and be ready to move. No long dresses or fancy shoes."

"What about new passports, identities, and citizenship documents?"

"That'll come later. The extraction team needs to get you onto one of our ships."

"Where will you take us?"

"We'll figure that out. The important thing now is your safety. We'll talk once you're on board." Teague paused, then said, "This is permanent, Omar, you need to know that. There's no going back."

"I understand."

"Okay, then, we're set."

"Thank you, Mr. Teague."

"Thank *you,* Omar. You've risked a lot to help us."

Once Teague ended the call, Trent patted him on the shoulder.

"Good work. Keep me posted," he said.

"Yes, sir," said Teague. He waited until Trent was gone, then glared at Zoe. "I told you to go *home.*"

"Did you hear what Omar *said?*"

"Did you hear what *I* said?"

"He overheard plans to kill Tyler and Qaderi. Not only that, I want to know why Tyler's name keeps popping up. Why does Majli want him killed?"

Teague rubbed the bridge of his nose.

"Qaderi, I can understand," continued Zoe. "He owns the tablet and Abu Nazer wants to steal it. But why Tyler?"

"Don't you have a social life? Don't you get tired? I'm tired. I want to go home."

"There's got to be a reason! Some kind of a connection."

With a sigh, Teague picked up his phone.

"Yes, sir?" a voice asked.

"Two coffees. Big and strong."

"Right away, sir."

Teague hung up, then leaned back and gestured for Zoe to continue.

"This is what baffles me," she said. "Toy Soldier alerts us that Tariq flies to Saudi Arabia to meet with Abu Nazer. Instead, he meets with Majli and gives him the information. Does this mean Majli and Abu Nazer are working together? Could Majli be Abu Nazer?"

"What do your instincts say?"

"We've known about Majli for some time, so if he and Abu Nazer were one and the same, I think we would have heard. That leads me to conclude the two of them are working together, and that Majli is probably Abu Nazer's front man."

Zoe watched Teague for a reaction. But, as usual, his expression revealed nothing.

Teague stared at Zoe for a moment, then stood and began pacing the floor. "Give me a rundown on what we know. Aside from the obvious fact that Abu Nazer's a religious nut."

"Actually, we don't know that."

Teague stopped and looked pointedly at Zoe. "What do you mean we don't know that? Abu Nazer was involved in the assassination of Yitshak Rabin. Obviously, he hates Jews."

"What about those Omani businessmen he killed? They were Muslims."

"Who were working with a team of Americans, one of whom was a Jew. Without doubt it was a retaliation against Arabs who could be viewed as religious traitors. Not only that, we know that Tariq's in Mecca plotting the deaths of two men. Why not Frankfurt or London? I'll tell you why. Because Mecca's a religious center. Which makes Abu Nazer a religious zealot."

"I disagree," Zoe replied, suddenly feeling the heat of Teague's stare.

"Then paint me another picture!" growled Teague, as two large cups of coffee were brought in.

Zoe watched him take a gulp of his coffee as he stalked back and forth.

"I'm waiting!" he said, his neck muscles veined and taut. "Convince me that you're right and I'm wrong."

Teague was openly challenging her and Zoe felt herself starting to wilt. Obviously, he had spotted some flaw in her logic and she was about to get another one of his lectures. Here she was, four years out of university – a virtual rookie – and she had dared challenge the Deputy Director of Operations, a man with over twenty years of experience.

Still, Teague had once said he had not hired her to be a doormat.

With rising confidence, Zoe took a sip of her coffee, then calmly turned to meet Teague's stare with a resolute expression of her own.

"Well, it's true only Muslims are allowed in Mecca," she said, "but Mecca might have been chosen simply to mislead us. Unlike most religious fanatics, Abu Nazer has never made any kind of religious claim. Most terrorists of that ilk are motivated by some kind of twisted ideology, and they use religious diatribe to justify their actions. Not so with Abu Nazer. It's a negative space that speaks volumes. Plus, while it's true that most Muslims have traditionally been Middle Eastern, that pattern is changing. There are many more Western believers. Bottom line: apart from conjecture, we know very little about who he is or why Mecca was chosen for this meeting. We simply don't have enough information."

Zoe took a nervous sip of coffee and waited for Teague's rebuttal.

"Well done," he said with a nod of approval. "Step to the head of the class."

Zoe's mouth dropped open. "Are you telling me this was a test?"

"To be honest? Yes, it was."

"Mind telling me *why?*"

"Because I'm catching a lot of heat and I needed to know now if your methods would produce data that could stand up to that heat."

"I wish you'd shown me some faith."

"I do have faith in you, Zoe. It's why you're on this case. But the pressure's on me to catch Abu Nazer and I'm banking on you to do what no one else has been able to do – identify him. But when evidence is scant and people are yelling at you to come up with something, it can be tempting to extrapolate conclusions based on the accepted rumors. If that's what you were doing, I needed to know now rather than when I'm in front of a sub-committee. You know my axiom: base conclusions on facts, not assumptions."

A halfhearted nod was Zoe's reply. She'd heard that before. Like a million times.

After patting her on the shoulder reassuringly, Teague returned to his desk. "Don't be angry. I had to be sure. Abu Nazer's a master of contradiction. It's one reason he's never been caught. Aaron, by comparison, was different."

"The Israeli assassin?" asked Zoe.

Teague nodded "While he, too, was never photographed or identified, we know he was an Israeli."

"Before my time," said Zoe.

"Seven years ago, just north of Gaza, he took a fatal bullet from Abu Nazer. The two were mortal enemies."

"Same mindless quarrel between the Arabs and Jews."

"You're making assumptions," said Teague. "Yes, Aaron used a Hebrew name, and he even used a Hebrew calling card – Aleph – the first letter of the Hebrew alphabet. He had it printed on a business card that he left at or near each scene where he claimed responsibility. But these were not what identified him as an Israeli. It was his targeted retaliatory pattern that linked him undeniably with that nation. Aaron's pattern was eye-for-an-eye."

"Don't you mean, life-for-a-life?"

"I guess I do, although Aaron was never known to initiate an unprovoked strike. Unlike the terrorists of today, his assassinations were always against actual perpetrators of violence against Israel. Aaron was old school, and never to our knowledge were any of his victims innocent bystanders."

"How do you know he was male?"

"Good question," said Teague with a flicker of a smile. "Probability is high that he was male because of his physical strength. On one occasion he tracked down two killers, took them out, then quietly bent the barrels of their rifles to prevent others from using them. On another occasion, on the Syrian coast, he actually lifted a terrorist up and impaled him on a meat hook. It was a gristly act which – like the bent rifle barrels – suggests the strength of a male."

"And Abu Nazer?"

"No such clues. Which is why we have to be careful in what we assume. Abu Nazer might not be the Arab in that Arab-versus-Jew scenario you just mentioned. As you pointed out, his name could actually be a deliberate ruse chosen to fuel the public perception that terrorists are all wild-eyed fanatics from the Middle East. And unlike Aaron, we don't know that Abu Nazer isn't a woman. Rifles and bombs are user-friendly to both genders. Again, public perception is that terrorists tend to be male; however, in the final analysis, we can make no assertions about Abu Nazer's nationality, gender, skin color, height, weight…"

"Like I said – apart from conjecture, we don't know squat."

"As far as his personal profile is concerned, that's true. Abu Nazer is still a phantom. But when it comes to his behavioral profile, we do have a lead."

"Tariq Yassin?"

"Bingo. Toy Soldier tells us Tariq was in Saudi Arabia delivering information to Abu Nazer, and we have Omar's confirmation that the meeting took place with Majli."

"What do we do next?"

"You tell me."

"Obviously, we need to slap surveillance on Tariq so that we can begin recording his behavioral patterns. If Omar heard right, then Tariq's got Majli's phone number and plans to call him from Cairo. That means we can put a tracer on his phone, get Majli's number, and maybe get a fix on where he is. We still don't know how Abu Nazer makes contact with Tariq, but it's probable he uses the internet. If he does, then Tariq's computer would have copies of old e-mail correspondence and a list of addresses, although web-based e-mail addresses can be obtained anonymously and changed quickly, so that may not lead us anywhere. Still, it's worth a try. Also, by contacting

Tariq's Internet Service Provider, we should be able to intercept and monitor any future correspondence."

"Anything else?"

"Flag Tariq's bank accounts and see what happens."

Teague nodded. "Anything else?"

"Knowing that Tyler and Qaderi are targets, I think it makes sense to profile them. I also think we should question Tyler. See what he knows. Figure out why Abu Nazer wants to kill him. I think we should place Tyler under surveillance. Find out who he hangs with, what he talks about, what his activities are — again, to flesh out his profile so that we can determine why Abu Nazer wants to kill him. Plus, if and when Abu Nazer does try something, we'll be there, thus increasing our chances of nabbing Abu Nazer and saving Tyler's life."

"Anything else?"

"That's all I can think of."

"Then go ahead and get the ball rolling. Start with Tariq, then the profiles."

"What about surveillance on Tyler?"

"I'll approve a level one, but only to help you flesh out his profile. Liaise with the surveillance team directly; but remember, Tyler isn't our focus, Abu Nazer is. This is temporary and it terminates once we find the connection. Also, when you phone Tyler, I want Cooke in on the call as your technical back-up. Stick to the basics and keep it casual."

"Yes, sir."

"Now, back to this business about Armageddon."

"That's only if the tablet proves genuine, which no one will know for certain until Dr. Eaton and her experts have had time to study it."

"Which gives us some breathing room. Abu Nazer won't risk stealing it until he knows whether or not it's real."

"Maybe, maybe not," said Zoe. "It's too early to make that call. Guesses aside, we're still not sure why he wants it."

"Then find out. When's this study supposed to take place?"

"Don't know that either, but I'll find out."

"Find out tomorrow. I want you to go home."

"Can't I at least get the ball rolling? Thirty minutes. An hour at most."

"Go home, Gustaves!"

"Then at least tell me how he figured it out."

"How who figured what out?" asked Teague.

"Abu Nazer. That what went on at San Gabriel was a trap."

"He has a knack for things like that."

"It couldn't have been the money. We laundered those funds through more than a dozen offshore accounts."

"Like I said, he has a knack."

"No one's that good," said Zoe.

"He is."

"Maybe somebody tipped him off?"

"Nobody tipped him off," said Teague.

"Then how did he know?"

"For the last time, go home."

Teague walked over and opened the door.

"Someone had to have talked," said Zoe, finishing her coffee. "Maybe not intentionally, but someone did."

"I like your tenacity, Gustaves. It's one of the reasons I hired you. But you need to learn when to back off. Especially when I'm telling you to back off."

"Yes, sir, of course. I'm simply trying to—"

"I know what you're trying to do! And I'm telling you to drop it. Now, go home."

Zoe started to protest, but Teague intensified his glare.

With an impatient sigh, Zoe marched out the door.

Once Zoe had gone, Teague closed the door. He stood there for a moment with pursed lips, his hand on the door knob, his brow furrowed with concern.

Gustaves was becoming a problem.

CHAPTER 6

"My God, it's nearly seven!" exclaimed Tyler, glancing at his watch.

"Your other engagement?" asked Sharifa.

"Yeah. And if I'm late, Johnny Bill Sandborn turns into Godzilla."

"Are you free afterwards for dinner? I still have a number of questions. Specifically about taking photographs of the tablet."

"Tonight'll be late. How about tomorrow?"

"I'm leaving tomorrow."

"But you just got here."

"I'm on a very tight schedule. So, late is fine, I really don't mind."

Tyler eyed Sharifa for a moment. "Do you like chocolate-pecan fudge cake?" he asked.

"I beg your pardon?"

"I reckon you will. Come on, we can talk on the way."

"Dr. Tyler, I really don't think—"

"No time to argue. We've got to hurry."

Grabbing Sharifa by the hand, Tyler led her through the crowd and out to his pick-up truck in the parking lot. He unlocked the passenger door and scooped some loose tools and fixtures off the floorboard.

"Sorry about the mess," he said, tossing the tools in the back.

Sharifa noticed the door was missing its handle and window crank. It lacked mats or carpet, and the floorboard was nothing more than exposed sheet metal.

"Here," Tyler said, handing her the door handle.

Sharifa looked at him guardedly before accepting the handle and climbing in.

Tyler slammed the door, hurried around the front of the truck, and was just sliding behind the wheel when his cell phone rang. He checked the caller ID and took the call.

"Hey, Val, what's up?" he said, listening for a moment. "Presents? That's right, I forgot." A pause then a grin. "You're a lifesaver! Be there in five."

They arrived at the Sandborns' ranch-style house twenty minutes after seven, not noticing the white service van parked a short distance away. The driver of the van got out, slid open the side door and brought out several orange cones. He placed them around the van. He then used a crowbar to lift open a manhole cover. He returned to the van, reappeared with some tools and wire, and began working.

After handing Sharifa one of the two brightly-wrapped packages, Tyler led the way down the driveway toward the rear of the house. Large, stately oak trees fronted the Sandborns' house, their huge branches arching high into the air.

At the end of the driveway, Tyler opened a high, slatted gate.

"*Dad, Mom, it's Uncle Tyler!*" screamed two kids, enough out-of-sync to make it sound like an echo. "He's here and he brought her!"

They scrambled out of the swimming pool and ran screaming toward Tyler, who handed Sharifa his package. He knelt and opened his arms. Seven-year-old Ben plowed into him like a runaway truck, knocking him onto his back. He then scrambled on top of Tyler and pinned his arms.

"You give?" demanded Ben.

"I give, I give!" laughed Tyler.

Ben released Tyler, climbed off and sat beside him. "Is she really from E-jumpt, Uncle Tyler?" he asked.

"It's *Egypt*," corrected precocious Jenny, age nine.

"Gen-u-ine article," answered Tyler. "Those Egyptians, they sure make 'em pretty, don't they?"

The kids giggled.

Tyler glanced up at Sharifa, who was staring down at him with amused disbelief.

"Sonuvagun, you're early!" declared Johnny Bill, pushing open a screen door, a longneck in one hand. "Go on, you kids, leave Tyler alone. You can pester him later. Throw him in the pool, if you want."

"*Yeah!*" screamed Ben and Jenny, leaping up and jumping back into the water, where four other kids greeted them with vigorous splashes.

"Early? I thought you said seven," Tyler replied, climbing to his feet.

"I did, ya polecat. But everybody knows not to tell you the real time 'cause you're always runnin' late. Hell, we didn't figure on seeing you 'til at least seven-thirty. So that means you're early!" Johnny Bill laughed and slapped Tyler on the back. "Now git on in here and introduce us to your girlfriend."

"She's here on business," said Tyler.

"Riiight."

"Come on, Johnny Bill, you know why she's here! Don't go stirring things up."

Johnny Bill laughed and pulled open the screen door.

Tyler looked back at Sharifa. "I'm really sorry about this."

"It's okay. I really don't mind."

"Look who's here!" Johnny Bill called out.

While introductions were being made, a phone buzzed inside the white van.

"Charlie nine," the technician said.

"How's it looking?" asked Zoe from Cooke's office at Langley.

"All set up and ready to go," answered the technician, flipping some switches. "How's it looking at your end?"

Zoe checked the flow graphs on the monitors. "Household audio streaming loud and clear," she said. "What'd you do, pin mikes on their lapels?"

"New budget, new toys," replied the technician. "Hey, Zoe, since I got you on the phone, any way you can order us some pizza and charge it to your account?"

"In your dreams," said Zoe, ending the call. After a quick peek to make sure Teague wasn't prowling the corridor, she moved to another computer, entered a command and brought a search window up on the screen. She entered Tyler's name and hit "Enter." By the time Johnny Bill was dishing out barbecued ribs an hour later, Zoe had watched three of Tyler's celebrity interviews and read more than a dozen of his articles.

"Very interesting," she mused after reading Tyler's earliest magazine article, *The Holy Circle of Hatred,* which was a scathing rebuke of warfare in the name of religion. "What caused an intelligent guy like Tyler to quit writing gutsy pieces like this in favor of celebrity gossip and glitz? What happened to that righteous anger?" She stared at the article for awhile, then shrugged and clicked on the next one.

Back in Austin, Sharifa carried her dishes into the kitchen.

"Thank you for a wonderful meal," she said.

"We're so glad you came," Johnny Bill's wife, Gloria, replied. "Them kids have been dyin' to meet you ever since they heard Tyler's girlfriend from Egypt was in town."

"I really am here on business."

"Honey, I know that. We would've heard about you long before now if you were really his girlfriend. Johnny Bill always exaggerates stuff like that."

Gloria placed the dishes in the sink.

"How is Tyler related?" asked Sharifa.

"Oh, he's not really Ben 'n' Jenny's uncle. They call him that 'cause they love him so much. We've all been real good friends ever since he moved here."

"When was that?"

"Gloria paused, sponge in hand. "I'd say five, six years ago. He showed up at Johnny Bill's garage one day needin' some work done on his truck, and the two of 'em struck up a friendship."

"Where did he come from?" asked Sharifa.

"Somewhere in New Jersey. I knew right away he was from back East 'cause he pronounced his words funny, like Easterners do. He said his parents died when he was young and he was sent to New Jersey to live with relatives. I guess it was kinda tough on him, though he don't talk about it much. Tyler's that way – likeable, but he keeps his distance. Anyway, our kids took to him like pigs take to mud. And you can see how he spoils 'em rotten. Tyler's terrific. He even sponsors Ben's Little League team – though I must say I've never met a man as athletic as Tyler who's so clumsy at swingin' a bat. Can't throw a football, either."

"Everyone seems to like him."

"That's 'cause he's so generous. Right after we met, he offered to take some pictures of us with his new camera, which was one o' them fancy types with a big lens. He did it for free, and it's still the best shot anyone's ever taken. Same with my Aunt Pauline. She was so thrilled with hers she introduced Tyler to her old friend, Governor Conroe. Tyler asked the Governor if he could do an interview about his work with troubled kids. The Governor agreed, and Tyler talked one of the local TV stations into lettin' him use their studio. The interview went over so well it was run across the state, and it helped Governor Conroe win reelection. To show his appreciation, the Governor introduced Tyler to his old friend, Vice President Baker, who Tyler's interviewed several times on national TV."

"All that from taking a photo?"

"Funny how things work out sometimes, isn't it? Why, Tyler could pick up the phone right now, call Washington, and get put right through. He's even got a special password of some kind."

Out in the van, the surveillance technician picked up the phone and dialed Zoe.

"Gustaves," she answered seconds later.

"Did you hear that?" asked the technician.

"Hear what?" asked Zoe.

"About Tyler and Vice President Baker. It's possible Baker's the target and Abu Nazer's using Tyler to get to him."

"He's an amazing journalist," Sharifa was saying inside the house.

"He's a lot more than that," replied Gloria.

"In what way?"

Suddenly self-conscious, Gloria looked away.

"What is it?" asked Sharifa.

"Nothing."

But there was obviously something, and it had to do with Tyler. But what? An affair?

"Did I say something wrong?" asked Sharifa.

Several moments passed.

"Gloria?" Sharifa asked.

"You didn't say nothing wrong," Gloria replied, turning toward Sharifa, but avoiding her eyes. After an emotional sigh, she said, "A few years back, Jenny got sick. The doctor did some tests and told us it was leukemia. We didn't have any insurance, and of course we didn't know what to do." She paused, tears welling in her eyes. "Johnny Bill mentioned our situation to Tyler, and Tyler called the doctor and told him Jenny was to have everything she needed, that he'd pay for it. To make a long story short, Jenny got her treatment, and because they caught it early, she was cured. All up, it cost Tyler over two hundred and sixty thousand dollars."

"My God!"

"And Tyler said he wouldn't take a dime of it back until our horse won the Kentucky Derby."

Gloria wiped her eyes and went back to washing dishes.

"I'm so glad Jenny's all right," Sharifa said, picking up a dishtowel.

Gloria silently nodded.

"Tyler didn't tell me you and Johnny Bill raised horses."

"We don't."

"But I thought…"

"That's just Tyler's way of not embarrassin' us. Look, I know Tyler has a doctorate and all, but he never makes us feel like we're poor or dumb. Neither Johnny Bill or I have ever been to college – which you can probably tell," she added with an insecure laugh. "But that Tyler, he's always been there for us. We just love him, we really do."

A long moment of silence passed while Sharifa reflected on what she had just learned.

"You 'bout ready for dessert?" Gloria asked, drying her hands on the mallard duck apron given to her last Christmas by Johnny Bill. She took off the apron, stepped over to the table, and picked up a large round cake. "Johnny Bill's actually the one who requested the chocolate-pecan fudge. Them kids don't really care, so long as it's made with butter and sugar."

"Is Tyler for real?" asked Sharifa. "I mean, he seems too good to be true."

"Honey, he's for real."

"Makes me wish I weren't leaving tomorrow."

"We're headin' out to the Broken Spoke later on tonight. Why don't you come along?"

"The Broken Spoke?"

"Local hotspot and world famous honky-tonk."

Sharifa looked quizzically at Gloria.

Gloria laughed. "Country music. Best on the planet."

"I wouldn't want to intrude."

"Nonsense! And I got just the clothes you can wear. Mind you, I haven't been able to get into them for – well, I won't tell you how long – but I'm bettin' they'll fit you just fine."

"Are you sure?"

"Absolutely. Now come on, let's serve up this cake."

CHAPTER 7

With the final fanfare blast of Johnny Bill's Firebird echoing across the parking lot, Tyler guided his pick-up past Johnny Bill and into a vacant space near the back fence.

"Like I was saying," he said, switching off the ignition. "A good country tune plucks the heartstrings, not cello strings. There aren't a lot of intricate note patterns – unless the fiddle player gets warmed up – but the melody's rich and satisfying, like sorghum on grits."

"But all this lamenting about love gone wrong. Isn't that depressing?"

"Heartache's a part of life, and a good country song isn't afraid to capture that. But other songs capture different emotions – the exhilaration of a kiss, the magic of a night, the hope of a better life… Come on, I'll show you what I mean. Stony Lonesome's in town and he's the best. I've got all his CDs."

After locking his truck, Tyler led Sharifa toward the entrance.

"Hey!" a voice called out.

Tyler glanced toward the voice. Leaning against the tailgate of a black Chevy pick-up was a muscular, bald-headed man. With him were half a dozen of his friends, all wearing the usual blue jeans and hats, all drinking beer.

"You talkin' to me?" asked Tyler.

"Damn right I'm talkin' to you."

"What's the problem?"

"You can't park there."

"Why not?"

"'Cause we don't like Fords."

The remark elicited howls of laughter from the man's friends.

"Right on, Lenny!" one of them shouted.

Tyler shook his head and kept walking.

Lenny rushed over and halted Tyler with a hand to the chest. "You hard o' hearing?" he asked, giving Sharifa the once-over before leveling his gaze at Tyler.

"We're not looking for trouble," replied Tyler.

"Then move that piece of crap."

Grinning with expectation, Lenny's friends all gathered around.

"Fine, it's not worth the hassle," said Tyler, leading Sharifa back toward his truck.

"Come to think of it, we don't much like spics around here, either," said Lenny. "So when you move that shit heap, why don't you keep on going. 'Less, o' course, you want to pass the dark meat around. If she's any good, we'll let you stay."

"Too boney!" one of Lenny's friends called out.

"Ain't enough there to pass around!" shouted another.

More coarse laughter.

Tyler stopped, looked down, took a calming breath.

"Don't…" Sharifa whispered.

"Go inside. Find Johnny Bill," said Tyler.

"Let's just leave, okay?"

"Go on. I'll be fine."

"There's seven of them!"

"Better listen to your bitch," said Lenny.

Tyler turned and faced Lenny.

Sharifa grabbed Tyler by the arm.

He turned and took her by the hands reassuringly. "Go on. While I straighten this out."

Sharifa shook her head.

"I need you to go inside," he said.

Sharifa saw the seriousness in his eyes. She nodded and started for the entrance.

"Grab her," said Lenny.

Wearing a sleeveless white t-shirt, Teddy Elwood was a cocky sophomore fullback already into his second hour of drinking. He spat a brown stream of tobacco juice onto the gravel then grabbed Sharifa by the arm.

"Ain't never had any spic meat before," Teddy said with a broad, toothy grin. "Come to Daddy. Let's see what ya got."

It was a graceful pirouette – arm up and around, spinning, bending, twisting easily from Teddy's grasp. A second pivot brought her under Teddy's outstretched arm.

"What the—" was all Teddy could say in that instant before Sharifa hammered an elbow into his diaphragm.

Teddy staggered, mouth open, chest heaving, for four wobbly steps. Then his knees buckled and he fell to the ground.

"You fucking *whore!*" shouted Lenny.

Lenny lunged for Sharifa, teeth bared, hands like claws.

Tyler's left hand clamped down across the top of Lenny's wrist, his right hand swinging up and grabbing Lenny firmly above the elbow. With a quick twist, Tyler yanked Lenny's arm up behind his back, kicked the rear of his knee and drove him facedown into the gravel.

With an enraged bellow Lenny tried to wrench free, just as Mitch and Woody, two of Teddy's football buddies, charged Tyler.

Bending at the waist, Tyler stepped over Lenny, keeping Lenny's arm in place. Tyler's back kick snapped high, boot meeting teeth, spraying blood in a mist as Mitch's head jerked back and he crumpled to the ground.

Woody collided with Mitch's tumbling body and fell with him. Tyler recoiled from the kick and spun, one hand still holding Lenny in place, his other hand like an axe as it chopped down across the back of Woody's neck.

With an expulsion of air, Woody went limp.

Lenny again tried to wrench free, but Tyler lifted his arm. Lenny screamed and cursed and immediately went slack.

Tyler felt a gun barrel press against his head.

"Let him go, asshole. Or I blow your brains all over the parking lot."

Tyler looked slowly around. He saw a skinny man holding a chrome revolver, arm stiff and fully extended, fingers itching to pull the trigger and call it self-defense.

"I said, let him go!" the skinny man demanded.

Tyler recognized the pistol. It was a .38 caliber Rossi – a handsome, compact weapon that could be stuffed easily in the back of one's jeans, as this one had been.

But Tyler was also aware of something else. There had been no audible click, meaning the pistol had not been cocked. But a double-action revolver like the Rossi didn't need to be cocked, because whenever the trigger was pulled, a linkage inside the frame automatically cocked the hammer before releasing it to fire.

Which meant double-action revolvers had stiff triggers, precisely because of this "double action" feature.

Tyler's fist exploded upward into the skinny man's armpit, striking the radial nerve bundle that lay just below the skin. It temporarily paralyzed his arm. Launching upward, Tyler seized the immobilized arm, stepped inward and hammered a fist into the man's groin, then up into his face as the gun fell from his grasp.

Lenny watched the skinny man fall unconscious beside Mitch and Woody.

He then saw the pistol on the ground.

Lenny grabbed for the Rossi, but Tyler stepped on Lenny's wrist, scooted the pistol out of reach, then dropped onto Lenny's back with both knees, again pinning him on the ground.

Craning his head around, Lenny saw Tyler glaring down at him, fist drawn back.

"Your move," said Tyler.

Lenny shook his head.

Tyler looked at the others, who were standing around them in stunned silence.

"You boys mosey on," he said. "I have a few things to discuss with your friend."

The others all looked at one another, unsure what to do.

"Tell them," Tyler said, grabbing Lenny's arm and lifting it higher, sending a fresh spasm of pain through his body. "Tell 'em we need to talk."

With his face mashed into the gravel, Lenny could only grunt.

"He said, 'Beat it,'" Tyler told them. "And take those morons with you."

Seeing how easily their friends had been defeated, the remaining members of the group dragged their unconscious bodies back to their truck.

Tyler took out a handkerchief and picked up the pistol.

"I'll make sure this gets to the police," he said.

He then grabbed Lenny's wallet out of his pocket and opened it. In a plastic window was his driver's license. Tyler recited the address.

"This where you live, Leonard?" he asked.

Lenny nodded.

"Well, now I know."

Tyler replaced the wallet in Lenny's hip pocket.

"So if I come out later and find even a tiny scratch on my truck, well, let's just say you and I will have further discussions. But if you decide to call it a night and leave things alone, then maybe one day we'll have a beer together and a laugh about all this. What do you say?"

Lenny nodded.

"Now, before we wrap this up, does my date have your sincere apology for the way you insulted her?" Tyler looked up at Sharifa, who was staring down at him.

Lenny nodded one more time.

"Glad to hear it," said Tyler, releasing him. "Come on," he said, taking Sharifa by the hand. He led her across the parking lot to the Broken Spoke.

"Are you all right?" he asked near the entrance.

Sharifa smiled and nodded.

"Where did you learn to fight like that?" he asked. "A lot of brown belts don't have your kind of reflexes."

"It wasn't easy growing up in the poorer parts of Cairo," Sharifa replied. She gazed across the parking lot at Lenny and his friends arguing. "So, where did you learn to fight like that?"

Tyler shuffled nervously.

"Gloria said you had a rough time growing up," she said.

Tyler shrugged.

Sharifa smiled and took Tyler by the hands. "We may be from opposite sides of the planet, but it sounds like we have a lot in common."

Tyler chuckled. "I guess we do."

"I'm a good listener if you ever want to talk," she said. "Now, come on. Let's go inside and see if you know what you're talking about when it comes to music."

Tyler laughed and opened the door.

After handing in the pistol to management, Tyler led Sharifa into the main hall, where he paused and searched the hundreds of faces filling the galleries along each side of the long wooden dance floor. He spotted Johnny Bill and Gloria off to his left, laughing with several other couples. Johnny Bill waved and pointed to a pair of empty chairs. Tyler waved back and led Sharifa across the crowded dance floor.

"About time you showed up!" Johnny Bill said when they reached the table. "Hell, I was just offered twenty bucks for these seats I been saving."

"He'd-a sold 'em, too," Tyler told Sharifa.

Johnny Bill looked wounded. "Aw, hell, Tyler, don't go sayin' stuff like that. You know I wouldn't-a sold 'em. Not for less than thirty."

Everyone laughed. Then they heard three microphone thumps over the loudspeaker.

"Good evenin', y'all, I'm Stony Lonesome," a voice boomed out.

Responding with applause, the crowd gazed up at the stage, where an enormous man in a cream fedora sat balanced on a barstool, an electric guitar resting on his lap. Overlapping rolls of flesh hung beneath his chin, while across the chest of his Western shirt were two embroidered mustangs, one on each side.

To his left was a thin man with tinted glasses and a ponytail, wearing a plain white t-shirt and blue jeans. He sat expressionless before a rectangular, steel guitar mounted horizontally on a tubular metal rack. Behind him, in a fortress of drums and bronze cymbals, sat a young man with long curly hair and an infectious smile, nodding enthusiastically to the crowd. Near the drummer stood a shorter man wearing a worn cowboy hat that had been crumpled and bent to fit, holding a bass guitar. And to the right of Stony Lonesome stood a frizzy, red-haired young woman clutching an old brown violin.

As Stony Lonesome readied his guitar, the clapping died away. When it was quiet, he rotated his ponderous head and gave a nod to the red-haired girl. She brought the fiddle up and positioned it between her chin and shoulder. Suddenly, the bow skipped across the strings and the fiddle yipped like a coyote before settling into a low whine. The steel guitar then began its lament, dipping mournfully for a few beats before billowing into a full swell of sound just as Stony Lonesome joined in.

Within moments the tempo had picked up in classic bluegrass style and what had been a scattering of applause became an epidemic. Moments later, listeners began to stomp their boots. Whistles and cheers came next.

Abruptly, the fiddle stopped, the steel guitar receded and the focus was on Stony Lonesome.

Obese and slow, the native Texan was famous for telling audiences how cold molasses could outrun him in a race. But his speed on a guitar was another matter. His agile fingers became a blur, and the audience of more than three hundred people fell silent while Stony Lonesome and his flat pick performed magic. Like a butterfly, the notes climbed in a gentle flit, then soared higher and held like a ballerina whirling on tiptoes. Then, off the pinnacle, the notes came in a tumbling zigzag, until a crash on the drummer's cymbal brought the fiddle and bass back in. The steel guitar created a swelling cloud of harmony, from which a powerful crescendo exploded on the trans-fixed audience. And a moment later, it was over.

Leaping to their feet, the listeners thundered their approval. On and on the ovation stretched, with Stony Lonesome's efforts to silence it only fueling people more. The cheering became so boisterous waitresses had trouble delivering drinks – including Tyler's pitchers of margaritas.

Eventually, the noise died down, the drinks were served, and Stony Lonesome laid aside his guitar. Then, while the others played accompaniment, he removed the microphone from its stand and began singing about life's lonesome roads – the song for which he was famous.

Tyler handed Sharifa a frozen margarita.

"What's this?" she asked.

"A local specialty."

Sharifa took a cautious sip and brightened. "This is fantastic!" she said, taking several quick gulps. "What is it?"

"Trouble, if you don't slow down."

Sharifa laughed, then refilled her glass.

While the others talked, Sharifa continued to drink, and within minutes was again refilling her glass.

"That's it, come on," Tyler said, taking her by the hand.

"Where are we going?" she asked.

"To do the two-step," he said.

"The what?" asked Sharifa, the mellow warmth of the tequila bringing an involuntary giggle to her lips.

Leaning close to her ear, Tyler explained the dance, and while he spoke, Sharifa found herself becoming aroused by the heat of his breath. Goosebumps crawled up her thighs.

"I don't understand," she said.

"Not a problem. I'll teach you," he replied.

Sharifa looked at the couples moving around the dance floor to the lively embrace of the music.

"The two-shtep?" she asked, suddenly tickled at her fumbled pronunciation.

"You got it. Come on."

Tyler led her onto the floor and showed her where to place her hands. "Okay, here we go," he said.

Staring down, Sharifa tried to keep step. She stepped on Tyler's boots several times, then tripped and nearly fell.

"I can't do this!" she said.

"Don't look, just feel," he replied.

"Tyler, I can't do this!"

"Yes, you can. Just close your eyes."

Sharifa scowled doubtfully up at Tyler, but his blue eyes were warm and confident.

"Trust me," he said. "Close your eyes."

She did.

Tyler drew Sharifa to him.

"Good. Now, feel the music," he said.

They began dancing again, this time with Tyler counting softly in her ear. Seconds later, they began moving as one, gliding and turning, faces close, bodies closer.

Suddenly, Sharifa stopped and pulled back.

"What is it?" he asked.

She started to speak, then glanced away.

"What?" he asked again.

Sharifa looked back at Tyler. "I'm scared," she murmured.

"Of what? Those bozos outside?"

She hesitated then said, "Of you."

Tyler laughed. "You can't be serious!"

"Look at the way we're dancing. And I don't dance!"

"That makes absolutely no sense whatsoever."

"Exactly! This makes no sense."

"You've lost me."

Sharifa touched a button on Tyler's shirt. "I just met you and yet I feel like – like I've known you all of my life. What's happening here, Tyler?"

The predawn morning was humid with anticipation as Tyler laid Sharifa on the cool sheets of his bed. A soft breeze drifted in through the window. A chorus of insects sang in the darkness.

Stretching out beside her, Tyler brushed the hair from her face.

Sharifa smiled then drew Tyler to her.

It was a gentle kiss at first. Soft and slow. They parted, then kissed again, this time lingering before Sharifa pushed Tyler onto his back, rolled on top and straddled his waist. Her breathing was erratic as she peeled his shirt up over his head and tossed it away. She kissed him again on the lips, then glided down over his neck, bare chest, and stomach to the buttons on his jeans.

Tyler reached out to stop her, but Sharifa pinned his arms and stared down at him in the darkness, her face inches from his. She then lowered herself down slowly to kiss him again on the lips, before moving tantalizingly down over his chest. Moments later, they lay naked in the darkness.

With intertwined legs, they began exploring one another in a slow dance of touch. Lips frolicked up legs, over hips, and along backs. Then came the tickles, more kissing and coaxing as they tumbled across the bed. An hour later, unwilling to bridle restraint any longer, Tyler brought Sharifa to him, their playful prologue now turning furious.

They reached the pinnacle, rode the moment, then freefell through space, floating and drifting. Minutes later, they peeled apart, perspiring and exhausted before snuggling together in a satisfied embrace just as the first signs of dawn lit the eastern sky.

CHAPTER 8

Dappled sunlight was playing across the bed when Sharifa opened her eyes. It was shortly before noon and she was wrapped in Tyler's arms, her cheek against his chest, one arm slung over his stomach as it rose and fell with each breath.

She rose quietly and crept across the hardwood floor toward the bathroom. The floorboards squeaked lightly when she picked up her clothes. Twenty minutes later, showered and dressed, she emerged to find the bed empty.

"Good morning," Sharifa called out as she entered the kitchen. She broke into a laugh when she saw Tyler standing at the sink in his gray cotton briefs.

"Good *afternoon*," he replied with a grin.

She walked over and gave him a kiss. "Is that coffee I smell?" she asked.

"It all depends."

"On what?"

"How much you're willing to pay."

"That depends on the quality of the product."

"I buy cheap coffee and brew it in plastic."

"Sold," Sharifa declared. She reached up and kissed him again, then pressed herself against him, feeling his arousal.

Two minutes later, Tyler was carrying Sharifa and her coffee upstairs.

She took a sip. Said, "This is *dreadful*."

"Wait 'til you taste my bacon and eggs."

They made love, rose for a two o'clock breakfast, and before they knew it, were embracing again, this time at the Austin airport as the final boarding call was being made.

"The next three days will be an eternity," Sharifa said, taking Tyler by the hands.

"Then stay and fly over with me."

"I wish I could. But there will be a backlog of work as it is."

A mumbled protest was Tyler's response.

Sharifa gave Tyler a final kiss before boarding the plane.

Taking her seat, she peered out the window. Tyler was standing by the window where she had left him. Taking out her cell phone, she dialed a number. Seconds later, the connection was made.

"He's been recruited," she said quietly.

And with a contented smile, Sharifa ended the call, leaned back, and closed her eyes.

CHAPTER 9

The telephone rang in Dr. Philippa Eaton's paneled office in London.

"Yes?" she answered, her aristocratic voice a mix of displeasure and indifference.

Seated at her desk, Dr. Eaton was surrounded by stacks of books and papers rising like skyscrapers in a miniature city. A fluorescent lamp threw a wash of dingy yellow light over the clutter.

"Dr. Eaton, this is Youssef Qaderi," a voice announced, the English mildly accented.

Youssef was a handsome black man with light mocha skin and friendly brown eyes. In his late thirties, he possessed a strong, lean build and short, glistening hair. At the moment, he was seated at his desk on the fourth floor of his home on the Nile River island of Zamalek, in urban Cairo.

"Hello, Mr. Qaderi," Dr. Eaton replied, her face brightening into a stiff smile. "I trust you're well?"

"Yes, doctor, and you?"

"Very well, thank you," she said. "How is the weather?" she then asked, not really caring, but engaging in the usual trivialities as a courtesy to the man about to turn the world of politics and antiquities on its head.

"Sunny and hot," answered Youssef. "Is everything set for next week?"

"Indeed, and I'm very much looking forward to it."

"I'm ringing because I'd like to make sure my additions meet with your approval. Is your copy of the list close at hand?"

"One moment," Dr. Eaton replied, laying the phone down and removing several books from one of the piles. She rifled through some papers until she found it. "Yes, I have it," she said.

"What are your thoughts?" he asked.

"As you know, we've secured Dr. Nadia Burke, from the University of Pennsylvania. She's a recognized authority on Egypt's Middle Kingdom, which is my estimate of the corresponding time frame for your tablet. I've also secured Dr. Cameron Cushing, professor of Old Testament history at Princeton Seminary. Then there's your own

68

Dr. Faisal Mostafa, from the Egyptian Museum in Cairo. In addition to being an expert in proto-Sinaitic hieroglyphics, he's an excellent sculptor. Museums from around the world call upon him regularly to identify forgeries of ancient Egyptian art. As for your additions, I see you've recommended a valuation expert with Sterling Crest Gallery."

"Dr. Allan Woolley," said Youssef. "His specialty is ancient Egyptian literature."

"A solid choice. But are you certain you wish to include Dr. Rubin Yehuda? As a Zionist, he may cause trouble."

"It's a risk I think we should take. With the possible exception of yourself, his knowledge of ancient Near-Eastern literature is unparalleled."

"Yes, but there are other considerations. If the tablet is authenticated, accusations will be made that he may have influenced the outcome."

"And if it is not? Dr. Eaton, have you forgotten who owns the tablet? An Egyptian! Who has an expert from the Cairo Museum on the panel. For something of this magnitude, I believe an Israeli of Dr. Yehuda's stature is required. He's an excellent scholar and I don't want there to be any question of bias from either direction. Diversity is our strength."

"As you wish."

"I'm curious about your impressions of the tablet," said Youssef.

"Since I've not yet been able to study it, you'll understand my reluctance to respond."

"But you've studied Sir Edmund's journal."

"And my conclusions have already been published."

"Please. I'd appreciate hearing what you have to say."

Dr. Eaton sighed. "All right. But I must stress how my views cannot be construed as anything more than a preliminary appraisal."

"Of course."

"Well, in light of the details recorded in Sir Edmund's journal, your tablet shows all indications of being genuine. The colophon, of course, is the key to its value."

"What exactly is a colophon?" asked Youssef.

"A mark used in literature to identify the author or publisher of a work. In books today, we see this in the form of a publisher's logo on or near the title page, along with other pertinent information about the author, copyright and so on. In a handwritten letter, the colophon is the signature at the end. Similarly, in ancient Near-Eastern literature, the colophon was also a signature – either by the author or owner – at the end of the document. We see this evidenced in a number of famous examples from that era: the Code of Hammurabi, the Epic of Gilgamesh, and so on. Your artifact, which has been designated ES 34-30, for Egypt, Sinai, and the coordinates quadrant in which it was discovered, is a diorite tablet of imprinted text which duplicates the seventh section of Genesis, spanning chapters 11:27b through 25:12."

"What do you mean, the seventh section?" asked Youssef, just as Mrs. Fedje, his housekeeper, served him a tiny cup of the thick black syrup that was Egyptian coffee.

"Genesis, unlike any other book in the Bible, can be divided into sections quite distinct from the modern chapter headings with which we're all familiar. The more natural, ancient divisions are identified by the colophons, which are still visible today in the phrases, 'these are the generations of,' or 'this is the genealogy of,' followed by the name of the author – Adam, Noah, Shem, and so on. Your tablet is an exact duplicate of the seventh section, with the colophon coming at the end just as it does in other examples of ancient Near Eastern literature. This colophon identifies Ishmael as the author; and of course the tablet itself is written in proto-Sinaitic, which was the language of the Sinai Peninsula during the time Ishmael lived there."

"What's the significance of that?"

"Contrary to what Sir Edmund believed, your tablet does not prove that Genesis was copied from the Egyptians. In fact, it proves quite the opposite – namely, that Ishmael authored that portion of Genesis. Written in the local language – the lingua franca, if you will – your tablet testifies to the historicity of Genesis. Centuries later, Moses gathered this and other tablets into a single book, which we now know as Genesis."

"I'm more intrigued by your statement that the tablet could spark Armageddon. That seems a bit extreme."

"I said that because ES 34-30 makes reference to the original Promised Land: Israel and Palestine, including Jerusalem, plus parts of Egypt, Jordan, Syria, and Lebanon. But your tablet also records Ishmael, founding father of the Arab nations, declaring this land to be the inheritance of Isaac and his descendants, the Jews. Bear in mind, those two brothers – Ishmael and Isaac – worshipped the same God as their father, Abraham, from whom Muslims and Jews claim ancestry. But, as we know, the descendants of these two brothers have been fighting over that land ever since."

With his cordless phone to his ear, Youssef walked out onto a balcony overlooking the tamed waters of the Nile. Beyond, Cairo floated in a haze of pollution.

"Forgive me, Dr. Eaton," he said, "but I don't see why the tablet will stir up such controversy if, as you say, it's simply a duplicate of what's already found in Genesis."

"Most people regard Genesis to be historically questionable, if not downright unreliable. Thus, unless corroborated by outside evidence, claims made from its text can be accepted only by faith. One cannot prove, for instance, that Creation took place in six days. Similarly, one cannot disprove it, either. Which, of course, illustrates my point: it's open to interpretation. Your tablet, however, closes the gap between faith and fact. It's an original, eyewitness document, written by the father of the Arab nations, which – if authenticated – substantiates the Jews' claim on the land. I need not tell you the reactions this will generate, depending on whether one is an Arab or a Jew. That's also why possession of the tablet is so important. It's a corroborating, historical document that proves ownership over the most hotly contested real estate on earth. If, however, the tablet is destroyed, then any claim remains a matter of faith, which can be contradicted by other religious documents."

"No wonder I've been receiving threats," said Youssef.

"A situation that's likely to intensify."

"Which brings me back to your assessment. The gallery has made a number of statements about the tablet's cultural and historical value, but wouldn't offer a dollar value until after they've reviewed Dr. Woolley's report."

"Ahh, the heart of the matter…"

"Forgive me, but I am a businessman," said Youssef. "A simple estimate will suffice."

"You must realize that any figure I give you is nothing but speculation."

"I understand."

Dr. Eaton was silent for a moment.

"Well, assuming Dr. Woolley concurs," she said, "I suppose I could estimate its value to be in the neighborhood of forty to fifty million dollars."

"My *God!*"

"Yes, and you'd better hope your God is watching over you. For if your tablet is indeed authenticated, there will be no shortage of people willing to kill you in order to possess it."

CHAPTER 10

The moon over the Red Sea was like a wedge of Camembert cheese – soft creamy yellow, a perfect half circle, hanging low over the water. The darkness shimmered. The wind blew light and warm. The waves lapped silent swells, rising and falling, lungs breathing. Alive.

The rush of water past the bow was the only sound, apart from the deep churning rumble of the USS George Washington's four giant propellers. The massive nuclear-powered carrier had slowed its speed to a virtual crawl for the extraction, with radar and satellite coverage providing real-time data on any and all possible threats.

Except for Omar's darkened taxi parked near the water, the beach was deserted when the two Zodiacs came ashore. Dressed in camouflage fatigues and wearing PVS-14 night vision goggles – the kind that covered one eye in order to leave the other eye functional in case of a sudden burst of light – ten Marines fanned out and secured the area.

"Perimeter secured," First Sergeant Troy Black reported into his microphone.

"Copy that," Lieutenant Shane Reilly replied from the Zodiac.

First Sergeant Black and two Marines approached the car, their M-4s at the ready. Inside, four heads were visible as dark shapes in a luminescent greenish glow.

Black tapped his gun barrel on the driver's window.

No movement.

He tapped again.

Still no movement.

He then saw the rivulets of thickened blood. Propped upright, all four of them had been executed. Single shots to the head.

"What's the status of the package, come back?" asked Reilly.

"Located," answered Black.

"Bring 'em in. We're almost out of time."

"Sorry, sir. Their time's run out. All four of them are dead."

CHAPTER 11

"Val, I need you to reschedule my appointments for the next two weeks," Tyler said when he entered the converted downstairs bedroom that was his office. It was Monday morning.

"The interview with Qaderi?" asked fifty-two-year-old Val, removing her glasses. Cut trendy and short, Val's hair was the color of plum.

"I'm to meet him Wednesday in Cairo."

"Isn't that kind of sudden?"

"Qaderi sent his PA as inducement," said Tyler with a smile. "Needless to say, I was induced."

Val was not amused. "I don't need to remind you to be careful."

"You don't, but I'm sure you will."

"This isn't a game, Tyler!"

"I'm not saying it is."

"She spent the night here, didn't she?"

"How'd you know that?"

Val rolled her eyes.

"Come on, Val! How'd you know?"

"Tyler, you don't do that kind of thing! And I'm not referring to safe sex, either."

"I don't know, we just kind of…connected. Like we've known each other for years."

"Oh, please!"

"Come on, Val, you know what I mean. I don't do this kind of thing."

"What do you think I've been trying to tell you?"

"And I'm telling you this is different. You, of all people, know what it's been like. How long it's been. How I've never let anyone get close. How I couldn't let anyone get close. But Sharifa and I, we've got things in common – backgrounds, experiences…"

"She works for *Qaderi!*"

"I know that."

"Then you know the danger of getting involved."

"Look, this wasn't planned, all right?"

"Planned or not, you let it happen."

74

"Some things you can't control."

"Someone's not thinking with his brain," muttered Val, just as the phone rang. "Dr. Tyler's office, this is Val," she answered.

"Is Dr. Tyler available?"

"May I ask who's calling?"

"Zoe Gustaves, CIA."

"CIA?" repeated Val, the surprise causing a noticeable lilt in her voice. "Uh, just a moment, please."

Zoe wondered what kind of guy Tyler would be. Having read most of his articles and seen several of his interviews, she knew he was good looking and intelligent. At least that's how he came across on camera.

Which meant he would either be aggressive as hell or a milquetoast, which journalists usually weren't. At least, not if they played in the big leagues, which Rutherford Tyler most certainly did.

Thus far, the basics had been fairly easy to ascertain. Published interviews revealed Tyler to have been born in Ohio then reared by relatives in New Jersey. Transcripts from UCLA showed him to have been an average student, after which he moved to Austin and started taking photos and writing articles. Until, that is, luck handed him a career as a TV journalist.

"This is Rutherford Tyler. May I help you?"

"Dr. Tyler, this is Zoe Gustaves with the Central Intelligence Agency. I'm phoning because I need to ask you some questions. However, in order for you to verify my identity, I'd like you to hang up and call our one-eight-hundred number. Ask for Zoe Gustaves. They'll put you through."

"That won't be necessary," said Tyler, realizing that if such an invitation were being made, it was probably a legitimate call. "What's this about?"

"It has to do with a case I'm working on."

"How am I involved?"

"I'm not at liberty to divulge anything other than the fact that your name appeared on a list of individuals who may possess knowledge which could affect our investigation."

"That doesn't tell me a heckuva lot, does it?"

Zoe smiled. "No, it doesn't. And I hope you'll believe me when I say I wish I could tell you more. It would make my job a whole lot easier."

"I understand. At times, I have to do the same thing with people I'm interviewing. They want to know what it is I'm investigating and I have to tell them something that's really a lot of gobbledygook. Not that what you just said is gobbledygook."

This time Zoe laughed.

"How can I be of assistance?" he asked.

"First, a few preliminary questions to make sure I've got the right person. Are you Rutherford Birchard Tyler?"

"Yes, I am."

"May I digress for a moment and ask how you got that name? It's certainly unusual."

Tyler explained how he was named after the nineteenth president, Rutherford Birchard Hayes.

"I don't have anything nearly that interesting to tell people."

"Count your blessings. Being a teenager named Rutherford had its drawbacks."

Zoe chuckled, then asked the names of Tyler's parents and his date of birth, all of which Tyler provided.

"Okay, thank you," she said. "Now, do you know a man named Tariq Yassin?"

"Should I?"

"All I'm asking is whether or not you recognize the name."

"No, I don't. Who is he?"

"Sorry, I can't say. Do you know a Youssef Qaderi?"

"I've heard of the man, although I've never met him."

"What have you heard?" asked Zoe.

"That he's a collector living in Cairo."

"Anything else?"

"It seems he owns an ancient Egyptian tablet."

"How do you know this?"

"His personal assistant."

"You've had contact with Qaderi through his PA?"

"Yes," replied Tyler. "After reading that he owned the tablet, I wrote to him to request an interview. As you know, I'm a journalist who makes his living beating other journalists to stories and this one looked hot. Anyway, his assistant, Ms. al Rashid, came to Austin to tell me Qaderi was interested. I'm to meet him in Cairo on Wednesday."

"You're telling me she flew all the way from Cairo to advise you, in person, that Qaderi was interested in an interview?"

"That's right."

"Why didn't she just phone?"

"I don't know."

"Doesn't that seem odd?"

"Should it?"

"I'm asking what you think."

"And I'm telling you I don't know. Look, I realize you can't talk to me about your investigation, but you're with the CIA and, well, all these questions are starting to make me a little nervous."

"Why is that?"

"You track down terrorists, right?"

"Dr. Tyler, you know I'm not at liberty—"

"Come on, Ms. Gustaves! Cairo's in the Middle East and the Middle East is a volatile place."

"Actually, it's in North Africa."

"Whatever. Point is, I want to know if something's going on over there that I should know about."

There was a long moment of silence.

"Please! Will I be in some kind of danger if I take this assignment?"

"It's possible," was Zoe's measured reply.

"Should I withdraw? Tell him I'm not coming?"

"I'm not in a position to give you advice."

"Is there something about Qaderi that I should know? Come on! If there is, I need you to tell me."

The compassionate side of Zoe told her she should say something. Tyler was, after all, the subject of an assassination plot and her inclination was to pass on a warning.

Yet, as a profiler and analyst with the CIA, she knew she could not. Not without clearance from Teague.

"Ms. Gustaves?"

"I'm here."

"I don't want to be associated with Qaderi if he's a dangerous man."

"That's not it," said Zoe.

"Then what about that other guy, Tariq? Is he some kind of a terrorist?"

Zoe was about to answer when Tony Cooke ran into her cubicle and pulled a finger across his throat. Zoe stared at him, confused. Tony repeated the gesture emphatically before motioning for her to hang up.

"Ms. Gustaves?" asked Tyler in the absence of a reply.

"Dr. Tyler, you've been very helpful. Someone from our office will be in contact if we need additional information."

"But you haven't told me what kind of danger I'm in!" he said as the line went dead.

"What's going on?" demanded Zoe in her cubicle at Langley.

"You let him take control," said Tony. "Don't ever let a subject start asking questions like that."

"He was concerned for his safety."

"Come on, Zoe! Journalists are a tough bunch. You never hear them fret about traveling to locations where tourists go by the thousands."

"Not many journalists have the CIA phoning with veiled inquiries about their work. You heard what he said. He was worried about Qaderi. A man whose name, along with his own, is on Abu Nazer's hit list."

"But Tyler doesn't know that. I think he was strumming your strings to get information."

Zoe shot out of her chair. "Strumming my strings?"

Tony held up his hands and backed away. "Sorry. That came out wrong."

"Sorry doesn't *cut it!*"

"I apologize. I was out of line."

Zoe stood there, hands on her hips, glaring at Tony.

But what if Tony was right? What if Tyler *had* been milking her for information? Tony was a geek with the social skills of a fence post, but he knew linguistic subtleties like no one else.

"Really, Zoe, I'm sorry," said Tony. "You're the last person I'd ever want to offend."

"Then why did you say it?"

"I seriously don't want to go there," he said.

"Come on, Tony, you know what I do all day. I'm an analyst. I write profiles. I crunch facts. I need to know why you think Tyler took advantage of me."

"I'm not sure I can explain that and stay out of court."

"Please, as a friend," she said.

Tony took a deep breath. "You're friendly and kindhearted and I think Tyler used that against you."

"How? He doesn't know the first thing about me."

Tony did not reply.

"Come on, Tony – give!"

"Look, I know it's not politically correct to talk about interaction dynamics on the basis of gender, but the fact is, we generally respond more favorably to someone of the opposite sex, especially when they send out friendly vibes. Your hesitation, your inclination to help, the sympathetic tone to your voice – these were all indicators."

"Of what?"

"That you're not a hardboiled agent. An experienced journalist would detect that."

"So you're saying he took advantage of me because I'm a woman."

Tony shrugged, clearly uncomfortable.

"Tony!"

"Okay, yes, I'm saying he took advantage of you as a woman. But it goes the other way, too. Women often play men."

"But he seemed so nice."

"He probably is. But some of it was an act."

"How do you know?"

"Come with me."

Tony led the way down the hall to an office lined with consoles and computers.

"Have a seat," he said, plopping down in front of a terminal. He entered some commands on his keyboard while Zoe wheeled a chair over to his desk. She sat down next to Tony and noticed a large pile of Snickers wrappers and paper cups under his desk.

"Are you, what, starting a landfill under here?" she asked, scooting aside the trash with her foot.

"Check this out," he said.

Zoe saw four small polygraph grids appear on the monitor. Tony moved the cursor up to the "Replay" icon and clicked it. Seconds later, they were listening to the telephone conversation between Zoe and Tyler, while all four graphs responded with synchronized lines representing the tonal variations in Tyler's voice.

While the conversation played, Tony pointed to the first grid.

"That was brilliant asking him about his name," he said. "I needed at least twenty seconds of casual conversation from which to construct a baseline."

"Baseline?"

"A standard of truthful intonation against which to judge the rest of his speech flow. The baseline's there, in grid one. Now, watch the other three grids. In a second you'll ask him if knows Tariq."

Zoe's voice asked the question.

"Look at those tracings," said Tony when Tyler gave his response. "And watch what happens when he tells you that he doesn't recognize the name. There – look at those spikes!"

"What do they mean?" asked Zoe.

"They signify intense vocal stresses at the emotional, cognitive, and physiological levels."

"Tony, what does that mean?"

"It means Dr. Tyler was lying."

CHAPTER 12

There are cities, there are great cities, and there is Jerusalem.

Able to make small men feel great and great men feel small, Jerusalem is forever a passion for those who believe, a marvel to those who do not. At times holy, at times harlot, this ancient city crowns the rocky heights of Palestine with a spackled beauty that is far from pristine but every bit as alluring. It is a city where the memories and dreams of Jews, Muslims, and Christians mingle together in precarious equilibrium. It is a city united, but always divided.

At the same time as two Arabs in *kaffiyah* head cloths were carrying a suitcase into an apartment block south of Jerusalem, Dr. Rubin Yehuda was hurrying along one of the narrow streets in the Old City.

Rubin was not a man of great physical stature. At sixty-seven years of age, he was no more than five and a half feet tall. Possessing a high forehead of receding gray hair, he had long ago lost the athletic physique of his youth.

The telephone call from Dr. Eaton had come as a shock. Although he had known the woman for nearly twenty years, he had never liked her. Nor did she like him. Dr. Eaton reminded him of a horse, except that he admired horses and felt the comparison was degrading to the animals. Plus, she – not he – was recognized as the world's leading authority on colophons, a reality that continued to rankle him.

Which made it all the more startling that she had asked him to sit with her on a panel that would soon be judging the authenticity of ES 34-30.

ES 34-30. The Ishmael tablet. The most important archaeological find since the Dead Sea Scrolls.

Dr. Eaton, of course, had been widely quoted as saying that, if proved genuine, the tablet could ignite war in the Middle East. This had led to a flurry of investigative reports on Sir Edmund George Clayton's journal and his alleged discovery. The question on every journalist's mind was why this ancient tablet – which had never even been thought to exist – could have such an impact.

At least that's the way it was phrased to Rubin when a reporter from the *Jerusalem Post* had telephoned for his opinion.

Not having taken the matter seriously until that phone call, Rubin had managed to defer responding until he had "finished his own investigation," which he then hurriedly began.

And what he discovered left him speechless and trembling.

For if this most remarkable tablet were indeed proved authentic, then Muslims everywhere would have no option but to concede ownership of Palestine, including Jerusalem, to Israel. None of Ishmael's Arab descendants would have any claim on the land – a fact made clear by Ishmael himself.

The colophon was the key, for the colophon was nothing less than Ishmael's signature, and as such provided the basis for the tablet's authority.

If it were proved genuine.

And there would certainly be those committed to making sure that it was not.

Rubin knew that few Westerners could understand the passion felt by the Jews for Jerusalem. For one thing, Westerners – in particular the hoards of tourists who trampled Israel in search of trinkets and sentimentality – compartmentalized faith as though it were a room to be entered or vacated at whim. But to the Jew – and, admittedly, to the Muslim – faith and life were inseparable.

Plus, Jerusalem was no arbitrary plot of soil. It is – and has been from the beginning – the very essence of the Jewish people, housing its collective soul in the same manner that bodies of flesh housed human souls. And a soul without a body is a ghost, just as all Jews since the first century had been ghosts.

Until 1948, that is, when Israel was reborn and the Jews were rightfully returned to the land from which they had been forcibly driven.

Rubin clenched his hand into a fist. This land is ours, he thought as he pushed his way impatiently through a mob of tourists clogging the narrow street. They had stopped to listen to a large, jewelry-laden woman haggling vociferously with a merchant selling embroidered Holy Land shawls.

Wretched shegetz! Of course these loathsome gentiles did not comprehend the Jews' refusal to be forced again from their land, which the barbaric Romans did two millennia ago, and which the

Arabs still endeavor to do in their incessant cries for a Holy War. How can one expect understanding, much less fairness, from nations who cheated and slaughtered their own indigenous populations?

That was why Israel must stand on its own, and why he, Rubin Yehuda, had aligned himself with the *gibburim* – a sect of zealots named after King David's famed Mighty Men. Thus would the hated Muslims experience the wrath of holy *war!*

While one of the Arabs in the apartment south of Jerusalem readied himself with fervent prayers, a young man in the Old City bumped against Dr. Yehuda before disappearing quickly into the flow of pedestrians filling the narrow street. Rubin paused in the shadow of a stone doorway, reached into the pocket of his suit jacket and withdrew the slip of paper placed there by the young man. He opened the note. Scrawled on the page was the number eighty-two. It meant the *gibburim* would be meeting tonight at eight o'clock, location two.

The first Arab in the apartment finished his prayers and watched the other Arab – a bearded, slender man with delicate features – complete the assembly of a Russian-made SVN-98 sniper's rifle. Mounted on a black metal bipod, the .50 caliber weapon had virtually no stock and an enormous barrel with an optical scope. It was one of the few rifles in the world with an accurate range of 1800 meters, or well over a mile.

Moving to the window, the sniper looked through binoculars at a group of high-rise apartments in a distant Jewish community. Built of blond Jerusalem stone on land sequestered from Palestinian settlers, the development resembled a fortress.

"You said you would pay in dollars?" the first Arab asked.

"The money is in the suitcase," the sniper answered. "You may count it if you wish."

The first Arab hurried to the suitcase, opened it and pulled out a bundle of American dollars, which he eagerly counted. Meanwhile, the sniper continued observing activity around the apartment complex.

Slowing his pace in the Old City, Rubin thought about the *gibburim* – the true Israel – and their steadfast refusal to be deceived by the West's hollow promises of land for peace. Land for peace? *Never!* Peace would only come when—

"Rubin, is that you?" a voice inquired from behind.

Cramming the note into his pocket, Rubin whirled around to see the wrinkled face of Ariel Cohen, a man of similar age, but shorter and heavier.

"Don't look so alarmed," Ariel told him with a smile.

Rubin laughed nervously.

Ariel shook his head.

"Rubin, Rubin, I can read you like this morning's paper," he said. "You play with petrol when you play with the gibburim."

"What do you mean?"

"This news of the tablet and how you will be expected to influence the panel."

"Where did you hear that?" demanded Rubin, pulling Ariel into a doorway.

"When it comes to whispers, the walls of Jerusalem are thin."

"Then you know the importance of this tablet, and why it will enable us to finally rid Israel of all foreigners! *Especially* the Arabs."

"And that is where you are wrong. You, of all people, should know this. I do, and I am no scholar."

The rebuke stung and Rubin pulled away.

Ariel placed a consoling hand on his friend's shoulder. "You and I have gone through much together, and while we do not always agree, we always listen to what the other has to say."

"And so you *insult me?*"

"I would never do such a thing. But a smog of hatred has settled over this land. It poisons us against one another and blinds us to the truth. And the truth is this – Arabs have as much right to be here as we. So do Christians."

"*No!*" hissed Rubin as he spun angrily toward Ariel.

"Read the Scriptures," said Ariel. "For if this tablet is your new weapon of sovereignty, then your appeal is based on Moses. The tablet documents both the accuracy and the authority of Moses."

"My appeal is *not* based on religion! I have discarded such myths and you would be wise to do the same."

Ariel smiled. "Are you so sure?"

"The tablet is a declaration which the Arabs must heed!"

"And why is that?"

"Because their founder, Ishmael, witnesses ownership of the land being given to Isaac and his descendants. The Arabs have no claim –

by Ishmael's own admission!"

"Given by whom?"

With an exasperated huff, Rubin turned away.

"Given by God," Ariel said gently. "The text of the tablet comprises one of the eleven sections of *bereshith,* or what the West calls Genesis, which is one of the five books of Moses – our Torah. And the Torah says that while the land is indeed the inheritance of Israel through Abraham and Isaac, all nations – including our brothers, the Arabs – must be allowed to come here and live. All are welcome. And do you want to know why? Because we are supposed to be a light to the nations, a testimony of God's faithfulness and truth. Are we a light, Rubin? Or has the light within us become dark?"

"I will not listen to this!"

"You must listen."

"No, *you* listen!" Yehuda fired back, speaking in a low, angry voice. "Do we strap bombs to ourselves and kill innocent children? The Arabs have vowed to drench this land with our blood. Look how many times we have been attacked since 1948. Holland does not attack us. Mexico does not. It's the Arabs! They are the mongers of hatred, and they teach it to their children."

Ariel put his arm around Rubin's shoulder and began ushering him along the crowded street. A pair of Israeli soldiers strolled toward them, their automatic rifles slung across their chests, their suspicious eyes roving the crowd.

"Few would dispute our right of defense," Ariel said once the soldiers had passed. "But I repeat, the land must be shared."

"The Arabs kill innocent people," spat Rubin contemptuously.

"As do we. When will it end? The willingness to stop has to start somewhere."

"We stop when they stop," declared Rubin.

"But no one ever stops! And that is the problem."

To the south, the sniper surveyed the large crowd gathered near several limousines parked in front of the Jewish apartment complex. More than two dozen uniformed soldiers were also present in the crowd, along with more agents in plain clothes.

Standing near the entrance, in front of four Secret Service agents, Vice President Sam Baker was speaking about the dividends of peace.

Recognized around the world for his fairness and objectivity, Baker had made two similar visits to Israel over the last six months, and was known throughout the region for his "among-the-people" initiatives, which allowed ordinary citizens the opportunity to provide input into the peace process. Behind him, several families from the apartment complex stood listening, including two mothers with infants. One of them was singing an old Yiddish lullaby to her five-week-old daughter.

"*Pot-she, pot-she, kee-che-lech.*" Clap hands, clap hands, little cakes.

"Mr. Vice President!" a monastic scholar shouted, raising his hand. He was dressed in a black caftan, with long spiraling side locks hanging from beneath his black hat.

Baker pointed to the scholar.

"A stone tablet written by the patriarch Ishmael decrees Palestine to be ours," the scholar said. "You, on the other hand, say we should work cooperatively to share the land, as we did prior to the Six Day War. So tell me, Mr. Vice President, why should we Jews surrender to the Arabs that which is ours by Arab decree?"

"Because brothers share with brothers!" the leader of a group of Israeli moderates shouted before Baker could answer.

"This land is our *inheritance!*" the scholar shouted back.

"Gentlemen, please," said Baker, holding up his hands for calm. "The tablet you refer to does not exist."

"Then apparently you have not seen this," said the scholar, holding up a full-page newspaper ad written in Hebrew, Arabic, English, German and Italian. It read:

PALESTINE BELONGS TO JEWS,
DECLARES ISHMAEL TABLET

The headline was followed by an announcement of the discovery of the tablet followed by a synopsis of its content.

"This ad will run tomorrow in the *Jerusalem Post*," said the scholar. "So I ask again, Mr. Vice President, why should we Jews surrender to the Arabs that which is ours by Arab decree?"

Many Palestinians in the crowd countered with cries for *jihad* – holy war – saying the land was theirs.

Baker called again for restraint, but the back-and-forth shouting only grew louder. Tempers began to flare.

Looking to his left, Baker nodded and a sound engineer turned a dial. A deafening screech reverberated out of the speakers like amplified thunder, subduing the mob.

"Listen to me, all of you!" Baker shouted. "Even if such a tablet has been discovered, no one has verified whether or not it is genuine. And even if it were authenticated, such a tablet must be viewed in an historical context before judging whether or not it relates to our present situation."

While the Vice President continued to speak, the sniper focused the crosshairs of his scope on Baker's chest.

"Make the call," he said quietly.

Bringing a walkie-talkie to his mouth, the other Arab uttered a command.

Suddenly, in the distance, staccato bursts of gunfire erupted from a diversionary group of protesters shooting AK-47 assault rifles into the air.

"Shhh…" the young mother whispered to her infant daughter, who had begun to whimper.

"*Pot-she, pot-she, kee-che-lech.*"

The sniper drew in a breath, exhaled slightly and gently squeezed the trigger. An enormous detonation thundered out of the barrel and echoed across the countryside, where it became lost in the other gunfire.

Reacting to the sound of the AK-47s, one of the Secret Service agents signaled Baker. When Baker stepped over to confer with the agent, the .50 caliber bullet missed its target and hit the young mother standing behind him. Blood sprayed everywhere as she collapsed backward and fell dear to the ground, her infant daughter landing on top of her before rolling gently out of her arms.

Leaving the rifle where it was, the sniper moved quickly away from the window. While the other Arab continued to watch the ensuing chaos through his binoculars, the sniper walked over to the suitcase and lifted out a false bottom.

"The authorities will be here soon," the first Arab remarked, lowering his binoculars. He glanced around to see the sniper pointing a 9mm Jericho pistol at his chest.

"*No!*" was all he had time to scream before the sniper fired.

Seconds later, the diversionary shots in the distance sputtered to a stop.

Dropping the pistol, the sniper placed the SVN-98 beside the dead Arab, making sure that his fingerprints were all over it. The sniper then hurried into the bathroom, removed a pair of latex gloves, false beard and skullcap wig.

Shaking her hair loose, the sniper – a woman of thirty – cut the beard and wig into small pieces and flushed them down the toilet, along with the gloves. She then went to the suitcase, put the money inside a briefcase and removed two changes of clothing. Two minutes later, dressed as a conservative Arab woman in a headscarf and long dress, she left the apartment. Ninety minutes later, she stepped out of a taxi at the Tel Aviv airport.

Inside an airport toilet stall, the woman stripped off her conservative clothing and put on a skirt and jacket. Fifteen minutes later, her red lipstick a dramatic contrast with her navy suit and long dark hair, she stood in the cordoned-off line at the ticket counter, a French passport in the name of Lydia Ardois in one hand, her briefcase in the other.

Suddenly, a squad of Israeli soldiers burst into the airport. In the hands of the commander was a stack of posters with an artist's drawing of an Arab man.

Lydia stiffened at the sight of the soldiers while watching them disperse throughout the airport. She wondered if anyone had reported seeing a woman.

"Next," the ticket agent called out.

Lydia stepped up to the counter.

"One business class ticket to Frankfurt," she said.

Over the loudspeaker, announcements regarding departures echoed through the terminal.

"Will this be charged to a credit card?" asked the agent.

"Yes," answered Lydia, handing it to him with her passport.

Glancing casually to his right, the agent nodded.

With the indifferent expression of a seasoned traveler, Lydia glanced in the same direction and saw two Israeli soldiers start toward her. Maintaining her façade of indifference, she placed her briefcase on the counter, clicked open the latches, and lifted the lid.

Although Lydia appeared to be leafing through some papers, her hand was actually retrieving what appeared to be a pack of French cigarettes. But there was no tobacco inside the pack. Instead, it was filled with C-4 explosive. When armed with a special ballpoint pen detonator, the explosive could be set off by an electronic signal from Lydia's wristwatch. Anyone within a ten-meter radius would be killed, those within twenty meters severely injured. Lydia had rehearsed the routine many times.

Except now she was in Tel Aviv, and few airports in the world were as heavily guarded.

Lydia readied the ballpoint pen. She looked casually at the approaching soldiers.

Their eyes met hers.

"All ready, Ms. Ardois," the agent said, drawing Lydia's attention. He placed Lydia's credit card, passport and boarding pass on the counter and recited her departure information.

Without taking her eyes off the agent, Lydia inverted the pack and prepared to insert the detonator.

"Have a nice flight," the agent said. He then turned to the soldiers. "Okay, let's eat."

The agent joined the soldiers and the three men ambled away.

Breathing a sigh of relief, Lydia returned the detonator to its pocket and closed the briefcase.

And with her documents in hand, she turned toward the gate.

CHAPTER 13

There will be hell to pay, Ariel thought as he watched the grim-faced reporter on the television. Someone had just tried to assassinate Vice President Baker, and accusations were flying from all directions.

Israelis were blaming the Palestinian faction, *Qamat*, and calling for Wassim Jafar to reign them in. Palestinians, of course, claimed Israelis were behind the deplorable act, as evidenced by the discarded Jericho pistol. Radicals on both sides were shouting chants of vengeance, with moderates expressing worry that the *gibburim* had actually carried out the attempt in order to provoke military action against the Palestinians.

Ariel switched off the TV and shook his head. What the world did not need were groups like *Qamat* and the *gibburim* fanning the flames of hatred. The result was always the same – new waves of killing. When would the madness end?

It would end only when ordinary people chose friendship over hatred. Only then could this fragmented land have any hope of lasting peace.

Thankfully, many people were trying. An article on the third page of the Post reported how several young Arab men had helped a Jewish family search for their missing teenager, who was eventually found drowned on a beach near Haifa, apparently from a late-night drunken swim. Another article showed Israeli families handing out emergency supplies to displaced Palestinian Christians who had been victims of religious hatred.

Yet he – Ariel – was but an old man, and what could an old man do?

He could write letters to the newspaper, that's what! He could inspire others to speak out against the mindless killing.

Ariel hurried to a small wooden desk and folded down its front panel. The compartments inside were stuffed with envelopes and papers. An old tumbler held pencils and pens. He pulled some papers from one of the pigeonholes and they spilled across the desk.

"You clumsy old fool," he muttered, gathering them together.

Suddenly his eye caught a glimpse of something, and Ariel instinctively sucked in a breath. His weathered hands, blotched with brownish age spots, began to quaver as he carefully separated out a business card on which was printed the solitary first letter of the Hebrew alphabet: *Aleph.* It was a calligraphic character resembling an "N," but with fat tips on the vertical legs and a thick diagonal main stroke. Ariel stared at the card for a long moment, recalling how *Aleph* had once been the most feared and revered symbol in all of Israel.

For *Aleph* was the signature of none other than Aaron, the legendary Israeli assassin.

A sad smile formed on Ariel's lips, for although Aaron had been a dispenser of death, by the same token he made aggressors think twice. His retributions were always swift, and word about him had spread far beyond Israel. However, because of international pressure, the State Department had finally offered a reward for Aaron's capture.

Undeterred by the increased efforts to find him, Aaron continued to operate by his famous code of honor, whereby he never took action without clear provocation. Aaron did not kill indiscriminately, and never with explosive devices that injured or killed innocent bystanders. His eventual death at the hand of Abu Nazer had left a tragic void.

A void the *gibburim* was desperately trying to fill.

But the *gibburim's* tendency to kill whomever they saw fit, whenever they saw fit, meant they were now part of the problem.

Without question, there were times when fighting was one's only choice. With the *gibburim,* fighting was always their only choice. Like *Qamat,* they were simply thugs.

It had been different with Aaron. Yet in the end, he was still an assassin. A mercenary. A killer.

Which brought Ariel's focus back to the card he now held in his hand.

Whenever Aaron took responsibility for a kill, somewhere on or near the victim would be found one of these cards. Only twice did copycat killers try printing their own cards in an attempt to shift blame for their crimes. In each instance, Aaron hunted the men down and made them pay with their lives.

Aaron had been a genius marksman, but even that remained shrouded in mystery, since his famous rifle was never recovered. And because no one ever saw him use the rifle, the exact make and model were never known. A joint Jordanian-Israeli ballistics team thought it was probably custom-made judging from the specially chambered

.380 subsonic bullets pried from the skulls of two Syrian terrorists ambushed outside of Al Mafraq.

Jordanian authorities had captured the pair trying to cross into Syria and were returning them to Amman for questioning when the hit took place. The party had stopped beside the road to allow the Syrians a toilet break. The officers guarding the pair neither heard nor saw anything other than the two urinating Syrians dropping to the earth like severed marionettes. The next day, two Aleph cards were discovered on the very spot where the Syrians had been killed.

Ariel, a retired printer, knew this because he had been the one who printed the cards for Aaron – a man he had never met but with whom he had talked many times on the phone.

Through the years, Ariel often wondered what had prompted Aaron to call and ask if he would print the cards. He wondered even more what had prompted him to agree. But he had done it, and recalled the night he tucked the first bundle of cards into a cranny along a darkened Jewish Quarter street. The night had been hot and still, with the day's heat radiating off the walls of thick stone. He remembered looking around to see if anyone was watching. Seeing no one, he went back home. Several days later, he found one of the Aleph cards – along with a month's wages in cash – in an envelope inside his front door.

A door he always kept locked.

Those were the days, Ariel reflected with melancholy fondness, remembering how Aaron's voice had become familiar and comforting, especially when the assassin addressed him simply as Ari, which in Hebrew means "lion."

But that was then and this was now. Ariel pushed the card back into the pigeonhole with the rest of the papers.

The ringing phone caused him to jump.

Aaron, he thought, then rebuking himself when the phone sounded again.

He picked up the receiver. "Allo?"

"I have news I think you should hear," Yehuda said.

"What kind of news?" asked Ariel.

"Six o'clock, our usual place. Take care that you are not followed."

CHAPTER 14

"Look, the walls glow," Ariel told the young Israeli soldier sitting next to him on the bus.

The soldier looked up from his newspaper and viewed the Old City as they rounded a bend. In the afternoon sunlight, the ancient walls appeared as if basted in honey.

"Aren't they beautiful?" asked Ariel.

"I suppose they are," responded the soldier. "To tell you the truth, I've never noticed."

"You noticed today."

The soldier chuckled. "I guess I did."

On occasions like this, Ariel sensed the people of this land might one day be ready to cease quarreling and breathe in such moments of beauty. If they did, most certainly they would relish the fragrance. But lately such occasions had been rare, for resentments as ancient as the stones themselves were staining the beauty of Jerusalem almost beyond recognition.

And he feared it was about to get worse.

Stepping off the bus, Ariel entered the Old City through the Jaffa Gate and made his way along a series of narrow streets to the café where he and Rubin often met for coffee. The establishment was small, the walls cluttered with numerous photos of the popular Israeli actor, Topol.

"Sit. We do not have much time," Rubin said.

Ariel pulled out a chair.

"Have you heard about Vice President Baker?" Rubin asked, signaling for two espressos.

"Was it the *gibburim?*" asked Ariel.

"They were not involved," answered Rubin.

Ariel responded with a suspicious frown.

"You have my word," said Rubin. "But that is not the problem."

"I assume you refer to this ad the Post is going to run asserting Jewish ownership of Palestine?"

"Worse," responded Rubin, looking around to make sure no one was listening. "We think Abu Nazer was responsible," he said quietly.

"For the ad?"

"For the shooting," said Rubin. "Though it would not surprise me if he were behind the ad. A terrorist like him thrives on hatred and violence."

"Why do you think he is behind the shooting?" asked Ariel.

"Because the attempt on the Vice President's life was made with a large caliber, experimental weapon called the SVN-98. It is one of the longest-range sniper rifles in the world. It's nearly impossible to find and costs a small fortune. The body of the alleged sniper has been identified as a *Qamat* hothead who was full of hatred and eager to prove it. However, friends who knew him say there was no way he could have afforded such a weapon. More importantly, no one but an expert marksman could have made such a shot from that distance. If Baker hadn't moved, he would have been killed. However, someone was seen going into the building with the sniper. And this, we believe, was the real assassin."

"Did you get a description?"

"Bearded male, mid-twenties, slender build."

The two men fell silent while the owner of the café, a stocky woman with thick gray hair and a dull print dress, placed two small cups of espresso on their table. As she walked away, each man stirred in sugar.

"Assuming it was Abu Nazer," said Ariel, "who would have hired him? And why?"

"I do not have answers, only questions. Vice President Baker is a friend to the Arabs, so it makes no sense for the Arabs to want him killed. A forensics team found fibers from what they think is a synthetic beard, so the assassin was not only a brilliant marksman, but also skilled with disguise."

Both men took sips of their espresso.

"Why am I here?" asked Ariel.

Rubin ran an anxious hand across his face and again looked around to make sure no one was listening.

"Tomorrow, the Post is going to run a comprehensive story on the tablet," he said.

"And the *gibburim* – what will they do if the tablet is found to be genuine?" asked Ariel.

"They are pressuring me to make sure such a determination occurs. They want to use the tablet to drive the Arabs from the land. To destroy their mosques."

"Rubin, you must not allow that to happen!"

"I never thought things would go this far. Naturally, part of me wants the tablet to be genuine. But part of me is terrified at the prospect. Which brings me to my problem."

"I fear to ask what it is."

"The tablet is owned by an Egyptian named Qaderi. He is certain to become a target for extremists like *Qamat,* who want to destroy the tablet. You must warn him."

"I doubt he would listen to a Jew."

"Qaderi's going to be interviewed by an American journalist named Rutherford Tyler. Call this journalist. Have him pass on the warning."

"Why not phone him yourself?"

"As a member of the panel, I cannot be involved. That is why you must do it. There is no one else I can trust. The tablet must not fall into the hands of *Qamat.*"

"Nor the *gibburim.* I won't help you if that's what you're planning."

"No, no, nothing like that."

Ariel looked skeptically at his friend.

"You have my word! Now, please, I beg you. Will you phone this journalist?"

Ariel thought for a moment then nodded. "All right," he said, "I will do it. Pray that he heeds my warning."

"I quit believing in prayer a long time ago."

Ariel shook his head sadly.

"Do not worry, my friend," said Rubin. "This is why I have you. You pray for the both of us."

CHAPTER 15

"Quit being so dang picky," Tyler complained over the irritating sound of a Gene Pitney sound track. With an annoyed scowl, he reached over and switched off the music.

"Then quit ending your sentences with prepositions," Val replied, switching it back on.

"I write like people talk," he said, switching it off again.

"'What are you up to?' That's a double preposition."

"I told you, that's the way people talk."

"Do you include every belch of profanity just because it's the way people talk? Of course not. You edit those into an acceptable written standard, which today isn't much, but is what you hired me to do. Now quit hovering. You make me nervous."

"You're ruining quality literature."

"And you, my dear boy, are dreaming."

"You started that sentence with a preposition!"

"*Tyler.*"

With a victorious laugh, Tyler headed for the door.

"Anyway, it was a conjunction, not a preposition," she muttered.

"Back in five," he said.

"Where are you going?"

"To the toilet, if you must know. All that coffee you pour down me's gotta go somewhere."

"That is definitely more information than I needed to hear."

With a chuckle, Tyler climbed the stairs, his boots clomping loudly on the hardwood steps.

Val switched on Gene Pitney again and resumed editing. Less than a minute later, the telephone rang.

"Dr. Tyler's office, this is Val," she said.

There was no response.

"Dr. Tyler's office," Val said again.

"Allo?" the accented voice of Ariel Cohen asked hesitantly. "Is this the office of Doctor Rutherford Tyler?"

"Yes, it is."

"Good, yes, thank you. My name is Ariel Cohen and I am telephoning from Jerusalem."

"May I help you, Mr. Cohen?"

"I wish to speak with Dr. Tyler."

"He's not available. May I take a message?"

"It is very important that I speak with him."

"I'm sorry, but he's not available."

"Please, I am calling from Jerusalem."

"I'm aware of that. May I ask what this concerns?"

"Forgive me, but I must speak with Dr. Tyler. I know he is going to Cairo. What I have to tell him may well save his life."

"Is this some kind of a prank?"

"No! What I am telling you is the truth. I must speak with Dr. Tyler."

"Why don't you tell me what this is about."

"Very well, I will explain the nature of my call," Ariel said, and with measured speech, he told Val what he knew about the tablet and its implications for the ownership and control of Palestine.

"Whose interests do you represent, Mr. Cohen?"

There was a pause.

"Your reservations are understandable," he said. "I do not hide the fact that I am a Jew, and that Jews will gain the most from this tablet. However, the terrible killing between my people and the Arabs is disgraceful. It must stop."

"How does this relate to Dr. Tyler?"

"Arab militants like *Qamat* will want to destroy the tablet. Israeli militants like the *gibburim* will want to use it to drive Arabs from the land. These madmen will do anything to achieve their goals, which is why Dr. Tyler must warn Mr. Qaderi to take extra precaution. One mistake may cost them their lives."

"Why not tell Qaderi yourself?"

"I doubt an Arab would trust the word of a Jew."

"Why should I trust you?" Val asked just as Tyler strode into the room. Hearing the acerbic question, he paused and looked at her quizzically.

"Surely you must sense that I am telling the truth," said Ariel. "I have nothing to gain from urging Dr. Tyler to be careful."

"I'm going to place you on hold for a moment," Val said. She pushed a button that suspended the call.

"What's going on?" asked Tyler.

"This man is phoning about a possible terrorist attack on you and Qaderi."

"I already know about that."

"This may be something new."

Tyler walked over and picked up the receiver. On the console, the light was blinking. "Does the man have a name?" he asked, reaching for the button.

"Ariel Cohen," answered Val.

Tyler slammed down the receiver. "Ariel Cohen? From Jerusalem?" he asked.

"Yes. How did you know?"

"Because I've heard about him in connection with some right-wing radicals. Tell him you'll take a message."

"Don't you want to hear what he has to say?"

Tyler turned and headed for the door.

"Tyler, the guy sounds legit," tried Val.

"Take a message," said Tyler, disappearing down the hall.

"At least listen to what he has to say!" Val called out.

The front door closed. Tyler was gone.

CHAPTER 16

"Break time! How about a coffee?" Tony asked, leaning into Zoe's cubicle. In his hand was a half-eaten Snickers bar.

Zoe pushed herself away from her desk, her angry eyes glaring at the passport photo of Tyler on her screen. "He played me. The bastard played me!"

"Now's obviously not a good time."

"And it's *really* pissing me off!"

"Seriously. I'll come back later."

"So I started asking myself, what's his motive? There's got to be something that he's getting out of it. And then it hit me. He gains time! Don't you see? He gains time! Why is that important, you ask?"

With a sigh, Tony took a bite of his Snickers and fell into a chair.

"It's because he *knows* there's a connection between Tariq and Abu Nazer. Why is *that* important, you ask? Because Tyler's planning on doing what no other journalist has ever done – get a scoop on the world's most elusive terrorist. How he managed to link Tariq with Abu Nazer, I haven't a clue. But Tyler lied about knowing Tariq because the last thing he wants is us following him around. At the very least, it ruins his story. At most, it gets him killed."

"I thought he was going over there to interview Qaderi."

"If that were the case, why would he lie?"

"Maybe he found out he's on Abu Nazer's hit list. Maybe he thinks Tariq's out to kill him."

"Then why lie? A normal person would have answered truthfully and asked for our help. Not Tyler. He lied, and voice analysis proved that. So we know he's not afraid for his safety, in spite of that little show he put on. Which reinforces my conclusion that he's after a story on Abu Nazer and is using the interview with Qaderi as cover. Don't forget, Abu Nazer has his eye on the tablet, so an interview with Qaderi places Tyler in a perfect position."

Tony thought about what he had just heard. Zoe's theory was far-fetched, but logical. What journalist wouldn't go after the unobtainable story, just like Zoe went after the unobtainable profile?

"Assuming you're right, what's next?" asked Tony.

"Tyler's the common denominator, so we make him our focus."

"Common denominator, how?"

"He's on Abu Nazer's hit list, he knows about Tariq, he's got an interview with Qaderi – supposedly about the tablet, which Qaderi owns and Abu Nazer wants to steal. Trouble is, we don't know why he's the common denominator. Too many negative spaces. And that bothers me."

"Too many what?"

"Negative spaces," answered Zoe. "Profiles are like art – a combination of positive and negative spaces. Confirmed facts versus an identifiable absence of facts. One of the positive spaces in Tyler's profile is that he's an educated journalist with an honorary doctorate. In support of this I found his academic record on file at UCLA. That's a positive space, a confirmed fact. The negative spaces are that no photo of him exists in any yearbook, nor did he write for any university publication. This is slightly irregular, for it would be logical for those facts to exist positively rather than negatively. However, the same can be said about me as a psych major at Columbia. It was a large school, I disliked preppy publications such as yearbooks, and I disdained clubs and organizations. Hence, I'm not attaching any importance to these peculiarities because they're not that much out of the ordinary. But when facts are absent, my job is to discover reasons and degrees of abnormality."

"So what's your problem with Tyler?"

"He's too squeaky clean."

Tony raised a skeptical eyebrow.

"Where are the quirks?" asked Zoe. "The flaws and habits that make us human? I mean, look at you. You've always got girlfriend trouble, you blog all sorts of geek-speak crap on the internet, you're a Snickers junkie who never seems to gain weight, and you're more than three months overdue with the phone company."

"Hey!"

"But with Tyler, there's none of that. No late payments, no former girlfriends telling all, no fetishes for anything other than a zillion Stony Lonesome CDs charged on his AMEX card."

"Stony who?"

"Tony, you're missing the point!"

"Maybe."

"Maybe's got nothing to do with it. He's too squeaky clean. End of story."

"Want to know what I see in all of this?"

"What?" asked Zoe with an impatient sigh.

"You want Tyler to look like a bad guy."

"I don't trust him!"

"Why? Because he made you mad?"

"He made me look like a fool."

"And it pissed you off."

"Damn right it pissed me off!"

"Think maybe that's clouding your judgment? Causing you to manipulate facts into a foregone conclusion?"

Zoe folded her arms and looked away.

"Look, I'm not saying he isn't up to something. I'm just saying be careful about making more of those positive and negative spaces than is actually there."

Zoe tapped a button and Tyler's photo disappeared.

"How about we focus on Tariq?" said Tony. "Give Tyler a rest."

"Can't. He's off the grid."

"Didn't he take a flight back to London?"

"Not that I can tell. His name isn't on any of the manifests, which leads me to believe he's headed for Cairo, probably by car."

"Then we've lost him. We're sunk."

"O ye of little faith," said Zoe. She tapped another button and Tyler's photo reappeared.

"Our common denominator!"

"And he's accessible. Which makes it all the more important we find out what he's up to."

"You two – in my office!" barked a voice.

Zoe and Tony looked up, and saw Teague.

"This doesn't sound good," Tony whispered as they followed Teague down the hall. When they reached Teague's office, he opened the door, allowed them to enter, then closed the door behind them.

"What's the latest on Tariq?" he asked, crossing to his desk.

"He's disappeared," answered Zoe. "And there's no record of him either leaving Saudi Arabia or landing in London."

"Find out if he's in Jerusalem," said Teague.

"He may be headed for Cairo."

Teague yanked a classified report out of a printer tray and handed it to Zoe.

"What's this?" she asked.

"Someone just took a shot at Vice President Baker and I want to know if it was Tariq."

Zoe read the report.

"Whoever it was fired from nearly a mile away using an SVN-98 sniper's rifle," explained Teague. "The bullet would have killed Baker if he hadn't moved."

"Then Baker is the target!" exclaimed Zoe.

"You're assuming again," said Teague. "What our surveillance team heard in Austin is suggestive but inconclusive."

"Then we need to keep digging. Find out!"

"To make matters worse," added Teague, "the assassin shot his accomplice with an Israeli pistol. Israeli forensics found synthetic fibers and traces of adhesive, so we think he used a disguise."

"How do you know the perp was a male?"

"Witnesses recall two men entering the apartment block where the shots were fired."

"Any evidence it was Tariq?" asked Zoe.

"That's what you're going to find out. See if there's any record of him having entered the country, charged anything on a credit card – you know the drill. Involve Mossad. They'll help all they can."

"What about this Jerusalem Post ad about Palestine belonging to the Jews? Why would they run something like that? The whole Middle East could go up in flames."

"That's just it – the Post didn't run it," said Teague, retrieving a copy of the ad from his desk and handing it to Zoe. "Someone had a bunch of these tear sheets printed and distributed them around Jerusalem with a rumor the Post was going to run it. The culprit obviously wants to stir up trouble, but no one's claimed responsibility. The Post is working overtime to dispel the rumor and find out who was responsible."

"Was Abu Nazer behind it?" asked Zoe.

"Knowing what we know, it's a serious possibility."

"But?"

"It's too early to tell with any certainty. We need to keep digging."

Zoe nodded and made a note.

"Now, what's this I hear about you letting Tyler take control of a conversation?" asked Teague.

Zoe whirled toward Tony, who suddenly became preoccupied with his shoelaces. She glared at him for a moment before looking back at Teague. "It just happened, sir," she said.

"And what did you learn?"

"That I screwed up. Big time. But it won't happen again, sir. Ever."

"I don't care about that," said Teague. "I want to know what you learned."

"What I learned?"

"About Tyler."

"Well, I learned that he knows Tariq, or something about him, although I'm not sure exactly what. I also learned he plans to interview Qaderi on Wednesday in Cairo. So we now have a link between Tyler and Qaderi, but no real explanation as to why he's on Abu Nazer's hit list. I think we should continue surveillance, maybe increase it a notch and follow him to Cairo."

"I'll approve a level-two domestic, but following him to Cairo is out of the question. We don't have enough assets over there for something like that. Besides, I'm not even sure it's warranted. As of now, San Francisco's our focus. Dr. Eaton and her team will be meeting there next week to study the tablet."

"Isn't it possible some nut may try and steal it before it leaves Cairo?"

"Unlikely until after the results of that study are in."

"Unless you're an Arab," said Zoe. "They're not going to want to take the chance of it being authenticated, since it hands Jerusalem back to the Jews. And the best place to steal it's in Cairo."

"A reasonable deduction, except you're forgetting about Omar's report. He heard Tariq and Majli discussing San Francisco."

"But we don't know in reference to what."

"We can reasonably deduce that it has something to do with the tablet. If San Francisco's important to Abu Nazer, then it's important to us. Not only that, next week President Fitzgerald will be addressing a Middle East peace congress there. Arab leaders will be attending along with the Israeli Prime Minister. So I repeat – San Francisco's our focus. It's the one place where everything comes together."

"Can't we at least give them a heads-up in Cairo? Omar overheard Tariq tell Majli that he'd call him from there."

Teague thought for a moment. "I suppose I can have our man there, Tim Odell, pass on a warning."

"Why not have Odell stake out Qaderi's house?" asked Zoe. "Look for anyone suspicious hanging around."

"Out of the question."

"But what if Abu Nazer decides to try something?"

"He'll pass on a warning."

"Not even for a few days?"

"No!"

"But if Abu Nazer decides to try something—"

"I said, no, Gustaves, now drop it!"

Zoe bit her lip.

"If there's nothing else…" Teague began.

"Actually, there is," said Zoe.

An impatient sigh was Teague's response.

"As you know, seven years ago Abu Nazer killed Aaron," she said.

"Your point being?"

"I may have found a witness."

Teague's irritation suddenly turned to interest.

"When I left here last night," Zoe continued, "I started asking myself what proof we had that Aaron was actually killed. I mean, if nobody knew his identity, how do we know he's dead? No corpse was ever discovered, and yet no one doubts that it happened. Why? Because the retaliations stopped. So that led me to wonder if the incident actually *was* reported, but because the victim seemed to be some ordinary guy, the authorities didn't know who he really was."

"And?"

"According to an article in the *Jerusalem Post,* a New York magazine editor named Stephen Kappelmann was murdered one night north of Gaza. He was vacationing in Israel with his wife, Louise, when they were drugged in a nightclub and taken to a remote stretch of dunes, blindfolded and bound. The couple was robbed and Kappelmann was murdered. Later that night, a gunfight broke out between the killer and an Israeli soldier, who had come to their rescue. The soldier was wounded and later died. The unidentified killer, who was also wounded, escaped and never was caught. Louise, who survived the ordeal, was quoted as saying she and her dead husband lay taped together on the beach for over an hour before the shooting started. She then had to wait another hour before the authorities arrived."

"Where is this leading?" asked Teague.

"If robbery were the killer's motive, why did he wait around for an hour? And why did he shoot Kappelmann but not his wife?"

"To set a trap."

"That's right. The killer *knew* Aaron would show up."

"So the Israeli soldier may have been Aaron?"

"Yes, sir."

"Any evidence to support this theory?"

"I just gave it to you."

"You gave me conjecture, not evidence. Besides, you said the wife was blindfolded."

"She may have heard something, smelled something, touched something."

"You're reaching."

"Maybe. But it's a lead I think we should follow."

"What happened to her?" asked Teague.

"Returned to New York, quit work and mysteriously disappeared."

"How do you know she's even alive? If she did witness something, there's a good chance Abu Nazer may have already silenced her."

"That's what I'd like to find out. It's possible she changed her identity in order to protect herself."

"All right, I'll allow it," he said.

"Yes, sir."

"That's all. Dismissed."

Tony started to leave but Zoe remained standing where she was.

"Don't tell me there's something *else*?" asked Teague, glancing at his watch.

"Sir, have you ever heard of a covert operation called Nightingale?"

"What's this got to do with anything?"

"It relates to what we're doing."

"I don't see how. Nightingale was never anything more than

right-wing hawk talk. It never got off the ground."

"I think it did."

"It didn't."

"With due respect, sir, I think it did. The project was conceived—"

"I know what it was! And I'm telling you it never got off the ground."

"Again, with due respect—"

"I don't have time for this, Gustaves! More importantly, neither do you. Now, drop it and get back to work."

"If you'll just hear me out."

"What part of *drop it* don't you understand?"

"At least listen to what I have to say."

Teague slammed his hand on the desktop. "That is enough! I've been willing to cut you some slack because of what you went through. But bomb blast or not, enough is enough!"

"Yes, I was in that blast. But I'm okay. So – with respect, sir – I don't want you cutting me slack because I'm the daughter of Diane Gustaves."

"The Congresswoman's got nothing to do with this."

"I think she does."

"And I'm telling you she doesn't."

"Then hear me out."

Teague looked up and took a calming breath. "I hired you because you're talented and determined," he said. "But there is a thin line between an asset and a liability. I want team players – people who know how to take orders – and I do not tolerate insubordination, or backtalk, from *anyone*."

"You hired me because my mother pushed you to hire me. She pushed you the same way she pushes me, and as much as I hate who my mother is and what she stands for, I've become just like her. And I hate myself for it. But it's the only way for a woman to get anywhere around here. By pushing harder than the next guy."

"And I'm telling you that is not the way it is. Nor is it the reason I hired you. I hired you because—"

"Of my mother."

Teague threw up his hands. "Why am I arguing with you about this?"

"Because—"

"This conversation is over!" shouted Teague. "You *will* learn to do what I tell you and you *will* learn to control those impulsive tendencies before you make a *rash* decision at the *wrong* time and someone gets *killed*. This has got nothing to do with gender or who your family is or what kind of issues you have with your mother. It's an issue of attitude, self-control and being part of a team. My team! Do you hear what I'm saying?"

Zoe looked away.

"Do you hear what I'm *saying?*"

"Yes, sir."

"Good, because you're taking next week off to think long and hard about what I just told you. Officially, you'll be on stress leave, but make no mistake, this is a warning. Go sit on a beach, go hiking – I don't care. I want you to do a one-eighty with the attitude, put a zipper on your mouth, and come back ready to work. Now, get out of here. Cooke can take over your files."

"You can't do this!" shouted Zoe.

Teague whirled and pointed to the door. "Get the hell out of here now!"

Out in the hall, Tony tried keeping pace with Zoe as she stormed along the corridor.

"You really crossed the line in there," he said.

"So did you when you told him about Tyler!"

"I don't know how he found out."

"Bullshit!"

"All right, so I might have let something slip."

Zoe kept marching, irate.

"Look, I'm sorry, all right?" said Tony.

"It's not all right!" said Zoe. "You owe me. *Big time.*" She stopped and grabbed Tony by the arm. "And I'm going to collect, starting now."

"What do you mean?"

"For starters, you're going to keep digging on Nightingale," she said, pulling Tony with her while she walked. "For some reason, Teague doesn't want me near it and I want to know why. I also want you to find out who printed that fake Jerusalem Post ad. Who gains from something like that? I also need you to track down Louise Kappelmann and find out what happened to her. I also want information on Qaderi, Tariq, Tyler, and any connection Tyler may have with Tariq, or why he would have heard of him. And don't forget Vice President Baker. Someone tried to kill him and I want to know who it was.

Maybe there's a connection to the assassination of Senator Ashford."

Tony whimpered as she propelled him down the hallway.

"Email any and all updates to my Agency address," said Zoe. "It's encrypted and I can access it from where I'll be."

"Where exactly will you be?"

"Cairo. I hear the Pyramids are beautiful this time of the year."

CHAPTER 17

"Yes, Mr. Cohen, I gave him your message," said Val.

"This is the second time I have phoned," Ariel replied. "Please, I *must* speak with Dr. Tyler. It is a matter of great urgency!"

"Dr. Tyler is aware of the danger. He was aware of it long before you called the first time."

Val glanced over at Tyler, who was gazing out the window at Lake Austin. Out in the water, a speedboat was pulling a skier. But Tyler's attention was not on the boat.

"I beg of you!" pleaded Ariel. "I believe Abu Nazer or *Qamat* may try to kill him while he is in Cairo. You must allow me to speak with him!"

"I'll tell him you called," said Val.

She hung up the phone, glanced disapprovingly at Tyler, and shook her head. "I still don't see why you wouldn't take his call."

Tyler closed his briefcase and stood.

"Whatever you say," Val said with a wave of surrender. "For the record, he reiterated his concern. He thinks Abu Nazer or *Qamat* may try to kill you in Cairo."

Briefcase in hand, Tyler headed for the door.

"I think you should take the mallet," she said.

Tyler stopped and looked back at Val. "The mallet would jeopardize everything I'm trying to do."

"I'm not sure you know what that is."

Without another word, Tyler left the room.

CHAPTER 18

Between the Connecticut coast and the open waters of the Atlantic lies an island. This wooded outcrop was home to the Algonquian people for thousands of years. In the early 1600s, the Dutch named it *Lange Eylandt,* although it is recognized around the world today by its English translation: Long Island.

From space, Long Island looks like a minnow trying to take a bite out of North America. The mouth of this minnow is filled with Atlantic seawater and is known as Jamaica Bay. Where the gullet would be is arguably the premier gateway into the United States – John F. Kennedy International Airport. Like insects flying in and out of the mouth of the minnow, hundreds of airplanes take off and land at JFK each and every day.

Threading her way along the crowded concourse, Zoe again focused on the purpose of her trip: to identify and stop Abu Nazer. But in order to do that, first she needed to find him. And to do *that,* she had to follow Tyler, whom she knew would be on her flight. For by staying close to Tyler, she realized she had a good chance of catching the man who wanted to kill him.

Zoe veered out of the flow of pedestrians and into an airport lounge. Like most, this one was dim and quiet. Dressed in a boot-cut, navy-blue pant suit, and with her carry-on bag slung over one shoulder, she stepped up to the polished hardwood bar and ordered an orange juice spritzer with a twist. A few minutes later, she was sitting at a table enjoying her drink.

It felt good to relax after her run-in with Teague.

Initially, she had been furious at having been ordered away for a week. Her reaction had been to head straight for the shooting range and take out her frustration.

As usual, Big Jack was in "The Bunker" – as the firing range was affectionately known – wearing his usual, solicitous, crooked smile.

When she first started working for the Agency, Zoe had taken offense at Jack's suggestive remarks. However, at an overweight sixty-something years of age, talk was about all Jack had going for him. Yet as a marksman, he could dot an eye at a hundred paces, and knew handguns like Kansas knows wheat. Sure, he could be annoying with his recital of endless facts and statistics. But he possessed an eye like a neurosurgeon when it came to sighting faults in technique.

"Well, well, what have we here?" he asked with a lecherous twinkle. "A SIG-Sauer Pro, I do believe. Nine millimeter, double action, polymer frame – the first for SIG, I might add – with a fifteen round capacity. Your little friend comes equipped with a stainless-steel slide, interchangeable grips and custom-threaded barrel to accept a silencer. Powerful, accurate, and comfortable in the hand. Just like the cannon I carry, if you know what I mean."

At this point Jack reacted to his own remark, as he always did, with a coarse laugh.

Zoe usually rolled her eyes and responded, "in your dreams." But not today. Today she just nodded tensely.

Jack sobered quickly. "You all right?"

"Fine," was Zoe's curt reply as she grabbed some protective eye-glasses and earmuffs.

"Taking out frustration on anyone in particular?" Jack inquired, grabbing a large sheet of paper with a black torso printed on it. He swaggered over to a loop of cable strung the distance of Zoe's shooting aisle, like a clothesline. After clipping the paper onto the cable, he punched a button on an electrical box located high on the wall. The target reeled rapidly to the far end of the practice range and stopped.

Zoe donned the protective gear and loaded the SIG's magazine with ammunition from the full box placed in front of her. When finished, she snapped the magazine into the handle and pulled the slide, sending a fresh cartridge into the chamber. Lifting the matte-black SIG to eye level, she took aim, her second hand supporting the one that held the weapon.

She squeezed the trigger and a quick succession of loud shots echoed through The Bunker.

There was a sneer of satisfaction on Zoe's face when she saw all fifteen bullets had punched holes in a small pattern in the center of the head, where eyes and a nose used to be.

"Again," she called out.

Without a word, Jack hit the button. The target whizzed toward them for replacement while Zoe reloaded.

Zoe remembered feeling better after that session. She took a sip of her spritzer and smiled. Had she and Teague not butted heads, she would not be tailing their one remaining lead.

And yet, in the back of her mind, she wondered if she was doing the very thing Teague warned her about. Was she being rash? Was she being careless? Would she get someone killed?

A dull vibrating noise sounded from her carry-on. Zoe took out her cell phone and put it to her ear.

"Gustaves," she said into the instrument.

"It's Tony. I'm glad I caught you."

"What's up?" she asked.

"Remember how Teague said President Fitzgerald was scheduled to speak at the Middle East peace conference in San Francisco? Well, the White House isn't going public with this, but Vice President Baker will be there as well, conducting behind-the-scenes negotiations prior to the conference."

"That just upped the ante."

"We also intercepted an email to Tariq."

"Who from?" asked Zoe.

"Anonymous, from one of those throwaway webmail addresses. The sender informed Tariq that the meeting was confirmed for Cairo, same time and place."

"That must have been what Tariq and Majli were talking about in Mecca."

"That's my take. We also just got an interesting wiretap report on someone named Ariel Cohen. He phoned Tyler from Jerusalem to pass on a warning."

"About what?"

"That Abu Nazer and/or *Qamat* may try to kill him in Cairo. His assistant Val took a message. She said Tyler was aware of the danger."

"I knew it! Tyler knows he's a target!"

"I'll let you know who Cohen is once I find out."

"Listen, I need another favor."

"What now?"

"Contact our embassy in Cairo and have someone meet me at the airport with a pouch."

"What for?"

Zoe lowered her voice. "Because I'm carrying my SIG and I'll need help getting it past customs."

Tony nearly choked. "Don't tell me you're *carrying?*"

"Of course I am."

"Are you cleared for that?"

There was no immediate reply.

"*Zoe!*"

"All right, so I don't have clearance. But I've got a license and my Agency ID."

"That's not enough and you know it!"

"Then help me out. Have someone meet me in baggage claim. I'll stick my gun and files into the pouch. Diplomatic privilege will get them through."

"What about security there at Kennedy? Even if they allow you on board because of your ID, you can't just pull out a pistol in the Cairo airport, drop it into a pouch and expect to get away with it. You're risking immediate deportation and one hell of a lot of trouble!"

"I'll be discreet, all right?"

"Discreet? You've got to be kidding!"

"Look, I don't have time to debate this. Send an email to the embassy and tell them I'm coming. Company channel, so they know it's official."

"But this isn't official. You're not official!"

"Then make it look like I am."

"I could get in a lot of trouble for this!"

"Just do it, okay? Say that I made you do it. Any heat that occurs will be mine."

"Yeah, right."

"You said Tyler knows he's a target?"

"That's what his assistant told Cohen."

"And yet here he is, trying to finesse a story on the man who wants to kill him. I mean, think about it: tracking the man who wants to kill you? That takes balls."

"You're starting to sound like a fan."

"Don't be stupid. Any word yet on who printed that fake *Jerusalem Post* ad?"

"Not yet."

"What about Louise Kappelmann? Anything from the IRS?"

"Not yet," said Tony. "They can't do much without a Social Security number. I had them run a name search but that went nowhere."

"Don't they have her old tax records on file?"

"I'm sure they do somewhere, but they're not exactly overstaffed. Which means a request like this one gets shoved into the too-hard basket."

"But this is important!"

"They're all important."

"What about the publishing company where she used to work?"

"They destroy files that are more than eight years old."

"God, we're coming up empty. Keep trying to locate a Social Security number. We need to find her, and fast."

Zoe ended the call just as a group of businessmen passed by on their way out. A couple of them smiled at her just as a man in blue jeans squeezed past on his way to their vacant table. Zoe ignored them and finished her drink.

So who the hell was Ariel Cohen? Where the hell was Louise Kappelmann? And how the hell did Tyler find out he was a target?

Frustrated, Zoe stuffed her phone back in her carry-on bag and went to the bar.

"Another spritzer?" the bartender asked.

Zoe nodded, her mind on Tony's call.

Cohen had phoned Tyler from Jerusalem. Vice President Baker had been shot at near Jerusalem. Was there a connection?

Zoe caught a blur of movement out of the corner of her eye. She glanced around in time to see the man in blue jeans dash out of the bar with her bag.

"Hey!" she shouted.

With the bag tucked under his arm like a football, the man in blue jeans zigzagged through the broad river of people filling the busy concourse. He typically worked single females, primarily because they were soft targets. Not only that, most women's carry-on bags were treasure troves of jewelry and cash.

Hearing no shouts, he slowed his pace so that he appeared to be nothing more than a passenger in a great hurry.

What he did not know was that Zoe, a former sprinter at Columbia, had chosen to run quietly along the edge of the concourse, where there were far fewer people. Thus, when the thief slowed his pace, Zoe locked onto him like a tomahawk missile.

It therefore came as a complete surprise to the thief when he caught a blur of movement out of the corner of his eye. He glanced around the instant Zoe thrust out her foot.

Had this been Monday-night football, the catapulting thief would have probably scored a touchdown. Thrown higher than normal because of his leaping attempt to catch his balance, the thief actually appeared to be crashing over a collapsing defensive front line, with the ball – in this case, Zoe's carry-on bag – held securely in his arm. His face contorted was in shock as he cartwheeled through the air and landed flat on his back. Around him, nearly a dozen people screamed and tumbled to the floor.

Rolling painfully onto his side, the thief started to get up, then froze when he saw Zoe's nine-millimeter SIG staring him in the face.

"You just made a felonious attempt to steal Federal documents!"

The thief moaned and flopped down onto his back.

A patrolling security officer noticed people running in all directions. Some were scrambling away from whatever had happened. Others were hurrying to see what was going on.

"Airport security!" he announced, pushing through the ring of gawkers. "What the—! *Drop your weapon!*" he shouted, whipping out his pistol.

"Federal officer!" Zoe shouted back, without taking her eyes off the thief. She pulled out her Agency ID and held it in plain sight. *So much for anonymity.*

"Alister Einck, airport security," the officer said, stepping around to where Zoe could see him. "What's going on?"

"Attempted theft of classified documents."

"Warranting the use of a firearm?"

"Necessary to apprehend and prevent the loss of sensitive information vital to the security of the United States, so – yes – warranting the use of a firearm. Besides, the bastard's not hurt. The safety's on."

"I've got him covered, so holster that weapon."

Zoe eyed the large number of people surrounding them and stood, holstering her weapon. A moment later, two more security officers pushed through the crowd.

"What's happening here? What's going on?" demanded B.J., the more muscular of the two. He strode over to Alister with a barbell strut.

"The bitch attacked me!" the thief blurted out. "Drew a fuckin' *gun*."

"Who pulled a gun?"

"She did!" yelled the thief, pointing at Zoe.

"She's Agency," Alister explained.

B.J. ran his eyes over Zoe.

Stupid women's rights, he thought with a derisive snort. As far as he was concerned, women had no place in law enforcement unless they could type or make coffee. Allowing them to carry weapons was the crown of stupidity.

"Something wrong?" asked Zoe.

"Who gave you the authority to draw a loaded weapon in an airport?" demanded B.J.

"That man stole my carry-on bag. Witnesses in the bar where I was sitting will verify that fact."

"You pulled a gun because some guy stole your cosmetics case?"

"Because he stole classified *documents*," Zoe replied.

"No one carries classified documents in a carry-on bag."

"Evidently they do."

"I don't believe you."

"Too bad."

"It is for you until I'm satisfied you're telling the truth!"

"You're going to have to take my word for it," said Zoe.

B.J. reached for the bag but Zoe stopped him.

"Classified," she said, all too aware that her documents were not in fact officially *classified.* Sensitive, yes, but not classified. She just hoped these officers believed her.

B.J. jabbed a finger at Zoe. "You may think you're some high-flyin' skirt—"

"What the hell is your *problem?*" said Zoe, knocking his hand away.

"*You're* my problem! You and all the skirts who want to play by separate rules!"

"For the record, I operate by the same rules as you. But in case you've forgotten, I'm not the one who broke the rules. He did." She glanced at the thief, then stared hard at B.J. "And you know what? You did, too, with that offensive attitude and foul mouth."

A number of spectators clapped and cheered.

"So, the skirt wants to play tough," snarled B.J.

"Dial it down," said Alister.

B.J. seized Zoe by the arm.

"That's enough!" Alister commanded, removing B.J.'s hand. "She's Agency and you are *way* out of line."

"What do you mean, *I'm* out of line?"

"You've already violated several articles of conduct, so I think you should drop the matter before Ms. Gustaves and I take this up the ladder."

"She made a claim about classified documents and I want it verified."

"I've already given you my statement," said Zoe. "If you want it in writing – fine. But the contents of this bag are classified and that's as far as it goes. Now, is there anything else that you want? If so, make it fast, 'cause I've got a plane to catch."

"Hey, what about me?" yelled the thief.

"Joe, cuff that guy," Alister told the third officer, who pulled the thief to his feet.

"What about her?" shouted the thief. "Why ain't she in cuffs?"

B.J. grabbed Zoe by the elbow. "If I had my way, she would be!"

"I told you, I'm catching a flight," said Zoe, twisting free.

"Not until this is cleared up!"

"Then clear it up."

"Who's your supervisor? What's his number? I want his assurance that you're carrying classified documents and that you have the authority to carry a weapon."

Zoe's heart sank. *If he called this in, she was dead.*

But what could she do? Refuse to give him Teague's number? Give him a wrong number? Doing that would only exacerbate her problems, and she was in enough hot water as it was.

Zoe heard the crowd grow quiet.

With an unwavering stare, Zoe took out her ID and held it in front of B.J.'s face.

"Take a good look at this," she said. "I'm not trying to pick a fight, but if I miss my plane, a lot of angry people with badges just like this one will be looking to ream your ass." She closed the wallet and put it back in her pocket. "So if you want to ask me any more questions, do it while I'm walking to the gate."

She picked up her bag and turned away.

B.J. grabbed her again.

"That's enough!" commanded Alister.

"I want to talk to her supervisor!"

"Release her, B.J. *Right now!*"

With a roar, B.J. whirled away.

"Sorry about that," said Alister.

Zoe took a deep breath and nodded.

"Who's your supervisor, by the way?" he asked.

Zoe swallowed. "Jackson Teague."

"What's his number?"

Zoe recited the switchboard number, her voice cracking slightly as she tried to sound confident.

While B.J. paced angrily nearby, Alister wrote down the information. He then took out one of his cards and handed it to Zoe.

"Mind if I get one of yours?" he asked.

"Of course," she answered, giving her card to Alister. "Let me know if you have any more questions."

"I doubt that'll be necessary," he said.

"*What?*" exclaimed B.J.

"You heard me," said Alister.

"She thinks she's above the law!"

"She thinks nothing of the sort."

"Whose side are you on?"

"I didn't know we were taking sides. She offered her statement, has witnesses we can talk to, and we where to find her. Thank you, Ms. Gustaves, you may go."

B.J. whipped out his phone. "I'm calling this in!"

"You sure you want to do that?" asked Alister.

"Damn right I do! Simmons will have your *butt!*"

"B.J.," Alister said gently.

"*What?*"

"Simmons used to be with the Agency."

From his position behind a group of onlookers, Tyler watched the red-faced officer lower his phone and storm away. He then looked back at Zoe.

So that's the young woman who phoned me, he thought. And with a chuckle, he turned toward the gate.

CHAPTER 19

Feeling rested after his flight in First Class, Tyler stood waiting for his luggage in the Cairo airport, along with over two hundred other passengers. Although Val had pressured him into wearing a sports jacket and tie, Tyler had not surrendered the comfort of his jeans.

He strolled over to where Zoe stood waiting.

"That was quite a show you put on back at Kennedy," he said.

Zoe kept staring at the empty conveyor belt.

"Do you often tackle guys like that in public?" he asked.

A spontaneous chuckle was Zoe's reply, and she shook her head. Here she was, standing next to the man she was supposed to be tailing – a man she felt she knew, although they had never met. Still, from the profile she'd managed to compile since their telephone conversation, Tyler was definitely a man who intrigued her.

Too much, perhaps?

Don't be stupid, she told herself. Tyler was nothing more than an assignment and investigating him was part of her job. But no matter how many times she reminded herself of that fact, Zoe knew she wasn't convinced.

What was it about him that so attracted her?

Aside from his nationally-televised interviews, Tyler was a journalist whose articles and photographs had been published all around the world.

But that's not what impressed her the most. What impressed her most was his gutsiness in going after Abu Nazer – assuming that was in fact what he was doing, which she sensed that it was. Tyler was like a photographer stalking a lion. The lion was a dangerous predator, and the challenge was not merely in outsmarting the lion, but capturing him on film. To do that took courage and skill.

Anyone could hunt lions, but this particular lion – Abu Nazer – had eluded the most skillful of hunters. Somehow, she felt Tyler would succeed.

And now, with Tyler standing right next to her, Zoe felt a tingle of excitement.

But she had to remind herself that Tyler was also a man who had lied to her about knowing Tariq Yassin – or certainly knowing about him – and then played on her sympathies as a woman in order to milk her for information.

In short, Tyler might be nothing more than a seasoned actor.

Yet she also sensed that was not the case.

She thought about the things they had in common: a love of country music, good beer, photography, and going after the unobtainable. Not to mention he was dangerously good looking.

Zoe felt a sudden flush rising in her cheeks.

Stop it! You're here to do a job.

"I take it you're not just bumming around Egypt," Tyler remarked in the absence of a reply.

"No offense," Zoe said, "but it's not SOP for me to answer questions from strangers."

"Hey, I don't blame you," responded Tyler with an understanding nod. "It's not standard operating procedure for me to do that, either. Of course, I could always tell you my name, and you could tell me yours, and then we wouldn't be strangers."

"That's one option," Zoe answered, unable to suppress a smile. Just then the first wobbling bag came through a small opening in the wall on the conveyor belt.

And Zoe suddenly became aware that if Tariq or Abu Nazer happened to be watching, a prolonged exchange with Tyler could well blow her cover.

"Another option would be for us to remain strangers and go our separate ways."

"That's not exactly what I was hoping you'd say," Tyler replied, impressed by how blue Zoe's eyes were, especially when framed by that tangle of luscious brown hair. "I was kinda hoping we could become friends. Maybe go out for a drink."

Zoe shrugged.

"Didn't I hear one of the policeman back at JFK address you as Ms. Gustaves?" he asked.

"You have a good memory," she said.

"Only when it's convenient," he answered with a laugh. "Anyway, I guess that means we're not total strangers. After all, I know your last name. First name, too, if it's Mizz."

Another chuckle was Zoe's reply.

"By the way, folks call me Tyler," he said, sticking out his hand. "Tyler's actually my last name, but with a first name like Rutherford… well, you can see why I go by Tyler."

Zoe looked at the outstretched hand, then at the man who had offered it.

"Really, it's okay," he said. "We're not strangers anymore."

Zoe looked back at the conveyor belt. "You're certainly persistent," she said, aware that she shouldn't be enjoying this flirtation.

But in truth, she was.

"I really don't bite," Tyler said. "Honest. My dear old mama, God rest her soul, taught me there are certain times one shouldn't argue."

"Are we arguing?"

"I'm tryin' hard not to," he answered, sounding very Texan. He extended his hand once again. "But I keep offerin' and you keep refusin'. I hope you don't take that as arguin', because one should never argue with the cook, your surgeon, or a woman packin' a pistol."

This time Zoe laughed outright.

Tyler continued to stand there with an outstretched hand.

Finally, with a sigh of resignation, Zoe gave Tyler's hand a quick couple of shakes.

"That wasn't so hard, now, was it Mizz—"

"Zoe," she instinctively replied, then instantly regretted the mistake. She hoped Tyler didn't remember her from the phone call.

"Nice to meet you, Zoe," he said.

"Same here," she answered, looking toward the glass doors into the main foyer of the terminal. *Someone should be arriving soon from the embassy.*

A few seconds of silence passed by.

"Would you, by any chance, be the same Zoe Gustaves of the Central Intelligence Agency who phoned me recently with some questions?" he asked, leaning close and lowering his voice.

Zoe stiffened.

"The same Zoe Gustaves who hung up when I asked if my life was in danger?"

Zoe folded her arms into a knot.

"If that's the case," he said, "then we're really not strangers, are we? Because if you're indeed that same Zoe Gustaves, then you know a great deal more than you're letting on. I wonder if it's coincidence that we were on the same flight?"

The infatuation Zoe had felt a minute ago evaporated into a brutal awareness that, once again, he had been playing her.

How could you be so stupid? How could you let him do this to you? Zoe knew the answer. *You saw what you wanted to see.* She could hear Teague yelling at her now.

"If you really do know the danger I'm in," Tyler spoke so softly and close to her ear that she actually felt his breath, "then you also know that it only takes a mistake – one *simple* mistake, like that cowgirl act of yours back at Kennedy – to get someone killed. Maybe you should think about that before you go snooping around in other people's business. Now, if you'll excuse me, I see my bags." He started to leave, then paused. "By the way, I meant what I said. I was hopin' we could have become friends. Had a drink together."

"In your dreams," Zoe muttered bitterly as Tyler turned away.

After a brief hesitation, indicating that he had heard her reply, Tyler excused his way through the crowd, grabbed three large aluminum suitcases off the carousel and hoisted them onto a trolley. On his way to the customs counter, he passed a disheveled, twenty-something red-haired man racing in through a side door. The red-haired man paused, glanced at the photo in his hand, then scanned the crowd. *There! With the folded arms.* He rushed over and tapped Zoe on the shoulder.

Zoe jerked around.

"Ms. Gustaves?" he asked.

Zoe looked at the man's ID.

"Tim Odell, American Embassy," he said with a smile. "I'm here to take you through customs."

CHAPTER 20

Youssef Qaderi's ornamental residence immediately caught Tyler's eye as Sharifa's Mercedes coupe turned down the quiet, tree-lined street. Faced with gleaming white marble, the multi-storied building was bathed in a wash of floodlights, which were mounted discreetly in the shrubs.

The first two stories were fairly plain, while the more ornamental third and fourth stories were adorned with columns, arches and awnings. A covered balcony encircled much of the fifth story, with what looked to be a large cupola rising from one side of the flat roof.

"Now that's impressive!" Tyler remarked as Sharifa parked the Mercedes in front.

"Youssef purchased it several years ago from the owner of a transport company," she said. "Houses are not normally so elaborate, even in Zamalek, which is one of the most exclusive neighborhoods in the city. The balconies on the other side overlook the Nile, with the lights of the city beyond."

"You live here full time?"

"One of the privileges of working for Mr. Qaderi."

"How many employees does he have? And is there room for one more?"

Sharifa laughed. "Aside from me, there's Mr. Qaderi's cook, Mrs. Fedje, and a bodyguard."

"Bodyguard?" asked Tyler.

"Don't worry, you've got one, too."

"I do?"

"Me," Sharifa said. And with a seductive smile, she opened her door and climbed gracefully out.

The foyer of Qaderi's house was sparsely furnished. To the left was an elevator. Directly ahead was a corridor of travertine marble. On the right was an open staircase.

"Before I forget," Sharifa said. She handed Tyler a spare key, then led the way down the corridor. "Your bedroom is here, on the right," she said, pushing open a door. "If there's anything you need, I'm across the hall."

"Anything, as in *anything?*" he asked.

"I don't cook and I don't do laundry."

"I wasn't thinking of that."

"I should hope not," she said with a playful smile.

Across the river, Tim Odell showed Zoe into his office.

"Wait here. I'll check on the guest room," he said.

"No time, we need that boat."

"I thought you were kidding."

"No joke. We need it now."

"Don't you want to get settled in?"

"No time. Come on, let's go."

Tim shook his head and followed Zoe out the door.

"I'm so glad that you're here," said Sharifa.

"I'm glad to be off that plane."

"Youssef wanted me to extend his apologies for not being at the airport to meet you. He'll arrive back from London tomorrow."

"No offense to Youssef, but I'd much rather get a welcome kiss from you."

Sharifa laughed. "Come on, I'll make you dinner."

"You said you don't cook."

"How hard can it be? Mrs. Fedje makes it look easy."

"How about I take you out?"

"Let's stay in. Fix something ourselves."

"Are you sure?"

"Absolutely!" She took Tyler by the hand, led him upstairs, through the living room and out onto the deck, where a small table and chairs had been set up. "Room with a view," she said.

Tyler walked mesmerized to the balustrade.

Directly in front was the Nile, a massive, churning black ribbon of water, silent and restless, as timeless as the desert to which it gives life – or did at one time. On the river's surface were shards of color, skipping and dancing, reflections of the vivid lights of Cairo, spread out like an endless cinema screen as far as the eye could see. During the day, Cairo was a sooty crush of concrete and brick, a collision of ancient and obsolete. But tonight, as with each night, the city was ornamented in light, glowing majestically up into the night sky until the reality of dawn once again revealed its grimy monotony.

"I never get tired of it," Sharifa said, joining Tyler at the railing. "Most nights I come out here simply to stare."

"It's magnificent. Hypnotic."

"As Africa's largest city, Cairo has many problems. But at night, the problems disappear."

"At least for awhile."

"Look, over there," she said, pointing to a high-rise apartment lit up with hundreds of tiny rectangles. "The city is full of them. So many people, so many problems."

They stared in silence for several moments.

"Listen to me!" she said. "You just get here and already I'm on a – how do you say it – a detergent crate?"

"Soap box," he said with a laugh.

"What an unusual expression," she replied. "What does it mean?"

"It's from the days when a person wanted to stand above the crowd in order to make a speech – to get people's attention. One of the best ways to do that was by standing on a wooden crate. They were lightweight, portable, and sturdy."

"Well, I'm off of my soap box. Let's eat."

Sharifa led the way up a flight of steps into a spacious kitchen fitted with every imaginable gadget and utensil. The countertops were polished granite, the appliances stainless steel. Overhead was an array of skillets and pans hanging on metal racks.

"So this is where it happens," said Tyler.

"We could feed an army, but Mrs. Fedje rarely cooks for more than three. And that's when we're not dining out."

"Then let's give it a workout," said Tyler, rolling up his sleeves. "What do you want me to do?"

"Mrs. Fedje has an excellent collection of recipe books. Why don't we look through them, decide on a menu and I'll phone our grocer with a list of ingredients?"

"That is *way* too complicated. Let's check the fridge and see what's there. I can do wonders with leftovers."

"I can't feed you leftovers!"

"Ain't much you can't resurrect with a wok and some sweet chili sauce."

An hour later, seated on the deck, they pushed aside their chopsticks and empty bowls. A candle inside a colored jar flicked splashes of red on their faces.

"I can't believe you got your start by taking that woman's photo," Sharifa said, finishing her wine.

"It was definitely a lucky break."

"A Cinderella story – in boots – if I've ever heard one," she replied. "Orphan survives abusive relatives to become one of America's premier television journalists. But I've yet to see anyone interview you. How have you managed to stay out of the limelight?"

"By putting other people in it," answered Tyler, refilling their glasses.

"Very clever," she said.

"What about you? What's your story?"

Sharifa glanced at her watch. "Goodness, is that the time?"

"Oh, no you don't. You're not wriggling out of the spotlight that easily."

"Tyler, really – you must be tired. And tomorrow's a big day. Youssef's arranged a meet-and-greet at one o'clock with Doctors Mostafa and Woolley."

"Come on – spill! I want to know more about you."

"There is honestly not that much to tell."

"Don't give me that. Everything I've discovered about you so far is impressive."

"Impressive is hardly accurate."

"I think it is."

"How so?"

"You're an impressive fighter," he said. "So I know better than to ever pick a fight."

Sharifa laughed.

"You're also an impressive dancer."

"Now you are joking!"

"I am seriously impressed, I tell you. Not everybody can down that many margaritas and stay on their feet."

Sharifa slapped Tyler on the arm.

"All kidding aside," he said, "to have had it rough like you did as a kid and yet become what you've become…"

"Kind of like you," she said.

"Like both of us, I think. So, tell me something I don't know. Like what your parents do. How you landed this job. How you met Youssef."

"Like I said, there is really not that much to tell. Besides, it is all kind of boring."

"Let me be the judge of that."

"I met Youssef one day in the museum, we got to talking, and one thing led to another."

"There's got to be more to it than that."

Sharifa shrugged.

A long moment of silence passed.

"You really don't want to talk about it, do you?" he said.

"I do not want you getting the wrong idea."

"Will I?"

Sharifa stood and walked over to the railing. Tyler observed her for a moment then joined her.

They stood watching the reflections of light playing on the surface of the Nile. A gentle breeze rustled the fronds of some nearby palms.

"I know what you must be thinking," she finally said.

"I'm thinking you overcame some pretty tough odds to get to where you are. I'm also thinking this is making you *very* uncomfortable."

"People talk," she said. "They talk, and they do not care whom it hurts or how much."

"About what? You working for Youssef?"

"And living under his roof."

"People are always going to gossip about stuff like that. You can't let the stupidity of others bother you."

"You don't know Cairo."

"I know you can't run your life by what society thinks."

"What happens when that gossip hurts others?"

"Who are you referring to?"

"My parents. They hear what has been said. That I am Youssef's mistress. That I slept my way into this job."

"Easily fixed. Just tell 'em the truth."

Sharifa did not respond.

"You've tried, haven't you?" he asked.

Sharifa did not respond.

"Sorry. This is none of my business."

He turned to go, but Sharifa stopped him.

"I have not talked to my parents in years," she said.

"Why not?"

"They are Coptic Christians, and they..." Her voice trailed off. Tyler said nothing.

"They are *zabbaline*," she said at last. "Garbage collectors who make their living recycling trash. They live in a rubbish city in the Muqattam Hills."

"A rubbish city?"

"Built from recycled bricks, metal, wood – whatever they can find. I know what you must be thinking. How did I come to live in such luxury, while my family collects cans for a living?"

"What I'm thinking is that you need to quit being so hard on yourself."

"That is difficult to do when my father is so disapproving. He doesn't trust Youssef. I tried to explain how each of the staff has his or her own room, but it didn't make any difference. He had his mind made up, and was not about to listen. Things ended in a big fight, and we have not spoken since." Sharifa wiped tears from her eyes. "What am I going to do?" she said. "I feel so alone."

"We'll think of something," Tyler replied, giving her a hug.

"I am so glad I have you to talk to," she said, snuggling into him.

"Me, too," said Tyler.

He drew her close, and together they stood gazing across the river.

Had Tyler looked carefully, he would have noticed the small motorboat anchored offshore. In it were Zoe and Tim. In Tim's hand was a portable parabolic directional microphone and recorder. In Zoe's was a 32x day/night prismatic monocular.

"What a load of crap!" Zoe remarked, her voice turning whiny and sarcastic, "'What am I going to do? I feel so alone. I'm so glad I have you to talk to.' God, I want to throw up."

"Want to tell me what you really think?"

"He's here to do a *job!*"

"O-*kay.*"

"And there he is, up there on Qaderi's deck, acting all lovey-dovey. What the hell is he *thinking?*"

"And this upsets you because…?"

"It isn't *like him!* He doesn't *do* this kind of thing!"

"Looks to me like he does."

"She came on to him with that pathetic 'poor-little-me' routine and he bought it. I can't believe he's that *stupid.*"

"Maybe he likes her."

"I've profiled the guy and I'm telling you, he doesn't do this kind of thing! Something's not right."

"Why are you so angry?"

With a growl of disgust, Zoe put the monocular back to her eye.

With their attention on Tyler and Sharifa, neither Zoe nor Tim noticed the small boat farther out in the river. In it was Tariq Yassin.

Tariq directed his telephoto camera away from Tyler and Sharifa and onto the two people in the other boat. With a smile he brought them into focus.

Seconds later, he had taken more than a dozen infrared photos.

CHAPTER 21

After photographing Tyler, Sharifa, and the CIA surveillance team, Tariq returned the rented boat to its slip and made his way into the city on foot. He dashed across a busy street, turned along a sidewalk and threaded his way through the crowds in front of several nightclubs and coffee houses. After turning a corner, he took out his cell phone and dialed. Moments later the call was answered.

"I'm on my way," he said.

Tariq put the phone away and entered a narrow street that smelled of grilled lamb and onions. In the distance, he heard a group of laughing women. Their shrill voices pierced the night.

Turning another corner, Tariq passed the gutted space of an old building, its door broken open by years of trash and garbage being thrown from the windows of neighboring apartments. He heard voices in a darkened doorway and smelled the sharp odor of cheap cigarettes. He passed beneath a heavy stone arch before turning into a narrow alleyway that branched into a warren of even darker alleys.

With drawn daggers, the two men from the doorway ran after Tariq. With no streetlights in this section of the city, visibility was poor and no one would be able to recognize them. The high walls on each side of the alley were like a stone canyon that funneled sound.

The two men reached an intersection and paused.

"I hear him, in that alley, off to the left," one of them said.

The two men raced into the alley.

An explosion of white spots was all the first man saw before crumpling unconscious to the ground.

The second man stumbled over his friend's body, caught himself, then turned and looked down.

"What happened?" he asked. He knelt beside his friend and saw that he was unconscious.

Suddenly, movement in the darkness.

The man leapt up and slashed wildly at the fleeting shadow.

More movement! There! To his right!

The man slashed again.

Whirling full circle, the man slashed left, then right. Then left again. But no one was there!

A sharp pain shot through his wrist. The dagger was torn from his hand. The man turned to run.

A hand clamped like a vice around his neck, truncating his ability to scream. It lifted him off the ground and smashed him against a wall.

"You *dare* interfere with Abu Nazer?" rasped the robed figure of Majli.

His eyes bulging with fear, the man shook his head, his frightened orbs locking onto the blade of Majli's dagger held inches from his face.

"Pick up your companion," ordered Majli, releasing the man.

The man knelt slowly, expecting at any moment to feel the icy fire of Majli's dagger ripping open his throat.

He paused, and glanced up at the figure looming over him.

"You test me!" hissed Majli.

"No, great one!" the man replied. He roused his friend by smacking him lightly in the face, then helped him to his feet and led him away.

"This way," said Majli, slipping his dagger back in its sheath. He led Tariq toward a recessed doorway that appeared as a black semi-circle in a montage of other shadows.

A clank sounded and Majli pushed open the door.

"Per your instructions, a rifle and explosives," he said, handing Tariq a long narrow gun case. "It was not easy to obtain such a weapon."

"When will you have their schedules?" asked Tariq.

"Eighteen hours, maybe less. Once the job is complete, I'll wire your five-hundred-thousand dollars."

"Half tonight. My Swiss account."

"That was not our agreement!"

"It is now."

And with the gun case in hand, Tariq melted away into the darkness.

CHAPTER 22

After an exhausting night of surveillance, Zoe returned to the embassy with Tim to find more than a dozen emails waiting. Dealing with those took over an hour, during which time Tim transcribed his audio recording, which Zoe started reading.

Sunlight was streaming through a window when Tim poked his head in the door. Outside, a haze the color of dry mustard hung over the city.

"You look like hell," he said.

A sharp glance was Zoe's reply.

"Jetlag's harder on some people than others," Tim said. "Throws my rhythms out of whack."

Zoe yawned and kept reading.

"Want me to get you some coffee?" asked Tim.

"I've still got an acid stomach from the last batch you served."

"I never was any good at making coffee."

"No kidding."

"How about something else?"

"Got any bacon and eggs?"

"Pork rind and cholesterol, fried crisp. That should take care of the acid."

"You ever get punched for talking too much?"

"Not a good day unless I get punched," said Tim. "Especially by someone so charming."

A reluctant chuckle was Zoe's reply.

"I'll see who's open," said Tim. "But it won't be bacon and eggs."

"No fava beans," said Zoe.

"You really should give them a try. They mash them with garlic and egg at this little stand around the corner."

"No fava beans, Tim! Now, go!"

Tim grinned and ducked out the door while Zoe continued reading. *Thunk!*

Zoe jerked and sat up. She had fallen asleep and her head had fallen forward, hitting the desk. She glanced at her watch. Ten minutes has passed since Tim had gone.

Ten *wasted* minutes.

Time was slipping away and yet what could she do? She knew when and where Tyler was meeting Qaderi, but nothing else. What she needed was a way to listen in on their conversation and find out what they were planning. But how? A parabolic microphone in a boat at night was one thing. Broad daylight was another. Especially now that Tyler knew she was following him. It was a problem that needed to be solved if she were to have any chance of intercepting Abu Nazer.

Tim said he was working on something, but how long that would take was anyone's guess. If only she weren't so *tired!*

Zoe was packing away her laptop when Tim pushed open the door.

"Here you go," he said. "Smoked turkey and egg in some kind of goat lard pastry, or whatever they use in this land of no pigs."

Zoe snatched the croissant and devoured it in three ravenous bites.

"I should have bought half a dozen," remarked Tim.

"You should have," agreed Zoe, her cheeks bulging as she chewed. "Okay. Which way to a bed?"

"Care for a bit of dessert?" asked Tim with a twinkle in his eye.

An icy glare was Zoe's reply.

Tim grinned and held up a hand. "No, no, not that. Though I know I'm hard to resist. I'm talking about a deliciously sweet bit of news that just came in. I refer, of course, to the high frequency microwave interference shield that Qaderi's neighbor just won in a raffle."

"Tim, I'm too tired for drivel."

Tim touched a fist to his heart and looked hurt.

"*Tim!*"

"Okay, okay," he said. "Remember how I told you I was working on daytime surveillance? Well, we concocted this raffle story so that one of our technicians could install a directional microphone and transmitter on that neighbor's rooftop satellite dish. By one o'clock today, you'll be listening in on every word spoken by Tyler and Qaderi."

CHAPTER 23

The gray-haired old woman wore cheap clothing, a cheaper hat, and even cheaper makeup, which discolored her face, like old flannel.

"I'd like to see Ernst," she told the Credit Suisse bank clerk in a thin, whisper-like voice.

"To see Ernst requires an appointment."

"I need to make a withdrawal."

"You may do so at the machine outside."

"Your machine can access my account?"

"It can access any account."

"Thank you so much," the old woman said. "I didn't realize they serviced double-alpha accounts."

That got the clerk's attention. "Did you say double-alpha?" she asked, aware that double-alpha accounts were numbered and reserved only for the wealthiest of clients.

Two minutes later, the old woman was shown into Ernst's paneled office.

"Madam wishes to make a withdrawal?" asked Ernst, gesturing her to a chair. He was a small man, conservative and neat, with rimless glasses and a gray tweed suit.

"Yes," the old woman replied.

Ernst nodded politely, and with great formality slid a form across the desk. To his surprise, the old woman wrote the precise alpha-numeric account sequence – twice, as the form required – all from memory. She then wrote the amount she wished to withdraw and slid the form back to Ernst, who stiffened slightly when he saw the number.

"To process such a request will take at least seventy-two hours," he said.

"I have a train to catch," the old woman declared in her whisper-like voice. "If this takes more than ten minutes, I will cancel my withdrawal and the entire account will be moved to a more accommodating bank."

Ernst stared at the woman, who glanced pointedly at her watch.

"One moment," he said, clearing his throat as a discreet sign of protest. He then stood and strode briskly out of the office.

He returned eight minutes later with a lumpy cloth sack.

"Fifty thousand dollars, U.S.," he said curtly. "Please count it and sign here."

The old woman placed the sack in her bag, scribbled illegibly on the bottom of the form, then turned and left.

Outside, she took a cab to the Bank of London and deposited the money into another account. When finished, she hailed another cab and directed the driver to a restaurant across town. Once the cab was gone, she walked two blocks to a modest hotel on a cobblestone side street. She climbed a flight of creaking wooden stairs to the room she had rented earlier, where she washed off her makeup and brushed her hair back to its natural black color.

Fifteen minutes later, dressed in a tailored ivory business suit, Lydia left the hotel and hailed a final cab, this time traveling to the Zurich airport. Ninety minutes later, Lydia settled back in her Business Class seat.

"Would you care for a top-up on Champagne?" the male flight attendant asked once the plane had reached cruising altitude. He sat casually on the armrest of the seat next to Lydia, holding a starched linen napkin around the bottle.

"I have plenty," answered Lydia.

"It's freshly opened, so I can personally vouch for its sparkle."

Lydia did not reply.

"We'll be serving hors d'oeuvres in a few minutes," the attendant said.

Again Lydia did not reply, and the flight attendant, getting the message, moved on to serve other passengers.

Once he was gone, Lydia took out her laptop and connected it to the internet. She accessed a website, opened an email and typed: "Transaction complete." She clicked "Send" and the email disappeared. Lydia then shut down her laptop and stowed it away.

In Austin, Val cursed when she saw the glowing red numbers on the digital clock in Tyler's guest bedroom, where she stayed when he was away.

"Damn it, it's *three a.m.!*"

Val rarely swore, and she knew why she had – she was angry with Tyler. Muttering a string of complaints, she threw back the sheet and slid her feet into a pair of old moccasins. A few minutes later, she had stomped downstairs to the kitchen.

While a carafe of coffee steeped, Val went to the office to send a message to Tyler.

"I'm sending the mallet," she typed.

"Go back to sleep," he typed back.

"I can't, and you know why!"

"Try a sleeping tablet."

"As if that will solve anything!"

"You need to trust that I know what I'm doing."

"That's the problem, Tyler. I don't know what you're doing!"

"Well, I do, so quit worrying."

"How can you tell me to quit worrying when you're over there having a romantic fling? I think you've forgotten why you're there."

"This isn't the time."

"When exactly *will* be the time? Post-mortem? What if Abu Nazer's onto you? What if he knows what you're doing?"

"He's not onto me."

"You don't know that. I'm sending the mallet."

"Will you *please* quit pushing me on this?"

"I wouldn't have to push if you'd listen to reason!" Val shouted. She jumped up and began pacing in front of the monitor, fists clenched, fuming. Any halfwit could see what was going on, so why couldn't Tyler? Sharifa was a distraction, an involvement.

And that meant Tyler had a blind spot.

But what good was the mallet if he couldn't see the danger he was in? Did something terrible have to happen before he changed his mind?

Probably, Val thought with a sigh. And I just hope it's not fatal. "Have it your way," she typed.

"Thank you," was Tyler's response. "By the way, I met Zoe Gustaves, the agent who phoned from the CIA. After managing to get her carry-on bag stolen at Kennedy, she ran the thief down, tackled him in front of a hundred people, then held him at gunpoint until airport security arrived. She then had a run-in with one of the guards, and for a while it looked like they were actually going to duke it out. She's quite a handful, this Zoe Gustaves, and now she's here tailing me."

"For God's sake, be careful!" typed Val.

"I will. Now go back to sleep."

With a final shake of her head, Val logged off, went to the kitchen, and poured herself a mug of coffee. She stared at it for a moment then dumped it down the sink. Minutes later, she was upstairs in bed.

"I miss you, Sack," she murmured, calling her husband by the nickname she'd given him on their first date. She stared up at the darkened ceiling for a few moments until she felt tears trickling down her cheeks. With a sniff, she turned onto her side and closed her eyes.

While Val was drifting off to sleep in Austin, in Shady Oak, Virginia, Jackson Teague was being awakened by the ringing of his phone.

"Yes?" he answered hoarsely.

"Sir, this is Dispatch," said a voice. "We have a level three development in process."

"On my way," answered Teague. He stood and wiped the drowsiness from his eyes.

"What is it?" his wife asked sleepily.

"Another dog in a tree," was Teague's routine way of telling his wife something was happening that he couldn't discuss.

"Okay," she replied, shielding her eyes from the bathroom light that came on a few seconds later. Then came the hiss of the shower.

Ten minutes later, Teague was backing his Chrysler out of the garage, not bothering with coffee, which he knew it would be waiting for him at the office along with a selection of breakfast sandwiches.

"What have we got?" he asked, striding into the Situation Room forty minutes later, his intense gaze scanning the faces in the room.

His secretary, April, handed him a mug of coffee.

"Zurich," answered Alwinda Jones, Teague's European sector chief. "Our field agent, Friedrich Schmidt, barely missed a personal cash deposit of fifty thousand dollars into Tariq Yassin's account with the Bank of London."

"Did we get a name or description?" asked Teague, taking a swallow from his mug.

"One of the clerks said the deposit was made by a gray-haired old woman wearing lots of makeup."

"Anything from security video?"

"Negative. She wore a wide-brimmed hat and used it to keep her face shielded from the cameras."

"How about a sketch?"

"Doing that now. We did catch a small break from Credit Suisse though. Apparently, the old woman withdrew the funds from what they call a double-alpha account – big bucks, identified and accessed by a seven-digit alpha-numeric code. No names or IDs required."

"Meaning anyone can access the account so long as they have that code?"

"Yes, sir. Same problem, though, with the wide-brimmed hat and security cameras. But she managed to piss off the chief teller, so he gave us a fairly detailed description. It matches the description we got from the Bank of London."

"Will Credit Suisse allow us to flag the account?"

"Not without clear evidence it's linked to terrorist activity, which we can't provide. The manager did say privately, however, that the fifty thousand was withdrawn from the same numbered account that we inquired about before."

"Meaning the same one from which Tariq was paid the ten grand?"

"Yes, sir. Plus, Tariq's Internet Service Provider just notified us that an email was sent to him from a web-based account accessed from a commercial aircraft."

"What did it say?"

"'Transaction complete.' MI6 is getting us a list of passengers as we speak. Hopefully, they'll be able to match our description with a name."

"Conclusions?" asked Teague.

"Three possibilities," answered Alwinda. "A: Tariq is Abu Nazer and the woman is simply a drone who did the banking and sent him confirmation that funds from his numbered account were now in his operating account. B: The woman is Abu Nazer and was notifying Tariq that payment's been made for services rendered or about to be rendered. C: Tariq and the woman are both drones working for a third party, who may or may not be Abu Nazer."

"And D?"

"I don't have a D," said Alwinda.

Teague handed his mug to April and nodded for a refill.

"D: It's a set up," said Teague. "Abu Nazer knows that we're monitoring Tariq, and either personally or through a drone made the deposit as a gambit."

The others glanced at one another, perplexed.

"Gambit?" one of them asked.

Teague looked at the man standing quietly at the back of the circle. "Donald, what's a gambit?"

Tall and skinny, with a mop of unruly hair, Donald glanced nervously around as everyone turned to look at him.

"You, uh, want me to tell them what a gambit is, Mr. Teague?"

"Since you're the one who mercilessly stomps me into the ground whenever we play chess – yes, I'd like you to tell them."

A few people chuckled while Donald nervously wrung his hands.

"A gambit is, well, a maneuver in chess where a player risks or sacrifices one piece – usually an inferior one – to deceive an opponent and gain a strategic advantage."

Dropping his gaze, Donald smiled fleetingly at his definition while reflecting on how many times Teague had fallen for his gambits.

"So," said Teague, "to apply Donald's definition to our current situation, we must consider the possibility that Abu Nazer *wants* us to know about the deposit."

"To what end?" asked Alwinda.

"That's what we need to determine, which we can't do until we deduce which conclusion is correct: A, B, C, or D. Or E, or F, or G."

"But we don't—" Alwinda began.

"Precisely," Teague cut in just as April handed him a fresh mug of coffee. "So let's get to work. Sector chiefs, I want a summary of the facts, and I do mean facts. Barb, find out what Israeli intelligence knows. Where's Zoe? I need those profiles."

"Away on stress leave, remember?" said April.

"Dammit, that's right. Who's got them?"

"Tony. I'll check his desk."

While April hurried down the corridor, Teague entered his office and paused to sort through the various memos and pink slips piled in his basket.

Six calls from Congresswoman Gustaves.

Teague tossed those pink slips in the wastebasket and continued sorting through the others. His eye fell on one memo in particular.

"*April!*" he shouted.

April ran into the room. "Yes, Mr. Teague, what is it?"

"What the *hell* is Zoe doing pulling a loaded weapon at JFK? Where is she?"

"I don't know, sir."

"Get Cooke. I want to know what in the hell's going on."

"He's not on the level three list."

"He's on it now! Get him in here."

CHAPTER 24

Tony knew he was in trouble long before he walked into Teague's office.

The phone call from April had been bad enough, yanking him as it had from a deep sleep. But when he was told that Teague wanted to see him now, he knew it was bad.

"Are you in contact with Zoe Gustaves?" asked Teague.

"Isn't she away on stress leave?" answered Tony.

It was a statement Tony regretted the moment he saw the look in Teague's eyes.

"Let's try this again," said Teague, standing. "Are you in contact with Zoe Gustaves? I'm aware she's away on stress leave because I ordered her to take it. What I need to know is whether or not you've been in touch with her. Yes or no."

The unnerving calm in Teague's voice let Tony know which of them was the giant and which of them was Jack. Without a beanstalk. Tony swallowed and a lump seemed to lodge in his throat.

"Yes," he squeaked. He then coughed to cover his nervousness.

"Are you familiar with an incident at JFK involving Zoe drawing her weapon?"

Tony nodded and the lump nearly came up.

"We'll get back to that," said Teague, stepping over to a set of file cabinets. He picked up several folders brought to him earlier by April. He tossed them down in front of Tony.

"Recognize these?" he asked. He sat while Tony continued to stand.

Tony glanced at the various profiles that he and Zoe had been working on. Abu Nazer's was very prominently on top. "Yes, sir," he replied.

"Have you been forwarding information from these files to Zoe?"

This is where the shit hits the fan. "Yes, sir," he said. "Zoe asked me to help her fill in some blanks."

"And have you?"

"Have I what, sir?"

"Been helping her fill in the blanks."

"Yes, sir."

Teague nodded. But Tony could not tell if it was simply an

acknowledgment or just-what-I-thought-so-you're-fired.

"Where is she?" asked Teague.

"In Cairo," answered Tony.

Teague rose from his chair like a gristly bear eyeing dinner. "What did you say?" he asked.

"In Cairo," squeaked Tony.

"For what reason?"

"Stress leave."

"Cut the crap! Why is she there?"

"She's hoping Tyler will lead her to Abu Nazer. I don't know where she's staying, but she's working with Tim Odell."

"Odell? How'd she talk him into this?"

"You know Zoe," said Tony.

"I want a complete report on everything you know."

"When?"

"Right now. Grab a sandwich and plenty of coffee. I want you fueled; you'll be here awhile."

Tony was back in five minutes.

"The whiteboard is yours," said Teague.

After several quick bites, Tony picked up the marker and wrote Tariq's name.

"Based on Omar's call and information supplied by Toy Soldier," he said, "we know Tariq hooked up with Majli in Mecca and talked about killing Tyler and Qaderi. Conclusion: Majli is Abu Nazer and Tariq is a hit man planning to kill Tyler and Qaderi in Cairo. Supporting this is a call our embassy received from an arms dealer in Cairo. He reported the sale of a Russian-made SVN-98 sniper rifle. Cash deal, no names. The arms dealer didn't wish to identify himself but said he was trying to help stop the spread of terrorism."

"An arms dealer with a conscience. How quaint."

"The dealer said he remembered the sale because he never sells rifles like that. He said he heard an SVN-98 had been used to try to kill Vice President Baker. This could be the break we've been waiting for."

"Or a gambit."

"True, but if we walk the cat back over the facts, we can see the timing of this call lends credibility to my conclusion. After all, someone took a shot at Mr. Baker, so we can't rule out the possibility that it was Tariq, although we have no evidence that he was actually in Jerusalem. However, when I got here a little while ago, I saw a report that fifty thousand dollars had been deposited into Tariq's account. Which supports my conclusion that Tariq's our man. He's definitely been paid for something big."

"Did you ever stop to think that Tariq may not be working for Abu Nazer, but in fact is Abu Nazer? And that the others are working for him?"

Tony stared at Teague for a moment. "No, sir, I didn't," he said. "I guess I was focusing on my own conclusion."

"It's worth considering. What else?"

Tony wrote Tyler's name on the whiteboard, and beneath it wrote, "Journalist seeking a story?"

"Why the question mark?" asked Teague. "We already know he's in Cairo to interview Qaderi."

"As you know, voice analysis revealed that Tyler either knows Tariq or knows something about him, which suggests the interview may not be the only reason he's there. A wiretap confirms that he's very much aware of the assassination plot against him."

"You've got a record of that?"

"Yes, sir. Zoe believes Tyler's using the interview with Qaderi to bait Abu Nazer, since he knows they're on his hit list."

"To what end?"

"To capture him on film – or maybe do a story. He could retire on the money he'd earn."

"Yeah, six feet under."

"But what journalist worth his salt doesn't go after the big one? The aspect of danger increases its value. To the point of winning a Pulitzer."

"So Zoe's goal is to – what – intercept Abu Nazer when he tries to kill Tyler?"

"Yes, sir."

"You mentioned a wiretap report?"

"Yes, sir. Of a conversation between Tyler's assistant, Val Johnson, and an Israeli named Ariel Cohen. Cohen phoned from Jerusalem to warn Tyler that Abu Nazer may try to kill him while he's in Cairo. Cohen phoned twice, but both times Tyler was unavailable. However,

Ms. Johnson told Cohen that Tyler was well aware of the danger, even before he called. When we factor in Tyler having lied to us about knowing Tariq, it suggests that he knows about the link between Tariq and Abu Nazer."

"What do we know about Cohen?"

"Nothing. But I did forward the report to Barb."

"Okay, what else?"

"Our Cairo embassy just received an invitation to a black tie gala being hosted by Qaderi. I mention this because word has it he plans to make an announcement about the tablet."

"I didn't think anything was bring announced until San Francisco."

"Qaderi probably wants to capitalize on Tyler being in Cairo. I rang Sterling Crest Gallery in San Francisco – they're the ones hosting the study, as well as brokering insurance on the tablet – and I was told that one of their experts, a Dr. Allan Woolley, is in Cairo doing a preliminary evaluation. They also told me Qaderi plans on sending the tablet on a world tour once it's been authenticated – assuming, of course, that it is authenticated."

Troubled, Teague looked away.

"Want me to stay on that?" asked Tony.

With his brow furrowed in thought, Teague did not reply.

"Sir?"

"Yeah," said Teague, refocusing. "Any news yet on Louise Kappelmann?"

"We don't have a Social Security Number, so finding her's taking some time. Morgan Publishing, where she and her husband used to work, doesn't keep records from that long ago, so we're left with a name-only search. I've got a call into the IRS but they haven't gotten back with me yet."

"Place another call to Morgan Publishing and see if any of the old timers remember her. Ask what her maiden name was, has she remarried, do they have a forwarding address, et cetera. I want her found."

Tony nodded and made a note just as a discreet knock sounded on the door.

"Enter," Teague called out.

A long-haired blond of twenty-six entered. She acknowledged Tony with a nod then nervously approached Teague's desk.

"Is something wrong?" asked Teague.

"Sir, we just received word that Omar and his family have been killed."

Teague shot out of his chair.

"Executed," said Barb. "The extraction team went ashore and found them sitting in their car. Dead, all four of them, single shots to the head."

Teague walked over to the window. Nearly a full minute of silence ticked by.

"I convinced him we were a team," Teague said, staring out into the darkness. "That we were like the front line of the Redskins – everybody standing shoulder to shoulder, working as one, regardless of race, religion or nationality. And he believed me."

Barb and Tony said nothing.

"I even promised I'd take him to a Redskins game."

Teague continued staring out the window for another minute, then shook his head bitterly and returned to his desk.

"I wish I could have known him," remarked Barb.

"Yeah," said Teague. "Me, too."

"I've got news on Ariel Cohen," added Barb. "But if you'd like, I'll come back later."

"It's all right. Let's have it," said Teague.

"Mossad says he's a retired printer who lives in Jerusalem. Quiet, orderly, a political moderate who supports reconciliation with the Arabs. He is, however, a long-time friend of Rubin Yehuda, who's in league with the *gibburim*. Yehuda's one of the members of Dr. Eaton's panel."

"Is Cohen sympathetic with the *gibburim?*" asked Teague.

"Definitely not."

"What's his involvement with Tyler?"

"They're strangers from what we can tell."

"Then why'd he phone Tyler with a warning?"

"I'm guessing as a favor to Yehuda, since they're friends and Yehuda wouldn't want the tablet to fall into the hands of *Qamat*."

"Why didn't Yehuda phone Tyler himself? Or go straight to Qaderi?"

"Probably to avoid compromising his role on the panel."

"Plus," added Tony, "being an American, Tyler might be viewed as more approachable than Qaderi, an Arab."

"Can Israeli intelligence confirm any activity on the part of the *gibburim?*"

"Yes," said Barb, "but it's not what one would expect. They're involved in an archaeological excavation near the Western Wall. Yehuda's directing the dig."

"Why would the gibburim be interested in archaeology?" asked Teague.

"We don't know."

"What about *Qamat*? Anything on them?"

"Nothing concrete."

"Meaning there are rumors?" asked Teague perceptively.

Barb nodded. "As you know, there are growing numbers of Palestinian moderates who oppose *Qamat*. Like their Jewish counterparts, they're tired of the endless killing. But they're also frightened of coming forward for fear of retribution. Still, according to what's being heard on the street – and I must stress these are unsubstantiated reports – some of Wassim Jafar's people are bragging about how they'll soon be in possession of the tablet."

"How soon?" asked Teague.

"We don't know."

"Find out."

"Yes, sir."

"Anything else?" asked Teague.

Barb shook her head.

"Good work. Dismissed," he said.

Barb and Tony turned to go.

"Not you, Cooke," said Teague.

Tony stared dejectedly after Barb until the door clicked shut. When he turned around, he found Teague standing inches from his face.

"I want to know what the hell Zoe thinks she's doing pulling a loaded weapon at JFK!" growled Teague.

"I, uh, heard safety was on," stammered Tony. *How can he move that fast without making a sound?*

"And what happens if the perp takes the gun away? Safety *off*. Bang, bang!"

"I hadn't thought of that."

"It's why you're not authorized to carry anything more than a ballpoint pen. Zoe is and I'm not sure her license shouldn't be *revoked*." Teague whirled away and began pacing the floor. "I have a mind to yank her out of there. But as much as I hate to admit it, she may have stumbled onto something by following Tyler to Cairo. Especially if the tablet gets a preliminary stamp of approval."

"Do you think Abu Nazer may try something in Cairo?"

"We can't rule it out. And this gala makes an attractive target. Contact Zoe and tell her she's back on the case. Then call the embassy and get her name added to the guest list. Odell can give her a hand. Tyler may well be our best shot of cracking this open."

"Isn't Zoe away on stress leave?"

"Cancelled."

Tony shifted uneasily.

"You got something you want to say?" asked Teague.

"No, sir."

"Then get *moving!*"

Tony started for the door then paused. "Before Zoe left, she told me to keep working on Aaron's profile."

"Shelve it. We don't need a profile on Aaron. Instead, I want you to cross-reference each name on the flight from which Tariq's deposit confirmation was sent to the names of all passengers leaving Tel Aviv the day the Vice President was shot at. See if we get a match."

Tony returned to his office and plopped down in front of his terminal. "I should have said something," he mumbled while checking his inbox. "But say what? That I don't agree with him leaving Zoe in Cairo?"

It wasn't that Zoe wasn't smart. She was. And her instincts were good. But here she was – an analyst – doing *field work*. Zoe wasn't trained for that. *And Teague knows it.* So why is he allowing it? Doesn't he remember the last time he sent her into the field? How she almost got *killed?*

Tony opened the latest wiretap report. This one was a transcript of Val's IM chat with Tyler.

So Val Johnson is worried that Abu Nazer may be onto Tyler. Onto him about what? And what's this mallet they keep mentioning?

Tony forwarded a copy of the report to Zoe, adding that he would run a search on whatever this mallet might be.

After updating her on his grilling by Teague, he signed off by saying, "Remember how you wanted me to find out who might have wanted to kill Vice President Baker? Well, get this: I discovered he's been investigating Nightingale! I know Teague said the operation was nonsense, but I think this proves otherwise. But that's not all. Senator Ashford was working on it, too! That means her death and the attempt on Baker may well have been because of Nightingale. BTW, Teague ordered me to shelve the profile on Aaron, but I think you should know what I found. In response to one of your enquiries, a reporter from the *Jerusalem Post* emailed his account of what happened that night on that beach north of Gaza. He said he was the one who covered the incident, and he remembered meeting the Palestinian family who called the police. He withheld their names from the article because they feared reprisals from Qamat. Anyway, the husband recounted how he heard gunfire and later ventured down to the beach, where he found Louise Kappelmann lashed to the body of her dead husband. But get *this!* The husband's name was *Ismail Yassin.*"

CHAPTER 25

On most tourist maps of Jerusalem they are designated simply as "archaeological excavations" and there are several of them in and around the Old City. One site lies just outside the southern wall of the Temple Mount at the base of the *al Aqsa* mosque, where excavations were begun in 1971 but later closed. The reason: the excavations had accessed a network of ancient tunnels running beneath the mosque.

Tunnels that could be filled with explosives.

Rubin Yehuda scanned a detailed map of the tunnel system spread out before him on the table. Standing beside him were two uniformed men and a woman. The leader, who went by the name of Adino, was in his forties, while the other two were both in their twenties.

Although their uniforms were standard-issue for the Israeli army, the three were not in the military. They were highly trained killers for the *gibburim*.

The basement in which Yehuda and the others were meeting belonged to a holocaust survivor who lived in the Jewish Quarter. The old survivor was undeniably disturbed by the violent initiatives of the *gibburim*. But she reluctantly supported the radical faction because she saw little alternative to the growing pressure to surrender more and more of their land. That was why she allowed the *gibburim* to dig each night in her tiny basement. Muffled generators powered fans and furnished light for the narrow shaft that angled sharply away to the east. Rock and debris dug from the tunnel were quietly removed then later scattered across remote desert spaces in the Negev.

"In addition to this project, we have men working in a tunnel along the Western Wall," Adino advised his two colleagues. Dark-haired and dark-eyed, Adino was lean and muscular, but because of an old bullet wound, walked with a cane. "The fact that Dr. Yehuda is directing the digs allows us permission to excavate. More importantly, it focuses attention away from our activities here."

"How much longer before we access the tunnel network beneath the Temple Mount?" asked Rubin.

"A matter of days. Once the tablet has been authenticated, we will pack the shaft with explosives and reduce *al Aqsa* to gravel."

Seventy-five kilometers to the southwest, Wassim Jafar was pacing the floor of a concrete house on the outskirts of Gaza. Before him sat more than a hundred militants – most of them in their late teens and twenties. Assault rifles rested against their knees or lay on the floor.

"Who is on the panel?" asked the sixty-year-old leader of *Qamat,* who was wearing a Saville Row suit and his trademark red-and-white *kaffiyah* head cloth.

Jafar's lieutenant, a former French commando named Philippe, unfolded a sheet of paper. Philippe was Parisian Lebanese, and had wavy black hair. "Chairing the committee is Dr. Philippa Eaton, from King's College, London," he said.

Snide murmurs about the English could be heard from the militants.

"Dr. Allan Woolley, an Englishman, is also on the panel," he continued, "as is Dr. Faisal Mostafa, from the Egyptian Museum in Cairo."

Remarks of approval followed for Mostafa.

"Then there is the pig, Rubin Yehuda."

A chorus of angry shouts erupted against the Jews. Jafar lifted a hand and the group fell silent.

"Last are the Americans, Cameron Cushing and Nadia Burke."

More insulting remarks could be heard, this time against the great Satan, America.

"Can we control the decision of the panel?" asked Philippe. "Perhaps through Mostafa?"

"It is doubtful," Jafar replied. "Dr. Eaton believes the tablet to be genuine and Yehuda and the Americans will agree."

"Maybe Qaderi will give us the tablet?"

"Unlikely," answered Jafar.

"But he is an Arab," Philippe pointed out.

"Whose loyalty is to affluence and status."

Philippe nodded, although he knew Jafar to be much the same. Glancing to his right, he spotted Lydia in the crowd. He smiled and Lydia smiled back.

"In the meantime," Jafar said, "we have before us an opportunity. An opportunity to be heard. An opportunity to be felt. An opportunity for *jihad!* We will show them whose land this is!"

While the assembly cheered and jabbed rifles in the air, Jafar leaned close to Philippe. "Remain after the meeting," he said. "I have an assignment."

"Of course," answered Philippe. "What is it you need me to do?"

"Get that tablet. Do whatever it takes."

"I doubt Qaderi will cooperate."

"Did you not hear me? Whatever it takes. You leave tonight."

CHAPTER 26

At the very same moment Tyler was stepping into the shower, on the rooftop next door a CIA technician was opening his toolbox. By the time Tyler had slipped into his clothes fifteen minutes later, the technician had finished installing a compact parabolic microphone, transmitter, and sixteen-hour rechargeable solar battery.

Downstairs, the owners of the new "high-frequency microwave interference shield" were being shown the "improved reception quality" on their television by a second technician.

"The picture looks the same," the husband said.

"Which is the beauty of this unit," the technician replied while adjusting the contrast to sharpen the image. "The equilibrium capacitor on the motherboard adjusts pixel oscillation automatically in order to eliminate visual extremes. This brings the image back to the optical range you're comfortable with so that you can watch more programming without retinal fatigue. Isn't that great?"

The husband and wife gave each other confused looks.

"Don't worry, you'll love it. Congratulations!" the technician said, patting the husband on the shoulder as he departed.

Next door, Tyler climbed the stairs and entered the living room. The floor was travertine marble with large Persian rugs. The furniture was contemporary and divided into three seating arrangements of sofas, stuffed chairs and coffee tables. In the center of the room was a circular bar.

"Good afternoon, Dr. Tyler," said Mrs. Fedje. "Please help yourself to some refreshment. Mr. Qaderi and the others will be with you shortly."

Tyler nodded and walked over to the coffee table. On it were sandwiches, wine, water, orange juice, coffee, and a large bowl of cashews. Grabbing a handful of nuts, he ambled over to a display case, which housed a golden head bust of Queen Nefertiti. Above her slender, graceful nose, Nefertiti's vacant eyes stared serenely off into eternity.

After admiring the statue for a moment, Tyler strolled out onto the deck. Sparkling in the sun, the Nile was full of tour boats and felucca, the simple sailboats used along the river for millennia.

Finishing his cashews, Tyler walked back inside, again being drawn to the statue of Nefertiti. There was sensuality to the curve of her cheeks, a hint of a smile on her lips. It was as if she were flirting with a lover – indeed, with everyone who gazed on her face.

"She is quite delicious, is she not?" a cultured voice asked from behind.

Tyler turned to see the lean figure of Youssef Qaderi standing beside him, his hands clasped behind his back, a faraway smile on his face.

"Even her name – Nefertiti – means 'the beautiful one is come.'" Youssef extended his hand. "Dr. Tyler, it's a pleasure to meet you. I'm Youssef Qaderi. Welcome to my home."

Tyler shook Youssef's hand then looked back at the statue. "Her beauty is exceptional. But why is she bald?"

"The bust is actually a wig stand, most probably found in a hidden chamber in the tomb of Amenhotep II. As far as I can tell, it was then traded to French adventurers in that brief window of time when Napoleon ruled our land. It ended up in a private collection in Paris, where I discovered it several years back. Thankfully, I was able to tempt the owner to sell." Youssef then leaned close and lowered his voice. "But it cost me a bloody *fortune.*"

"Isn't it illegal to own ancient treasures like this?"

"All I can say is this: there are exceptions to every rule."

Tyler chuckled and both men stood gazing at the statue in silent admiration for several moments.

"May I pour you some wine while Doctors Mostafa and Woolley finish their bickering upstairs?" he asked.

"Sounds good," answered Tyler. "What are they bickering about?"

"It's actually quite petty," said Youssef, filling a glass. "A contest of egos, I believe. But they are leaders in their fields and must be allowed their eccentricities."

Youssef handed Tyler the glass then poured some for himself. "To a successful and enjoyable visit," he said.

"And to your generous hospitality," added Tyler, clinking his glass to Qaderi's.

Qaderi smiled and nodded his thanks.

"Cairo's a beautiful city," remarked Tyler.

"Come now, Dr. Tyler, we must do something about that formality. It encourages you to exaggerate terribly for the sake of good manners."

Tyler laughed. "You must have heard that before."

"Actually, not a lot, which is the reason I saw right through it. Intense, crushing, a dust-coated tapestry of extremes – these are descriptions of Cairo. But never beautiful."

"Well, your house is certainly beautiful."

"That I will accept."

From the stairwell came a duet of voices locked in friendly argument. Tyler turned to see two men enter the room. The taller Englishman, Dr. Allan Woolley, was demonstrating his disagreement with a theatrical wave of his hands. The shorter Egyptian, Dr. Faisal Mostafa, was laughing heartily. Following behind was Sharifa, who was shaking her head.

"Still fussing?" Youssef called out.

"Your countryman is being most obstinate," Woolley declared, striding ahead of the others. Dressed in a rumpled brown suit, Woolley was in his mid-fifties and overweight. His brown hair was salted with gray.

"I am declared obstinate simply because I do not agree?" asked the compact Faisal Mostafa. Sporting a short moustache and neatly combed black hair, he wore a blue sports coat and contrasting tan slacks.

"Sharifa will attest to the benefits of English culture upon Cairo," said Woolley, grabbing up the wine and filling a glass.

"Leave me out of this," Sharifa replied, smiling brightly at Tyler. She nodded at his choice of clothing and walked over to him, hand extended. Tyler shook her hand, which she continued holding while offering her cheek, which Tyler kissed.

A slight wrinkle appeared on Youssef's brow.

"Imperialism aside, how can one argue against such benefit to the city?" asked Woolley, gesturing with his glass.

"I do not decry the beauty of English Colonial architecture," replied Faisal, pouring himself a tumbler of orange juice.

"Aha!" cried Woolley triumphantly.

"The fact is, it was forced upon us," said Faisal, "and to that I object. Whatever direction our culture would have taken – for better or worse – it would have been ours. That is all I am saying."

"Gentlemen," said Youssef with a quick glance at Sharifa, who was picking a loose thread off Tyler's shoulder, "may I present Dr. Rutherford

Tyler? He will be taking photographs of the tablet as well as conducting interviews with each of you."

"Dr. Tyler, it's an honor," said Faisal, stepping forward and shaking Tyler's hand. "Your reputation has most definitely preceded you."

"Allan Woolley," the Englishman added.

"The honor's mine," replied Tyler. "To meet the Cairo Museum's world-renowned Egyptologist alongside the author of the acclaimed commentary on *The Tale of Sinuhe* is humbling indeed."

Both Woolley and Faisal stared open-mouthed at Tyler.

"I do believe this is the only time I've seen the two of you speechless!" exclaimed Youssef with a laugh. "Bravo, Dr. Tyler!"

"How on earth did you know that?" asked Woolley.

"I'm not the only one with a reputation," answered Tyler.

Woolley nodded appreciatively.

Youssef suddenly turned serious. "Gentlemen, as you're aware, my tablet has been attracting some undesirable attention."

He picked up a remote control and touched the power button. A large flatscreen television blinked to life. Youssef replayed the local Cairo news, which showed a small crowd of protestors arguing with police. Several carried placards accusing Qaderi of worshipping money rather than Allah.

"Fortunately, few people know where I live," Youssef said, switching to the international news, where a confrontation in Jerusalem over the tablet was taking place. Another click showed a crowd of protesters outside the Israeli Embassy in Washington. The camera focused on signs accusing Israel of neo-Semitism against the Arabs, while other placards defended the tablet as evidence of God's divine purpose for Israel as a light to the nations. Streaming along the bottom of the screen were ticker tapes carrying the latest news bites: *Ishmael tablet says Palestine belongs to Israel. Protests in Paris and London. Violence in Gaza.*

Youssef switched off the TV.

"But what really surprised me were these," he said, opening a folder and taking out a stack of letters, which he dealt like cards onto the table. "From Oman, the Emirates, Dubai, Saudi Arabia, America – private organizations, universities, even governments – all wanting to buy the tablet. The response from the Jewish sector has been much the same. We have bids as high as seventy five million dollars."

"Seventy five *million?*" asked Woolley.

"And climbing," responded Qaderi. "Nothing like controversy to stimulate interest."

"This is unbelievable," said Woolley. "Until now, its value has been estimated to be no more than a few million, max. Your offers blow those figures out of the water!"

"At what cost, though?" asked Tyler. "Protests, riots, death threats…"

"As much as I hate to admit it, you're absolutely right," said Youssef. "And the danger appears to be growing. Your embassy phoned earlier with a warning."

Said Faisal, "Youssef, this is getting out of hand!"

"There's not much I can do," Youssef replied, glancing sharply at Faisal but maintaining a smile.

Disturbed, Faisal looked away.

"We could have avoided all this if the gallery would have allowed me to ship the tablet earlier," Youssef remarked.

"Let me guess," said Tyler. "They wanted a declaration of authenticity plus a valuation before they would issue a letter of coverage."

"You've dealt with insurance companies before."

Tyler nodded. "Can't live with 'em, can't live without 'em."

"They're requiring photographs as well," said Youssef.

"Got it covered," said Tyler.

"Once documentation has been received, the insurance company will issue a letter of coverage and we can ship the tablet. Therefore, I'd like to conclude business as soon as possible so the tablet can be shipped before the gala on Saturday night."

"Gala?" asked Tyler.

"Black tie, at Mena House, near the Pyramids," said Youssef. "What started out as a press conference has turned into a formal event for more than three hundred people."

"What's the occasion?" asked Tyler.

"Once word began to spread that you were in town, we began receiving calls from people wanting to meet you."

"Are you serious?" asked Tyler.

"Fans, reporters, government officials…"

"I'm surprised people know who I am."

"You are much too modest. You will be pleased to know you have a considerable following here in Cairo. Most of your articles have been translated into Arabic and, of course, we love watching your television specials."

Tyler acknowledged the compliment with a nod.

"But you must tell me something," said Youssef. "How did Vice President Baker react when you asked him about the Green House?"

"The Green House?" asked Faisal.

"The office and residence of the U.S. President is, of course, the White House," explained Youssef. "But I'm sure we all remember the last election where candidates Baker and Fitzgerald were running against each other for their party's nomination. Fitzgerald won, but in an extraordinary move, selected Sam Baker to be his running mate. After they won a landslide election, Dr. Tyler interviewed Vice President Baker and remarked how heated the primary had been with its mudslinging." Youssef looked over at Tyler. "Is this the correct term – mudslinging?"

Tyler nodded.

"Mr. Baker, of course, downplayed his clashes with Fitzgerald, after which you asked one of those trademark questions, which I shall never forget. You turned to the Vice President and mentioned a newspaper headline that proclaimed Baker to have been 'green with envy' at having lost his party's presidential nomination. Mr. Baker, I believe, merely smiled. And then you asked, 'Now that you're Vice President, does this make your residence the "Green House"?' Tell me, Dr. Tyler, how did he react?"

"I have to give Sam Baker credit for some really quick thinking," said Tyler, "because my question was actually a humorous play on words intended to add a bit of life to an otherwise humdrum interview. Pursing his lips, Baker looked at me and said, 'Tyler' – and he did indeed call me by my last name, which showed that he, too, had done his homework – 'I guess that means our conversation is an example of greenhouse gas.' With that, the audience came apart. Once the laughter died down, Baker looked me straight in the eye and said, 'I beat you to the punch line, didn't I?' The audience loved it, and once things had again grown quiet, he narrowed his eyes and added, 'Or did you hand me that one on purpose?' I smiled and told the Vice

President that I wouldn't think of doing that any more than he'd think of letting Senator Bakeman win at golf. With a final laugh, Baker stood and offered me his hand. 'I like a man who lets me win a round now and then,' he said. 'You're always welcome at the Green House.' And after waving to the audience, he walked off the stage."

"Brilliant!" cried Youssef.

"It was for him," said Tyler. "He really did beat me to the punch line."

Faisal and Woolley both laughed.

"Your ratings soared," said Youssef, "and that interview became the talk of the world. Even here, in Cairo. Stories like that are why people want to meet you."

Tyler acknowledged the compliment with a nod.

"Hats off to you, Tyler, that was a damn clever question," Woolley remarked, slapping Tyler on the shoulder. Woolley then started to refill his wineglass.

"Before you become too relaxed," Youssef told Woolley, "I'd like you and Dr. Tyler to get straight into your interview."

"Now?" asked Woolley.

"Short notice, I admit, but we must push our timetable forward so that we can get the tablet on its way." Youssef looked over at Tyler. "Providing you're up to it, of course. If you're jetlagged, I'm happy to wait."

"Not at all," said Tyler. "But is it possible to have the use of your office? I'll be videotaping these interviews and I'd like Dr. Woolley in an office setting – desk, computer, some bookshelves, that sort of thing."

"Of course. And I do hope you'll forgive me for propelling you so quickly into your work."

"Not at all. It's why I'm here."

"I've arranged a cameraman to assist you, of course."

"No need. I'll run things myself."

"Are you sure?"

"Do it all the time. But what about those still shots you want of the tablet? Do you prefer digital or film?"

"Digital, if you don't mind."

"I'll get my things."

"Before we dismiss," said Youssef, "I'd like to introduce my new chief of security. And while I don't think we're in any immediate danger,

I wanted you to know I'm taking these threats very seriously." He turned to Sharifa. "Will you ask him to join us, my dear?"

Sharifa nodded and left the room.

"I never thought something like this would happen!" said Faisal.

"Don't worry," said Youssef. "If anyone is a target, it is I. However, your safety is the reason I hired the man you're about to meet. Sharifa's known him for some years and insisted we bring him aboard. She says he's the best."

Footsteps in the hall drew everyone's attention. Seconds later, Sharifa came through the door. Behind her was a tall, gaunt Arab. He wore a flowing jellaba, and his unfriendly eyes scrutinized each face in the room.

Especially Tyler's.

"Gentlemen, may I present Majli?" said Youssef. "Our safety is now in his hands."

CHAPTER 27

After setting up his video camera, Tyler positioned Woolley behind Youssef's desk and clipped a microphone on his lapel.

"When do you think this will air?" asked Woolley.

"Hard to say," answered Tyler, running the wire inside Woolley's jacket and down to the transmitter in his pocket. "Probably in conjunction with the U.S. portion of the tour. My editing team will integrate your interview with the others into a docudrama, which will be narrated by a Hollywood celebrity."

"I hear it's all about ratings."

"It's more about viewers. They expect a lot, and if we don't hook 'em up front, they'll switch channels."

"The power of the remote."

"Which can work for us or against us. A good interview can make a tour the same way a bad one can break it."

"How do you think this one will do?"

"The tablet's controversial, so that's good. A lot depends on what the other channels are running. My last special ran against stiff opposition and still drew twenty million viewers."

"That'll make Youssef happy."

Tyler knelt beside Woolley and adjusted the position of the microphone. "Is that important? Making him happy?"

"Well, no, of course not. I just know a successful interview is something that he wants."

Tyler nodded while Woolley frowned thoughtfully.

"How long have you and Youssef been friends?" asked Tyler.

"Is this leading somewhere?" asked Woolley.

"Merely idle chitchat while I finish the prep. I'll keep my mouth shut, if it bothers you."

Woolley eyed Tyler for a moment.

"Youssef and I are not actually friends," Woolley said. "I like him, of course, but I'm here purely on behalf of the gallery – to assess the value of the tablet for insurance purposes."

Tyler nodded again.

"Working for Sterling Crest Gallery must be pretty cool," he said. "They're one of the top galleries in the world."

Woolley shrugged.

"There, that should do it," Tyler said, tucking the wire inside Woolley's jacket. "Being in front of a camera won't make you nervous, will it?"

"I've been in front of them before."

"That's what I like to hear."

Tyler stood and glanced at his watch.

"How about a glass of wine?" he asked.

"Are you sure that's okay?"

"Who's running this interview?" asked Tyler.

Woolley grinned. "That's what I like to hear!"

"Mind grabbing us a bottle from downstairs while I make some final adjustments?"

Woolley sprang from his chair and left the room.

Once Woolley was gone, Tyler grabbed a tiny, cylindrical wireless modem from his briefcase and hurried over to Youssef's computer. After a quick glance toward the door, he disconnected the keyboard cable and plugged the modem into the jack. He then plugged the keyboard cable into the modem. When Woolley returned, Tyler was standing outside on the balcony.

"This white shiraz looks good," Woolley said, filling two wineglasses.

Tyler stepped back inside, closed the door, and accepted a glass from Woolley.

"Cheers," said Woolley.

"To your health."

And they drank.

Tyler gestured Woolley to a chair. "What made you become interested in Egypt?" he asked.

"It all started when I read Alf Layla wa Layla," answered Woolley.

"*The Thousand and One Nights*," said Tyler.

"You know Arabic?" asked Woolley with surprise.

"I know *The Nights*. What kid doesn't?"

"I've yet to meet one who knows its title in Arabic."

"Most kids aren't journalists."

"Are you telling me you were?"

161

"Of course not," said Tyler with a laugh. "I read the stories as a child, but learned the Arabic title in my travels to the Middle East."

Woolley nodded and took a drink.

"So *The Nights* is what sparked an interest in Egyptian literature?" asked Tyler.

"I had actually planned on pursuing a doctorate in classical mythology. But *The Nights* captured my imagination and I was hooked."

"What led you to write such a remarkable exposition on *The Tale of Sinuhe?* It was an extraordinary commentary on a fragmentary and, some say, unimportant work."

"You're both kind and very well informed. Being in the club yourself, you know the pressure to publish original research."

"My doctorate was honorary, but – yes – I understand."

"As any good journalist would. Anyway, I chose *The Tale of Sinuhe.* Very little had been written about it, which meant it was a chance to make a name for myself."

"Which it certainly has. That's got to be a big part of why Sterling Crest Gallery keeps you on retainer. They're lucky to have someone like you."

Woolley shrugged and took another drink.

"Your expertise must have earned them millions," said Tyler.

With a cynical snort, Woolley took a larger gulp.

"To say nothing of the value your name has added to their reputation," Tyler added.

Woolley looked away bitterly.

"Top gallery like that's got to be paying you – what? Six figures and shares?"

"They're paying me bloody tripe, is what they're paying!" snapped Woolley. "A *grade-school teacher* makes more than me!"

"That doesn't sound fair."

"It's not!"

Tyler nodded understandingly and reached for the bottle.

Upstairs in Youssef's bedroom, Sharifa was keyboarding information on her laptop when Youssef came in from the verandah, where he had been talking on the phone.

"Another media request," he said.

Sharifa did not reply.

Youssef looked over Sharifa's shoulder at what she was keyboarding.

"Finances, I see," he observed, noticing the subtle whiff of spice. He leaned close and took another sniff.

"What are you doing?" she asked, feeling the heat of his breath.

"Investigating," he whispered, noting how the complexity seemed different today.

"You know this fragrance. It's the one you bought me at Harrods."

"I know it well, my beautiful one." What made the scent so unique, so alive? Youssef suddenly realized what it was. Arousal had brought it to life. Arousal for him? Youssef considered the possibility for a moment. He had known Sharifa for many years, and never once had he sensed such an erotic chemistry. What made it so potent today?

The answer came like a slap.

Tyler!

Youssef kissed Sharifa on the neck.

She shrugged him off.

Youssef kissed her again, catching sight of Sharifa's slender thighs. He peeled back the collar of her blouse.

"Not now," she said.

Youssef kissed her a third time, then ran his fingers over her collarbones, where he felt the smooth cloth of a lightweight silk bra.

He slipped his hand under the material.

Sharifa emphatically removed his hand.

Youssef straightened and managed a laugh. "I gather it's not good time."

"No, it's not a good time! There isn't a whole lot of money left in the account, so now's really not the time you want to be distracting me."

Youssef stared hard at Sharifa before turning and walking away.

Across town, Zoe was typing furiously on her laptop. "Teague wants me to do what?"

"Attend Qaderi's formal with Odell," answered Tony.

"There's *no way* I'm going to a formal dressed in ruffles and lace!"

"You don't have to look like a wedding cake. Try something sleek and plain. Simple elegance will compliment your eyes."

"Cut the frilly sweet-talk crap! I haven't worn a gown since high school and I'm sure as hell not starting now."

"Shall I forward your refusal to Teague?"

There was a noticeable pause.

163

"If you mention this to anyone," wrote Zoe, "and I do mean anyone, I will personally barbecue your carcass over an open fire."

"Cut the frilly sweet-talk crap," was Tony's reply.

Zoe was both cursing and laughing when a knock sounded on the door. "What?" she shouted irritably.

The door pushed open and a uniformed Marine named Brad Henschel entered.

"I was told to bring you this, ma'am," he said, handing Zoe a sheet of paper. With a brisk nod he turned and left.

Zoe scanned the report.

"*Shit!*" she exclaimed, tossing aside the report and sliding her laptop toward her. "Latest audio surveillance on Tyler just came in!" she typed. "Majli is Qaderi's chief of security and *Sharifa's* the one who hired him!"

"Come back?" Tony replied.

"Sharifa hired Majli! Qaderi said the two of them have a long history, which means that Sharifa and Majli may both be working with Abu Nazer, and that she brought him into the house to kill Tyler and Qaderi." Zoe paused, then added, "It could also mean Sharifa's being exploited."

"Meaning Majli approached her, rather than the other way around?"

"It's possible," answered Zoe.

"How could she not know about Majli?" asked Tony. "It's no secret he's a terrorist."

"How well do any of us know the people we call friends? What to us is a terrorist is to others a freedom fighter. He may have a different reputation over here in Cairo."

"I don't know. The idea of Sharifa being duped is hard for me to swallow."

"There's also a third option," said Zoe. "Qaderi was lying."

"Why would he lie about something like that?"

"It's simply a possibility, that's all I'm saying. I'll send you a copy of the audio recording for analysis."

"What's that going to prove?"

"I don't know. Just run it, okay?"

"I really don't see the point."

"Which we *can't* know until it's been analyzed! So will you just run the damned thing?"

"All right, but it may take awhile. Teague's got me loaded down."

"As soon as you can, then. But hurry! Now, any news on Louise Kappelmann?"

"I'm about to phone Morgan Publishing to find out if anyone there remembers her."

"Let me know what they say. I also need you to find out if Ismail Yassin had a son named Tariq. And don't forget to send me anything you find on this mallet. Run a word search and see if Tyler mentions mallet or something similar to that in any of his articles. People often create symbolic names based on special words, places, or events."

"And you need this by when?"

"Tomorrow."

"Come on, Zoe! *No way* can I get all this done by tomorrow."

"You have to."

"And I'm telling you *I can't.*"

"Not even if I promise to make you one of those chocolate ice cream tundra cakes you like so much?"

"That's blackmail!"

"Actually, it's bribery, but who cares? So long as the job gets done."

"Teague'll *kill* me if he finds out!"

"But you'll die happy. Come on, I need this!"

"Dude, you are going to owe me sooo big."

CHAPTER 28

"Let me put you through to Mr. Mayer's office," the clerk in human resources told Tony. "Both he and his assistant, Mrs. Hill, have been around here for years. One of them should remember."

"Thanks," said Tony.

The wait was not long.

"Mr. Mayer's office, this is Geneva," a woman's deep, smoky voice answered.

"My name is Tony Cooke and I work for the Central Intelligence Agency. We're trying to locate a former employee who we believe has information pertinent to one of our investigations. However, in order for you to verify the legitimacy of this call, you may hang up and phone our one-eight-hundred number. Ask for Tony Cooke. They'll put you through."

"That won't be necessary, young man. I'm happy to help so long as I'm not asked to violate anyone's privacy."

"I'm sure that won't be necessary."

"And if it is, you'll slap me with a subpoena. Right?"

"Sounds like you watch the same television shows that I do."

Geneva responded with a raspy laugh. "Ask away, Mr. Cooke."

"First, may I get your name?"

"Geneva Hill."

"How long have you worked for Morgan Publishing?"

"Let me see, now. That would be twenty-three years, next July."

"Do you remember Stephen Kappelmann?"

"I certainly do. You know he was murdered, don't you?"

"Do you remember his wife?"

"Of course. It was awful what the killer did, taping Louise to Stephen's body like that. How she managed to survive, God only knows."

"Do you know where she is?" asked Tony.

"My goodness, no. After Stephen's death, she tried coming back to work but couldn't. I haven't seen her in years."

"Any idea where she is?"

"Does this have something to do with her husband's death?"

"Sorry, but I'm not allowed to talk about our investigation. We just need to find her."

"I wish I could help, but I haven't heard from Louise since she left."

"Do you remember her maiden name?"

"I really didn't get to know her until after she and Stephen were married."

"How about any schools attended, her hometown, any known relatives?"

"Sorry."

Tony sighed. "Thanks for trying."

"I wish I could've been more help."

"May I speak with Mr. Mayer?"

"Sorry, but he's not available. Shall I have him return your call?"

"Do you know when that might be?"

"His meetings can sometimes last for hours. I'll be sure and pass on your message and have him get back to you as soon as he can."

"I'd appreciate that."

After ending the call, Tony checked the various graphs displayed on his monitor. There really hadn't been enough normal conversation to get an adequate baseline on Geneva Hill. Consequently, the voice analyzer couldn't determine with any degree of accuracy whether or not she had been lying.

With a sigh of frustration, Tony grabbed his mug and went for a coffee.

After hanging up, Geneva Hill dug through her purse until she found her address book. Inside the back cover was a number. Picking up the phone, she dialed that number.

Geneva listened to the beep of the answering machine, then said, "The CIA – they called. They're onto you!"

CHAPTER 29

Tariq finished the remainder of his tonic water, then stretched in the late afternoon heat. Around him, oiled sunbathers lay motionless on their towels.

It had been a relaxing day by the pool, although even sunbathing became tiresome after so many hours. He looked at his watch. It was half past six. Majli should have been here by now.

Tariq slipped into a plush terrycloth robe, slid his feet into some hotel sandals, and strode across the concrete deck. Pulling open a door, he entered the luxurious interior of the Cairo Marriott.

Approaching the front counter, Tariq paused in front of a television to watch the latest BBC news coverage of the clashes between heavily armed police and mobs of angry youths. A reporter ducked at a staccato burst of gunfire in the background, then turned to the camera. "Tensions are escalating here in Gaza over claims that an ancient tablet written by the patriarch Ishmael cedes ownership of Palestine to Israel. In related news, the *Jerusalem Post* stringently denies running an ad—"

"May I help you, Mr. Yassin?" asked the clerk, drawing Tariq's attention.

"Any messages?" asked Tariq.

The young man handed Tariq an envelope.

After a final glance at the television, Tariq took the elevator up to his room. Once inside, he tore open the envelope and read the enclosed information. Tyler and Qaderi would be taking a bus tour on Sunday.

Tariq smiled and tore up the note.

The countdown had begun.

CHAPTER 30

The day began like a lazy yawn – chirping birds, pleasant breezes, the sun shining through the trees. Not even the local news station could find anything bad to report, and so had used filler stories to complete the morning's broadcast. Which meant the program was palatable, because filler stories usually focused on achievement rather than catastrophe.

Thus, today, while she fried an egg in one of Tyler's blackened cast iron skillets, Val enjoyed listening to a report about a Christian rehabilitation program for young addicts that was actually working. After five years, nearly eighty-five percent of them had remained drug free.

"Too bad you're only filler," she remarked, flipping the egg.

Ordinarily, Val liked cottage fries with her eggs. But since she needed to drop a few pounds, the fries were out – at least for today. She sipped from a second mug of coffee and waited until the egg was firm but not hard. Then she slid it onto her plate, turned off the burner, and removed two slices of toast from the oven.

She liked staying at Tyler's house when he was away. It was peaceful here by the lake, although during summer the speedboats were out earlier than the birds. But while Tyler was away – especially on an assignment that took him to the other side of the planet – it was easier to remain near the computer in order to accommodate all the phone calls, emails and rough drafts, which could come at the oddest of hours.

Sliding behind her desk, Val sliced off some egg and guided it mechanically into her mouth. She then jiggled the mouse and her computer screen winked to life.

What occurred next was a spontaneous decision that forever changed the course of her life.

With a slice of toast dangling in her mouth, Val impulsively picked up the telephone and dialed her home number. After several rings, the answering machine clicked on, instructing her to leave a message after the beep. Using the telephone touchpad, Val entered her access code and the machine began replaying her messages.

The first was from a marketing firm conducting a survey.

Beep.

The next was an apology for a wrong number.

Beep.

The third was from a woman who did not identify herself, and whose voice Val would not have recognized were it not for what she said.

"The CIA – they called. They're onto you!"

Val froze as the final beep occurred.

The toast fell from her mouth.

Slamming down the phone, Val ran to the bathroom and vomited what little she had eaten. Leaning over the sink, she caught her breath, then ran some water and rinsed her mouth.

"How could this have happened?" she moaned. She had been so careful. But to remain hidden forever, especially from the CIA, was pushing her luck. She knew that. So what had tipped them off? What did they want?

Val knew what they wanted. They wanted information on the death of her husband. Abu Nazer had killed him and they wanted to find out what she knew.

The perverse brutality of Stephen's murder had nearly driven her insane.

"Sack" was the pet name she had given him because of his initials, S.A.K. They had become soul mates shortly after she – Veronica Angelica Louise Johnson – had been hired as a young writer at Morgan Publishing. Fresh to New York with a Bachelor's Degree in computer science and a Master's Degree in journalism, she had captured Stephen's attention with an article she had written on stolen identities. She remembered being called into his office one morning. Waiting for her was Karen Post, her senior editor, who proceeded to launch into a scathing review of the article. Dressed in a black turtleneck and slacks, the dark-haired Stephen stood gazing out the window, his hand positioned thoughtfully across his mouth, while Karen ranted and criticized. Her closing statement was the denigrating act of tossing Louise's final draft into the air, the pages turning loops and fluttering unceremoniously down to the floor. Karen then threatened Louise with termination unless her attitude changed and her writing improved.

That's when Stephen turned and asked Karen what specifically was wrong with Louise's writing.

Karen stammered momentarily, then repeated her previous remarks, citing attitude as the dominant problem.

"I'm just not sure Louise is cut out for this job," Karen said.

"So attitude, not skill, is the problem?" asked Stephen.

Karen agreed.

Stephen nodded and turned back to the window, where he stood thinking for nearly a full minute, his back to the two women, who looked silently on.

"It seems others have said much the same thing," Stephen said, stepping over to his desk.

Karen replied with a wicked smile. Folding her arms, she glanced over at Louise, who stood nearby, her face sagging with dejection.

Slowly Louise knelt down and began gathering together the pages of her article.

"Regarding your attitude, Karen, not hers," said Stephen.

"*What?*"

"I have watched you rip into other journalists in the same insulting manner with which you just belittled Louise, who – by the way – is a gifted writer with an important perspective. You, on the other hand, produce nothing but negativity. Negativity and noise. Lots of noise."

"But it's my job to hammer inferior text into the high standard that you demand. That the *public* demands."

"Your job, Karen, is to challenge and polish. We've been over this before."

"The journalists weren't responding! I had to get tough."

"You can be tough so long as you're fair. Demanding so long as your leadership inspires writers to push old boundaries and achieve new heights. No magazine can keep producing incisive material when editors trample the wills of good journalists."

"But—"

"No buts, Karen. Take your demeaning tactics elsewhere."

"What are you saying, Stephen?"

"That you're fired."

The memory of Karen Post cleaning out her desk brought a fleeting smile to Val's face.

But that was then and this is now, and "now" posed some very serious problems.

Val dried her face and ran back down the hall.

Tyler had to be warned.

Thankfully, before quitting Morgan Publishing she was able to hack into the computer system and expunge her records. Few people today would remember how, after she and Stephen were married in a strictly religious ceremony, she had chosen to retain her maiden name in all business dealings. In the eyes of one another and the public, she was Louise Kappelmann. In the eyes of the IRS, she was Louise Johnson. No marriage certificate had ever been filed, since they were of the opinion that such documents were unnecessary and irrelevant. Which meant that anyone searching a database for Louise Kappelmann would come up empty. And what had originally been her way of maintaining a professional identity as Louise Johnson, the writer, became the accidental backbone of a "witness protection program" that allowed her to hide from Abu Nazer and anyone else trying to find her.

It had not been easy to do, suffering as she had from a whole spectrum of emotions: denial, rage, fear, resentment, plea-bargaining with God, indifference, and a galvanized determination to bring Abu Nazer to justice.

Abu Nazer. Did the CIA know what really happened that night on the beach? How she lay there for what seemed like an eternity, taped to the corpse of the man she loved? If the brave and kindly Ismail Yassin hadn't found her when he did, she would have died, and in some ways she wished that she had. Even now, she still found herself waiting for Stephen to walk through the door. At night, she could almost feel him sleeping beside her, lying on his side with his cheek in his hands.

So many wonderful memories.

And yet they were only memories because of a monster named Abu Nazer.

A monster she vowed to kill.

But in order to do that, she first needed to create a new identity that would allow her to operate without being recognized.

Hence, Veronica Angelica Louise consolidated her initials into VAL and, using her maiden name, became Val Johnson. She then left New York for Texas.

Tyler, of course, knew the full story and had provided her with the cover she needed. They shared what each felt was a righteous indignation against terrorism and violence. Each had their own reasons, but it was their common bond.

Unfortunately, over time, Tyler became part of the problem, for in his success as a television journalist, he lost his rage. And to make matters worse, there was this unexpected distraction with Sharifa.

A distraction that could well get him killed.

Sitting at her desk, Val took a few deep breaths. Anger was a luxury she could not afford. And yet each breath came out as a hiss. She was angry. Angry at everything she had lost. Angry that her plans to get even with Abu Nazer were in jeopardy. If only she could trade places with Tyler and get close enough to Abu Nazer to do to him what he had done to her.

Trading places with Tyler, of course, was not possible.

But rekindling his anger certainly was.

That was it! She would make Tyler angry! She had invested too much in this quest to let things fall apart now.

Grabbing her keys, Val ran outside, jumped in her station wagon, and roared away. Fifteen minutes later, she screeched to a stop in front of a large metal shed.

Engulfed by an ear-deafening blast, Johnny Bill was bent under the hood of a Corvette he'd just restored. His burly arms smeared with grease, he released the throttle and allowed the rebuilt V-8 to idle back to a deep, powerful rhythm. He cocked his ear for a moment, then straightened, a broad grin lighting up his bearded face.

"Purrs like she's had a good lay," he said to snorts of laughter from two young men standing nearby. Spotting Val, he grabbed a rag and began wiping his hands.

"Hey, kiddo, what's up?" he asked, his eyes squinting with laughter. "Don't tell me you blowed a clutch out drag racin' again!"

When Val didn't laugh, Johnny Bill grew serious. "What's wrong?" he asked.

"I'm in trouble. I need your help."

While Val was talking with Johnny Bill, a heated telephone conversation was taking place between Teague and Zoe.

"And I'm telling you to look at the *facts!*" shouted Teague. "Tariq discussed killing Tyler and Qaderi with Majli in Mecca. Tariq is now in Cairo – where Qaderi lives and Tyler is visiting. Tariq received fifty thousand dollars, in all likelihood from Abu Nazer. When we factor in this latest news about Sharifa hiring Majli to work as Qaderi's chief of security, we're left with what I think is an inescapable conclusion: Tariq is Abu Nazer and he's in Cairo to kill Tyler and Qaderi. But not before he gets Sharifa and/or Majli to steal the tablet."

"Then why hasn't somebody made a move?" asked Zoe. "Both targets are together in one place – unprotected! The tablet's right there for the taking. Yet no one's made a move. Why?"

"Obviously, because they want to wait and see what the preliminary findings will be on the tablet."

"But Tyler lied about knowing Tariq! Not only that, he was aware of the danger *before* Ariel Cohen phoned. I think something else is going on and Tyler's pulling the strings."

"We know only that he lied about his recognition of Tariq's name. We cannot extrapolate *what* he knows, or if he knows anything beyond that."

"Regardless, we need to warn him," said Zoe.

"Tyler is already aware that he's a target."

"But he doesn't know about Majli. And he sure as hell doesn't know about Sharifa! We at least need to let him know what we know."

"If we do that, we risk him saying or doing something stupid that could allow Abu Nazer to slip through our hands."

"Catching Abu Nazer isn't as important as protecting a man's *life*. Tyler needs to be *warned!*"

"And I'm telling you that's not going to happen. The best way to protect Tyler is to stop Abu Nazer, which we can't do if Tyler screws up the works. No warning! Is that clear?"

Zoe did not respond.

"Is that *clear?*"

"Yes, sir," mumbled Zoe. "But may I have some latitude to keep digging?"

"I'm inclined to say no."

"Please! It may well help us find out why Abu Nazer wants to kill Tyler. Which in turn could give us a jump on when and where he'll strike."

There was a long pause. "All right," Teague said at last. "But you are on a very short rope, Gustaves, and I mean that. I'll yank you out of there in a New York minute if you pull another stunt like the one at JFK."

"Yes, sir. Thank you, sir."

Teague then proceeded to tell Zoe about Val Johnson's identity.

"Louise Kappelmann is Tyler's *assistant?*"

"That's right," said Teague. "Tony's call to Morgan Publishing must have spooked one of the secretaries, who left a message on Val's recorder that we were looking for her. We wouldn't have picked it up except that Val decided to check her recorder using Tyler's office phone, which of course is tapped. The phone company confirmed the number to be Val's, and the IRS confirmed that Val Johnson is actually Veronica Angelica Louise Johnson, who resided at the same address as Stephen Kappelmann before his murder."

"Are you going to question her?" asked Zoe.

"In due course."

"In due course? Sir, we need to question her *now!*"

"I'll take care of it when I'm ready. In the meantime, Odell and a Marine sergeant named Brad Henschel are going to be giving you a hand."

"With what?"

"Everything."

"I can handle it."

"This isn't a request."

"Does this mean they'll be following me around?"

"You'll get used to it."

"They'll get in the way!"

"Work around them."

"I don't need babysitters!" exclaimed Zoe.

"This isn't a democracy! Now, have you bought a gown yet for that party?"

"Are you kidding? You broke that joyful news to me – what? – an hour ago?"

"Well, don't forget. The embassy will foot the bill but are going to be charging it back to me. So find something inexpensive."

"An inexpensive gown? Those two words are so antithetical they don't belong in the same sentence."

"Just watch it, all right?"

"I'm not wearing cheap upholstery."

"I don't want you in Gucci, either. Inexpensive. I gotta go."

Before Zoe could reply she heard the dial tone in her ear.

"God, he makes me mad!" she shouted, slamming down the phone. Just then her laptop announced the arrival of an email. She moved her finger over the touchpad and opened the message.

"I ran 'mallet' through our various dictionaries," Tony's message read, "and got the standard definition across the board: a hammer, usually of wood. Matching it against words with at least a sixty-percent tonal similarity, I found the Mediterranean island of Malta, or Melita; the Spanish port of Malaga; the Israeli town of Ma'alot; and the West African republic of Mali. Further details on each is attached."

Zoe's eyes fell on the name: Ma'alot.

"Mallet...Ma'alot. The two words sound almost the same," she murmured to herself. "Where have I seen Ma'alot before?"

Opening the attachment, Zoe read about the small town in Northern Israel, where a massacre of schoolchildren had occurred in 1974. Zoe then remembered where she'd seen the name: in Tyler's article – *The Holy Circle of Hatred*. Was it a coincidence that Tyler's "mallet" – which Louise Kappelmann wanted him to use so badly – sounds so much like Ma'alot?

Zoe closed the attachment and opened the Kappelmann file. It contained some old photos, IRS records, and passport applications. Also in the file was an English translation of the Jerusalem Post article about Stephen Kappelmann's murder, plus copies of the reporter's handwritten notes, which – unlike the newspaper version – listed details about Ismail Yassin and his family. As she read the notes, Zoe's eyes suddenly widened.

Ismail Yassin had a son named Tariq!

CHAPTER 31

Holding an empty wineglass, Tyler stood at the railing of the deck, pondering what he had learned. Although Woolley was an esteemed expert, he harbored resentment about his lack of success. The gallery prospered while he struggled along. Stepping inside, he set his wineglass on the table. Some light jazz was playing on the stereo and Mrs. Fedje was vacuuming the floor. Suddenly, the music stopped, the vacuum whined down and the lights in the house snapped off.

"What's going on?" he asked.

"A blackout," Mrs. Fedje replied. "We get them in Cairo all the time."

"Will the electricity be off for long?"

"Five minutes, five hours. Who knows?"

"Great," mumbled Tyler with a frustrated sigh.

He was again standing at the railing when Sharifa approached him from behind.

"Deep in thought?" she asked.

"Hey! How's it going?" he smiled.

"Couldn't be better," she replied. She stepped up to his side and took his arm. Behind them, the marble façade of Youssef's house rose several stories to the covered verandah that encircled the top floor.

"This blackout has fouled things up," he said. "Without power, there's not much I can do."

"Then why don't you come with me?"

"Where to?"

"Here and there. I've got errands to run."

"I've still got a lot to do. I need to transcribe Allan Woolley's interview, send an email to Val…"

"Which you can't do without electricity. Come on! It beats sitting around here. Let me get my briefcase and I'll meet you downstairs. Besides, there's some people I want you to meet."

"Who?"

Sharifa smiled. "My parents."

"Are you serous? Last night, you seemed pretty stressed about that."

"I know. But after talking with you, I began thinking that maybe

I need to quit being so stubborn and make the first move. I mean, they're my parents – the only ones that I've got. I'd hate it if something happened and I never got to see them again."

"Sounds like you've done some thinking."

"I have. And I've got you to thank. That's why I'd like you to meet them. And them to meet you."

"This sounds like something you may want to do on your own."

"I wouldn't be going to see them at all if it weren't for you. Please, I'd like you to come."

"Are you sure?"

"I've never been so sure of anything in my life."

"All right," he said, "let's go."

He turned toward the slider but Sharifa stopped him.

"What is it?" he asked.

"This," she said, throwing her arms around his neck and giving him a deep, passionate kiss.

Upstairs, on the top floor verandah, Youssef stood out of sight near the railing. He had heard every word, every moan.

With clenched fists, he rushed inside and over to his desk, grabbed his cell phone and dialed a number. Seconds later, the connection was made. "Majli, it's me! Sharifa – she's downstairs kissing Tyler."

"Calm down," instructed Majli.

"Did you hear what I *said*? She's downstairs *kissing him.*"

"I heard."

"What do we do?"

"Leave it to me. I'll take care of it."

"I don't want them hurt."

"Don't worry, I'll take care of it," said Majli.

"What do I do in the meantime?"

"Act as if nothing has happened."

"Are you *serious?*"

"Very. They mustn't know."

CHAPTER 32

Zoe was busy at her laptop when Tim burst into her office.

"Wait'll you see this!" he said, slapping a surveillance report on her desk.

Zoe read the report. "No question about accuracy?" she asked.

"Clear as a bell. Sharifa asked Tyler to go with her to meet her folks and planted him with a kiss. Qaderi must have seen them, freaked out and phoned Majli. We don't know what Majli offered to do, since we only have audio of what's spoken out loud in Qaderi's house. But Qaderi responds that he doesn't want them hurt, obviously because he has a thing for Sharifa. I don't know what Majli's planning, but whatever it is, it doesn't sound good."

Zoe walked to the window and stared outside for several seconds, arms folded, lips pursed. Abruptly, she turned, walked over to the desk, and picked up the phone.

"Who are you calling?" asked Tim.

Zoe dialed a number and put the phone to her ear. The wait was not long.

"Hello?" a voice asked.

"Is this Val Johnson?" asked Zoe.

"Are you *crazy?*" hissed Tim in a harsh whisper. "Teague will kill us!"

"Yes?" answered Val.

"Ms. Johnson, this is Zoe Gustaves of the Central Intelligence Agency."

Zoe could hear Val draw in a quick breath.

"Ms. Johnson – Louise – we need to talk. About you, about Tyler, about Cairo…"

Val knew it was futile to try to run. They had finally tracked her down. "I'm not sure what you want me to say," she responded, knowing her remark would require Zoe to make the opening move.

"For starters, what should I call you?"

"Let's stick with Val."

"Sounds good. You can call me Zoe."

Val did not reply.

"There are a couple of things I need you to know," Zoe said.

179

"First, we're on the same side. You and I, we want the same thing. If you don't believe me – well, naturally, you can postpone the inevitable by hanging up. You can even try running. Federal officers would, of course, track you down and take you into custody. But even more serious would be the time wasted as a result. Events are unfolding quickly over here and lives may be lost – or saved – depending on whether or not you cooperate."

"Cooperate, how?" asked Val.

"If you recall, I originally phoned Tyler because of an investigation I was working on. Do you remember?"

"Your point being?"

"I still need information. And because I don't have a lot of time, I'm going to bend the rules and tell you some of what I know. By confiding in you this way, I'm hoping you'll understand the seriousness of the situation and help me fill in some blanks. If you do, then I think we can save some lives. Including Tyler's."

"I'm listening," said Val.

"I'll begin by telling you that we've been monitoring your communications in accordance with Federal law. I'm sorry this has been necessary, but we believe Dr. Tyler has information that's vital to our investigation."

"What kind of information?"

"When I talked with him previously, I asked him whether or not he recognized Tariq Yassin's name. He said he did not. Voice analysis indicates Dr. Tyler may not have been telling us the complete truth."

Zoe had purposely not accused him of outright lying because she needed Val's help. Alienating her with inflammatory language would accomplish nothing. A little diplomacy, on the other hand, might win her over.

"In other words," said Zoe, "Tyler either knows Tariq or knows something about him, and sooner or later I'll find out what it is. But you can shortcut that process by telling me the truth."

"Look, Ms. Gustaves, I can't – and won't – speak for Tyler. That's not my place. And I'm not about to let you try and pit one of us against the other, so if that's why you called, you've wasted your time."

"Then let me ask you the same question I asked Tyler: Do you know Tariq Yassin, son of Ismail Yassin, the man who called the police the night your husband was murdered?"

Val closed her eyes.

"Val?" Zoe asked again. "Do you know Tariq Yassin?"

"Yes," whispered Val.

"Do you know Ismail, his father?"

"Yes."

"Does Tyler?"

"Yes. But you'll have to ask him to what extent."

"Val, I need you to tell me what he knows."

"And I repeat: You'll have to ask Tyler. I recognize both names because of the reason you mentioned. I probably owe Ismail my life. Tyler knows the names because of what happened to me. But how much he knows beyond that is a question only he can answer."

"Then tell me this: Is Tariq a terrorist?"

"How would I know?"

"Because you met him! The profile we have paints him as a terrorist. Yet now we find out he's the son of the man who saved your life. Who is he? What's he doing?"

"I have no idea. When I met him, he was little more than a teenage kid living at home. Quiet. Kept to himself."

"Do you think he's a terrorist?"

"I don't know."

"Val, please…"

"I don't *know!*"

"Okay," said Zoe, backing off. She paused and took a breath. *I am dead meat if I blow this,* she thought. "Look, I'm sorry to have to do this, but I need to revisit the murder of your husband. Do you remember anything at all about that night?"

"After being drugged in a nightclub, we were taken unconscious to the beach. I don't know who drugged us, who transported us, or who taped Stephen and me together. I was blindfolded when I regained consciousness, so the only person I saw that night on the beach was Ismail, after he rescued me."

"Maybe you heard something?" asked Zoe.

"I heard gunfire and shouts – that's all."

"What kind of shouts? Men or women's voices?"

"I don't know, just shouts and shooting. Then silence. Except for the storm."

"But nothing identifiable?"

"No."

"Nothing specific you heard someone say? Maybe a word, an accent of some kind?"

"No."

"Returning to the subject of Tyler," said Zoe, "we've been monitoring the interaction between him and Sharifa, and it seems to have gotten pretty intimate."

"Unfortunately, yes," answered Val.

Zoe made a note of Val's disapproval.

"We've also established what we think is a link between Sharifa and a killer named Majli."

"*Majli?* Is he in *Cairo?*"

"You've heard of him?" asked Zoe.

Val silently berated herself for speaking too quickly. "I really can't say," she replied.

"Please! Do you know Majli?"

Silence.

"Val, we're wasting *time*. We know Majli's plotting something against Tyler, but we don't know what. But whatever it is, it's going to happen soon. So, if Majli and Sharifa *are* working together, then Sharifa's leading Tyler into a trap. If not, then both of them may be in danger. Now, please, what do you know?"

Val ran a hand across her forehead. *How much should she say?* If what she had just been told was true, then Tyler was in far more danger than he realized. "I know basically what you just told me," she said. "That Majli works for Abu Nazer."

"How do you know that?" asked Zoe.

"Abu Nazer murdered my husband, in case you'd forgotten!"

"I don't mean to sound insensitive, but Tyler's neck is on the line and I'm scrambling to figure out who wants to kill him. Is Majli working alone? Is he working with Sharifa?"

"I don't know anything about Sharifa. I do know Majli works for Abu Nazer."

"Where exactly did you hear that?"

Val hesitated. "From Tyler," she said.

"*Tyler?* Where did he get that information? Who's his source?"

"I don't *know*."

"Dammit, Val, level with me!"

"I don't know, okay?"

Zoe swore under her breath. She suspected Val was lying but knew she couldn't force the issue without destroying all hope of her continued cooperation.

"Then why is Tyler in Cairo?"

"He's a journalist on an assignment."

"Come on, Val, quit playing games!"

"Tell me how you think I'm playing games."

"I know he's a journalist, and, yes, he's in Cairo to interview Qaderi. No argument there. But I think there's more to it than that. I think he's using the interview as a ruse in order to track down Abu Nazer. For what reason, I'm not yet sure. I used to think it was for some kind of a story, or maybe to snap his photo. But the more I think about it, the more I think it's got something to do with you. Abu Nazer did, after all, murder your husband. That's why I think you quit work and changed your name. You needed to disappear and Tyler offered to help. How you met Tyler, I haven't a clue. But I think you're planning something together – like maybe *revenge*? So before Tyler gets himself killed, will you *please* tell me what you're *planning*?"

"Why do we have to be planning something? Don't you think it's possible Tyler simply wanted to help me disappear?"

"Then tell me why you – a journalist with a Master's Degree – are working as an *office assistant*. A high school graduate could do what you're doing!"

"I'll let you answer that when you've gone through what I've gone through," Val said, her voice cracking slightly. "Are we through now?"

"Not quite. What's this mallet you and Tyler keep arguing about?"

"It's not important."

"Obviously, it is. You want Tyler to use it and he keeps refusing. What is it?"

"I can't say."

Zoe knew she had to keep pushing.

"In Tyler's article, *The Holy Circle of Hatred,* he mentions a town called Ma'alot. Is Ma'alot connected with mallet? The two words sound almost the same."

Silence.

"Val! Are the two words connected?"

"Yes, there's a connection," said Val.

Zoe scooted forward in her chair. "What is it? What's the mallet?"

More silence.

"Years ago, there was an incident where a bunch of school children were killed at Ma'alot. Did you know that?"

Val's answer was barely a whisper. "Yes."

"Is the mallet a gun?"

This time the silence was deafening.

"That's it, isn't it? Tyler's in Cairo to track down Abu Nazer, not to do a story, but to put a *bullet in his head.* Your motivation for wanting him killed, I can understand. But what's Tyler's? Did you talk him into this? Is Ma'alot where Abu Nazer got his start?"

"I think I've said enough."

"Tell me – is the mallet a gun?"

"Good-bye, Ms. Gustaves."

"*Tell me!*"

The line went dead.

CHAPTER 33

"What the *hell* do you think you're doing phoning Louise Kappelmann?" Teague shouted over the phone. "*You stepped way over the line*, Gustaves, and I'm ordering you out of there on the very next plane. When you get back, I'll determine the extent of disciplinary action."

"Fine," answered Zoe. "But you should know I was counting on you listening in."

"You were what?"

"Counting on you listening in. By way of the wiretap. I needed you to hear everything Louise Kappelmann told me. From her lips, not mine."

"If you're trying to sidestep your way out of this…"

"I'm not trying to sidestep out of anything. You heard what she said. The mallet's a gun, and Tyler's in Cairo to kill Abu Nazer!"

"Actually, I didn't hear her say that," said Teague. "I heard you say it. And I've warned you before about jumping to conclusions."

"But it makes sense! She admitted knowing about Majli. She knows Tariq, although I'm not sure who's side he's on anymore. You heard the silence when I asked her if the mallet was a gun. If it is, then we need to check with the airlines and make sure she hasn't already sent it. We can't let Tyler go through with this."

"You're operating on assumptions again."

"Which illustrates my point! We simply don't have enough information to make a clear judgment. That's why I need to keep digging. To find out what's going on."

"Forget it. You're out of there. An experienced team will leave here tomorrow."

"There's no time for that! I know Tyler, know his behavior. If you send in a new team, I don't care how experienced they are, they'll be coming in blind and playing catch up. Not to mention the attention they'll attract. The last thing we need right now is the international community pissed off with us any more than they already are. Please! Allow me to stay on this. I'm already here. I blend in. Let me find out what Tyler's up to so that you can focus on San Francisco."

185

"Are you seriously suggesting that Tyler's planning to kill Abu Nazer instead of the other way around?"

"If the mallet's a gun, then – yes. Which we can determine by phoning the airlines and checking to see if Val shipped him a gun. Sir, please. You said you trusted my instincts. If I screw this up, then go ahead and hang me out to dry. But if I'm right…"

Zoe allowed the sentence to dangle.

Teague exhaled with exasperation. "All right. I'll ring the airlines and see what they say. If there's a gun on the way, you can stay."

"Thank you, sir!"

"This isn't over. Don't thank me yet."

CHAPTER 34

Soaking in his hotel room bathtub with his eyes closed, Philippe reflected on why he had been sent to Cairo. He was to use whatever means necessary to locate and destroy the tablet. If he failed, then he alone would bear the consequences. If he succeeded, then Wassim Jafar would take the credit.

Jafar, Philippe thought bitterly. He was more concerned with his own media status than with the plight of the people he claimed to represent. These days, one saw him more in the department stores of Manhattan than the sparsely furnished shops of Gaza. And for what? Advancement of the Palestinian cause? What a mockery! And yet that's what people believed.

That's also why most of Palestine was little more than a slum. Other than terrorism, what did they have? Manufacturing? Export? Agriculture?

We have none of these, Philippe thought angrily.

And yet Jafar did not suffer any of the deprivations his followers did. Closets full of new suits. Steak and wine at every meal. Donations from all over the world. And what did he give back? Unending violence. Poverty. And death.

Philippe climbed out of the tub, wrapped himself in a monogrammed towel, and went to switch on the TV. He poured himself a cup of coffee, then picked up the remote control and touched the power button. A headline filled the screen.

LAND BELONGS TO ISRAEL, ISHMAEL TABLET DECLARES

This was followed by stock footage of an Israeli helicopter firing missiles at a building. The camera then cut to a shot of the burned-out hull of a bus. Beside it lay a row of charred bodies covered with sheets. In the background, sirens wailed, red lights flashed and medics rushed about.

Martyr kills twenty-seven, the caption read. The camera then cut to Jafar in front of a mob of reporters. Behind him, a dozen men in ski masks brandished assault rifles.

"*Qamat* will not stand for this latest attempt by Israel to drive us from our land!" he cried. "This is only the beginning! *Jihad* will *not* stop until the tablet is destroyed!"

With a growl of disgust, Philippe switched off the TV. *Those murdered Israelis were innocent.* Unfortunately, Jafar was right about one thing. If the tablet was not destroyed, fanatics would use it to drive every non-Jew from the land. Which, of course, was why he was here.

The plan was to have a quiet talk with Qaderi about surrendering the tablet in exchange for a leadership role with Qamat. If he declined, then more forceful measures were to be used.

If he declined. Did Jafar honestly expect him to accept? Philippe shook his head. *This is madness.*

A knock sounded on the door.

Grabbing his pistol, Philippe tiptoed to the door and peered through the peephole. His face broke into a smile at the sight of a woman in sunglasses and a hat.

"Lydia?" he asked, pulling open the door.

The silenced Beretta coughed three times. Philippe was dead before his body hit the floor.

CHAPTER 35

With the exception of a few wealthy enclaves such as Zamalek, a cloud of poverty hung over Cairo like industrial exhaust. It was suffocating, acrid, and relentless.

The sun had just dipped below the horizon when Sharifa directed her Mercedes off the Ring Road and headed east. Pollution had turned the western sky the color of cheap rouge, while before them the rugged Muqattam Hills were shrouded in a gray, smoky haze.

"You're very quiet," remarked Tyler.

"I'm nervous," Sharifa said.

"How long has it been?"

"Too long."

Sharifa slowed the Mercedes for a donkey cart on the road. The cart was a huge wooden crate on wheels. Sitting on its front bench was a barefooted girl in a faded green dress. She wore a red scarf and a string of yellow plastic beads. Piled on top of the cart's large mound of cans were several baskets of colored scraps of cloth.

The girl switched the donkey with a thin branch, steering it to one side. With a brief wave, Sharifa passed by her and continued along the bumpy road.

"That was me, when I was a girl," Sharifa said, glancing in the rearview mirror.

Tyler looked back. "*Zabbaline?*"

Sharifa nodded. "Dressed in the scraps she's collected. These hills are where she lives."

Staring out the window, Tyler saw masses of squat, unfinished buildings surrounded by ridges of bricks and rubbish. Many buildings had second and third-story pylons jutting into the air. Others had partial staircases climbing to nowhere, while still others were roofless and in shambles. The whole area had a bombed-out feel.

"Most structures never reach completion," Sharifa explained. "The government gives people a tax concession during the construction of their homes; so to keep this low rate for as long as possible, owners keep slowly adding on. That's why the whole area looks incomplete.

Sometimes buildings fall apart faster than they get built."

"And this is where you grew up?"

"You see now why I didn't want to talk about it?"

"Coming from a poor neighborhood is no reason to be embarrassed."

"I know that now," Sharifa said, steering around a pothole. "The fact that you had such a difficult time growing up in New Jersey made me realize how much we had in common. That I wasn't alone. Trouble is, I'm not sure what I'm supposed to say when I see them. What if they're angry? What if they don't want to see me?"

"Ever known a parent to be angry when a wayward child comes home?"

Sharifa looked sideways and saw Tyler grinning.

"Wayward child, huh?" she said, punching him on the arm.

Tyler laughed. "Eyes on the road! We wouldn't want our wayward child to have an accident!"

Minutes later, in the waning light of the day, Sharifa stopped in front of a single-story hut with a flat roof and shutters. Beside it was a walled area covered by a corrugated iron roof. Under the roof, an old man was seated beside several piles of cans. Wearing a black turban and striped shirt, he was operating a pair of long-handled sheers that split open the cans, which he then flattened. Across the barren lot, a woman in a long dress was separating aluminum cans from the steel. A wooden cart similar to the one they passed earlier stood near the street.

As the Mercedes stopped, the couple paused to look. When Sharifa climbed out, their curiosity erupted into joy.

They ran over and embraced Sharifa, hugging and kissing her again and again, then pulling back as if to verify that it was really she who was standing there – that they weren't dreaming. Then more hugging. And tears. And laughter. Once the emotional welcome had subsided, Sharifa motioned for Tyler.

"This man is the reason I'm here," she explained tearfully in Arabic. "He made me realize…"

Sharifa burst into tears.

Her father opened his arms, drew Sharifa to him, and allowed her to weep.

"I long time dream for this moment," he said to Tyler, his smile revealing several missing teeth. "We not see her for many tall ages."

"For many years," Sharifa said, drying her eyes.

The old man grinned. "My English, not so good!" He kissed Sharifa, then beckoned them to follow. "Come, we eat."

Arm-in-arm, Sharifa and Tyler walked toward the house. Before entering, Sharifa pulled Tyler aside.

"This means more than you'll ever know!" she said.

Brushing a wisp of hair from Sharifa's face, Tyler recalled the hypnotic effect Sharifa had had on him the moment she stepped out of the taxi. It had been impossible not to stare as she strode down the sidewalk and into the Hula Hut. It was no different now.

"What are you looking at?" she asked.

He touched her cheek then leaned down and kissed her.

"We eat now!" a voice called out.

"Coming," Sharifa replied. She gave Tyler a final kiss before leading him into the house.

From the top of a distant pile of rubble, Majli watched through a pair of binoculars. Silhouetted against the dusky red sky, his black jellaba flapped in the wind.

Lowering the glasses, Majli checked his watch.

He would soon be making his move.

CHAPTER 36

Majli glanced at the dashboard clock just as Sharifa's Mercedes drove past. It was well after two in the morning and most households would now be asleep.

Reaching under his *jellaba,* Majli brought out his pistol and screwed on a silencer. He then slid back the cocking lever that fed a cartridge into the chamber.

Opening his door, Majli climbed out of his car and started toward the house. In the distance, a single can toppled from a mound of cans, clanking lightly as it tumbled to the ground. Moving silently over the gravel, he set a course for the small brick hut.

Inside, two naked bulbs filled the room with harsh light.

"She looked happy," the old woman remarked while her husband dried a plate.

"She had the same look in her eyes that you had in yours," the husband replied, sliding the plate onto a stack of others on a shelf made of lettuce crates.

"What do you mean?"

"You had the same look in your eyes the first time I met you," he said. "I could tell that you desired me. Do you not remember how you followed me around?"

The wife swatted her husband on the arm. "It was you who followed me!" she scolded. "One look and I could tell what you desired. And it did not show just in your *eyes.*"

They laughed and the old man kissed his wife.

The door swung open and Majli fired.

CHAPTER 37

The nightmare struck like a summer storm and moved furiously across the landscape of Tyler's dreams.

First came peals of laughter. Heavy laughter, laden with mockery, the kind bellowed by men of cruelty. Bursts of gunfire followed.

Then came the images: corpses of children tumbling toward him in slow motion, their faces frozen in agony. One in particular – that of a young girl – had tears in her eyes.

Shackled by sleep, Tyler fought to wrestle free from the haunting vision as bodies hurtled by him. He wrenched to the side, kicked off the sheets and tore at his inability to move. He begged the gunmen to stop, but they would not. It was a massacre – soldiers against children.

"*No!*" Tyler screamed, bolting upright in bed, a slick of perspiration coating his skin.

The dream dissolved like rotting fabric.

Panting heavily, Tyler swung his feet down onto the floor and sat hunched over in the darkness. Finally he stood, walked unsteadily to the bathroom and splashed handfuls of water on his face.

Shutting off the tap, Tyler stood alone in the darkness, his hands on the rim of the sink. He then heard the creak of the door.

He turned toward a faint rectangle of light. Silhouetted in the doorway was a shadowed figure visible only for a second.

"Who's there?" he asked.

"It's me," Sharifa whispered.

"Here, let me turn on the light."

"No! I'd rather say this in the dark."

"Say what?"

Sharifa tiptoed over, took Tyler by the hands, and led him to the bed. "What is it?" he asked.

"Have a seat," she said.

They sat.

"I need to tell you something and I'm not sure how," she explained.

Tyler did not reply.

Finally, she said, "Youssef and I…we've been lovers for several years."

"I wondered about that."

"When I came to Austin, my assignment was to ensure that you took this interview. Youssef's got a lot riding on it and he wanted to make certain you didn't back out. But something happened. I fell in love. And believe me when I say that was not in the plans! But that's what happened, and for me it was like discovering chocolate for the very first time. You listen to people talk about how good it is, but until you let a piece melt in your mouth, there's no way you can understand what they're talking about."

"You lost me."

"When Youssef hired me as his assistant, he rescued me from a horrible life of poverty. And it didn't take long for me to learn what he expected in return."

"You don't have to do this," said Tyler.

"Yes, I do. Just hear me out."

She took a steadying breath.

"And while I suppose I did love him for helping me turn my life around – at least that's what I told myself to keep what little self-respect I had left – in the end, I felt like a prostitute. Someone who slept with her boss."

"Sharifa…"

"Then I met you, and I discovered what real love felt like, what it sounded like, and tasted like. You're my piece of chocolate, Tyler, and I love you like I've never loved anyone before. That's also why I know I have to break things off with Youssef. Trouble is, I'll get fired over this. But that's okay! My heart and body can't live in two worlds. Your world is where I want to be."

"Are you sure about this? I mean, really?"

"Absolutely. I plan to tell him as soon as this business with the tablet is finished. I'm sick of the tension, the jealousy, the worry about terrorists, how much money he'll make…"

"How well do you know Youssef?" asked Tyler. "I mean, I understand everything you just told me. But how well do you *really* know him?"

"Well enough, I guess. Why?"

"When you break things off, do you think there's a chance he'll hurt you? Do something violent?"

"Good heavens, no. At least I don't think so. Majli, on the other hand, scares me. I hate it that he lives here in the house."

"I thought he was a friend."

"God, no."

"Youssef said you've known him for years. That you recommended him for the security job."

"Youssef hired Majli, not me. He's only been around here a few weeks. I never met him before Youssef brought him on as his chief of security."

Tyler did not respond.

"Are you sure that's what Youssef said?" she asked.

"Maybe I misunderstood."

Sharifa thought for a moment. "Unless…"

"Unless what?"

"Unless he knows about us. Maybe he said that to try to drive a wedge between us. To make you suspicious of me. Youssef has a horrible temper."

"That's why I asked how well you knew him. Because when you finally do break things off, I want to be certain he won't freak out."

"I never would have thought so before," she said. "But now, I'm not so sure."

"Let's not worry about it right now," he said. He wrapped an arm around her shoulder and drew her near. "Hey, what's this?" he asked, feeling a welt on her shoulder.

Sharifa chuckled. "I once had a tattoo with the name of – can you believe it? – a local rock star, foolish girl of sixteen that I was. The removal clinic left quite a scar."

"I never noticed it before."

"I guess you were focused on other things."

Tyler laughed. "I guess I was."

Sharifa stood and pulled off her shirt. Against the faint light of the window, Tyler gazed at her silhouette.

"What about now?" she asked, pushing Tyler down onto his back and sliding on top of him. "Any chance I can recapture that focus?"

"I think that can be arranged."

Out in the corridor, Majli stood listening.

CHAPTER 38

Shortly before ten, Faisal was shown into the living room by Mrs. Fedje. He was about to pour himself a cup of tea when Tyler walked into the room.

"Do we have time?" asked Faisal.

"Absolutely. Mind if I join you?"

"Of course. I heard the popularity of coffee with Americans started in Colonial days, as a protest against the British and their propensity for tea."

"And all along I thought it was bourbon! Man, I've been dunkin' my doughnuts in the wrong *stuff*."

Faisal laughed and handed Tyler his tea.

"I thought we'd conduct your interview at the museum," explained Tyler, taking a sip. "Once we're finished, I'll shoot some footage of artifacts that people will recognize: King Tut, a few mummies, that sort of thing."

"Isn't that being sensationalistic?"

"Not at all. You're a famous Egyptologist whose expertise is sought by museums all over the world. That footage will serve to illustrate the environment in which you work."

Faisal nodded.

"Being in front of a camera won't make you nervous, will it?"

"I've been interviewed before."

"Did Youssef tell you this interview will be seen around the world?"

"Several times. It's something that makes him extremely happy."

Tyler caught the edge in Faisal's voice.

"Have you and Youssef been friends for long?" he asked.

Tightening his jaw, Faisal averted his eyes. Suddenly, he became aware that Tyler was watching him.

"I wouldn't say that we're friends," said Faisal. "I've known him professionally, of course, for many years."

Tyler nodded.

"It's a small world, antiquities and art."

Tyler nodded again, then said, "I should probably explain the kinds of questions I'll be asking. As you'd expect, we'll talk mostly about the tablet, but I'd like to introduce you with a recap of your background."

"Such as where I went to university, subjects studied – that sort of thing?"

"Plus a little about you and your family. Youssef told me you have two daughters."

Faisal suddenly grew very uneasy.

"They're what – eleven and nine?"

"I wish to keep my family out of this," said Faisal.

"But your family is an important part of who you are, what makes you tick. Besides, viewers love pretty faces. Not that yours won't charm the ladies!"

"Dr. Tyler, please…"

"But Youssef told me—"

"I really must insist. Whatever else you ask is fine. But nothing about my family."

"Not even a few photos of you together?"

"I am quite emphatic! Nothing about my family!"

"Okay, whatever you say. I can fill in with some shots of you examining artifacts, conferring with colleagues, et cetera, then cut to you in your office, probably at your desk. We'll then begin talking about the tablet. How's that sound?"

A terse nod was Faisal's reply.

Tyler smiled. "Faisal, it's all right. Nothing about your family. I promise."

Another terse nod.

"Now, back to the tablet. If I happen to ask a question and think your answer is too technical, I'll ask you to rephrase."

"I thought you wanted my technical expertise."

"I do. But the viewing audience might not understand technical jargon, so we'll need to phrase it in language they can understand. For instance, you might remark that the tablet is diorite. When I ask what diorite is, rather than giving an answer about volcanic processes and mineral compositions, simply explain that it's an extremely hard igneous rock, similar to granite. If you want, you can add how diorite was used by ancient Persians, Babylonians and Egyptians to carve tablets and figurines. Similarly, I might ask in what language the tablet was written. After saying it's proto-Sinaitic, you could add how this was the language of the Sinai Peninsula during the time Ishmael lived there. Stuff like that."

Faisal nodded.

"I'll also ask about forgery techniques, and the criteria by which you judged the tablet to be genuine."

Troubled, Faisal looked away.

Tyler clasped Faisal on the shoulder. "Relax, Faisal. Nothing about your family; I promise. Let's finish our tea and get going."

While Tyler and Faisal were finishing their tea, a white sedan was speeding across the 26th of July Bridge toward Zamalek. Behind the wheel was Sergeant Brad Henschel, wearing jeans and a sports shirt. In the passenger seat was Zoe Gustaves, her arms folded defiantly.

"You're an embassy guard, right?" she asked.

"Yes, ma'am."

"I don't need a guard."

"Yes, ma'am."

"I know how to drive."

"Traffic can be tricky in Cairo."

"Bullshit."

"Yes, ma'am."

"Quit 'ma'amming' me, Sergeant. I hate it!"

"Yes, ma'am."

With a huff, Zoe looked out the window.

She knew Brad Henschel's annoying mannerisms were not the real reason she was angry. What really bugged her was Tyler, plus this latest intel on Lydia Ardois.

Lydia Ardois, of course, was a known member of *Qamat*. No surprise there. What raised eyebrows was the fact that Lydia Ardois had been a passenger out of Tel Aviv the same day someone tried to assassinate Vice President Baker. Coincidence? Perhaps. And allowances for that had been made. But what really set off alarm bells was the fact that she had also been a passenger on the same flight where Tariq's deposit confirmation had originated.

What didn't make sense was her leaving Switzerland without any record of her having entered the country. Not only that, the two flights almost overlapped, with differing points of origin and destination. So how could she be in two places at roughly the same time? Either she was traveling under a variety of names, or someone else was using her identity.

The sedan squealed around a corner. To the left was the salmon-pink Cairo Marriott while in the distance were the tufted tops of the palm trees skirting the Gezira Sporting Club's lushly irrigated grounds. Within five minutes, Brad was switching off the ignition in front of Qaderi's residence.

"Man, this is some pad!" he remarked, peering through the windshield. "I could handle a week in a place like this. Strolling that upper balcony with a bottle o' Wild Turkey in one hand, a babe in some of that see-through material in the other..."

"I am not even going to comment," said Zoe, climbing out and slamming the door.

She bounded up the steps and pushed the bell button.

"May I help you?" asked Mrs Fedje, opening the door.

"Zoe Gustaves, American Embassy. May I speak with Dr. Tyler?"

"He is with someone."

"This is urgent. I won't be long."

Mrs. Fedje invited Zoe to enter. The wait was not long.

"Ms. Gustaves, how nice to see you!" Tyler called out as he came down the stairs.

"We need to talk," said Zoe.

"I guess we can skip the pleasantries."

"Val – I know who she is."

"My assistant. No secret there."

"But that's not quite the whole story, now, is it?"

Tyler looked quizzically at Zoe.

"She's *Louise Kappelmann*, Tyler!"

"Where did you hear that?" Tyler demanded, grabbing Zoe by the arm and forcing her into his bedroom.

"Let go of me!" she said, twisting away.

"Where did you *hear* that?"

"The game is over!"

"Tell me! Where did you *hear* that? Who else knows about this?"

"The game is *over!* I know what you're *planning!*"

"Who else *knows?*"

"No one!"

199

"Someone told you. Who was it? Your boss?"

"I'm not answering your questions!"

"Didn't I tell you one mistake could get someone killed? Do you think Val changed her name for the fun of it? She's a *target,* Zoe! Abu Nazer *murdered her husband!* So either you start talking and tell me who else knows about this, or we've got nothing more to say and you're leaving."

Zoe met Tyler's angry stare with a defiant one of her own.

"Fine. You're out of here," he said, grabbing her by the arm and leading her toward the door.

"All right! My boss. So what?" said Zoe, twisting away.

"What's his name?"

"None of your business."

Tyler grabbed Zoe again. "Dammit, what's his name?"

"Jackson Teague," she said, pulling free. "And if you ever lay a hand on me again, I'll knock your teeth down your throat."

"Who else did he tell besides you?"

"No one."

"Do you have *any idea* what you've done?" said Tyler, snatching up his cell phone and dialing a number. Within seconds, his home phone was ringing.

"Hello?" a groggy voice answered.

"Val, thank God you're there!"

"Where else would I be at this hour?"

"The CIA! They know who you are."

"I'm aware of that," said Val, switching on a light. "Zoe Gustaves phoned earlier."

"You need to get out of there."

"She's kind of pushy, but in an odd way I like her."

"Val, you need to get out of there! *Now!*"

"She said Sharifa could be working with Majli."

"That's an Agency screw-up. She's not."

"Zoe knows about the mallet. She's smart, Tyler. Top of her class. I ran a background check."

"Val, I want you to get out of there!"

"Tyler, I'm fine. Nobody knows that I'm here."

"The Agency knows!"

"And they're all asleep, like I should be."

"Word may have leaked!"

"I'll think about it in the morning."

"Dammit, Val—"

"I love you, Tyler. You're like the son I never had. So don't take this personally when I tell you I'm going to hang up. I need a full eight hours, and you know how cranky I get when that doesn't happen."

"Val, wait!"

"Good bye, darlin.'"

The line went dead.

"Shit!" shouted Tyler, throwing his phone on the bed.

"Don't you think you're overreacting?"

"Didn't I tell you one mistake can get someone killed?"

"Will you chill out? Nothing's going to happen."

"Obviously, the word *Nightingale* means nothing to you."

Zoe grabbed Tyler by the arm. "Where did you hear that?" she asked.

Tyler looked pointedly at Zoe's hand and she removed it. "None of your business," he said.

"I'm making it my business!"

"We're finished here," said Tyler, heading for the door. "You can show yourself out."

"I guess we can do this the hard way," said Zoe, taking out her phone. "I'll have Val brought in for questioning."

Tyler whirled and grabbed for the phone.

Zoe stepped back and held the phone out of reach. "Either you talk or I dial. What's it going to be?"

With a growl, Tyler stormed to the window.

"I'm waiting!"

Tyler did not reply.

"Your choice," she said, punching buttons.

"All right!" said Tyler. "It's a covert group of assassins funded by the CIA. But they're so deep and dark few people know they even exist. Even fewer know that Abu Nazer is one of them."

"Tariq and Majli – are they with Nightingale?"

"No idea."

Zoe held up her phone and gave Tyler a warning look.

"I don't know," he said.

"Where did you hear about Nightingale?"

"Someone I once knew was approached by them for recruitment."

"Who?"

"I'm not revealing the names of my sources."

"And I'm not trying to make you. But I need you to tell me what you know about Nightingale."

"Why?"

"Because I've been trying to find out who's behind it but keep getting stonewalled."

"Consider yourself lucky. Most people simply get killed."

"What do you mean?"

"Senator Ashford. She got too close."

"How do you *know* this?"

"Don't take this personally, but I don't really trust you all that much. Abu Nazer killed Senator Ashford and her daughter. He nearly killed Vice President Baker. He wants to kill Val. And someone at Langley is protecting him."

"So you're here to even the score, is that it?"

Tyler rolled his eyes.

"Don't play games with me, Tyler. I know about the mallet. I know you're planning to kill him."

"You really have lost the plot."

"Then tell me why a *rifle* just happens to be on its way to you."

Tyler looked skeptically at Zoe.

"We phoned the couriers. FedEx confirmed it."

"I am *not* here to kill Abu Nazer."

"Then why are you here? And don't tell me it's to do an interview!"

"Then I've got nothing to say."

"Look, we don't need to be at odds over this," Zoe said. "If you're not here to kill Abu Nazer, then tell me why you're here."

Tyler did not reply

"I'm not kidding, Tyler. I *will* have her brought in for questioning."

Tyler heaved a sigh. "I'm here to expose Abu Nazer. To get proof of his identity."

"Then you do know who he is." A statement more than a question.

"Not yet."

"So what's the deal with the rifle?"

"Val's idea. She thinks I need it because Abu Nazer's planning to kill me. I told her not to send it, but she didn't listen."

"Why would Abu Nazer want to kill you?"

"I know what he's planning to do."

"Which is?"

Mrs. Fedje appeared in the doorway. "Everything is all right?" she asked.

"Fine," answered Tyler, forcing a smile.

"Dr. Mostafa, he is still waiting."

"Tell him I'll be there in a minute."

"Mr. Qaderi has also just arrived," said Mrs. Fedje. "He phoned to say he will go with you to the museum."

"Thanks."

Mrs. Fedje looked warily at Zoe, then went back upstairs.

"What's Abu Nazer planning to do?" asked Zoe once Mrs. Fedje was gone.

Outside, a car door slammed.

"Tell me!" said Zoe.

"Qaderi's coming."

"Quit stalling!"

"I'm not stalling. Qaderi's coming and I can't talk. I'll explain everything as soon as I can."

"When?" asked Zoe.

"I'm busy the rest of today. And tonight's out because of this party."

"I'm on the list. Tonight'll be fine."

"It's not like I'll have loads of free time."

Zoe jiggled the phone in her hand. "I'm sure you can squeeze me in."

A frustrated sigh was Tyler's reply.

The deadbolt clicked.

The front door opened.

"Thanks so much for the update, Ms. Gustaves," Tyler said in a loud voice, stepping into the foyer. He reacted with apparent surprise upon seeing Qaderi and Majli. "Youssef! I'm glad you're here. Ms. Gustaves was just following up on the threats that were made against us. She thinks something might happen tonight."

"Oh?" responded Youssef, eyebrows arched as he looked Zoe over.

"Zoe Gustaves, American Embassy," she said, offering her hand.

"That's very considerate, Ms. Gustaves," said Youssef, stepping past Zoe, "but you needn't worry. Security will be more than adequate." He turned to Majli. "Be with you shortly."

After a quick glare at Zoe, Majli went upstairs.

"Then I won't trouble you any further," said Zoe.

"Thanks again for stopping by," said Tyler, pulling open the door. Zoe nodded and left.

Tyler watched her descend the front steps and return to the waiting sedan.

"Since when does your embassy make house calls?" asked Youssef.

"Since that tablet of yours began turning the world upside down."

Upstairs, Majli stared open-mouthed at the two emails that had just arrived. The first was infuriating. Tariq was demanding his other quarter of a million dollars. The second, however, was catastrophic. *Louise Kappelmann was alive.*

"Are you certain?" Majli typed back.

"Absolutely," was Nightingale's reply.

"Take care of her. $50K."

"LOL."

"All right, $75K."

"$1M. My Swiss account."

"You know we don't have that kind of money!"

"Not my problem. Kappelmann is, after all, the only person who can possibly identify you."

"She's your problem, too!" replied Majli, glancing toward the sound of voices echoing up the stairwell. "If we go down, so do you."

"Don't ever threaten me like that again or the arrangement between us terminates, the trail disappears, and you die a slow, painful death. One million, take it or leave it."

Majli stormed to the window. He had no choice but to pay! For not only was Nightingale their only remaining source of funding, but also their protection.

And Nightingale was very clearly reminding him of that fact.

Seething with resentment, Majli returned to the computer.

"Agreed," he typed.

Nightingale's reply was instantaneous.

"Contract will be fulfilled within twenty-four hours. Have a nice day."

CHAPTER 39

Youssef led Faisal, Majli, Sharifa and Tyler through a maze of ramshackle streets so narrow most saw no direct sunlight. After several turns the street opened into a tree-lined quadrangle filled with the sounds and smells of a market. Hundreds of locals – mostly women, a few with headscarves – were crowded around dozens of wooden stalls and push carts piled high with fruits, vegetables, freshly baked flat breads, spices, copper pots, tubs of fish, cages of chickens, buckets of flowers, and stacks of vividly colored goat-hair pillows. In the center of the quadrangle, clumps of skinny men stood smoking while the women shopped.

Skirting the shoppers, Youssef led the others down an alleyway and stopped in front of a heavy door. On the wall beside the door was an illuminated twelve-digit keypad. He punched ATEN 37 and the door clicked open.

They entered a dimly lit corridor that smelled dusty and stale. The walls were plastered brick, and painted green. The floor was tessellated tile.

The group followed Youssef along the corridor to another door. Overhead hung a metal alarm box.

Youssef stuck a key into a lock and twisted. The door pushed open. Inside was a darkened stairwell. Youssef flipped a switch and a light came on. Seconds later: a high pitched squeal. Youssef entered a code on another keypad and the piercing noise stopped.

Leading the way down a flight of worn limestone steps, Youssef unlocked yet another door and switched on the lights.

"Welcome to my vault," he said.

Tyler entered and glanced around. The walls were insulated concrete and what used to be three windows near the ceiling had long ago been bricked shut. Wooden racks held numerous paintings, while reinforced metal shelves held statues and relics. A hush of filtered air maintained a constant temperature and humidity.

Youssef walked over to a heavy steel case and pulled open a padded drawer, which glided out smoothly on ball-bearing hinges.

Motioning to Tyler, he folded back a blue felt cloth.

Tyler approached the drawer, and stood silently staring at the dark gray monument etched with hundreds of tiny proto-Sinaitic hieroglyphs. The primitive characters – many of which resembled stick figures – were packed in tight rows across the dull surface of the slab.

"It is both disappointing and magical, is it not?" remarked Youssef, with an expectant smile.

"You think it's going to be more than it is, then realize it's four thousand years old and written by Ishmael himself. It's inanimate, yet living… Spectacular, yet ordinary."

"And now worth a hundred million dollars."

Tyler stared openly at Youssef.

"Seems we are in the midst of a bidding war," he said, "which of course must be reflected in the amount of insurance required to protect it."

Tyler looked back at the tablet, studying each striation, feature, and hieroglyph. He glanced at Faisal, who looked away.

Sharifa suddenly removed her jacket and moved to the other side of the drawer. She bent over to get a closer look. When she did, Tyler could see that she was wearing no bra.

She looked up, and saw Tyler looking. After a quick glance at Youssef to make sure his attention was on the tablet, she silently mouthed, "Later," then looked back down at the monument, making no effort to adjust her position.

Concentrate, Tyler told himself. *And not on the outline of her nipples.* "I should probably do what I came here to do," he said. "Is it possible to lay the tablet on one of your worktables?"

"I'd rather not," Youssef replied. "If it's a matter of visibility, the sides of the drawer fold down."

"That'll do."

While Youssef unlatched the sides, Tyler opened his aluminum camera case and took out two light stands and a frame. He assembled the stands, then attached the camera to the frame and positioned it over the tablet. He then switched on the lights and took several meter readings. After adjusting the camera's settings, he began to shoot.

Across town, in the American Embassy, Brad Henschel opened Tim's office door and allowed Zoe to enter.

"Look what just arrived," said Tim, nodding toward the gun case on the table. "A locksmith is on the way."

"Got a screwdriver?" asked Zoe.

"What for?"

"Have you got one or *not?*"

"All right, already!" said Tim. He opened a drawer, found a screwdriver and handed it to Zoe. She slid it under each of the hasps and popped them open.

"No *way!*" she said, opening the case and lifting out an old, single shot .22 caliber bolt-action rifle.

"Is that the mallet?" asked Tim with a dubious frown.

"No way could Tyler use a relic like that to bring down Abu Nazer," snapped Zoe, dropping the rifle in its case.

"Maybe he's a really good shot."

"No one's that good," said Brad. He picked up the rifle, made sure the chamber was empty and shouldered it. "My grandfather used one of these."

"Exactly!" said Zoe.

"Meaning what?" asked Tim, looking confused.

"Meaning he's *messing* with us, that's what!"

"Why would he do that?" asked Tim.

"Because he's frigging *Tyler,* that's why!"

CHAPTER 40

At 4:40 AM, the black government van drove slowly down the tree-lined lane toward Tyler's house. With its headlights off and tires crunching softly on the gravel, the van rolled to a stop twenty feet from the garage. As expected, the house was dark.

The doors of the van opened quietly and five commandos climbed out. They were dressed in black fatigues and their faces were smeared with camouflage paint. Each carried a holstered .45 caliber semi-automatic pistol. Without saying a word, the men put on 7-Bravo night vision goggles – the kind that covered both eyes – and latex gloves.

One commando went to the front door, three went around back, while a fifth kept watch up the lane. The driver remained in the van. Each of the men wore a tiny earphone/microphone headset.

The lock on the kitchen slider was not difficult to force, and in less than a minute the three commandos were inside.

They moved silently to the stairs. Their rubber-soled boots barely made a sound. The squad leader paused and held up a hand. Old wooden stairs often squeaked. He made several hand signals indicating points of danger before leading the way up.

At the top, the leader pointed toward a half-open door, where the cadence of deep breathing could be heard. He touched his weapon and reached for the door.

A floorboard creaked.

Val stirred and opened her eyes. Was that a noise or had she been dreaming?

She leaned up on one elbow and listened, then looked at the clock. It was a quarter to five. That meant it was early afternoon in Cairo, which meant Tyler would have had time to read the email from Toy Soldier that she had forwarded to him. And by now he should have replied.

Might as well get up and read it.

With a yawn, Val switched on the bedside lamp the same instant the door swung open.

To someone wearing Bravo-7 night vision goggles, the sudden burst of halogen light from that small bulb was like staring into a

208

thermonuclear blast. Momentarily blinded, the commandos ripped off their goggles.

Val scrambled to the other side of the bed before realizing she would be trapped there. Her only chance was to run. She kicked away the sheets and sprang for the door.

Although his vision was little more than a field of chaotic white spots, the leader saw Val dash for the door. He grabbed for her but she knocked away his hand. She ran out the door and down the stairs.

"Subject is loose!" the leader shouted into his microphone. Rubbing his eyes, he staggered after her, his boots thumping awkwardly on the wooden floor.

Val tore through the kitchen, out the slider, and across the patio onto the back lawn. Looking behind her, she saw another man charge around the corner of the house.

Weaving her way through the trees, Val knew she had a good chance of escaping if she could reach the lake. In her youth she had been a good swimmer.

But Val was now fifty-two years old and in poor physical condition. Panting from her short sprint, she was no match for the fourth commando, who tackled her to the ground.

She tried to scream, but the commando slapped tape over her mouth. He rolled her over, braced her in that position, handcuffed her wrists and then taped her ankles and knees.

By now the others had arrived. They hoisted Val inside a body bag and zipped it shut. Picking the bag up, they ran to the van.

The leader slid open the door and the others heaved the body bag inside. Two of the commandos grabbed a small briefcase and ran back into the house. Within three minutes they had returned and the van drove quietly away.

The time was 4:55.

Once they were on the highway, the squad leader took out his phone and dialed a number. It rang twice before it was answered.

"Phase one complete," said the leader.

"You know what to do. Teague out."

209

CHAPTER 41

After photographing the tablet, Tyler packed away his equipment and gave the camera's memory card to Sharifa for conversion to disk. Forty minutes later, he was again lifting his camera cases out of the trunk of Youssef's Mercedes, this time in front of the Cairo Museum.

Tyler shut the trunk and looked toward the street, where a mob of angry protestors were shouting at the line of policemen keeping them away from the museum.

"The tablet," explained Youssef quietly, "and this inflammatory ad about ownership of the Holy Land. It's provoking all sorts of reactions."

Tyler glanced sideways at Youssef. He then picked up his camera cases and headed toward the museum.

With its neoclassical style, the Egyptian Museum did not look at all Egyptian. Built in 1900 by a French architect, the entrance resembled a miniature *Arc de Triomphe,* around which had been built a symmetrical, rectangular warehouse.

Faisal cleared the group through the security checkpoint and led them into a cavernous two-story interior congested with statues and sarcophagi. Thick columns along each side of the atrium supported high spanning arches.

The group followed Faisal down a corridor to his office, their footsteps echoing against a backdrop of murmured conversation.

"I have other business I must attend to," said Youssef, just as Faisal unlocked his office door, "so let's meet at the house in an hour."

"Better make it two," said Tyler.

"Two hours it is. See you then. Majli will remain here to assist you. He'll call a cab when you're ready to leave."

"That's really not necessary," said Tyler.

"No trouble at all. I insist."

And with a wave, Youssef turned and left.

Tyler surveyed the office. It was crammed with artifacts, bookshelves, and display cases full of cuneiform tablets and pottery. Numerous maps hung on racks near louvered windows that cast lined shadows across the floor. A massive wooden desk was crowded with more relics and journals.

"How about we shoot over here?" asked Tyler, walking over to Faisal's desk, where he noticed a framed photograph of two girls. "Your daughters?" he asked, picking it up and looking at the image of two smiling girls standing beside Mickey Mouse.

Faisal took the photo and placed it in a drawer.

"All right if I rearrange things on your desk?" asked Tyler.

Faisal nodded and Tyler removed several stacks of journals. He then rearranged the artifacts. Once Faisal had been seated and wired for sound, Tyler returned to his camera and made a few final adjustments.

"Okay, we're set. Are you ready?"

Faisal nodded.

Tyler began the interview with a few lighthearted questions about food, then steered the conversation to Faisal's educational background, research interests, and a discussion of the various techniques used by forgers. Faisal's description of a counterfeit wooden panel from Byzantine Egypt provided a natural transition for Tyler to ask about the tablet.

Faisal provided a simple, non-technical description, citing comparative rock inscriptions from other sites on the Sinai Peninsula. He then elaborated on stylistic parallels from other examples of ancient Near Eastern literature.

"The tablet is unquestionably genuine. It dates from approximately 1900 BC."

"Does radiocarbon dating support your assessment?" asked Tyler.

"Radiocarbon dating can only be performed on organic matter," said Faisal, "such as a piece of charcoal or wood. The tablet, being rock, could only be dated by radiometric means, such as potassium-argon or uranium-lead. But this still wouldn't help us, because it would reveal only the age of the slab itself and not the date it was inscribed. To ascertain that information, we must use other methods. Being familiar with proto-Sinaitic text, I compared the tablet with other tablets whose dates we can confirm because of the known historical events they record."

"How do you know the tablet's not a forgery?"

"Because I scrutinized each hieroglyph under a microscope for more subtle features of aging such as erosion, calcification and discoloration. The tablet is definitely authentic."

"Okay, that's a wrap," said Tyler. "All I need to do now is shoot some footage around the museum."

Tyler removed the video camera from its tripod.

"We won't be long. Would you call me a cab?" he asked Majli, who stepped over to the door and opened it. "Was that a yes or a no?" he asked.

"You are under my protection," Majli responded in a firm, deep voice. "You do not leave my sight."

"We're safe here in the museum. Right, Faisal?"

Faisal glanced uneasily at Majli, whose virulent glare dominated the room like a loose cobra.

"Right, Faisal?" Tyler asked again.

"The museum is quite safe," said Faisal.

Without responding, Majli waited beside the open door.

In less than forty minutes, Tyler had finished filming everything he needed and was pulling away from the museum in a taxi. The cab squealed left, then right into the traffic, adding its own trail of fumes to the city's noxious haze.

The taxi was speeding toward the Tahrir Bridge over the Nile when Tyler suddenly told the driver to go back.

"You want go back?" asked the driver.

"Yes. I left my microphone and transmitter on Faisal's jacket."

The driver nodded and careered the taxi across all lanes of traffic, eliciting an outraged blare of horns from other drivers. Within minutes, they were back at the museum.

Tyler told the driver to wait. Jumping out, he entered the museum through the main entrance, cleared security, and hurried down the corridor to Faisal's office. He rapped twice on the door and entered.

He froze at the sight of Faisal being held by two men in ski masks.

Faisal's hands had been tied behind him and a thin cord had been looped around his neck. The man standing behind Faisal was twisting the cord, causing Faisal to choke. The man in front held a gun to Faisal's head.

The men jerked around and stared at Tyler when he entered.

"Who are you?" the man with the gun demanded.

Tyler held up his hands.

"You told me the door was locked," the man said to his companion in Arabic.

"You said the door was locked!" responded the second man in Arabic.

"There's no need for a gun," said Tyler.

"American! The man is American!" the second man said.

"Put the gun down. Let him go," said Tyler. He could see Faisal struggling to breathe.

"This man is not your concern!"

"He can't *breathe*. For God's sake, let him go!"

The masked man was in front of Tyler now, the pistol aimed straight at his face. "You will leave, or we do same to you."

"We cannot allow him to leave!" the second man called out in Arabic. "He will phone the police."

"Majli took care of that," the first man replied.

Tyler saw the panic in Faisal's eyes.

"What do you look at?" demanded the man with the gun.

Tyler did not reply.

"You want I should kill you, too?"

"This man is American! We cannot hurt him!" the second man said in Arabic.

"I go, but Faisal goes with me," said Tyler.

"This man is not your concern!" For emphasis he jabbed the gun in Tyler's face.

"I am *really* tired of people sticking guns in my face," growled Tyler. He snapped his forearm right, blocking the pistol away from his face and looping his hand like a corkscrew around the masked man's forearm. He yanked upward and the arm snapped like a twig. The man opened his mouth to scream an instant before Tyler slammed a fist to the side of his head, knocking him out cold. Tyler caught the pistol as it fell, then released the man's arm and allowed him to slide to the floor.

Seeing Tyler coming toward him, the other man swung Faisal in front of him. "Drop gun or I kill him!" he shouted, cinching the cord tighter.

"Let him go," said Tyler evenly.

Faisal's eyes were bulging now.

"Then I kill him!" screamed the man, inhaling for the strength needed to complete the garrote.

In one smooth motion, Tyler lifted the gun and fired. The bullet sliced off half the man's ear and sprayed blood into the air. The man grabbed his ear and screamed, releasing Faisal, who fell gasping to the floor.

Tyler sprang toward the masked man, grabbed him around the neck and smashed his head against the wall. When he let go, the man crumpled to the floor.

After tossing the first man's gun in the trashcan, Tyler helped Faisal to a chair. "Are you all right?" he asked.

Gulping air and rubbing his throat, Faisal nodded.

Tyler picked up the phone and dialed security.

Dealing with the police took a tedious two hours and accomplished little. A gun had been discharged – a very serious matter in Cairo – but justifiable given the possible endangerment to Dr. Mostafa by some of the protestors.

"*Possible* endangerment?" queried Tyler. "One of them tried to *garrote* him! The other held a gun to his head!"

The policemen shrugged.

"How the hell did they get past security in the first place?" demanded Tyler. "And what are you doing to locate *Majli?* I heard one of them mention his name."

"We know of no such person."

"He works for Qaderi! Call him!"

"The police will investigate the matter in due course."

"In due course? You need to act now!"

"The police will investigate the matter in due course."

"You're *morons,* all of you!" shouted Tyler as he was escorted out of the museum and over to his waiting taxi.

Half an hour later, Tyler was standing on the front porch of Youssef's house banging on the door. Then he remembered his key.

He had just let himself in when Youssef came bounding down the stairs. "I just heard what happened!" he exclaimed.

"Where's Majli?"

"He's disappeared."

"What do you mean, he's disappeared?"

"He's not answering his phone," said Youssef. "Sharifa's with the police now. They're trying to locate him."

"Sharifa's with the police?"

"She offered to help as soon as we heard. Faisal phoned and

wanted me to tell you he's still planning on attending tonight's gala."

"You're not planning to go through with that, are you?"

"Faisal insisted. A policeman will remain with him until Majli is found."

Tyler stared at Youssef in disbelief.

"I suggested putting things off," explained Youssef, "but Faisal responded by saying the longer we delay getting the tablet on its way, the more danger there is of more violence."

Tyler continued glaring at Youssef and did not reply.

"Why don't you take a few minutes," Youssef said gently, "while I take your cases upstairs. Let's meet in, say, half an hour?"

A cynical snort was Tyler's reply.

Youssef smiled and took Tyler's camera cases up to the office.

Tyler went into his room and sat on the bed. *If he hadn't gone back for his microphone and transmitter…* He stood and walked over to the small desk by the window. He opened his laptop, logged onto the internet, and saw that Val had forwarded him an email from Toy Soldier.

"Payment has been made, the date has been set," the message read. "Abu Nazer plans to have you killed Sunday, on a bus tour."

"So payment's been made," repeated Tyler. He minimized the email and opened the surveillance program on his laptop that had been receiving data from the modem on Qaderi's computer. Powered by the processor itself, the modem could broadcast information to a distance of up to fifty meters.

He took a quick glance at the nearly forty pages of transmitted text. *You're in there somewhere,* he thought.

After reading Toy Soldier's message again, Tyler noticed an added paragraph at the bottom.

"I've sent the mallet," Val said. "I know you said you didn't want it, but I sent it anyway. I'm afraid for you, Tyler – afraid you'll get yourself killed. Sharifa's been nothing but a distraction, and since meeting her you're behaving like this is some kind of vacation. Have you forgotten the reason you're there? Have you forgotten what Abu Nazer did? That bastard ripped out my heart! I thought you understood but I don't think you do. Not anymore. You've become a celebrity like the celebrities you interview. Popular – yes – but what's the point? Thank God for Zoe Gustaves, that's all I can say. I see in her what I used to see in you – passion. And if she seems impetuous, well, in my book that's forgivable, because at least she's over there trying to stop that monster. I wish I could say the same about you. But I can't. You've grown comfortable with your success. You don't care anymore. You've lost your rage. I wonder what kind of tragedy it will take for you to finally get it back. How many people does Abu Nazer have to kill before you get angry again?"

Tyler sat there, staring at the screen, not breathing, not blinking, his mouth open in shock. Suddenly, he sprang from his chair. "Lost my *rage?* Not *care?* How *dare* you!" he yelled, grabbing his phone. "You want anger? I'll give you anger! I'll give you a serving you'll never *forget!*"

CHAPTER 42

The phone kept ringing and ringing. *Where was she?* Tyler hung up and dialed again, but still there was no answer. He tried phoning Val's home number, but all he got was her answering machine. He finally tried calling her cell phone, but it was switched off.

Dammit, where the hell is she?

It was, of course, possible that Val had taken his advice and gone away. But surely she would have said something. But she hadn't. Not a peep. Something was wrong.

Stop it! You're overreacting. She's probably in the shower.

Climbing the stairs, Tyler tried forcing away the worry. But like a demon, it turned on him with graphic images of Val fighting for her life.

Youssef was waiting patiently by his desk when Tyler entered.

"Sorry I took so long," he explained. "I tried phoning my assistant, but no one was home. It's got me worried."

"The incident with Faisal has shaken me, as well," replied Youssef. "I'm sure she's all right."

"She should have been there."

"Perhaps she's with a friend?"

"It's still early morning in Austin, and we were messaging back and forth late last night. She should be home."

"Would you like to have someone go check on her?"

"I'll try her again once we're finished. She probably went out for breakfast."

"Are you certain? I really don't mind."

"Thanks. I'm sure she's all right."

Youssef nodded and took his seat.

The interview began much like Faisal's, with Tyler asking several introductory questions before turning to the subject of the tablet.

"Where did you acquire it?" he asked.

"In an Italian junk shop, if you can believe that!" replied Youssef with a laugh. "I had actually gone in for directions and saw this unusual coffee table in the corner. It had a gray stone top, which of course grabbed my attention, and when I looked it over, I noticed some inscriptions on the underside. I made an offer, which the owner accepted, and while helping me carry it to the car, he confided how glad he was to get rid of the ugly thing."

"If proved genuine, your tablet will create a firestorm of controversy. How does that make you feel?"

"Excited that we've discovered something written by the son of Abraham. Sad at the reaction of extremists wanting to exploit it. Look at what's happening already – riots, attacks, suicide bombs – it's out of control."

"Does this tempt you to destroy the tablet?"

"Isn't the destruction – or distortion – of truth what causes problems like this in the first place? No, we must press forward. I can only hope its message will bring peace and reconciliation to the world."

"Perfect, that's a wrap!" said Tyler, giving Youssef the thumbs-up. "That quote will be heard 'round the world."

"I wish I could take all the credit," said Youssef. "Good quotes are the result of good questions."

Tyler acknowledged the compliment with a nod.

A knock sounded on the door before it was opened.

"There is a telephone call for you, Dr. Tyler," said Mrs. Fedje. "Someone in America. A woman."

"Thanks. I'll be right down."

"You may take the call here, if you wish," said Youssef. "I'm off to meet with the director of the shipping company, to tell him we've been delayed. I'm assuming we'll have our letter of coverage by morning and can ship the tablet tomorrow."

"Are you sure you don't mind?"

"I insist." And with a wave, Youssef left the room.

Tyler picked up the phone and hit the lighted button on the console. "Val, is that you?" he asked.

"Tyler, it's Gloria. Your cell phone was switched off and I had to reach you."

"Hey, Gloria, what's up?"

"Something's happened – to Val – and it's bad."

Tyler stiffened.

"We were supposed to meet at our house for coffee," she said, "but Val never showed. I tried calling but couldn't get an answer. So I came over to see if she was all right. I thought maybe she'd fallen and broken her leg. When I went around back, the slider was open. When I went in, there was blood. The police are here now."

"I *told* her to leave town!" said Tyler.

"What do you mean, you told her to leave town?"

"I *begged* her to leave, but she wouldn't listen."

"Tyler, what's going on?"

Tyler sat and closed his eyes.

"Tyler?"

Tyler did not reply.

"Tyler!"

"Val and I – we've been working on something and it started getting dangerous."

"Working on what?"

"I can't say."

"What do you mean, you can't *say?* Val may be *dead* and the only thing you can say is, 'I can't say'?"

"I can't say, Gloria, all right? All I can tell you is things started getting dangerous and I told her to leave town. To go someplace safe."

"And she didn't."

"And she didn't."

"Who did this, Tyler?"

What should he say? What *could* he say? That Val was really Louise Kappelmann? That her husband had been murdered by the same killer who finally tracked her down?

Val was right. I've lost my rage.

Tyler remembered what Val had written in her email: *"How many people does Abu Nazer have to kill before you'll finally get angry again?"*

She'd seen it coming. Why hadn't he? How could this have *happened?*

It happened because someone had talked. Someone had told Abu Nazer who Val was and where she was. But who?

What was it Zoe had said? "My boss, Jackson Teague."

My God!

"Tyler, are you there?" asked Gloria.

"Where are you calling from?" asked Tyler.

"Your office. That's how I got this number."

"I need you to do me a favor."

"Name it."

"I need you to phone the Vice President."

"*What?*"

"Call the Vice President. His number's in the Rolodex on my desk."

"You mean, of the United *States?*"

"Use the code word 'Greenhouse' and they'll put you through. Tell the Vice President's secretary that you're calling for me."

"Tyler, I don't know..."

"Gloria, you have to do this!"

"Why don't you call him yourself?"

"I can't, not without explaining things I can't talk about right now. Please, you've got to do this."

"What do I tell him?"

"That the CIA has a leak. And his name is Jackson Teague."

CHAPTER 43

Vice President Sam Baker was in a special meeting with the President and left instructions that he was not to be disturbed.

A seasoned veteran of the cleverest attempts to circumvent those kinds of instructions, the Vice President's assistant, Dorothy Farmer, had listened to the full spectrum of excuses from Senators, Ambassadors, Generals, and everyone in between and beyond. Dorothy Farmer had heard it all.

Until today.

The telephone trilled politely amid the pattering of fingers on keyboards. Aides and secretaries, mostly young and eager, rushed along hallways with purpose in their step.

"Office of the Vice President," Dorothy answered. She had been sticking small yellow tabs on a document that indicated where Sam Baker was to sign.

"Yes, hello, my name is Gloria Sandborn," Gloria said. "I'm calling at the request of Dr. Rutherford Tyler. Is the Vice President available, please?"

The caller's courteous manner let Dorothy know she was not talking to a bureaucrat. But how did a private citizen get hold of this number?

"I'm sorry but you should ring the switchboard," Dorothy said. "Someone there will be able to help you."

"Please, I must speak with Vice President Baker. It's an emergency!"

Emergency. In Dorothy's books, the "e" word was almost as insulting as the "f" word. And virtually as inane.

"Do you have the switchboard number?" asked Dorothy.

"This is for Greenhouse," said Gloria, remembering the necessity of quoting that code word.

"I beg your pardon?" asked Dorothy, suddenly attentive. She set aside the document and moved her mouse to the "Clearance" icon, which brought a listing up on her screen.

"This is for Greenhouse," repeated Gloria.

Dorothy scrolled down the list until she saw "Greenhouse." She clicked once, and Tyler's details appeared. Dorothy read the information, noting that Rutherford Tyler had been given clearance to be put through.

"Your name again?" asked Dorothy, seeing Val Johnson as the other name listed with Tyler's.

"Gloria Sandborn. I'm Dr. Tyler's assistant."

"I'm sorry, Ms. Sandborn, but I don't see your name."

"But this is important! Dr. Tyler's in the middle of an emergency and asked me to give Mr. Baker some information."

"What's the nature of this emergency?" Dorothy asked, one eyebrow raised skeptically. *There was the "e" word again.*

"It has to do with a leak at the CIA involving someone named Jackson Teague."

At that moment, in an Agency jet high above the Great Plains, Jackson Teague was talking on the phone with the CIA dispatcher. "This woman – what's her name?"

"Gloria Sandborn," answered the dispatcher.

"Has Ms. Sandborn been put through?"

"She's talking with his secretary as we speak. Something about you and a Company leak. A text version of the conversation is being transmitted to your printer."

"Initiate intercept. Priority one."

"Yes, sir."

Dorothy Farmer again read the information on her screen. Rutherford Tyler and Val Johnson were the only people with Greenhouse clearance. And Dorothy was not about to put through a crank call about a leak at the CIA.

"You have my sympathies, Ms. Sandborn," Dorothy said diplomatically.

"I don't need your sympathies!" shouted Gloria. "I need to speak with Mr. *Baker!* Please! Dr. Tyler asked me to make this call."

"Why didn't he ring Mr. Baker himself?"

"H's in Cairo and probably couldn't get a line out of the country. All I know is when I phoned him with some bad news, he asked me to call the Vice President. And that's what I'm trying to do."

"I'm sorry, but you'll have to submit your request through the proper channels. As a courtesy, I'll take your name and number. Alternatively, you can try the State Department."

"For God's *sake!*"

"I'm afraid that's all I can do."

A brief burst of static occurred on the line.

"This is a priority one intercept," the CIA dispatcher said. "Go ahead, please."

"Ms. Farmer, this is Jackson Teague. Thank you, Ms. Sandborn, I'll take it from here."

"But—"

Gloria's connection was abruptly terminated, leaving Teague on the line with Dorothy Farmer.

"Ms. Farmer, my clearance is Juliet, November, Eleven," he said. "I repeat: Juliet, November, Eleven."

Dorothy Farmer closed the "Greenhouse" window and moved the cursor up to the CIA icon. She clicked it and a menu was displayed. She chose "Juliet" and another menu appeared. She clicked on "November" and found number eleven.

Jackson Teague.

Dorothy clicked on Teague's name.

The word "paperclip" appeared on the screen.

"Your password, please," requested Dorothy, knowing these words were updated weekly and sometimes daily.

"Paperclip," answered Teague.

"You've been confirmed."

"Patch me through to the Vice President."

In the paneled White House Situation Room, the President and Vice President were seated at a large table with CIA Director William Green, Director of Operations Philip Trent, General Noah Thomas, and several other advisors. All eyes were on General Thomas, who was giving an assessment of the escalating Middle Eastern crisis. Behind him, a digital map of Israel glowed on an illuminated screen. To one side was the circular Great Seal of the United States.

"Qaderi's tablet is electrifying fanatics like the *gibburim*," the general was saying. "They claim it's their license to get rid of the Arabs."

"Assuming the tablet's authenticated," said the President.

"Yes, sir. If that happens, *Qamat* has promised suicide bombings like we've never seen. They just blew up a bus in Tel Aviv, and Wassim Jafar is promising more. Israel wants our latest intel on the location of Jafar's training camps. They're proposing a surgical strike. Neat and clean."

"It's never neat and clean," said Baker. "We need to calm things down.

Get both sides talking."

"Israel's past that," Thomas replied. "The USS George Washington is already in the Eastern Med and I've placed it on alert in case things escalate."

"Which they probably will if we don't defuse the situation," said Baker. "Mr. President, we've got to stop Israel from retaliating. It won't solve a thing."

"They see it as justice," said Thomas.

"Has justice ever been achieved by retaliation?" asked Baker. "Do the books ever get balanced?"

The General did not reply.

"Exactly!" said Baker. "Look, I'm not suggesting we do nothing. Of course there needs to be accountability. And, at times, restitution. And there are diplomatic channels to carry that out. But we've got to go deeper. We've got to change the way people think. Revive the concept of community. Of treating others the way they want to be treated. And to do that, we need to get people talking. And listening! And not just the leaders, but people on the street. I've seen it happen. It can happen again."

The President looked at Director Green. "Bill, what's DCI's take on this?"

A tall, lean man with thinning hair, Green sat forward. "*Qamat* wants the tablet destroyed and sources tell us they've got someone in Cairo trying to get Qaderi to hand it over."

"Is Qaderi sympathetic to their cause?" asked the President.

"It's unlikely he'll cooperate," said Green, who then turned to Trent. "Philip, what's your assessment? Your people have been working on this."

"Qaderi's a collector," said Trent, "A businessman."

"How much do we know about him?" asked the President.

"Intel is pretty sketchy. He seems to have popped out of obscurity almost overnight. He's wealthy and lives in a ritzy part of Cairo."

"Is he Muslim or Coptic?" asked the President.

"Secular," answered Trent.

"So he has no religious aspirations for the tablet?"

"Everything we know thus far suggests he's in it for the money. If so, surrendering the tablet to Qamat would be counterproductive.

That being said, Qamat may simply put a bullet in his head and take a sledge hammer to the thing."

"Which may not be such a bad thing," said Green. "Not that I'm hoping Qaderi takes a bullet, but if that tablet gets destroyed, a lot of problems will go away. Take this fake Jerusalem Post ad…"

"Why would someone do that?" asked the President. "Who stands to gain from a stunt like that?"

"Qaderi, for one," said Trent. "The furor it's created has increased the value of his tablet exponentially. It's now said to be worth over a hundred million dollars."

"Where does Abu Nazer fit into this?" asked Baker, just as the phone in front of him buzzed.

"We know he wants the tablet but we're not sure why," answered Trent.

"Isn't it obvious?" asked General Thomas. "Inflaming religious tensions creates all sorts of opportunity for a terrorist with his kind of skills."

Baker's phone buzzed again and he picked it up. "Yes?" he said in a low voice, turning discreetly away from the others.

"A priority one intercept from the CIA, Mr. Vice President."

"Put it through."

"Mr. Vice President, this is Jackson Teague. We have a crisis."

The Vice President listened to what Teague had to say.

"One moment," Baker said, looking over at the President. "Mr. President, may I redirect this to speaker? It's priority one, from Jackson Teague."

The President turned to the others. "Will you excuse us, please?"

"Of course, Mr. President."

Green and Trent remained seated while the others rose.

"You, too, Bill," said the President.

"But Teague is one of mine," Green replied.

An unwavering stare was the President's answer.

"Of course, Mr. President," said Green.

He and Trent left with the others.

"What's going on?" the President asked Baker once the room was clear.

"It involves Rutherford Tyler."

"The journalist?"

Baker nodded. "He's in Cairo and he's in the middle of a situation that relates directly to what we've been talking about."

"Switch it over."

Sam Baker punched a button and replaced the receiver.

"Mr. Teague, we're now on speaker," said Baker. "I'm alone with the President and he can hear everything we have to say."

"Please forgive the intrusion Mr. President, Mr. Vice President. It was imperative that I speak with you immediately."

"What's going on?" asked the President.

"We've been monitoring a call from a woman claiming to be Rutherford Tyler's assistant. This woman is lying about her position; however, the purpose of her call is genuine."

"And that is?"

"A leak at the Agency."

"Press leaks are part of the game," said the President.

"This isn't a press leak," replied Teague.

"Then what are we talking about?"

"Sir, are you aware of a covert operation called Nightingale?"

In the dim lights of the paneled Situation Room, Sam Baker and the President looked at one other.

"Did I hear you correctly?" asked the President.

"Yes, sir, you did."

"I think you'd better explain."

"Sir, we have circumstantial evidence which suggests the Nightingale program has metastasized."

"That program was proposed during a previous administration and never approved, for obvious reasons. The United States, apart from military operations in times of war, does not employ or sanction the use of assassins."

"Yes, sir."

"Then how can a non-existent program metastasize?"

"Because certain individuals within the CIA – I don't yet know who – decided to incubate the concept without anyone's knowledge or approval. I heard about it from Senator Ashford, who was trying to track down those responsible. I also found out that she was working with you, Mr. Vice President. Sir, I don't need to point out the consequences of what happened as a result of those investigations. Senator Ashford was assassinated, and you nearly were. It goes without saying that someone does not want Nightingale exposed."

"Where is this leading?" asked the President.

"Nightingale has been training and protecting a team of terrorists. One of those terrorists is Abu Nazer."

"So this leak you're referring to—"

"—Is protecting Abu Nazer. Telling him when and where we've set a trap, how close we are, what we're planning next."

"And you're trying to identify this leak?"

"Yes, sir, very quietly. Which is why I've been keeping my people away from this. I don't want them asking questions and setting off alarms."

"What's this got to do with Tyler?" asked Baker.

"He's in Cairo and he's planning to kill Abu Nazer."

Baker bolted from his chair. "*Tyler?*"

"Yes, sir. Thanks to monitored communications out of his office, we became aware that a rifle was recently shipped to him."

"Are you sure about this?"

"FedEx confirmed it. And we've since confiscated it."

"But Tyler's a journalist."

"Who's using his interview with Qaderi as a cover for a plot that we believe was hatched by his assistant, Val Johnson, also known as Louise Kappelmann, widow of murdered editor, Stephen Kappelmann."

"I can't believe it," said Baker.

"Tyler's foolish if he thinks he can kill Abu Nazer. The best agents in the world haven't been able to do it, so it's both ludicrous and suicidal of Tyler to think he could succeed. That said, and despite the odds against him, it's vital that he not be given the chance to try."

"Why is that?" asked the President.

"We need Abu Nazer to identify Nightingale. And because Abu Nazer is somewhere in Cairo, I want to spread the word that we'll make him a deal."

"What kind of a deal?"

"Immunity in exchange for his cooperation."

"That's negotiating with a terrorist!" declared Baker. "And not just any terrorist, but the most wanted name on the list!"

"Sir, this isn't a hostage situation, so offering a deal doesn't necessarily violate policy."

"That's one hell of a stretch!" said Baker.

"Which nets us the people responsible for training and protecting

Abu Nazer and other terrorists like him. In other words, we kill the head of the serpent."

"You're actually proposing that we allow Abu Nazer to go *free?*" asked the President.

"As a last resort. The offer of immunity may be enough to force Nightingale into committing an error."

"And it may not," said Baker.

"Then we have no choice."

"And Tyler? What about him?"

"We'll be keeping a close eye on him. Intel leads us to believe Abu Nazer will try to take him out tomorrow, while he's on a bus tour."

"*What?*" shouted Baker.

"Don't worry, Abu Nazer won't succeed," Teague added quickly. "My people will be there to protect him."

"What if they fail?"

"Like I said, my people will be with him all the way. And by sticking with Tyler, we'll be in a perfect position not only to foil the attack, but also communicate the deal."

"You're using the man for *bait?*"

"Sir, I know that Tyler's a friend—"

"Watch yourself, mister! His being a friend has nothing to do with it."

"This isn't as calloused as it seems. Tyler went to Cairo to conduct an interview, and in doing so placed himself in this situation. In the process of tracking Abu Nazer, we became aware of the plot against Tyler, and we will do everything possible to protect him."

"How do you plan to do that when you're not even sure which of your people is working for Nightingale?"

Teague ran a hand across his forehead. He realized his career – and Tyler's life – was in the hands of an analyst he sent away on stress leave. "Gentlemen, I have the utmost faith in my people."

"And they'll protect Tyler at all costs?" asked the President.

"You have my word," said Teague.

"Are you certain there's no other option?"

"No, sir, not in my view."

"You're placing a lot on the line here," said the President. "Your career is going to take a nasty – and perhaps fatal – fall if something goes wrong."

"I'll risk it."

"Tyler's risking a hell of a lot more," said Baker curtly.

"And my people will be with him all the way," reiterated Teague. "Not only have we never come this close to identifying Abu Nazer before, but this operation could remove him from the mix. Not only that, we have the chance to identify Nightingale, who supplies and protects dozens of these kinds of killers."

"What do you think, Sam?" the President asked Baker.

"My concern is how the CIA can guarantee Tyler's safety when they can't even be sure which of their people is the leak? The person Teague thinks is watching Tyler's back may well be the one who tries to kill him."

"Like I said, I have the utmost faith in my people," Teague said again.

"I don't like it," said Baker.

"I don't think we can afford to pass up this opportunity," responded the President. "Abu Nazer may be our only means of identifying and stopping Nightingale."

Baker made a gesture of surrender and sat.

"I've asked you this before, but I'll ask it one more time," said the President. "Do I have your full assurance that you'll protect Tyler?"

"Absolutely," said Teague.

The President nodded. "Then go ahead."

CHAPTER 44

Mena House is one of the world's most enchanting hotels – and for good reason. An oasis of romance and splendor, it can easily transport one into the pages of the Arabian Nights, where jasmine-scented breezes swirl around mysteries as ancient as the desert. Originally built in the 1800s as a hunting lodge for the King of Egypt, the renovated and expanded Mena House of today resembles the legendary Hanging Gardens of Babylon, with its stepped terraces, graceful arches, palm trees, pools, and shaded balconies.

Tonight, however, the enchantment was tempered by the presence of over two hundred Egyptian soldiers and riot police patrolling the grounds.

Not only had they sealed off the hotel from a crowd of protestors chanting anti-Israeli slogans, but they were especially noticeable around the main entrance. Extensive television coverage had been lured not only by the anticipated announcement about the tablet, but also by the spectacular guest list. Dignitaries from film, television, music, business, industry, arts and antiquities would be present, along with five different ambassadors – among them, U.S. Ambassador Marjorie Reynolds.

With the majestic floodlit Pyramids illuminated against the evening sky, the black limousine crept slowly up the drive and stopped, its mirrored windows reflecting a line of international reporters speaking into cameras. English, Arabic, Hebrew, German, French, Chinese, Spanish – the world media had descended on Mena House.

The limousine stopped and a uniformed attendant opened the door.

The first to step out was Qaderi, who waved to a crowd of carefully chosen supporters and fans. A smiling Sharifa followed after him, looking poised and elegant in a white gown that accentuated an emerald necklace. The last to step out was Tyler, looking tense.

Several reporters pushed forward into the brilliant wash of light.

"Mr. Qaderi, is the tablet genuine?" one of them called out, as more than a dozen microphones were thrust forward.

A burst of gunfire erupted in the distance and with it a din of shouting. Everyone paused and looked nervously around, then again focused on Qaderi.

"I will not preempt Dr. Woolley's exciting announcement," Youssef replied.

"Exciting in what way?" asked the reporter.

Youssef wagged a finger and smiled, and a series of additional questions quickly followed. Mr. Qaderi, we've heard the tablet is now worth over one hundred million dollars. Is that true? Mr. Qaderi, is it true the Saudis want to purchase the tablet? What about the American Jewish League? Have they made a bid?

"In due course, my friends, in due course," replied Youssef. "What I can say, however, is how honored I am to have one of the world's most respected journalists on our team – Dr. Rutherford Tyler – whose photos of the tablet are on display inside. Dr. Tyler's photos are set to become the official images that will soon be seen around the world."

Lights and cameras focused on Tyler as another series of questions were shouted. Dr. Tyler, what was your reaction when you first saw the tablet? Do you think the tablet is genuine? If radical Jews try to use the tablet to drive Arabs from Palestine, what will the American government's response be?

Tyler held up his hands and the reporters grew silent.

"Youssef Qaderi owns the world's most exciting artifact, and this is his night." And with a terse wave, Tyler stepped past the reporters and started for the entrance.

Suddenly, over the cries of onlookers came a shout: "Tyler! Hey, Tyler – over here!"

Tyler stopped and looked at the crowd, where a hand was waving frantically. Tyler shook his head when he saw the familiar grin of Johnny Bill Sandborn. With a chuckle he approached the barricade just as Johnny Bill squeezed to the front.

Two soldiers moved quickly forward.

"It's okay, he's a friend," said Tyler.

"This man, he is known to you, Dr. Tyler?" asked one of the guards.

"Sure is. Mind letting him through?"

The guards parted the barricades to screams from Tyler's fans.

"Dang, it's good to see ya!" Johnny Bill exclaimed. He was dressed in blue jeans, checkered shirt and striped tie. His hair was tied back in a ponytail.

"What are you doing here?" asked Tyler. *And does he know about Val?*

"Business trip," answered Johnny Bill.

Tyler gave Johnny Bill a dubious look. "You? In Cairo? On business?"

"What, you think you're the only jetsetter in da 'hood?" He laughed and slapped Tyler on the arm. "Besides, I got somethin' for ya. Special delivery. Cameras and film."

Tyler grew serious. "Did you say cameras and film?"

"Val insisted I bring 'em over."

"Then you don't know about Val?" he asked.

"Know what?"

"Look, I need you to bring the case and meet me tomorrow at Al-Medina Tours," he said, guiding Johnny Bill toward the carpeted walkway, where Sharifa and Youssef stood waiting.

"You got it," Johnny Bill said. "By golly, is that Shay-reefa? Them kids o' mine is still talkin' about you!" He stepped over and gave her a burly hug.

"Johnny Bill Sandborn, meet Youssef Qaderi," said Tyler.

"Nice to meet ya," Johnny Bill said, sticking out a hand, which Youssef hesitantly shook.

"Come on, let's head on in," Tyler said, leading Johnny Bill toward the entrance.

"They got free liquor inside?"

"As much as you want."

"Hot damn!" said Johnny Bill, rubbing his hands together eagerly.

"Who is that?" Youssef whispered irritably.

"A friend of Tyler's," Sharifa replied. "From Austin. An auto mechanic."

"An *auto mechanic?* Who invited him? What's he doing here?"

"I've no idea."

Across town, in the darkened parking lot of Al-Medina Tours, Tariq held a tiny magnesium flashlight in his teeth while he worked under tour bus #7.

He warmed a lump of gray plastic material in his hands and mashed it up onto the undercarriage of the bus near the fuel tank. He then reached into his shirt pocket and withdrew a remote detonator. He uncoiled an antenna wire, pushed the detonator into the lump, then repeated the procedure with a second lump near the front of the bus.

Switching off his light, Tariq slid out from under the bus and climbed up into a crouching position. After scanning the parking lot to make sure no one was around, he moved quickly along the chain link fence to the gate. In less than a minute, he was gone.

From his position in the darkened doorway of a neighboring building, Majli waited until he was sure Tariq was out of sight. Dashing across the street, he entered the parking lot through the same gap in the fence Tariq had used.

He located bus #7 and slid beneath it. With his penlight, he inspected the undercarriage.

Majli smiled when he saw the two lumps of plastique explosive in place with their detonators.

Two lumps would be more than enough to incinerate everyone on the bus.

CHAPTER 45

The exotic strains of reed pipes and zithers mingled with the murmurs and laughter of nearly four hundred people filling the lavish grand ballroom. Tuxedoed waiters roamed the floor carrying silver trays piled high with hors d'oeuvres. Others followed with Champagne and sparkling pomegranate cordial.

While Youssef was being introduced to U.S. Ambassador Marjorie Reynolds, Tyler circulated through the crowd trying to find Zoe. It was not an easy matter, as people constantly stopped him to shake hands, make introductions or gush compliments.

He was making his way toward the lobby when he was confronted by three sisters in flowing, brightly-colored dresses. They curtsied, asked for Tyler's autograph, then launched into recollections of their favorite interviews. Keith Urban was mentioned and the sisters laughed at the memory of Tyler singing with Keith's band.

"Dr. Tyler, you are a very funny man," one of them giggled, after which they continued chattering, agreeing, disagreeing, overriding and interrupting one another.

Tyler looked on with a dazed expression.

"Forgive me, but I must steal Dr. Tyler," Sharifa said, stepping into their midst. She took Tyler by the arm and led him away.

The three sisters stared after them for several seconds before continuing their animated conversation.

"I really hate being rude," he said, "but greeting people is the last thing I want to be doing right now."

"I know."

"I tried reasoning with Val but she wouldn't listen."

"It's not your fault. You did everything you could."

"I should have tried harder."

Sharifa squeezed Tyler on the arm. "How'd they find out where she was?" she asked.

Tyler snorted bitterly. "The CIA."

"You mean that young woman who came to the house?"

"Not Zoe. Her boss," said Tyler spotting Zoe at about the same moment she spotted him. She waved and made her way through the crowd.

"Sorry I'm late," she said, shifting uncomfortably in her black gown. It was floor-length and tied around the neck, leaving her shoulders and upper back bare. Her hair was its usual structured mess.

Tyler stared at Zoe with an expression she couldn't quite read.

"Am I interrupting?" Zoe asked, looking back and forth between Tyler and Sharifa.

"Of course not," said Tyler. His eyes held Zoe's for a moment.

"Been a while since I've worn one of these," she said with an embarrassed smile.

"No room for a holster, I see."

"Whatever is a girl to do?"

"Tyler's forgetting his manners," Sharifa said, extending her hand. "Sharifa al Rashid, personal assistant to Youssef Qaderi."

"Zoe Gustaves, American Embassy."

"May we get you something to drink?"

"Thanks, but not right now. I'd like a word with Tyler, though, if I may."

"Of course," Sharifa said, turning to Tyler. "You're on after Youssef."

Tyler nodded and smiled.

"Nice to meet you, Ms. Gustaves."

"Same here."

Sharifa kissed her finger and touched it to Tyler's lips, then moved off to find Youssef.

"She's gorgeous. Are you two an item?"

"You look stunning," replied Tyler. He took Zoe by the arm and ushered her to the rear of the ballroom. To his left, he saw Johnny Bill talking to half a dozen Arab businessmen.

"You don't look half bad yourself," Zoe replied. "But we both know the reason I'm here, so why don't we get right to it."

"You don't let your guard down for a minute, do you?"

"You've already played me twice, Tyler, and it's not going to happen again. Now what the hell is going on? And please don't try screwing with me a third time because I will have Val brought in."

"I'm afraid it's too late for that."

"What are you talking about?"

"Val's missing. She's probably dead."

"*What?*"

"I just got the news."

"Who from?"

"A family friend who was supposed to have had coffee with her. When Val didn't show, she went to check on her and found the house had been broken into. There was blood all over the floor."

Zoe stared at him, stunned.

"Look, I know this isn't your fault," said Tyler. "But that asshole, Teague, is another matter."

"Whoa, hang on there, back up!" said Zoe. "Teague wouldn't do something like that."

"Other than you, he's the only person who knew where Val was. Knew *who* she was."

"I can't believe it. Not Teague."

"Believe it. He's not who he seems."

"I could say the same about you."

Tyler looked quizzically at Zoe.

"The *rifle,* Tyler!"

"For God's sake, lower your voice!" said Tyler. He led her into the lobby, past the elegant cinnamon and gold reception counter and down an empty corridor, where they could talk. A wall of plate glass windows framed by thick Arabesque arches looked out on the illuminated Pyramids.

"All right, start talking," said Zoe. "Tell me why Val shipped you a single shot twenty-two. You're messing with us, Tyler! I know it!"

"*I'm* not doing anything! It was probably the only weapon she could find."

"You argued back and forth with her about sending it, so don't tell me it's the only weapon she could find, as if this was some kind of impulsive decision. She told you she sent the mallet. It's even got its own special name. But then an old relic of a rifle arrives. Now, what the hell's going on?"

"For the last time, I am not here to kill Abu Nazer. I'm here to expose him."

"If you're playing me again…"

"I'm not, I swear."

"Expose him how?" she asked.

"That's where I need your help."

"What do you mean?"

"Are you any good with computers?"

"Good enough. Why?"

Tyler handed her a slip of paper.

"What am I looking at?" she asked.

"Numbers to a bank account in Switzerland."

"Whose is it?"

"I don't know."

"Where'd you get it?"

"From the small modem I plugged into the back of Qaderi's computer. It transmitted everything typed on his keyboard to my laptop."

"So you think Qaderi is Abu Nazer?"

"Him or Majli – I don't know. What we need is proof, which that number should provide."

"And you want me to – what – run a trace?"

"Wouldn't do any good. The Swiss will never release information about the owner of that account."

"Then what am I doing?"

"Hacking into the account and emailing a copy of the statement to Vice President Baker. It should provide some kind of clue as to who owns it, as well as provide a record of who deposited funds into it. If we're lucky, it'll lead all the way back to Nightingale."

"What about a password?" asked Zoe.

"Should be in his computer. The modem only gave me an account number, so I presume it's stored on the hard drive and automatically prompts whenever someone accesses the account."

"Either that or he uses a drag-and-click function from a flash drive."

"Well, what do you know? Brains on top of beauty."

Zoe raised a skeptical eyebrow. "Do not tell me you actually pick up women with that line."

"Why, are you wanting to be picked up?"

"Tyler, do not piss me off!"

"You're the one who brought it up."

"Shut up and tell me how I get into the house."

Tyler grinned and handed Zoe a key. It had smooth surfaces with lots of tiny holes.

"Pin lock – fancy and expensive," she said, looking it over. "I don't suppose he gave you the alarm code?"

"It'll be off. The housekeeper's home."

Zoe nodded. "When do I leave?"

"We leave after my speech."

"You mean I gotta sit through a speech?"

"What's wrong with that?"

"Don't you think we have more important things to do? As in stopping a terrorist?"

"It's not like I'm asking you to get a root canal."

"Wouldn't know. I've never heard you speak."

"I give my speech. Then we go."

"Look, no offense, but I'm assuming we don't have all night to do this. Why don't you stay here and do your thing, while I go and do mine?"

"Because we *are* trying to stop a terrorist and one of us needs to stand guard."

"Against whom? The housekeeper? For God's sake, Tyler, she's a Smurf. I remember her. Pudgy little thing."

"We both go."

"I'm trained for this. You're not."

"*We both go,* Zoe! Either we do this my way or I'll find someone else."

"Easy, don't pop a cork. You're the boss."

Tyler shook his head and led Zoe back into the ballroom in time to hear Sharifa tapping the microphone.

"Ladies and gentlemen, may I have your attention?" Sharifa announced.

The crowd grew quiet and turned toward the stage.

"Meet you back here when I'm done," whispered Tyler.

Zoe nodded and Tyler headed for the stage.

"First, I'd like to welcome each and every one of you on this very special night," Sharifa continued. "As you know, Cairo's own Youssef Qaderi has recovered what could well be one of the most important archaeological treasures of all time. To explain what I'm talking about, may I present the eminent scholar, Dr. Allan Woolley!"

The crowd broke into applause as a smiling Allan Woolley ascended the stage. Once the clapping had subsided, Woolley opened with a few lines from *The Arabian Nights,* after which he described the panoramic beauty of the northern Sinai and how it must have looked to Sir Edmund George Clayton in 1919.

While Woolley rhapsodized, Zoe slipped out of the ballroom, walked past the reception counter and out to where a line of taxis stood waiting by the curb. She hurried to the first one and opened the door.

"Zamalek," she said, climbing in.

Inside the ballroom, Woolley was saying, "Naturally, the question on everyone's mind is whether or not the tablet is genuine." He paused and gazed out over the hundreds of expectant faces staring back at him. This was his moment. "After careful analysis with my esteemed colleague, Dr. Faisal Mostafa, I am pleased to announce…the tablet is *real!*"

The crowd gasped just as Woolley swept a hand dramatically to his left.

"Ladies and gentlemen," cried Woolley triumphantly, "Mr. Youssef *Qaderi!*"

Beaming brightly, Qaderi stepped onto the stage to an explosion of flashbulbs and applause.

Tyler was applauding with those around him when Tim Odell stepped up to his side.

"Dr. Tyler, how nice to see you."

Tyler responded with a blank expression.

"Tim Odell. I work with Zoe."

Tyler nodded.

"Where is she, have you seen her?" asked Tim.

"Back of the room," answered Tyler. He caught a glimpse of Faisal standing off by himself, despondently staring at the floor, hands folded in front of him.

"Good evening, distinguished guests," Youssef said into the microphone, drawing Tyler's attention. "The Ishmael tablet has finally come home!"

The statement brought another round of thunderous applause.

It took just under twenty minutes for the taxi to reach Zamalek, and when they were half a block from Youssef's house, Zoe told the driver to stop. She paid him, got out of the cab and walked the rest of the way on foot.

Using Tyler's key, Zoe let herself in, being careful to close the door quietly. She tiptoed to the darkened stairwell and looked up. The blare of laughter spilled down the stairwell from a television set in the living room. With her shoes and purse in one hand, Zoe hoisted her gown and climbed quietly up the stairs to the third floor. Entering the office, she closed the door.

Without turning on a light, Zoe tiptoed over to the desk and sat down in front of the computer. When she moved the mouse, the screen came to life.

Operating by the light of the monitor, Zoe accessed the Credit Suisse website. She entered the account number, and a small window appeared with ten asterisks inside it. Zoe held her breath and tapped "Enter."

Accepting the prompted password, the Credit Suisse website lit up with page after page of deposits and withdrawals – mostly electronic, but sometimes cash – always in amounts exceeding one hundred thousand dollars. Some transfers had been made in Swiss Francs or Euros, as identified by the listed exchange rates, with the primary destination account listed as – Zoe's eyes widened – Youssef Qaderi!

"My God!" exclaimed Zoe, as she scanned nearly seven years' worth of transactions totaling more than two hundred million dollars.

She addressed an email to Teague, attached a copy of the file and hit "Send."

A thump in the stairwell startled her.

Zoe hit the monitor's power button, grabbed her purse and ran silently to the door. She pressed herself against the wall and took out her pistol.

A long minute of silence ticked by.

Zoe was just lowering her gun when her cell phone rang. Tearing open her purse, she grabbed her phone.

"*What?*" she whispered harshly into the instrument.

"Zoe, is that you?" asked Tim.

"What do you want?"

"I can barely hear you. What's going on?"

Tim's mouth dropped open when Zoe told him where she was and what she had found.

"Are you sure, I mean *really* sure?" asked Tim.

"Positive! And Tyler's the one who figured it out. Qaderi's Abu Nazer! We've got proof!"

"Tyler? But, how…?"

"Not now! Is he there?"

"Yeah, he just finished speaking."

"Get him!"

Tim took the phone to Tyler, who was receiving congratulations from a group of journalists.

"It's Zoe. She wants to talk with you."

"Where is she?" asked Tyler, excusing himself.

"Qaderi's house."

Tyler grabbed the phone and put it to his ear. "What the *hell* do you think you're doing?"

"Qaderi – he's Abu Nazer!"

"Dammit, Zoe—"

"It's all here, just like you said! Deposits, withdrawals, transfers totaling over two hundred million. He's hurting for money right now, though. Looks like he really needs cash."

"I want you to get out of there!"

"This is it, Tyler! The proof that we need!"

"Get *out* of there! Baker can take it from here."

Tyler could hear Zoe draw in a quick breath. "Tell me you sent Baker a copy."

"I was about to…"

"Zoe, you've got to do that! We need him to trace those numbers."

"I heard a noise. I had to hide."

"That's *exactly* why I didn't want you doing this alone!"

"It was probably the housekeeper. Everything's cool."

"Then send Baker that statement and *get out of there!* I mean it. No screwing around."

"Yes, Daddy."

"Will you quit—?"

"Hang on a minute, I heard something."

Tim eyed Tyler. "Is everything all right?"

"Fine," said Tyler, covering the phone.

"Did Zoe tell you what she found?"

"What did she tell you?" asked Tyler.

"She told me about Qaderi's bank statement and his numbered account! Tyler, we've got him!"

Tyler put the phone back to his ear. "Zoe, what's going—" He paused when he heard the sound of scuffling. "Zoe?"

Suddenly, a scream.

Then silence.

And what remained in that vacuum of silence was an echoing memory of the name Zoe had screamed.

Majli.

CHAPTER 46

The Gulfstream was starting its descent when an agent brought Teague a folder containing more than a hundred pages.

"What's this?" he asked.

"A bank statement from Gustaves," the agent replied. "She sent it to the office and April forwarded it on to us."

Teague read the statement over. "Get hold of Cooke and have him run traces on these numbers," he said, handing the folder back.

"Yes, sir," the agent replied.

Teague went to the galley, poured a cup of coffee and took it to the rear of the plane. He paused beside Val, who was staring angrily out the window.

"How you feeling?" he asked, offering her the coffee.

"I was assaulted by your men! How the hell do you think I'm feeling?"

Teague's normally stern features softened into a sympathetic smile. "I'm sorry, really I am," he said, sitting across from her. "But it was critical we make it look like you were murdered. We even splashed A-negative blood on the floor of Tyler's house. If Abu Nazer ever finds out this was a rescue, you're still a target."

"How did he find out where I was in the first place?"

Teague sat back, avoiding her gaze.

"Someone at Langley?" Val asked pointedly.

Teague eyed Val for a moment then nodded. Denial of something she probably already knew would only make him look foolish.

"And so, out of the kindness of your heart, you came to get me?"

"We were concerned for your safety," said Teague.

"That's a load of crap and you know it. I'm sitting here for one reason and one reason only: you need something. So why not drop the Good Samaritan act and tell me what it is?"

"All right," replied Teague, his expression hardening. "I want to know why Tyler's in Cairo."

"He's a journalist on an assignment."

"*That's* a load of crap and *you* know it!"

"What other reason would there be?"

"To kill Abu Nazer," answered Teague, his eyes fixed on Val, who looked away. "We confiscated the mallet, or whatever you call it. You didn't honestly think you could get away it, did you?"

"Who says I'm plotting to kill Abu Nazer?"

"You shipped Tyler a *rifle*."

"Does shipping him a rifle mean I'm plotting to kill someone?"

"Then why'd you send it?"

Val folded her arms and looked out the window into the night.

"Look," said Teague, softening his tone. "I can understand why you'd want Abu Nazer dead. What he did was unimaginable."

"That's not the reason I sent it."

"Then why?"

"Tyler's in danger. He needs protection."

"You don't expect me to believe that, do you?"

"Believe whatever you want."

"Well, I will not allow Abu Nazer to be killed. There's too much at stake."

"What, exactly, is at stake, Mr. Teague?"

"That's not your concern."

With a shrug, Val looked out the window.

Teague leaped to his feet and started to storm away. But Val was right. He did need something and he needed it now. With a calming breath, he sat back down.

Val looked at him coldly. "Something else?"

"I need to know who he is."

"Who?"

"Abu Nazer."

"What makes you think I know?"

"Because you were planning to kill him!"

"Your words, not mine."

"Will you quit being so evasive? I'm running out of time!"

"Sorry to hear that. But like you said, it's not my concern."

"You know I'm not at liberty to—"

"Then I have nothing to say."

Teague held up a hand. "To tell you any details of what's going on," he continued, finishing his sentence. "But I can tell you this: We need Abu Nazer, we need him alive, and we need him now. I'm not exaggerating when I say it's a matter of national security."

"How so?"

"I can't say. But I'm asking you to *please* tell me what you know."

"All right, I'll tell you what I know," Val said, folding her arms and staring impassively at Teague. "I know the CIA has a leak. And I'm betting you don't know who it is. I'm also betting this leak has connections to Abu Nazer, but because you don't know who Abu Nazer is, you need someone to identify him so that you can take him into custody and make him talk. And that's why you went to the trouble of rescuing me. How am I doing?"

Teague slumped back in his seat and massaged his eyelids.

"As much as I'd like to help," added Val, "the fact is, I don't trust you. How do I know you're not the leak?"

Teague chuckled and shook his head.

"I guess I deserved that," he said. "And I honestly don't know what I can say to convince you otherwise. Your friend, Ms. Sandborn, doesn't trust me and I know Tyler doesn't, either. He had her phone Vice President Baker to tell him that I was the leak."

Val looked guardedly at Teague.

"I intercepted the call," said Teague, "and described the situation to both the President and Vice President. And, yes, you're right. I do need you to identify Abu Nazer, because I want to take him alive and find out who the leak is. I'm also hoping to find a clue in a Credit Suisse bank statement I just received."

"Then Tyler got it!" exclaimed Val.

Teague stared dumbfounded at Val. "How do you know about that?" he finally asked.

"That's the reason Tyler's in Cairo. To locate Abu Nazer's bank account so that Vice President Baker can trace it to Nightingale."

"How the hell do you know about *Nightingale?*"

Val hesitated then said, "From Tyler."

"How did *he* find out?"

Val shrugged.

"So he's not there to kill Abu Nazer?" asked Teague.

"Don't get me wrong. I'd love for Tyler to put a bullet in that bastard's head. But that's not why he's there. He's there to hack into Abu Nazer's bank account and obtain proof of his identity. What happens next is up to you."

"And you've been in on this all along?"

Val nodded.

"Then you *do* know his identity?"

Val nodded again. "Yes, I do."

CHAPTER 47

"What is going *on?*" Tim demanded as he tried keeping pace with Tyler, who held Faisal by the arm as he marched out the door.

"Call the police," said Tyler. "Send them to Qaderi's house."

"What happened? Is Zoe all right?"

"I don't *know.*"

"Is she hurt?"

"I don't know," said Tyler, pulling open the door to a taxi. "Get in," he told Faisal.

"Dr. Tyler, I really must protest."

"Get in the fucking cab!"

Faisal hurriedly climbed in the taxi.

"Where are you going?" asked Tim.

Tyler jumped in the cab, signaled the driver and the cab sped away.

With a curse, Tim hurried back into the ballroom, found a waiter and scribbled a message on a napkin. He then told the waiter to give it to Qaderi. On it were these words: "I'm with Nightingale. Call this number."

In less than a minute, Tim's cell phone rang.

"Hello, *Abu Nazer,*" Tim said quietly. A tuxedoed waiter approached and offered him a glass of Champagne. Cheerful and gleaming under the bright lights, the flutes stood like soldiers at attention. Tim took one and nodded his thanks.

"Is this some kind of a joke?" asked Qaderi.

From his position behind a cluster of diplomats, Tim saw Youssef slowly circulating through the crowd. He was trying to locate the individual with whom he was speaking.

"It's no joke," Tim replied. "And before we go any further, I want you to stop where you are. I can see you trying to find out who I am. That isn't going to happen, and if you persist, I will hang up and you'll be dead before morning. Is that clear?"

Qaderi stopped in the middle of the floor. "What keeps you from killing me, anyway?" he asked.

"Because you're worth much more to us alive."

Eyes still scanning the crowd, Qaderi nodded.

"Walk back to the stage. Then we'll talk," said Tim.

Qaderi grudgingly did as he was told. He was briefly delayed by several people wishing to introduce him to their friends. Forcing a smile, he kissed the hands of two elderly women and shook several more hands before finally reaching the stage. "All right. Start talking," he said.

"Your cover's been blown," said Tim. "Zoe Gustaves hacked into your computer and accessed your Swiss bank account."

"Lots of people have Swiss accounts."

"Not ones we've paid millions of dollars into!"

A charged silence filled the next few seconds.

"What do you want?" asked Qaderi.

"Two witnesses know who you are. Agent Gustaves is the first. But she seems to have already met with some misfortune. The second person, however, needs to be eliminated."

"Who is that?"

"Your house guest, Rutherford Tyler."

CHAPTER 48

"How could I have allowed you to talk me into this?" muttered Faisal, as he led the way into the darkened alley.

"Because you know what'll happen if you don't."

They stopped in front of the locked door that led to Youssef's vault. Tyler knelt and searched along the base of the building.

"What are you looking for?" asked Faisal.

"Open the door," said Tyler, rising to his feet.

Faisal entered ATEN 37 on the keypad and pushed open the door. Once inside, Tyler led the way along the corridor until they reached the locked stairwell that led down to Youssef's vault. He made a quick inspection of the waist-high steel plate on the door.

"Here's where the lock is mounted," he said, pointing to four carriage bolt heads. He tore open the small package in his hand, removed a lump of plastique explosive and pressed it onto the middle of the plate. He then inserted an electronic detonator. "Okay, stand back," he said.

They flattened themselves against the wall. Tyler flipped a switch on the remote control and a tiny red light came on. He pushed a button, and a muffled explosion blew the door into the stairwell.

Racing through the smoke, Tyler led the way down the flight of steps to the second door, where he repeated the procedure. In less than a minute, they were lifting the tablet from its drawer.

Tyler hoisted the stone to his chest. It was heavy, but not unbearable. With Faisal in the lead, the two men climbed the stairs and turned left along the corridor to another door. Flashing behind them was the pulsating blue beacon of Qaderi's silent alarm.

Faisal unlocked the door, pushed it open and led Tyler into a clothing shop owned by one of his cousins. Without turning on the lights, they hurried into the office, where Tyler laid the tablet on a worktable.

"Are you sure you know what to do?" asked Tyler.

Faisal shrugged.

Tyler clasped him on the shoulder. "You're doing the right thing, you know."

"Am I?"

"Tell me what'll happen if you don't. Tell me what almost happened."

Faisal sighed heavily and nodded. "Are you sure this will work?" he asked.

"It will if we stick to the plan."

Back at Mena House, Youssef ignored the questions being shouted by reporters as he and Sharifa hurried toward the limousine. They ducked into the back seat and the driver closed the door. An instant later, Youssef's cell phone rang.

Youssef checked the caller ID and lifted the phone to his ear. "What is it?" he said.

The security dispatcher told him that his vault had been broken into.

"*What?* What was stolen?" shouted Youssef.

"Your tablet. They got away."

Youssef pounded his fist on the door.

"What's wrong?" asked Sharifa.

Youssef glared out the window and did not reply. Seconds later, his cell phone rang again. "What now?" he demanded.

"It's Tyler. Are you missing a tablet?"

Youssef's face flushed crimson with rage.

"I'm willing to trade," Tyler said. "The tablet for Zoe. Alive and unharmed."

So that's it, thought Youssef.

"Well?" asked Tyler.

"You seem to have me in a corner."

"Does that mean we have a deal?"

"I need to make a few calls," said Youssef. "To find out where she is."

"If anything's happened to her, your tablet is history."

"Call me in an hour."

Tyler ended the call then phoned Tim. Twenty minutes later, Tim was signing Tyler into the embassy through the after-hours gate.

"What's the latest on Zoe?" asked Tim.

"Majli's got her but I don't know how she is," Tyler replied. He stepped through the metal detector, then following Tim down a carpeted corridor.

"We've already been in touch with half a dozen ministers and the police. Naturally, we haven't told them who Zoe is, only that she's an

American citizen. To say this is a delicate matter is an understatement."

"I don't give a shit how delicate it is. Whatever it takes, I'm getting her back."

"It's not quite as simple as that," said Tim. "This will become a diplomatic nightmare – a diplomatic *catastrophe* – if word leaks that we've been conducting a covert operation on Egyptian soil without their knowledge. Ambassador Reynolds is already in overdrive. This has to be handled carefully. Through proper channels."

"You and your proper channels is exactly why I did what I did."

"What did you do?" asked Tim warily.

"Stole Qaderi's tablet. Which I've agreed to trade for Zoe. Unharmed."

"You stole his *tablet?* My God! *How?* Where is it?"

"Safe and sound."

"But how? How did you steal it?"

"It doesn't matter, Tim! Fact is, I've got it."

"Okay," said Tim, running a hand over his forehead.

"Look, if someone starts asking you questions, you can honestly say you didn't know."

"The less I know, the better. Wow, uh…yeah. That really helps a lot."

"That's the way it has to be."

"No, it's not. I can help you with this, Tyler, but you've got to fill me in."

"Not going to happen."

"What if something goes wrong? You can't do this alone."

"I told you I've got it covered."

"Tyler, we're on the verge of an international crisis! I need to know where that tablet is."

"What I'm doing is off the books, Tim. I'm not going to put you at risk."

"I'm already in over my head!"

"And I'm not adding to it. Be pissed off with me all you want. The tablet stays with me until I get on that bus tomorrow."

"Do you really think this will work?"

"Only one way to find out. And it begins by calling Qaderi. Are you in or out?"

"In."

Sixty seconds later, Qaderi was on speakerphone.

"Is Zoe all right?" asked Tyler.

Qaderi looked over at Zoe. She was blindfolded and tied in a chair, her ankles secured with a nylon cord that was strung tightly through the rungs and up to her wrists, which had been lashed behind her. She was shivering from the cold of the empty warehouse, but more from Majli and the brutal way he had tortured her with his eyes.

"She's fine," Qaderi replied.

"And I need proof."

"Say something," Qaderi said.

But Zoe refused to speak.

"Say something!" commanded Qaderi.

"I'm in a warehouse, center of town—"

Majli grabbed Zoe by the hair, yanked back her head, and jammed his pistol so far into her mouth she couldn't breathe.

"There, you heard for yourself," Qaderi said.

Tyler could hear Zoe gagging. "If you hurt her…" he shouted.

"Not likely, since we each have something the other one wants." He motioned for Majli to ease up, then said, "What assurances do I have that you won't doublecross me?"

"The same as I have with you," answered Tyler.

Qaderi laughed.

"A trap ruins it for both of us," said Tyler. "If Zoe dies, you're wanted for murder and you lose your precious tablet. It's win-win if we both play it straight."

Qaderi glanced at Zoe, who was slumped forward in the chair, gasping for air.

"Have we got a deal?" asked Tyler.

Qaderi let the seconds tick by. Making victims wait was a valuable tactic.

"Have we got a deal?" Tyler asked again.

"All right," replied Qaderi. "But I say when and where."

"I'm listening."

"Tomorrow, get on the tour bus as scheduled and have the tablet with you. We'll meet along the route and make the trade."

It was Tyler's turn to let the seconds tick by.

"I don't think so," he said. "Two cars. You bring Zoe, I bring the tablet. We make the exchange out in the desert. No bus. No innocent people."

"Oh, but I *want* innocent people!" countered Qaderi. "In the event you try something foolish, people can – and will – get killed. However, if things go as planned, then I won't have to shoot any innocent bystanders. Play by the rules and – as you say – we both win."

"So, I'm to get on the bus as scheduled," Tyler repeated, watching Tim unfold a map.

"The tour will go to the monasteries of Wadi Natrun by way of the Western Desert," explained Qaderi. "We'll meet somewhere along that highway."

"The monasteries of Wadi Natrun," repeated Tyler.

Tim circled them on the map and then whispered in Tyler's ear. Tyler smiled and nodded.

"Agreed," he said to Qaderi. "But I want you on the bus."

"So you can trap me? Not a chance!"

"Call it insurance," said Tyler. "No one from either side will start shooting so long as we're both on that bus. Majli brings Zoe and meets us along the route. He can choose when and where."

"If I so much as *smell* a trap…"

"I won't risk Zoe getting hurt."

Qaderi thought for a moment. "Agreed."

"Let me run through this again," said Tyler, "just so there's no misunderstanding. The bus will take the desert highway toward the Bahariya Oasis, then turn north into the Western Desert and head toward the monasteries at Wadi Natrun. We'll meet along that highway. When we see Majli, the bus will stop and we make the exchange."

"If anything goes wrong, people will die."

"If anything goes wrong, *you* will die."

Without responding, Qaderi hung up.

"He bought it!" said Tim.

"Good idea having him get on that bus."

"No ambush will take place so long as he's there beside you. For insurance, I'll be following out of sight with a team of Marines."

"Out of sight? You won't be much good if something goes wrong."

"We can't risk Qaderi seeing us."

"Then put 'em on the bus dressed as tourists."

"He'd see through that in a second."

"We're talking about a bus full of innocent people!"

"Quit worrying," said Tim. "Nothing is going to go wrong."

"You don't know that. I want those Marines on the bus."

"I can give you a couple, no more."

"Two Marines is not enough."

"It'll have to be."

"I don't like it."

"Look, just go with me on this. You said so yourself: if Qaderi smells a trap, he'll abort. He wants his tablet, and if he tries something stupid, everyone loses. Besides, we'll only be a few minutes away. Ring me when you've made the exchange."

Tyler shook his head and Tim gave him a reassuring slap on the shoulder. "Come on, I'll walk you out."

Once the taxi carrying Tyler sped away, Tim went back inside.

"Another late night?" asked the guard.

"Glutton for punishment," said Tim, his bow tie hanging loose.

With a laugh, the guard waved Tim through.

Tim walked down the hall to his office, stepped inside and locked the door. Sitting at his desk, he dialed a telephone number that directed his call through the embassy scrambler to a private number that would be recorded as a call to the CIA switchboard from a public telephone in Brooklyn.

Seconds later, Nightingale answered.

"Everything's set," said Tim.

"Including Abu Nazer?"

"He'll be on the bus tomorrow. But are you sure you want him killed?"

"He's become a liability."

"What about Tyler and Gustaves?"

"Collateral damage. They know too much."

"Are we still on for San Francisco?" asked Tim.

"We obviously won't be using Abu Nazer, but – yes – we're still on. Meanwhile, I want this incident with the bus to look like a terrorist attack."

"I have a team of mercenaries at a training camp out in the desert."

"Make sure they finish the job."

"By noon, they'll all be dead."

CHAPTER 49

April shut down her computer, turned off the lights and locked Teague's office door. It being Saturday, she had been able to work uninterrupted.

With her car window open, April accelerated her way onto the Capital Beltway and headed south. It was a beautiful evening, with feathery pink clouds high up in the sky. April had heard those kinds of clouds meant rain, but the forecast was for warm, sunny skies. Which, of course, meant nothing. No one but weather forecasters could be wrong so much of the time and still keep their jobs.

The eleven-mile drive normally took an hour, but tonight there was minimal traffic so the trip took only fifteen minutes.

"Honey, I'm home!" April called out when she opened the front door. She put her keys and purse on the hall table and peeked into the living room. The TV was on but the room was empty. "Carlos, where are you?"

She walked into the kitchen and flipped the light switch. Nothing happened. April groaned and headed for the fuse box, which was near the back door. As she rounded the corner, she saw the back door was open.

"Carlos, are you out there?" she called out.

Suddenly, from the shadows a man grabbed April.

April twisted and scratched his face.

"You fucking *bitch!*" he yelled.

April broke free and ran for the front door. The man caught her and tackled her to the floor.

"Somebody help me!" April screamed, jerking and kicking.

The attacker climbed on top of her and slapped a hand over her mouth. April bit him as hard as she could. The man cried out and grabbed his hand. April pushed him off and kneed him in the groin.

April scrambled to her feet and was running for the door when the attacker rammed her from behind. The blow smashed her against the wall and knocked a knick-knack shelf to the floor.

"*Carlos!*" April cried out, as the man's arm encircled her neck.

But Carlos could not hear her. His bullet-riddled body was in the bedroom.

The arm coiled tighter around April's neck. The man's other hand was on the side of her head. She couldn't breathe!

Snap.

The killer threw April's body to the floor, pulled out his gun and shot her twice, although she was already dead. With a curse, he shot her once more – retribution for the injuries he had sustained.

After wrenching the diamond ring off April's finger, the killer limped down the hall, found April's purse and rummaged through it. He took her credit cards and cash. He then went to the bedroom for the rest of her jewelry. When finished, he left by the front door.

As planned, he strolled casually to the end of the block, turned left and headed for the service station at the corner. As planned, a black florist's van pulled up beside him. The driver rolled down the window.

But instead of being handed a hundred thousand dollars, the killer received five muffled bullets in his chest.

Fifteen minutes later, the florist's van pulled into the parking lot of a nearby shopping mall. The driver switched off the engine, stepped out of the vehicle and walked away.

"This is Nightingale Six," the driver murmured into his cell phone as he reached the dark blue sedan parked several rows away. "Mission accomplished. I'm on my way."

CHAPTER 50

Tim directed the Range Rover into an angled parking space at Al-Medina Tours.

"I can't believe the police found nothing," said Tyler.

"Qaderi's house was clean. No one was there," said Tim.

"Not even the housekeeper?"

Tim shook his head.

"That doesn't make sense. She was there just yesterday."

"I'm only telling you what the police told me," said Tim. He clasped Tyler on the shoulder briefly before rotating in his seat to include sergeants Brad Henschel and Eric Jones. "Like I said, I'll be following the bus at a distance, so once you've made the exchange, call me and we'll move in."

"If that bastard hurts Zoe…" muttered Tyler.

"He won't if we stick to our plan," Tim replied.

Tyler opened his door and got out.

"Don't let him blow this," Tim said quietly.

"We'll do our best," said Brad.

Tyler went to the rear of the Range Rover, opened the hatch and took out a large brown suitcase. It had been reinforced with two leather belts and a makeshift handle.

Waiting impatiently near the office was Sharifa. When she saw Tyler getting out of the Range Rover she ran over to him.

"What *happened* last night?" she said, giving him a hug. "I saw you leave with Faisal. Then Youssef got a call telling him that his tablet had been stolen. Then he got another call that *really* made him angry. When I asked what was wrong, he told me to mind my own business. He then had the driver take me home."

"So you don't know where he went?"

"No. I waited up for hours, but you never came home. Where were you? What's going on?"

Tyler set the suitcase down and rubbed a hand over his forehead, not knowing quite what to say or how to say it.

"Tyler! What is going *on?*"

257

"Youssef," said Tyler. "He's Abu Nazer."

"What?"

Tyler nodded for Sharifa to walk with him and picked up the suitcase. "Zoe went to your house last night and hacked into Qaderi's computer," he said, heading for the bus. "She found bank records linked to a numbered Swiss account that we believe can be traced to a group of killers working for the CIA. Unfortunately, Majli caught her and would have killed her if I hadn't stolen the tablet."

"*You* stole Youssef's tablet?"

"Which I'm trading back to him, for Zoe, unharmed. We're to meet Majli somewhere along the tour route and make the exchange."

"Youssef is Abu Nazer? I can't believe it."

"The bank statement proves it. I was on the phone with him last night arranging the trade."

"I can't believe I've been working for a terrorist and didn't know it!"

"That's why no one's ever caught him. He fooled you, me, everybody. But his game is over. I've blown his cover. I've also backed him into a corner by forcing him to make this trade. So it's probably not a good day for you to be near me."

"I'm not staying behind, if that's what you mean."

"Sharifa, listen—"

"Forget it!"

"Will you listen to me for a minute? See those two guys over there?" Tyler pointed to Brad and Eric. "They're Marines and they're going to be riding along on the bus in case there's any trouble. Half a dozen more will be following out of sight."

"I don't care. I'm coming with you."

"It's a trap, Sharifa! They're going to take down Abu Nazer just as soon as we have Zoe. And that means there probably *will* be trouble."

"Like I said, I'm coming with you."

"Not under these conditions!"

"You are *not* leaving me here alone! Not with Majli on the loose."

"We're going to meet him out in the desert. In fact, he's probably out there already."

"And if he's not? What if he comes looking for me in order to get back at you? What happens if he's got friends?"

Tyler looked up and heaved a sigh.

"I am *not* staying here by myself!" Sharifa said.

A reluctant nod was Tyler's reply. Just then, Brad Henschel approached them with a phone.

"It's Val. She wants to talk with you."

Tyler stared at Brad for a moment then grabbed the phone. "Val? Is that you?"

"It's me. I'm all right."

"I thought you were *dead.*"

"The whole thing was engineered by Teague to throw Abu Nazer off my trail."

"Teague set this up? Are you sure?"

"I'm with him now."

"Val, I think he's with Nightingale!"

"He's not. He's one of the good guys. He knows you had Gloria phone Vice President Baker."

"Did she get through?"

"Teague intercepted the call and told Baker what was really going on – that he's trying to track down Nightingale using Abu Nazer. Tyler, he's on our side. We had a good talk and I believe him. By the way, the Credit Suisse bank statement got through. Teague's people are working on it now."

"Too little, too late, I'm afraid. Zoe's been kidnapped by Abu Nazer and we're trying to get her back. But I honestly don't have a good feeling about this. She may have made one rash decision too many."

"Is she still alive?"

"She'd better be, because I *will* kill Abu Nazer if she isn't."

"Listen, about those things I wrote…"

"Don't apologize. You were right."

"Out of line is what I was."

"Actually, you were right. I'd grown comfortable. I turned my back on what needed to be done."

"Just so you know, I'm disappearing for awhile. Teague's offered to put me up in a safe house."

"Don't you *dare* let him put you in a safe house! We don't know who Nightingale is, who's working for him, or who the hell we can trust. Go somewhere on your own. And don't tell anyone, not even me. No relatives. No colleagues from Morgan Publishing. No college roommates."

"Tyler, I get it."

"I mean it, Val. You've got to go deep and dark."

"I'll call you when all this is over."

"Take care of yourself."

"You're the one who needs lookin' after. Sometimes you don't have a lot of sense."

"Love you, too. Put Teague on, okay?"

Val handed the phone to Teague.

"Dr. Tyler, this is Jackson Teague. Sergeant Henschel filled me in on what's going on. Is there any word on Zoe?"

"Nothing yet. But I believe she's still alive. Qaderi wants his tablet and he knows he won't get it if anything happens to Zoe."

"I hope you're right."

"Me, too. Listen, about what you did for Val, saving her like that…"

"We moved as quickly as we could once I found out her identity had been compromised. She endured a bit of rough treatment but at least she's safe."

"I appreciate that."

"Vice President Baker and Congresswoman Gustaves have taken a personal interest in what's going on, so I've asked Sergeant Henschel to keep me informed. I understand Tim Odell will be following with reinforcements?"

"That's the plan."

"Good luck," said Teague.

Tyler returned the phone to Brad just as a taxi stopped in the street. Tyler saw Johnny Bill climb out with a black polycarbonate suitcase.

"Had a dickens of a time findin' this place," Johnny Bill called out. "Here's the case Val told me to bring ya."

The mention of Val's name drew Brad Henschel's attention.

"Val as in Val Johnson?" he asked, removing his sunglasses.

Johnny Bill did not reply.

"Any trouble with airport security?" asked Tyler.

"Not a lick. X-ray machines showed just what Val said they'd show – cameras and film."

"Did Val Johnson send you over here with this?" demanded Brad, kneeling to scrutinize the case. It was two feet by three feet by nine inches, with rounded edges and an eight tumbler, stainless steel lock.

Johnny Bill looked at Tyler. Said, "Who is this jerk?"

"He means well," answered Tyler.

Brad stood and faced Tyler eye to eye. "This is the mallet, isn't it? Not that piece of crap rabbit gun you sent over as a diversion, but the real thing."

"It's a camera case," answered Tyler.

"Bullshit!"

"X-ray machines don't lie."

"You knew damn well we'd call the couriers; so you had your assistant FedEx a decoy while your buddy here delivered the real thing."

"I don't reckon this is any o' your business!" interjected Johnny Bill.

"I'm making it my business," declared Brad.

Johnny Bill stepped forward, fists clenched. Tyler intercepted him and led him away.

"I can hold my own!" said Johnny Bill.

"Come on, I'll walk you to the cab," replied Tyler. To Sharifa, "Be back in a minute."

Tyler clasped Johnny Bill on the shoulder and walked with him to the waiting taxi. Johnny Bill paused before getting in.

"Val, or Louise, or whatever the hell she said her name was," Johnny Bill began, glancing back at the case then at Tyler. "She told me some stuff that's kinda hard to believe."

Tyler lowered his eyes.

"So it's true, then?" Johnny Bill asked.

"I'm not sure what she told you, but – yeah – it's probably true. Val's not one to lie."

"I won't kid you, Ty. When I first heard what she had to say, it kinda pissed me off. I mean, we've known each other a long while, and I figured we was friends."

"We are friends," Tyler responded. "You're the best friend I ever had. And I hope you believe me when I say this wasn't a matter of trust. It was a matter of me not wanting someone coming after you or Gloria. Or the kids. Still, I wouldn't blame you one bit if you—"

"Now hang on! I said when I *first* heard it. But later on, when I got to thinkin' about it, I realized if I'd been in your shoes I'd have done the same thing. So don't you go frettin' yourself none over this, ya hear? Fact is, no one's ever been a better friend to us than you have." He slapped a burly arm around Tyler's shoulder and lowered his voice. "So I really don't give a rat's ass if that case does have a gun in it. You go do what you gotta do and we'll see ya back home."

Tyler nodded and smiled. "Remember, I'm coverin' your costs."

"Already taken care of," said Johnny Bill.

"By whom?"

"By the Corvette I sold them A-rabs last night. Look after yourself." And with a wave, Johnny Bill climbed in the cab.

Tyler watched the taxi drive away, then returned to find Brad trying to open the case.

"What the hell's this thing made of?" asked Brad. He stood and kicked the case, like it was a tire. "Feels like it could handle a sledgehammer."

"It can."

"Which tells me it's not full of cameras."

Tyler shrugged and reached for the case.

Brad grabbed his arm. "Can't let you do it," he said.

"Do what?"

"Kill Abu Nazer. I don't for a minute believe that case is full of cameras."

"Believe whatever you want. And for the last time, I am *not* here to kill Abu Nazer."

"You're in way over your head here. This is a national security issue, which means I'm in charge. The case stays with me."

"Let's get something straight," said Tyler. "I'm here for one reason only and that's to make sure Zoe gets out of this alive. When that's accomplished, I'll step aside and you can flex your national security muscles any way you like."

"Fine. The case stays with me."

"Not without a warrant."

"This isn't the United States, Tyler. The case stays with me."

"If there's one thing I know about you, Sergeant, it's this: You know when to break the rules and when not to. It's part of the job of being a leader. But with Jackson Teague and the Vice President of the United States on the other end of my phone, this isn't the time to do something stupid. So I repeat, unless you've got a warrant…"

Brad glared at Tyler but did not move to stop him when he picked up both the camera case and the brown suitcase and continued toward the bus. Sharifa fell in step beside him.

"Why does he want that case of yours?" she asked.

"He's tense. We're all tense," said Tyler.

When they neared the bus the driver stepped out to meet them. He was a short man with wiry black hair. "Shall I place these on top for you, sir?" he asked.

"This case belongs to Youssef Qaderi," said Tyler, handing the brown suitcase to the driver.

The driver accepted the suitcase and had trouble picking it up. "It is very heavy!" he exclaimed with a grunt. "Too heavy to go on top of the bus. I must place it in the rear compartment."

"Sounds good by me," said Tyler. "The black case, I'd like with me."

"The black case must go on top," replied the driver.

"It's a camera case. I need it with me."

"Unfortunately, that will not be possible. The bus will be full, and the case is too large."

"I'll keep it out of the way."

Denial of the request seemed to pain the driver. "Regulations do not permit a case of this size to obstruct comfort and safety," he said. "Please, I will place it on the luggage rack on top."

Tyler opened his wallet and removed a fifty-dollar bill. "Can we talk about this?" he asked.

The driver shook his head sadly. "If only that were possible, generous sir."

"If only," remarked Tyler, sticking the money back in his wallet to the obvious disappointment of the driver.

After stowing the brown suitcase in the rear compartment, the driver paused to look sadly at Tyler. Then, with a sigh, he climbed up the tubular metal ladder and fastened the black case on top with the other luggage.

Finishing his call, Tim closed his phone and walked over to Tyler. "Has our man showed yet?" he asked.

"He probably won't appear until the very last minute."

Across the street, in a fourth-floor apartment, Qaderi and Majli stood watching.

"Blow the bus once I'm clear," commanded Qaderi.

"As you wish," answered Majli.

263

"Are you certain the explosives are in place?"

"Two lumps. I checked them myself."

"What about Gustaves? Where is she?"

"In the trunk of my car," answered Majli.

"And Mrs. Fedje?"

"I dumped her body in the desert."

"She never was much of a cook."

Several moments of silence ticked by.

"Where's the remote control?" asked Qaderi.

"Here," answered Majli.

Qaderi held out his hand and Majli gave him the control.

"Where's Tariq?" asked Youssef.

"I told him to come to your house tonight. When he does, an intruder will be shot, thus ending the life – and career – of Abu Nazer."

An icy smile formed on Youssef's face, which then vanished when he saw Sharifa reach up and kiss Tyler. He stared angrily at her for several seconds, then noticed the red-haired man standing next to her. Something about him seemed familiar.

Qaderi studied Tim for a moment and remembered where he had seen him: at Mena House, last night. He took out his cell phone and dialed the number given to him on the paper napkin.

Across the street, Tim's cell phone rang.

"Odell," he answered.

Silence.

"Odell. Hello?"

Hearing no response, Tim switched off his phone and put it in his pocket.

Across the street, Qaderi smiled and clicked off his phone.

"I'm outa here," said Tim, slapping Tyler on the shoulder. "Remember, we won't be far behind."

The bus driver sounded the horn.

"We're leaving. Where's Youssef?" asked Sharifa.

"Somewhere watching," said Tyler.

"Watching? How do you know?"

"Because I would be."

Sharifa shrugged and started for the bus. "Aren't you coming?" she asked.

"In a minute," Tyler replied.

Sharifa nodded and continued to the bus.

With his finger poised on the remote control button, Qaderi watched Sharifa climb onto the bus.

"She's getting on the bus!" said Majli, concerned.

Qaderi did not reply.

"Youssef, she's—"

"I heard you!" snapped Qaderi.

Majli saw the hatred in Qaderi's eyes and touched him on the arm. "If I do not leave soon, I won't be able to arrive at the exchange point before you."

For a long moment, Qaderi continued glaring at Sharifa. Then he tossed the control to Majli and left the apartment.

CHAPTER 51

The mountainous dunes of the Sahara lay beyond the smaller but equally hostile Western Desert, into which tour bus #7 was now driving, its air conditioner on high. The surrounding sand flowed in intermittent drifts, and where there was no sand, the barren earth was littered with rock.

Wen-Nabi, how I wish I would not have accepted this trip, the driver told himself. But the baksheesh – tip money – was good and he had many mouths to feed. Still, he would be happy when this day was finished. The final passenger, Qaderi, had arrived ten minutes late and boarded the bus without uttering a word.

But Qaderi's silence was not the concern. It was his eyes. Never had he seen eyes so full of hatred.

Wen-Nabi, I will be glad when this day was over!

The driver slowed the bus to a crawl and made a cumbersome right-hand turn onto a rough highway that stretched off into the sun-parched distance. The heat was intense. The road shimmered like a lake. The chattering families in front grew momentarily silent as the bus bounced slowly along over potholes. Before long, however, they accepted this as normal and began talking again.

Five minutes passed. Then ten.

With Tyler seated beside him, Qaderi stared angrily out the window. Sharifa and Brad were in one of the rear seats, with Eric across the aisle. The swaying of the bus caused everyone to rock back and forth.

Twenty minutes had now ticked by and the bus pushed steadily on. The driver rotated the steering wheel back and forth to avoid the large holes in the road. To the left was a high ridge of sand, to the right a rocky butte.

In the third seat, two of the kids began whining for something to eat.

"Shhh," their mother said. She turned around, offering them apples.

The kids wanted candy.

"No candy before lunch," said the mother.

"*Please*, Mom, this is a *vacation!*"

"No."

"*Pleeeeeease!*"

The mother finally gave in and the kids responded with fists pumped in victory.

Qaderi suddenly sat forward. Half a mile ahead, an old Mercedes was parked on the shoulder of the road. Its hood was raised. Beside the fender of the car stood a tall man in a *jellaba*. As the bus drew near, Majli waved his hand.

Qaderi discreetly checked the small revolver in his ankle holster. He would have killed Tyler by now and simply taken the tablet if it weren't for the Marines in the rear of the bus. No way would they let him get out of here alive.

"Pull over! That man needs assistance," he called out. He glanced coldly at Tyler and stood, waiting to be let out of his seat.

Tyler stepped into the aisle and allowed Qaderi to exit. Tyler then followed him to the front of the bus.

The driver stopped the bus and pulled a lever. The door hissed open. Qaderi jumped down onto the gravel, followed by Tyler

Three miles back, Tim pulled his Range Rover over and stopped to allow the utility truck that had been following to pull even with his window. Tim leaned out and handed the driver an envelope.

"No survivors," said Tim.

The driver opened the envelope and flipped through the stack of U.S. one-hundred-dollar bills. "You got it," he said. He jammed the gear stick into first and released the clutch. The truck lurched forward.

The Range Rover made a U-turn and sped away.

Standing in front of the bus, Qaderi turned to face Tyler. "Are you ready to conclude our business?" he asked.

"Once I verify that Zoe's unharmed."

"Get the tablet. I'll get the girl."

"The tablet stays where it is until I know Zoe's all right," said Tyler.

"Perhaps you didn't hear me."

"I heard you just fine. The tablet stays where it is until I know Zoe's all right."

Like dueling sabers, Tyler's cold gaze clashed with Qaderi's.

Inside the bus, Brad strode up the aisle and stopped beside the driver. "What the fuck's going on?" he muttered, his eyes on Tyler and Qaderi.

The two kids seated nearby looked at one another, their eyes wide with excitement. "He said the 'f' word!" one of them whispered.

The mother gave the children a scolding glance. "Driver, what's the delay?" she asked, standing.

Brad turned to the woman. "Stay seated. We shouldn't be long."

"I was speaking to the driver."

"Yes, ma'am. And I need you to stay seated," Brad replied.

"I don't take orders from you!"

"I'm *asking* you to stay seated." Brad removed his sunglasses and stared unwaveringly at the woman.

The woman turned to her husband. "Say something!"

The husband observed the brewing confrontation in front of the bus and pulled his wife down into her seat. She started to jump up again, but he held her in place.

A mile behind them, the driver was pushing his utility truck to its limit. Spotting the bus in the distance, he banged a fist on the roof.

Hearing the signal, the twenty-three mercenaries in the back of the truck threw off the tarp and began jamming clips of ammunition into their rifles. One of them hoisted a grenade launcher to his shoulder.

"This is ridiculous!" Sharifa said. She slipped past Brad and jumped off the bus.

"Sharifa, wait!" said Brad, grabbing for her but missing.

"Wait here. I'll get the girl," Youssef told Tyler.

Tyler looked over his shoulder when he heard the crunch of gravel.

"What is going on?" asked Sharifa.

"Go back and wait inside," said Tyler.

Tyler then noticed Sharifa looking past him with a surprised look on her face. He turned to see Qaderi running toward the Mercedes, where Majli was standing with his long, sinewy arm in the air. In his hand was a remote control.

"Now!" Qaderi shouted.

Tyler watched as Majli push the button.

Back down the road, the mercenary with the grenade launcher yelled a war cry as the truck closed in on the bus. With shouts of encouragement from the others, he aimed the tube. But sighting was difficult because the truck was jerking back and forth as it sped over the rough road. "Just a little closer," he said.

"Big trouble, six o'clock!" came a shout from the rear of the bus.

Brad looked to where Eric was pointing and saw the truckload of mercenaries heading toward them. He saw the grenade launcher. He then saw a puff of smoke.

"Eric, *grenade!*" Brad shouted. "Everyone *down!*"

Shouts followed, as parents ordered children down onto the floor. The driver curled up beneath the steering wheel. One of the fathers covered his two daughters with his body.

Majli stared with disbelief at the remote control in his hand. *Nothing was happening!* He pushed the button again.

Eric had just started up the aisle when a mammoth explosion ripped apart the rear of the bus. It lifted the vehicle off the road and bouncing it forward. Tyler's case somersaulted high into the air before hitting the ground in front of the bus and bouncing several times. The other luggage simply disintegrated.

Inside the bus, terrified families were crying and screaming. Shards of glass had sliced into the back of the father who had shielded his daughters. The girls were crying at the sight of his blood. They kept trying to wake him up.

The explosion that killed Eric smashed Brad against the dashboard. Struggling to his feet, Brad tore open his backpack, grabbed his cell phone and dialed Tim.

"Come on, come on, where *are* you?" he said to the incessant ringing.

The rear of the bus was a gaping hole. Through the smoke and flames Brad could see that the utility truck had skidded to a stop. Men in camouflage clothing were firing their assault rifles at injured passengers. A pair of German tourists was pummeled by the fusillade when they tried jumping free of the bus.

The shock of the blast had knocked Tyler and Sharifa to the ground. Majli was thrown back against the fender of the Mercedes. With a shout, Qaderi scrambled to his feet, sprinted to the passenger side of the car and pulled open the door.

Throwing the remote control to the ground, Majli whipped up his *jellaba* and pulled out an automatic pistol.

Rolling onto his hands and knees, Tyler began crawling toward his case.

One of the mercenaries opened fire. Explosions of sand stung

Tyler in the face.

Rolling to one side, Tyler looked back and saw passengers screaming and running. The mercenaries were gunning them down. The rear of the bus was in flames. Clouds of black smoke billowed into the air.

Lying on the barren earth in front of the bus, Sharifa groaned and tried to sit up.

"Lie still!" Tyler yelled.

He scurried forward to his case and began rotating the stainless steel tumblers. In the distance, he could hear Zoe's muffled cries from the trunk of the car.

A burst of gunfire shattered the windshield of the Mercedes.

"Get us out of here!" Qaderi screamed, diving inside.

"There are guns on the floorboard!" shouted Majli. "Join me. We will fight to the death."

"Get us *out of here!*"

Majli stared at Youssef in disbelief. *Qaderi was wanting to run!*

On board the bus, Brad looked back to where Eric had been standing moments before. More than a dozen people had already been killed trying to escape. On the floor of the bus were the remains of others. He put away his phone, opened his backpack and grabbed his pistol.

A mercenary peered through the gaping hole that was the rear of the bus. Brad gunned him down then leaped out the door. He hit the ground, looking right then left. He saw Sharifa crawling toward Tyler. A burst of gunfire ripped the sand beside her. Brad spun and fired, killing another mercenary. He dashed out and dragged Sharifa back to the relative safety of the bus.

"Stay here," Brad said.

Sharifa suddenly gasped.

Whirling around, Brad saw two mercenaries aiming their assault rifles at him.

The explosions that followed were deafening. Brad flinched as wet spatter hit him in the face an instant before the men's bullet-riddled bodies slammed against the grill of the bus. When Brad opened his eyes, he saw Tyler holding a matte-black rifle with a large magazine of ammunition curving out from beneath it. Tyler fired, panning left to right, the powerful gun recoiling smartly while ejecting a stream of empty casings into the air.

Tyler then swung the rifle toward Brad.

Whoom, whoom, whoom.

The mercenaries charging Brad were immediately cut down. One assault rifle in the grip of a mercenary continued firing until its magazine was empty.

Racing over to Brad and Sharifa, Tyler peered around the door. He fired once for a kill, then climbed up onto the bus. He fired several more times at the mercenaries climbing in through the rear.

Seeing how quickly the tide had turned, the remaining mercenaries jumped up onto the bed of the utility truck, which the driver was gunning away in a wide arc. Tyler lifted his rifle to pick them off.

Then, out of the corner of his eye, he saw Majli striding toward Brad, pistol aimed, his *jellaba* flowing behind him in the hot desert wind.

Tyler whirled and lifted his rifle in one smooth motion, the powerful weapon vibrating as a stream of bullets exploded the windshield into thousands of tiny chunks.

Majli was just pulling the trigger when the bullets from Tyler's rifle tore through him. He stared at Tyler in stunned shock for a split second before crumpling to the ground.

"You!" Tyler yelled to the driver. "Get the first aid kit and start treating the wounded. Have someone else put out that fire."

The driver nodded and clambered to his feet.

Tyler jumped off the bus, his rifle at the ready as he cautiously approached the body of Majli lying motionless on the ground. A pool of blood was soaking the barren earth around him, turning it the color of rust. Tyler knelt and felt for a pulse.

Majli was dead.

"Throw down your weapon!" came a shout.

Rising to his feet, Tyler squinted toward the Mercedes, where he saw Qaderi holding a gun to Zoe's head.

"Drop it or I kill her," yelled Qaderi.

Dressed in her gown from the night before, Zoe looked exhausted but unharmed.

"Are you all right?" shouted Tyler.

"I said, throw down your weapon!" Qaderi yelled again, pressing the gun against Zoe's head.

Maintaining eye contact, Tyler backed his way over to Brad and Sharifa. To Sharifa: "How are you feeling?"

"A few bumps but I'm all right," Sharifa said, climbing to her feet.

"I knew damn well that wasn't a camera case," growled Brad.

"Lucky for you it wasn't."

"What do we do now? Qaderi's tablet was destroyed by that RPG. You've got nothing to trade."

"Only one thing to do," answered Tyler.

"I told you, I can't let you do it!"

"We've got no choice."

"He's got a gun to her head! There's no way you can take him out with him standing behind her like that."

"Watch me."

"You're stupid if you think you can drop a man with a head shot at thirty meters while he's holding a hostage! At least try and talk to the guy."

"What's your rule about negotiating with terrorists?"

"At least *try!*" said Brad.

"He's right," agreed Sharifa.

"Qaderi won't listen," said Tyler.

"We don't know that," Sharifa replied.

"He won't listen, I tell you. Right now, he's plotting a way to get Zoe into that car and drive away without me shooting. I guarantee. He's in no mood to talk."

Sharifa stepped in front of Tyler. "Then let me try. Youssef won't hurt me. I know him."

"You didn't know that he was Abu Nazer! So don't tell me how well you know him."

"If I have to physically stop you from shooting, I will," said Brad, moving in front of Tyler.

"Zoe's got one chance of getting out of this alive and it's in the chamber of this rifle. Now get out of my way! Because if you decide to try something stupid, I *will* miss and Zoe will die. Do you want that on your head?"

Brad remained standing in front of Tyler.

"Get out of my way!" commanded Tyler. "Now!"

Spinning angrily away, Brad took out his cell phone and dialed.

"Last warning!" Qaderi shouted.

"Tyler, please! He's going to kill her!" Sharifa said.

"He's bluffing."

"How can you be sure?"

"Because Zoe's his protection."

"What if you're *wrong*? What if he sees you getting ready to shoot? He will kill her, Tyler!"

"And I'm telling you he won't."

Brad suddenly grabbed Tyler by the arm and held out his phone. "Here, before you really screw things up."

"I don't have *time* for this!"

"Well, you'd better make time. You're being patched through to Vice President Baker."

CHAPTER 52

Sam Baker was asleep when the phone beside him buzzed.

"What is it?" he answered in a low voice, trying not to disturb his wife.

The CIA dispatcher explained the situation.

"Put him through," Baker said, slipping into a robe. He padded quietly out of the bedroom and down the hall to his office. He switched on a desk lamp and sat down. Seconds later Teague's voice came onto the line.

"My apologies for awakening you, Mr. Vice President," said Teague, "but we have an emergency that requires your immediate intervention."

"What's going on?" asked Baker.

Teague told him.

"Patch me through, but stay on the line."

"Yes, sir," answered Teague.

Rifle in hand, Tyler was pacing the sun-baked earth in front of the smoking bus when he heard Sam Baker's voice. Behind him, the driver continued helping wounded passengers.

"Tyler, are you there?" asked Baker.

"Yes, Mr. Vice President, I'm here."

"I understand Abu Nazer's holding Agent Gustaves hostage."

"Yes, sir. I have him in my sights."

"Tyler, you need to stand down."

"Sir, did I hear you correctly?"

"You heard correctly," said the Vice President. "I need you to put away your weapon."

"Sir, Abu Nazer will kill Zoe if I don't take him out."

"And I can't risk agent Gustaves getting shot."

"I promise you, that won't happen."

"I appreciate your confidence, but we're talking about someone's life."

"Sir, like I said—"

"Tyler. We need him alive!"

"*What?*"

"We need Abu Nazer alive. Jackson Teague of the CIA is on the line. He'll explain why."

274

"Simply put," said Teague, "the man has information that we need. And we need him to talk."

"And you're planning to do that – how – by asking him nicely?"

"By offering him immunity."

"This man is a *butcher!* He knows it, we know it, and he *knows* that we know it. So he's not about to believe you'll let him walk free."

"If we can get him to listen to what we're offering, I think he will."

"I'm telling you he'll never fall for it. If you need him alive, then I'll give him to you that way. But let me take him down."

"I can't take the risk."

Said Baker: "Tyler, I'm asking you to put down your weapon."

"Sir, with all due respect, I don't think Abu Nazer will fall for Teague's proposal. I certainly wouldn't. For one thing, there's no way to communicate the deal without endangering someone else."

"He knows me. I could go," said Sharifa.

"Absolutely not!" said Tyler.

"Who said that?" asked Teague, overhearing the remark.

"Qaderi's assistant, but I won't allow it. It would give him another hostage."

"He won't hurt me," insisted Sharifa.

"We don't *know* that," responded Tyler.

"For God's sake, Tyler, I'm his *lover!*"

The remark was like a slap in the face and Tyler stiffened.

"Look, I'm sorry, I didn't mean it that way," Sharifa said, touching Tyler on the arm. "Just let me do this, okay? Youssef doesn't know yet that it's over between us."

"And what if he does? What if he knows more than you think?"

"He would have said something by now. Made some kind of a remark."

"I won't let you do it."

"You've got to! If I were to walk out there with nothing to offer, then, sure, he might figure he's got nothing to lose and take me as a hostage. But that isn't the case. Your government's offering him immunity. A chance to go free."

"Which I don't think he'll believe. One shot. That's all I need."

"What if you miss? Or hit Zoe? *Think,* Tyler! We don't have to take that risk."

With the barrel of his pistol pressed against Zoe's head, Qaderi watched carefully what transpiring. From this distance, he couldn't hear what was being discussed, but whatever it was, he could see Tyler didn't like it.

Tyler put the phone back to his ear. "All right," he said. "But *only* if Brad Henschel handles the negotiation. And if Qaderi harms Zoe, the deal is off."

"Whatever happens, you *must not pull that trigger!*" the Vice President said emphatically. "We cannot lose this opportunity."

"Sir, that man is a *monster*. And you're talking about turning him *loose*."

"In exchange for the other monsters. It's ugly, I know, but we have no choice. Without Abu Nazer, Nightingale goes free. Free to create and fund more Abu Nazers."

"Then Brad Henschel had better do some mighty smooth talking."

"Thank you," replied Baker with relief.

Tyler tossed the phone back to Brad.

"What did he say?" asked Sharifa.

"Abu Nazer goes free," said Tyler bitterly.

Sharifa took Tyler by the hand. "I know this doesn't seem fair, but it's the safest way for Zoe to get out of this alive. Attempting to shoot him only puts her at risk."

"The whole thing makes me sick."

"Okay, we're set," said Brad. "Teague's getting Ambassador Reynolds on the line to act as mediator. Qaderi met her last night and she'll verify the genuineness of the offer."

"What if he doesn't buy it?"

"Let's not play what-ifs just yet," said Brad.

With a cynical snort, Tyler looked away.

"You'll keep me covered, right?" asked Brad.

"They won't let me shoot, remember?"

"All the more reason to let me do it," said Sharifa.

"We've been over this before."

Sharifa turned to Brad. "Give me the phone," she said.

"Sorry, ma'am," said Brad.

"Things are less likely to go wrong if I do it."

She reached for the phone but Tyler stopped her. "Sergeant Henschel will take it out."

"You know as well as I do that if a soldier like Brad walks out there, Youssef will kill him. Just like he'd kill you. Tyler, please: don't make this worse than it is. Our objective is to get Youssef to surrender without getting anyone killed. I think I can do that."

"You can't be sure!"

"Under the circumstances, it's our best option."

Sharifa tried touching Tyler on the cheek but he pulled angrily away. With a sad smile, she turned to Brad and held out her hand.

Brad gave her the phone.

Sharifa kissed her finger and touched it to Tyler's cheek. Then, with a steadying breath, she started toward Qaderi.

"Remind me to kick your ass," Tyler growled once Sharifa was gone.

"What'd I do?" said Brad defensively.

With the phone held plainly in sight, Sharifa walked slowly toward Youssef. A hot desert wind was blowing from the south. It whipped Sharifa's hair about her face.

"Stop right there!" ordered Qaderi when Sharifa was ten steps away.

"I'm here to bring you this phone," Sharifa replied.

"For what reason?"

"The United States government wants to offer you a deal."

A cynical laugh was Qaderi's reply.

"It's true, Youssef," she replied.

Qaderi stared suspiciously at Sharifa. "What kind of a deal?" he asked.

"Immunity in exchange for helping them identify something or someone called Nightingale. I presume you know what that is? Ambassador Reynolds is on the line and will confirm what I just said."

Qaderi continued staring warily at Sharifa.

"I have no idea if the things they're telling me about you are true or not," Sharifa said. "It all seems so unbelievable. But if what they're saying is true, then I beg you to listen to what the ambassador has to say. It's a way to prevent further bloodshed."

"How do I know the person I'll be speaking with is really Ambassador Reynolds?"

"Ask her a question about last night. Something only she can answer."

Standing near the bus, Tyler watched anxiously.

"All right," Qaderi said, motioning her toward him.

Sharifa stepped forward with the phone.

But instead of accepting it, Youssef grabbed Sharifa and yanked her in front of him.

"No!" roared Tyler, aiming.

Qaderi bobbed back and forth behind the two women.

"Try shooting and one of them gets killed!" he shouted, backing toward the car. "Let me go and no one gets hurt."

Pulling open the door of the Mercedes, Qaderi told Sharifa to get in and drive. She climbed into the car, scooted across the seat and slid behind the wheel. When the engine started, Qaderi backed in, pulling Zoe with him.

"You and your goddamn plan!" Tyler shouted at Brad as the car sped away.

A hundred meters down the road, the passenger door opened and Zoe flew out. She hit the ground and rolled, landing face down on the gravel.

With sweat dripping from his face, Tyler sprinted toward her.

"Zoe, are you all right?" he shouted.

She did not move.

Tyler reached her and knelt beside her. He rolled her carefully onto her back and felt for a pulse. Groaning, Zoe groaned opened her eyes.

"Thank God!" Tyler exclaimed.

With her gown torn and dust covering her face, Zoe looked up at Tyler. "He let me go. He just…let me go," she said, looking around, confused.

"Take it easy. You're safe." He helped her sit up.

"I should have done something," Zoe said. "I should have done something when there were two of us in the car. I'm trained for that, Tyler, I'm trained for that!" She was talking rapidly now, her eyes darting wildly about. "Both of us could have jumped him! If only I'd given Sharifa some kind of signal."

"Shhh…" Tyler murmured gently.

"I should have done something!" Zoe said. She began to shiver.

Tyler hugged her then looked despondently down the empty road. A faint drift of dust was all that remained.

Zoe suddenly pulled away and spun around, panic in her eyes. "Where is he? Where's Majli?" she shouted.

"Calm down. Majli is dead."

"Dead? You're certain? You're sure?"

Tyler nodded.

"He stripped me, Tyler! He held a gun in my mouth and stripped me and tied me naked to a chair. It was a power play, I know that. He did it to try to break me, to see me fall apart while he was laughing and running the barrel of his gun over my body. But he couldn't do it! He couldn't break me! He couldn't make me cry."

"Well, it's over. You can cry, if you want to. He'll never touch you again."

"I will never let anyone see me cry. My mother said that. She said never let anyone see you cry. Ever! No matter how hard they try to break you. Majli tried, but he couldn't do it. He couldn't do it!"

"Easy. It's okay."

"It's *not* okay! It's a sign of weakness!"

"It's a sign of our humanity. It keeps us from imploding."

Zoe's eyes searched Tyler's for several seconds. Then, suddenly, she reached up and clutched him in a frightened hug.

An instant later, she began to cry.

CHAPTER 53

"You took an *hour* to get out to the bus!" Tyler yelled into the phone. His face was still dirty and streaked.

"Please calm yourself, Dr. Tyler," the Chief Inspector of the Cairo police replied. "Officers are currently at Mr. Qaderi's house, his photo has been distributed to the airlines and his name is in every computer. If he tries to leave the country, he will be detained."

"I don't care about Qaderi! What are you doing to locate Sharifa?"

"We are filling out the appropriate paperwork."

"You need to be out there *looking* for her."

"May I suggest you leave such matters to the police?"

"A woman's *life* is at stake! Have you sent up a surveillance plane? She could be out in the desert, injured!"

"I understand your concern."

"The hell you do!"

"My office will be in touch when we have further news."

"*Further*—?"

The dial tone hummed in Tyler's ear.

"Damn him!" yelled Tyler, slamming down the receiver.

"I know you're upset," said Brad.

"Someone needs to ram a hot poker up that jerk's ass!"

"Well, it ain't gonna happen, and yellin' at him like that only makes matters worse. The best advice I can give you is to go home. Let things run their course."

"Not without finding Sharifa."

"If I thought hangin' around Cairo would help, then I'd tell you to do it. But the truth is – it won't. You'll only get in the way. You're already gettin' in the way."

"I'll rent a car. Go looking for her myself!"

"Get real. If Qaderi's killed her, then her body may never be found. And if he hasn't – well, there is simply way too much desert for you to go traipsing around in. Let us handle things. *Go home!*"

"Letting you handle things is what created this mess in the first place!"

"I did what I had to do! So get off my back!"

While Tyler paced the floor, Brad stepped over to the worktable and opened Tyler's gun case. "The good news is Zoe's okay. The doc says she wasn't hurt."

"Emotional injuries cut a lot deeper than any flesh wound."

"She's tough, she'll get over it," said Brad.

"Ever had a gun stuck in your mouth?"

Brad looked over at Tyler then averted his eyes.

"I didn't think so," said Tyler. Heaving a frustrated sigh, he looked up. A long moment of silence ticked by.

"I wonder…" Tyler said.

"Wonder what?" asked Brad.

Tyler got up and walked over to the new computer sitting on Tim's desk. "Can I send emails with this?"

"Sure," said Brad, lifting Tyler's rifle components out of the case and examining the click-and-turn fittings. "Our techs seized Odell's old computer and replaced it with that one."

"Has anyone located Odell?"

"Found his Range Rover parked at the airport, so he's probably in Europe by now."

Brad lifted the rifle stock out of the case and held it for a moment. *Special alloy, lightweight and strong.* He picked up the firing mechanism and fitted it onto the stock – turn, click – then the shorter of the two barrels – turn, click. Then the scope, then the magazine – snap.

With a smile of satisfaction, he held up the weapon. Assembled in less than twenty seconds.

"Where'd you get this thing?" he asked, looking at the various types of ammunition. *Subsonics, supersonics, hollow tips, armor piercing… Something for every occasion.*

Tyler began typing an email.

"And what's the story with this case?" asked Brad, disassembling the rifle and placing each component back in its polyfoam slot.

Ignoring him, Tyler kept typing.

"Come on, Tyler, where'd you get all this stuff? And what the hell is this?" Brad rapped a knuckle on the flat metal box in one corner of the case. Coming out of the box were harnesses of colored wires that plugged into the lid and bottom half of the case.

"It's an electromagnetic generator," answered Tyler.

"What's it do?"

"Distorts x-rays. The microprocessor inside that box manipulates them into a 3-D holographic image by way of conductive and non-conductive implants in the laminate."

"I have no idea what you just said."

"On x-ray, whatever's in that case shows up as cameras and film."

"Because of electromagnetism?"

Tyler nodded.

"Where'd you get it?"

"Can't tell you."

"Then who made the rifle? I've never seen anything like it. Two detachable barrels, light as a feather…"

"Can't tell you that, either."

"Might as well. Our techs will find out soon enough."

"I don't think so."

"A gun case that goes undetected through airport security by projecting a false image? No way are we lettin' this out of here."

"That's exactly what you're going to do," said Tyler. "When I leave, that case leaves with me."

"Not if I have anything to say about it."

"Meaning no disrespect, but it's really not up to you."

"Let's just see about that," Brad replied. He picked up the phone and dialed.

"You need to get a little perspective."

"About what?"

"I could have waited a second longer."

The memory of wet spatter hitting him in the face made Brad shift uncomfortably. Tyler was right. If he hadn't gunned those two mercenaries down when he did, Brad knew he wouldn't be standing here today.

"Ambassador Reynolds' office," said a voice on the phone.

Brad stared at Tyler and saw Tyler staring back.

"Hello?" the voice asked again.

Without responding, Brad dropped the phone back in its cradle and walked out of the office.

CHAPTER 54

Teague picked up the phone and buzzed Tony.

"What's the latest on those traces?" he asked.

"You would not believe the maze of network encryption algorithms I had to crack!" said Tony excitedly. "Variant server dialects, two-fifty-six random bit mixes—"

"Cooke! Just tell me what you found."

"Yes, sir. Be right there."

Teague checked his watch three times in the twenty seconds it took Tony to walk to his office. Tony entered and handed Teague a fourteen-page report.

"Give me a summary," said Teague, tossing the report aside.

"Most of the money in Abu Nazer's account came from an offshore corporation owned by another offshore corporation owned by another and so on back to a parent company called Industrial Containers of Antigua. I discovered they have business contracts with over two hundred firms in North and South America, so running traces on all of them took even longer. Anyway, the funding stream zigzags around the world...several times, I might add, through those encryption shields that I mentioned. But I was able to follow the trail all the way back to – are you ready for this? – Rainbow Global Partners, a medical relief organization owned and sourced by Medical Plastics of Miami.

"Medical Plastics? As in our Medical Plastics?"

"Yes, sir."

"That means the pipeline—"

"Leads straight upstairs."

Upstairs, Philip Trent sighed as he hung up the phone. He hated killing good people. Except when they got in the way.

Senator Ashford had been the first, and by Abu Nazer's hand, no less, who himself must now be elimination. And all because of Teague and that nosey little agent of his. The fact that Gustaves had located Abu Nazer's Swiss bank account was as brilliant as it was infuriating. One had to assume she had read the statement, which meant she was a threat in the same way April Delgado became a threat when she received it. So April had been eliminated. The victim of a robbery gone wrong.

Or so it had been made to appear.

That left Teague and Gustaves. And, of course, Vice President Baker.

A minor mystery had been the unexplained death of Louise Kappelmann. Abu Nazer had been willing to pay a million dollars to have her eliminated, but someone had beaten him to it. Who would have done that? And why?

No matter, the job had been done.

Yes, he hated killing good people. Except when they got in the way.

High over the Rocky Mountains, the smell of fresh coffee awakened Qaderi, now bald, wearing glasses and sporting a moustache.

"Cup of coffee, Mr. Thibonais?" asked the smiling flight attendant.

"Better make it two," Qaderi said in a Jamaican accent. "How soon until we land?"

"A little over two hours," the attendant replied.

Qaderi accepted the cups of coffee and the attendant moved on.

Once the attendant was out of earshot, Youssef picked up the airline telephone, swiped a credit card and dialed a number.

"Scott Akron's office. This is Lisa," a voice answered.

"Is Scott available?" asked Youssef.

"May I say who's calling?"

"Youssef Qaderi. Regarding my claim."

"May I have your policy number, Mr. Qaderi?"

Youssef told her.

"One moment."

The wait was not long.

"Everything is in order, Mr. Qaderi. Dr. Tyler verified that your tablet was destroyed in an explosion."

"Come again?"

"Dr. Tyler verified that your tablet was destroyed."

"He actually said that?"

"As part of an embassy report. All we're waiting for now are verifications from the tour company and the police."

"Did they say when that would be?"

"By the end of the day. As soon as we receive those reports, the adjuster will fast-track your claim and the insurance money will be deposited into your account in Switzerland."

With a smile, Qaderi hung up the phone.

"Is everything set?" asked Lydia.

Qaderi nodded and took a sip of his coffee. All that remained now was to put a bullet in Woolley's head.

CHAPTER 55

Sterling Crest Gallery was an elegant, contemporary San Francisco auction house attired in blonde maple and stainless steel, with nineteenth-century exposed brick walls and tastefully painted ductwork and pipes.

The gallery consisted of two floors. The ground floor was where affordable *objets d'art* were sold to customers who wished to be seen carrying the coveted black-and-white plastic bag that was the gallery's hallmark. Up the cabled staircase, however, was the mezzanine, where more significant purchases could be made. Here Champagne was served, customers were referred to as "clients," and names were always remembered.

The mezzanine was also where valuations were made by experts like Dr. Allan Woolley, who had just finished a transaction with a smartly dressed fashion executive. Under her arm was a framed watercolor of some exotic flowers that looked remarkably sexual.

"Would you like us to have it delivered?" asked Woolley.

"That won't be necessary," the woman replied, putting her cell phone to her ear. "I'm ready, Brian, bring the car," she said into the instrument before ending the call and dropping it back in her purse.

Woolley watched her descend the staircase, her high heels smacking sharply on the polished granite steps.

"Dr. Woolley, please come to the office," a feminine voice cooed over the loud speaker.

Woolley headed for the office of Elizabeth Baring, owner of Sterling Crest Gallery. In all likelihood, the sale he'd just made was the reason Elizabeth wanted to see him.

"Hello Janine," Woolley said to Elizabeth's assistant when he entered the office.

"You may go right in, Dr. Woolley," Janine replied.

Woolley smiled and opened the door into Elizabeth's private office. He stopped abruptly when he saw the circle of people standing around Elizabeth's worktable.

The first was Dr. Philippa Eaton. She was wearing a boring brown suit and ruffled blouse. Beside her was Scott Akron, a thirty-something business type from the insurance company. Beside Akron were two large men Woolley did not recognize. Both wore serious scowls aimed straight at him. To Elizabeth's right was Tyler, dressed in his usual blue jeans and boots, and next to him was Faisal Mostafa. Standing beside Faisal was the portly Cameron Cushing, and beside him was Nadia Burke, a plain woman in wire-rimmed glasses. At the end of the table was Rubin Yehuda.

"I didn't think—" Woolley began, his voice trailing off the moment he caught sight of what was laying in the center of the worktable. An object he knew only too well.

ES 34-30.

Qaderi's tablet.

And very much in one piece.

"Shut the door," Elizabeth said.

Woolley stood motionless, blinking.

"Shut the *door,* Allan," she said again.

Woolley mechanically obeyed.

"Is there something you'd like to tell us?" she asked, removing her gold framed half-glasses. Elizabeth was a stylish woman with short white hair.

Woolley glanced nervously around the table.

"Well?" Elizabeth asked.

"The, uh, committee is meeting today?" responded Woolley, trying desperately to gather his composure.

"I brought them in early," said Elizabeth.

"Why wasn't I told?"

"Many reasons. Now, I'll repeat my question: is there something you'd like to tell us?"

Woolley again scanned the faces of the others. The only person not making eye contact with him was Faisal, and Woolley knew what that meant.

Faisal had talked.

Woolley glanced over at the two men he did not know. "I'm not sure I should discuss anything in the presence of strangers."

"Then allow me to introduce you to officers Sanchez and Benson. They have a long list of questions about your part in an insurance scam involving the tablet."

"I think I should call my lawyer."

Elizabeth watched as Sanchez and Benson placed Woolley in handcuffs and led him away. She then turned to Scott Akron. "I presume no charges will be filed against Dr. Mostafa?"

"That is correct," said Akron. "Abu Nazer forced him to carve the tablet by threatening to kill his family." He looked over at Faisal. "Dr. Mostafa, I can't thank you enough for coming forward with the truth."

Faisal nodded appreciatively.

"But I do have a question for Dr. Tyler," said Akron. "If the replica wasn't destroyed in the terrorist attack, then what was in the suitcase you placed on the bus?"

"Bricks," answered Tyler.

"You took quite a risk pulling a stunt like that. What would you have done if the bus hadn't been attacked and you'd been forced to make the trade?"

"Things wouldn't have progressed that far."

"What do you mean?"

"Just what I said. I wouldn't have allowed things to progress that far."

"How could you have prevented it?"

"Do I really need to spell it out?"

"I'm interested."

Tyler glanced around and saw everybody was looking at him.

"I would have killed him," he said.

Akron laughed until he saw Tyler's expressionless eyes staring back at him.

"You're serious?" he asked, swallowing nervously.

"The woman he held hostage was a friend of mine and I wasn't about to let anything happen to her. So, with a terrorist holding a gun to her head, and the real tablet on its way to San Francisco with Dr. Mostafa – you do the math."

Akron responded with an uneasy smile. He then gave a start when he looked at his watch. "My goodness, is that the time?" He smiled nervously and excused himself with profuse apologies for having another meeting.

"Anyone else?" asked Tyler once Akron was gone.

No one spoke.

Tyler turned to Dr. Eaton. "Have you come to a decision?"

Dr. Eaton gazed wistfully at the tablet in the center of the table. "Even without Dr. Mostafa's admirable confession, I have no hesitation in declaring the tablet to be a forgery," she said. "A very good one, I might add, but not without the distinctive evidence of fabrication."

"They you're all in agreement?" he asked, scanning the faces of the others.

"Yes," they nodded in response.

"I am extremely disappointed, of course," Dr. Eaton added with a sigh. "I was buoyant at the possibility that Sir Edmund's tablet had actually been discovered. You are not to blame, Dr. Mostafa, given the deplorable circumstances under which Abu Nazer forced you to fabricate this one. I only wish the dream had been real."

"I regret that it is not," said Faisal.

"Even so, I continue to dream," said Dr. Eaton. "Perhaps one day the real tablet will be found."

"I hope not," declared Cameron Cushing. "Look at the trouble it's caused. I wonder if anyone is capable of owning that land. All the killing: so futile, so senseless. Which is the last thing God intended."

Tyler turned to Yehuda. "Doctor, what are your thoughts?"

"A few days ago, I would have argued vehemently with Dr. Cushing over such a remark. Israel belongs to the Jews and I thought the tablet proved that."

"And now?"

"I will admit it has been difficult for me to accept that the tablet is a forgery. But I remembered what an old friend once told me – that the tablet repeats what is written in the Scriptures. And that made me think about God for the first time in years. I knew then that I could not be part of the madness any longer. The willingness to stop the killing has to start somewhere. I decided then it will start with me."

Spontaneous applause broke out around the table.

Yehuda held up a hand. "But there are those who, for their own reasons, want it to continue. Abu Nazer, *Qamat,* the *gibburim…* And Aaron."

"Aaron, the assassin? I thought he was dead," said Faisal.

"There is among the *gibburim* a man some of us believe to be Aaron," said Yehuda. "He goes by the name of Adino, but no one knows his real name. Years ago, he was badly wounded. Now, he walks with a cane."

Elizabeth suddenly turned pale. "My God. He's coming *here,* to the *gallery!*"

"What do you mean?" asked Tyler.

"Adino! He's on the guest list for this afternoon's meeting with Vice President Baker!"

Across the street in a coffee shop, Qaderi was about to phone Woolley to arrange a meeting, when he saw him being ushered out of the gallery in handcuffs.

"Your cappuccino's ready," the barista told Qaderi, who was staring out the window with disbelief at the sight of Woolley being placed in a squad car. "Sir, your cappuccino?"

Youssef ignored the attendant and ran out the door dialing his cell phone.

"Scott Akron's office. This is Lisa," a voice answered.

"Let me speak with Scott. This is Qaderi."

"One moment, Mr. Qaderi."

Qaderi continued hurrying along while trying to stay calm.

"I'm sorry, but Mr. Akron is unavailable," Lisa said. "May I ask what this concerns?"

"You know damn well what this concerns! Has my claim been approved?"

"One moment, please."

Qaderi cursed out loud at being put on hold again. His exclamation drew the surprised attention of several passersby.

Lisa finally came back on the line. "I'm sorry, Mr. Qaderi, but your claim has been denied."

"*Denied?* On what grounds?"

"Your tablet is a forgery. Dr. Mostafa delivered it to the gallery, where it was examined by Mr. Akron and a panel of experts. I'm told the police are—"

Youssef slammed shut his phone, turned a corner and ran toward the white BMW parked by the curb.

There's only one person who could have talked Mostafa into double-crossing me, he thought. He pulled open the door and climbed in.

"Where's Woolley?" asked Lydia.

"Start the engine. Our plans have changed."

290

CHAPTER 56

Philip Trent's secretary, Lori, stiffened when she saw the commanding figure of William Green striding into her office. With him were Teague and four agents.

"Director Green!" Lori exclaimed, jumping to her feet.

"Is he in?" Green asked.

"Yes, sir, but—"

Green swept by Lori and into Trent's private office. Trent looked up from a phone call as Green entered.

"I'll get back with you," he said, hanging up.

"Why, Philip?" demanded Green, slamming his hands on Trent's desk.

"What do you mean? What's this about?"

Teague nodded to one of his agents.

"Philip Trent, you have the right to remain silent. Anything you say can and will be used against you in a court of law..."

"You can't be serious," said Trent with a laugh.

"You better believe I'm serious!" replied Green, his eyes glowing with fury. "Of all people! How could you?"

Trent sat back, folded his hands across his chest and pressed his fingers together in a little steeple. "You're here about Nightingale," he said. He glanced icily at Teague then back at Green. "A program that has served this nation well."

"Served the *nation*? You're nothing but a mob of *killers!*"

"Who do this nation's dirty work," retorted Trent. "We clean the sewers. We handle what no one else has the stomach to handle."

"You killed Omar! You killed his *family!*"

"Collateral damage."

"And the USS Cole? The bombings of *embassies?* You took lives – *American* lives!"

"We needed to show a fat and lazy nation what the real world is like – what our enemies want to do to us – and *will* do, given the chance."

"I *trusted* you!"

"We needed to wake people up."

"Well, it's over. Nightingale is over."

"And you'll pay for what you've done!" vowed Trent, turning his glare on Teague. "Every last one of you will pay."

"Get him out of here!" hissed Green.

The agents led Trent away.

"My *God*," said Green. "He was one of *mine…*"

"We can't always tell where the rot is," said Teague. "Trent intended to deceive us, and he did."

"At least we've got enough to convict him."

"Right now we've got bigger problems."

"What could be more important than burying Nightingale?" asked Green.

"Abu Nazer is still out there. And we don't know how many other Nightingale killers there are to track down."

"We'll go through Trent's computer and find them. And I'll assign you a protection detail until we've caught every last one of them."

"I'm not the target," said Teague.

"Then who is?" asked Green.

"The person they tried to assassinate before: Vice President Baker."

CHAPTER 57

Zoe and Teague climbed out of the taxi in front of San Francisco's Moscone Convention Center. Flags atop a row of masts flapped lazily in the cool ocean breeze.

"How are you feeling?" asked Teague.

"I'm alive," replied Zoe, wrapping her trench coat around her to block out the wind. Beneath the coat, she wore her standard black pant suit and white shirt.

"Have you phoned—?"

"My mother?" asked Zoe.

"She's been phoning for updates on how you're doing," said Teague, leading the way toward the entrance.

"Tell her to mind her own business."

"Give her a call. She's concerned."

Zoe did not reply. The animosity between her and her mother was not anything she wanted to share. Teague may have his suspicions, but no one really knew what she knew: how her mother had played the grieving widow when her dad, Sergeant Major Mike Gustaves, was killed in action. In truth, her mother was planning to divorce her dad. Then he was killed. Then her mother bankrolled his heroic death and her newfound role as his grieving widow into a successful victory to the House of Representatives back in her dad's home state.

Her dad always told her to have her own opinions. To think for herself and form her own conclusions. So when Zoe did just that and said how she resented her mother's tactics, the conflicts began.

It was not that her mom was not a good at her congressional job. She was damned good. One of the best on the Hill, in fact. Zoe simply resented the way she got there. And her mother resented Zoe for having the audacity to say so.

"Any news on Sharifa?" asked Teague.

"No body, no clues," she replied.

"How's Tyler taking it?"

"You'll have to ask Tyler."

Teague noticed the sharpness in her voice.

"Are you sure you're okay?" he asked.

"Why wouldn't I be?"

"I don't know, you just seem...on edge."

"Do I?"

"Is this going to be one of those days?"

"What kind of day would that be?"

"I just asked how Tyler was doing."

"Can we talk about something else? Besides, where did he learn to shoot like that? And where did he get that rifle? And that gizmo gun case of his – what's the story on *that*? And where the *hell* did he meet Tariq? If you ask me, he's got some serious explaining to do."

"You're talking about him," Teague said.

With a huff of disgust, Zoe pulled open the door and marched inside. They paused in the spacious concourse. It was empty but full of echoes.

"Which way?" asked Zoe, glancing toward the sound of footsteps.

The man hurrying toward them was short, with a high forehead and scowling face. His dyed brown hair had been combed across a wide cranium and sprayed into a shell.

"Off limits, you'll have to leave," the man called out, waving them back toward the door.

"We're looking for Lester Moore," Teague replied.

"And you are?"

Teague took out his ID. "Jackson Teague, Central Intelligence Agency," he said. "This is Zoe Gustaves."

The man was suddenly all smiles. "Of course, Mr. Teague, I've been expecting you," he replied, extending his hand. "Les Moore, chief of security. I catch a lot of jokes about that. You know, Moore is Les and Les is Moore." He laughed.

Zoe glanced at Teague, then back at the idiot in the blue blazer.

Teague shook Moore's outstretched hand and followed him to a set of double doors.

"The Secret Service is already here," Moore explained, pulling one open one of the doors and leading the way inside.

Several agents were patrolling the cavernous auditorium. There was a large empty stage at the far end. High overhead was a catwalk and miles of pipes – all painted black. Near the ceiling was a row of windows.

"The President's motorcade will arrive through our underground garage," Moore continued. "We designed the convention center to accommodate heads of state, so areas of the parking garage can be sealed off. The President will then take an elevator that opens directly into a room behind the stage."

"Are those windows up there bulletproof?" asked Zoe.

Moore dismissed the query with a snort.

Teague looked directly at Moore. "Ms. Gustaves asked you a question and I'd like to know your answer."

Moore stiffened. "They're fixed, made of heavy-duty glass, with a mirrored film."

"But not bulletproof?" asked Teague.

"Unnecessary. Our rooftop is totally secure. Besides, the Secret Service is all over the place."

"Check trajectories from neighboring buildings," Teague told Zoe.

Zoe nodded and made a note.

"It would be impossible to find a high rise from which an assassin could fire a rifle," said Moore.

"We'll keep that in mind."

"You're wasting your time," insisted Moore. "Only Superman could see through our reflective glass and hit something."

"Want me to include choppers?" asked Zoe.

Teague nodded.

"The airspace around the center has already been restricted," Moore volunteered.

"Tell me about the kitchen, ductwork, ceiling access, stage cavity and wall density," said Teague.

"Don't forget floor thickness and penetrability," added Zoe. "Abu Nazer can shoot but he's also very fond of explosives."

"Did you say, Abu Nazer?" asked Moore, suddenly nervous.

"Name ring a bell?"

Beneath his shirt, Lester Moore began to perspire. "What were those questions again?"

While Teague repeated his list, Zoe walked up onto the stage and stood looking out over the voluminous hall. Workers were starting to wheel in trolleys of chairs and large round tables. She looked up at windows. Only a couple of neighboring buildings appeared to pose problems. However, if Abu Nazer had already been here, he would have anticipated someone standing where she was standing. He would know someone would calculate angles and trajectories. He would expect those buildings to be noticed.

Which meant he would try something different. Something unexpected. Zoe just hoped she could figure out what that was.

The afternoon passed quickly, and by 4:30 Zoe was sitting in one of the chairs at the back of the auditorium thinking about her encounter with Abu Nazer. Obviously, she had been spared not out of mercy, but as a calculated maneuver to distract Tyler, to keep him from shooting.

To keep him from shooting.

Zoe wondered what kind of weapon Abu Nazer would use against Vice President Baker – assuming, of course, that Teague was right about Baker being the target, which she was not entirely sure he was. A more logical target would be Tyler, the man who had robbed Abu Nazer of a hundred million dollars. Complicating matters – or perhaps simplifying them – was the fact that Tyler would be attending tonight's speech.

But the convention center was already swarming with CIA, FBI, Secret Service, and the SFPD. Teague tended to think this increased the attraction, that Abu Nazer was egotistical enough to want to penetrate such a concerted initiative. To do so would be an undeniable victory for his daring and skill.

While that argument was certainly logical, and it fit Abu Nazer's profile, Zoe could not quite accept it as a foregone conclusion. For one thing, it seemed counterproductive, even for a megalomaniac like Abu Nazer.

Outfoxing the world's best was never his real focus. Neither was killing Vice President Baker. His real focus, in her mind, was revenge: getting even with Tyler.

Zoe surveyed the huge room. Tyler would be seated out there tonight – which, of course, dovetailed nicely with Teague's argument. But Abu Nazer would not know where. So, other than at tonight's speech, where was Tyler most vulnerable?

"How are you doing?" Teague asked.

Zoe glanced over her shoulder. "We're pretty well covered, I guess."

"But?" asked Teague, detecting her lack of conviction.

Zoe shrugged.

"Let's have it," he said, sitting beside her.

"I think we're looking in the wrong direction."

The watch on Teague's wrist read 16:45 and he held it out for Zoe to see. "You're telling me this at quarter to five?"

"I know," she said. "But I can't help thinking Abu Nazer knows this is where we'll be concentrating our efforts. I think he'll try something different."

"Then what? And *where?*"

"I'm not sure. But I think Tyler, not Baker, will be the target."

"Aren't you forgetting about Trent? He told us Abu Nazer would hunt down everyone who helped ruin Nightingale. His implication was clearly aimed at Vice President Baker. And I think Abu Nazer's in town to finish the job."

"Did Trent actually say Abu Nazer would be the one to hunt down those responsible?"

"Who else would he be talking about?"

"Aren't you assuming?" asked Zoe.

Teague looked away with a snort.

"Maybe he was referring to another of the Nightingale killers," suggested Zoe. "Sir, Abu Nazer was inches away from collecting a hundred million dollars and Tyler's the one who ruined it. I think he'll want to get even."

"Then why not kill two birds with one stone? Both men will be here tonight."

"Because there's no way Abu Nazer can know where Tyler will be seated, and security will be impenetrable. Nor does he know which entrance Tyler will use. Or when he'll arrive. Plus, he knows we'll be expecting him to strike here. That's too many negatives."

"Those negatives increase the attraction."

"But outmaneuvering us is not his goal. In my view, his goal is to get even with Tyler, and he'll look for the easiest and surest way of doing that. Which has to include some means of escape. The convention center poses too many problems."

"Then *where?*" reiterated Teague, his frustration evident.

"Is anything happening before tonight's speech? Something that Tyler's involved in?"

Teague touched one of the speed dial buttons on his phone and held it to his ear. When his assistant answered, he said, "April—" then paused and took a breath. "Sorry. Heather, I need to know if you've got Rutherford Tyler on any guest list prior to the start of the peace conference."

Teague's new secretary pulled up a schedule on her computer screen.

"Five-thirty, Sterling Crest Gallery," she said. "There's a gathering of approximately three hundred people with Vice President Baker, Dr. Eaton, members of her panel, the media, and a host of Israeli and Arab diplomats. After an announcement about the tablet, the Vice President plans to urge all sides to renew their commitment to peace."

"Is Tyler's name on the guest list?" asked Teague.

"Yes, sir."

"What's the address?" asked Teague, glancing at his watch.

His secretary told him.

"Call the Secret Service and tell them 'Code Orange' for Vice President Baker and Rutherford Tyler. We've got a terrorist on the loose and he may strike during that meeting. The terrorist's name is Youssef Qaderi."

CHAPTER 58

Downtown San Francisco is not a good place to be at five o'clock, especially if you're in a hurry.

"Can't you hit the siren?" Teague asked the patrolman who was driving the car.

"Useless. No one can move."

"What's the holdup?" asked Zoe.

Visible over the tops of three lanes of stopped cars were some caution signs and a flashing arrow.

"Cable works," answered the officer. "During rush hour. Go figure."

Around them, bicycle couriers with walkie-talkies strapped to their lower backs darted between the gridlocked cars. Irate drivers, many of whom vented their frustration by leaning on their horns, tried inching forward, as though blocking the couriers would somehow speed things along. Farther ahead, words were being shouted at indifferent workmen standing behind a barricade stretching across two lanes of traffic. They remained oblivious to the angry drivers as they continued feeding a cable into a manhole from a giant spool on the bed of a truck. Two other workmen, their hardhats cocked back on their heads, stood talking near the edge of the barricade.

"We're running out of time!" said Teague.

"I could call for a couple of solos," suggested the driver.

"Solos?" asked Zoe.

"Motorcycle cops," answered Teague. He turned back to the driver. "How long would it take 'em to get here?"

"Ten, twelve minutes, depending."

"Too long. Anything quicker?"

"Not that I can think of. With three lanes funneling into one, we could be here for another twenty minutes."

Zoe touched Teague on the arm. "How much money have you got?"

"Why?"

"Give me a hundred. Or a couple of fifties."

"What are you going to do with it?"

"Sir, we're wasting time!"

With a growl, Teague pulled out his wallet and handed Zoe a hundred-dollar bill. She climbed out of the patrol car and threaded her way between the lines of cars.

"Where's she going?" asked the driver.

"I haven't a clue," answered Teague.

The two idle workmen saw Zoe coming toward them.

"Hardhat area," one of them said, thumbing toward a sign restricting entry.

"Big problem, we gotta get through," Zoe said, showing the workman her ID.

"No favors. Wait with the others."

Zoe closed the wallet, and when she did, the workman caught sight of the money. She put her ID away but kept the money discreetly visible.

"I need this lane opened so our squad car can get through," Zoe said. "We can't hit the siren 'cause no one can move. But it's critical that we get through. So, please, I'm asking for your help."

The two workmen glanced at one another. Indecision showed in their eyes.

"If you don't have the authority, point me to your supervisor and I'll ask him. No bullshit. This is important."

"Was that ID you showed me for real?" the larger of the two men asked, trying to read Zoe's expression.

"Hundred percent."

The pair again looked at one another and the larger one shrugged. "Okay, lady, you got it," he said. "I'll be the sucker."

Zoe extended her hand.

"Forget it, we're nearly done," he said. He scooted the first panel lazily toward the curb. "Where you headed? The airport?"

Not hearing a reply, the workman glanced back and saw Zoe's grave expression. He walked over and looked her square in the eyes. "You ain't shittin' me, are you?"

"This is for real. But I can't explain."

The workman stared at her for a moment, then turned and ran awkwardly toward the next panel. "Harry, give me a hand!" he shouted. "We need to move these barricades *now!*"

With a grateful wave, Zoe ran back to the patrol car to cheers and honks from drivers.

"What did you tell those guys?" demanded Teague once she was inside.

"I was tempted to keep this, you know." She held out the money and Teague snatched it back.

"Well?" he asked.

"I said we needed to get to the airport."

At Sterling Crest Gallery, dignitaries from North Africa and the Middle East were stepping out of chauffeured limousines under the watchful eyes of the Secret Service, newspaper, television, cable and internet news networks. Stationed on the rooftops of surrounding buildings were teams of snipers. Inside were half a dozen walk-through metal detectors, plus more agents with handheld scanners. Throughout the gallery were teams of Federal agents.

The mezzanine elevator doors dinged open and Adino and his aides stepped out. Adino approached one of the walkthrough metal detectors, laid his cane on the table, and limped through.

"Sir, would you please step over here?" asked an agent once Adino had picked up his cane.

"Why? The alarm did not sound."

"Please. Step over here."

"For what reason?"

"Sir, would you please step over here?"

"Do you know who I am? I was invited here by Vice President Baker!"

With a fixed smile, the agent gestured Adino toward a table.

Adino glared at the man, growled his disgust, and walked to the table. "You Americans and your silly games!"

Another agent with another fixed smile met Adino.

"Your cane, please," said the agent.

Adino surrendered his cane, which was handed to a third agent, who ran a metal detector over it.

Beep.

"It has a silver handle," Adino explained impatiently. "It does not take a metal detector to determine that."

The agent handed Adino a replacement cane.

"Did you not hear me?" protested Adino. "The handle is silver! It sets off alarms!"

"You may pick up your cane on the way out," said the agent.

"This is *outrageous!*"

"Standard procedure."

"I demand to speak with your superior!"

"Like I said, this is standard—"

"*Now!*"

"What's the problem?" asked another agent. He was similar in appearance to the others: physically fit, cropped hair, pressed suit, coiled ear wire.

"Who are you?" demanded Adino.

"The person you wanted to see. Now, what's the problem?"

"I refuse to be treated this way! I walk with the aid of a stick. It has a silver handle – which any *imbecile* can see. It always sets off alarms. That doesn't mean it's dangerous. Now, may I *please* have it back so that I can sit down?"

"We've supplied you with an adequate replacement. Your cane will be returned when you leave."

"I demand to speak with your superior!"

The agent took Adino by the elbow and escorted him several steps away. "Sir, you have two choices. You can either go in there and sit down with the stick we gave you or you'll be escorted off the premises."

"Are you afraid of a *walking stick?*" bellowed Adino. "The mighty Americans are afraid of a *walking stick!*"

The agent glanced around at all the people staring at them.

"See those people looking at us?" he asked. "They're wondering what kind of a troublemaker you are. And you know what? I'm beginning to wonder the same thing, too. Do you know what we do with troublemakers when it involves the safety of our leaders?" He paused and allowed his words time to sink in. "So I'll say this one more time. Either you go in there and sit down with the stick we gave you or I'm throwing your ass out of here. What's it going to be?"

Adino's nostrils flared with rage.

The agent raised an eyebrow.

With a growl, Adino snatched the cane and marched defiantly toward the main section of chairs.

Across the room, Vice President Sam Baker was shaking hands with Chaim Halevy, the Israeli Prime Minister.

"Mr. Prime Minister, how wonderful to see you," he said with a warm smile. "Thank you for coming."

"Thank you for inviting me, Mr. Vice President," the stocky Halevy replied, bowing slightly.

Halevy tensed when he saw Adino. He tensed even more when he saw Wassim Jafar in his familiar red and white checked *kaffiyah.*

Baker noticed Halevy's reaction.

"Mr. Prime Minister, you know why we're here," he said, placing a hand on Halevy's shoulder.

"Dialogue and peace, with them in the room?" asked Halevy cynically.

"They need to hear what we have to say."

"They are terrorists!"

"They are leaders who command a great deal of influence with a great many people."

"Mr. Vice President, you know as well as I do the number of unsuccessful peace proposals brokered by your various administrations – despite your good intentions. As you Americans say, it takes two to tango."

Baker smiled. "Then I trust you brought your dancing shoes with you today?"

The Prime Minister returned the smile. "Mr. Vice President, they never come off."

Across the floor, Tyler was speaking quietly with Dr. Eaton.

"The Vice President will open the meeting then introduce you and your committee. You'll be the one making the announcement about the tablet. I probably don't need to remind you, but please speak slowly and pause between sentences. This will allow translators time to communicate what you're saying. If you wish to call on other committee members for verification or comment, feel free to do so. You can then hand the meeting back to Mr. Baker and he'll open the floor."

"I admire what you're trying to do," said Dr. Eaton.

"I just hope it works."

Moments later, Sam Baker stepped forward and greeted the crowd, his welcoming smile melting into a somber frown when he recounted the recent escalations of violence.

"We all know who is responsible," declared Adino. He stood and pointed at Jafar. "The leeches of *Qamat,* that's who."

"I will not stand for such insults!" cried Jafar, springing to his feet.

"Gentlemen, please!" said Baker.

"Terrorist dog!" shouted Adino.

"Murderer!" Jafar shouted back.

"How *dare* you!" roared Adino.

Within seconds, the two men were locked in a shouting match, with news cameras filming it all.

"Stop!" shouted Baker. "Stop these insults and *listen*."

"Mr. Vice President, this is an outrage!" said Jafar.

"I speak the truth!" shouted Adino.

"You are like a polluted river," Jafar shouted back. "You bring death to our land."

"Jerusalem is ours! It belongs to the Jews! Arabs are like *vomit* on the land."

In the front row, Chaim Halevy shook his head sadly.

"I will not stand for this!" yelled Jafar.

Baker signaled his sound technician and a deafening screech reverberated through the gallery. Everyone shielded their ears. Another nod and the screeching stopped.

"Why do you force me to use such gimmicks?" said Baker. "We are not here for accusations!"

"We are *here*," thundered Adino, "because the Ishmael tablet says Palestine belongs to the Jews! We own it! It is *ours*! And that means the Arabs must leave. They have no place in *anything* that is ours."

"Then tell me why your founder, Moses, married a Midianite woman – a *Saudi*," said Tyler, stepping forward. "Tell me why your patriarch, Joseph, took an Egyptian wife."

"You dare lecture *me?*"

Jafar laughed contemptuously. "Jews are part Arab! I knew it!"

"Just as Arabs are part Jew," said Tyler. "Those women embraced their husbands, loved them, bore their children."

Jafar sat down with a growl of disgust.

"Enough of this nonsense!" said Adino. "Palestine is ours. The tablet *proves* it."

"I'm glad you brought that up," said Baker. "May I present Dr. Philippa Eaton? She chairs a committee of experts who have been studying the tablet."

"Tell them!" shouted Adino. "Tell them what the tablet declares!"

The room fell quiet.

"The tablet is a forgery," said Dr. Eaton.

"*What?*" screamed Adino. "Who is paying you to say such a thing?"

"It is true," Yehuda declared in his gravelly voice. "The tablet is a fake."

"You lie!" screamed Adino.

"He speaks the truth," said Faisal.

He nodded to the two gallery assistants standing to one side with a four-wheeled dolly covered with a sheet. The assistants wheeled the dolly over and Faisal removed the sheet.

There was a hushed silence as all eyes focused on the tablet. It was mounted on the dolly at an upright angle.

"Faisal took out a lighter, flicked it with his thumb and held the flame under the corner of the tablet. It bubbled and hissed and then melted into a blob.

He looked at the shocked faces of people staring back at him.

"The tablet is a fake," he said. "I know because I am the one who carved it from a slab of special polymer resin containing concentrates of oxides and stone dust. To the untrained eye, it is indistinguishable from a real slab of diorite."

"I knew it!" shouted Adino, waving his stick in the air while reporters hurriedly took notes. "The Arabs *deceive us.*"

"Dr. Mostafa had no choice," said Tyler. "Abu Nazer forced him to carve it."

"And Abu Nazer is an *Arab!*"

Across the mezzanine, Teague and Zoe stepped out of the elevator.

"My God, the place is *packed,*" whispered Zoe.

"Go left and I'll go right," Teague said quietly. "Don't forget, he may be in disguise."

"If Qaderi's here, we'll find him."

CHAPTER 59

Teague turned and nearly ran into Lydia.

"I beg your pardon," he said, stepping around her and moving on.

Lydia continued threading her way through the crowd toward Tyler. It had not been difficult to get her name on the official guest list. A quick phone call to one of Jafar's aides was all it had taken. All she had to do now was wait for Youssef's call.

The plan was simple. Youssef would inform Tyler that he had fifteen minutes to reach a particular pay phone at Fisherman's Wharf. If he refused, Sharifa would die. If anyone followed, Sharifa would die. If he called the police, Sharifa would die.

In other words, if he ever wished to see Sharifa alive again, he would follow the instructions to the letter.

He would never arrive, of course, because somewhere along the way he would be killed – the unfortunate victim of a drive-by shooting.

Lydia glanced at her watch. Just two minutes to go.

Zoe finished her half of the search and met Teague on the other side of the mezzanine. "No sign of him anywhere," she said.

"Keep looking. He's got to be here."

Zoe nodded and continued moving around the room.

Teague stepped over to the railing and scanned the floor below. Except for a few teams of agents, the downstairs area was empty. He made his way over to the pair of Secret Service agents standing near the staircase and asked about the likelihood of someone having hidden an explosive device in the gallery.

"We swept it completely," one of them said. "Electronically and with sniffer dogs. It's clean."

Teague thanked the agents and moved on.

Lydia excused her way to the front of a row of listeners and sidled in beside a bearded Saudi diplomat wearing a head cloth and tailored suit. When the diplomat glanced at her, Lydia nodded. The diplomat returned the nod before focusing again on Vice President Baker.

Unlike the diplomat, however, Lydia's attention was not on Baker. It was on Tyler, an arm's length away.

306

Tyler felt a nudge and turned to find Zoe standing beside him.

"Hey, how you feeling?" he whispered.

"Any sign of Qaderi?" she asked.

"The Secret Service advised me of the Code Orange, but I haven't seen him."

"Neither have I. And that bothers me." She moved off into the crowd.

Tyler watched her for a moment then saw Dr. Eaton signaling him. He nodded and circled discreetly behind Vice President Baker and over to where she was standing. The wide semicircle of agents protecting Baker parted slightly, allowing him to pass.

Lydia tensed when she saw Tyler move. *Youssef would be calling any minute!*

Knowing she had to remain close to Tyler in order to hand him the phone once Youssef called, she began circling around to where he was standing.

From the second row of chairs, a Jordanian diplomat raised his hand.

"Mr. Vice President, your next election is two years away. Will you be running again for President?"

A burst of applause swept through the gallery. Baker was often referred to as the *Sheik of State* because of his enormous popularity in the Middle East.

Baker smiled his appreciation and held up his hands. The room grew quiet.

"Some of you obviously remember the last election, and how spirited the campaign was," he said. "The press had a field day with some of my rather fiery outbursts."

Polite laughter rippled through the room.

"One journalist in particular took special delight in giving me a hard time."

Baker looked over at Tyler, who feigned innocence. Baker laughed and motioned for Tyler.

Tyler politely declined.

"May I remind you, Dr. Tyler, that you're surrounded by the Secret Service, the FBI, and the CIA?"

With a gesture of surrender, Tyler stepped to the Vice President's side.

Having just squeezed to the front of another row of listeners, Lydia panicked when she saw Tyler circle behind Baker and over to his other side. Cursing under her breath, she began sidling back through the same groups of people she had just pushed through moments before. Many looked at her with irritation as she stepped in front of them again.

"A free press keeps politicians like me honest," Baker declared. "And you can believe me when I say this man doesn't let me get away with a thing."

More laughter from the crowd.

Baker then turned serious.

"All joking aside, Dr. Tyler played an important role in bringing us together today, and I for one would like to thank him for what he has done."

Following Baker's lead, the crowd applauded. When the clapping had died down, Wassim Jafar raised his hand.

"Mr. Vice President!" he called out.

Baker pointed to Jafar, just as Jafar noticed Lydia pushing her way to the front of the row near Tyler. A look of astonishment came over his face.

"Lydia, Lydia Ardois? Is that you?" he said. "What are you doing here?"

Lydia stiffened at the mention of her name. She saw Jafar staring at her. Saw others turning to stare.

Saw Tyler turning to stare.

She looked down at the phone in her hand, willing it to ring.

Circulating through the crowd at the far end of the mezzanine, Zoe stopped when she heard Lydia's name.

Lydia Ardois was a member of Qamat. Lydia Ardois had been an airline passenger out of Tel Aviv on the same day someone had taken a shot at Vice President Baker.

Zoe pushed her way to the front of the crowd behind the main section of seats. She looked over the heads of those seated in the chairs and saw Lydia's eyes darting between Tyler and the cell phone in her hand.

Senator Ashford had been killed by a bomb inside a cell phone…

No wonder they hadn't been able to locate Qaderi. He wasn't here. *He was using a drone!*

"Everybody down, it's a *bomb!*" shouted Zoe.

There was a momentary hush, then chaos. People screaming,

running, dropping to the floor. Tyler whirled and tackled Vice President Baker.

Lydia saw Zoe sprinting toward her.

She turned to run.

Zoe caught her, grabbed the phone, and hurled it toward the front of the gallery.

The faint trill occurred a second after the phone left Zoe's hand. An instant later the gallery was a vacuum of brilliant white light.

The deafening blast slugged Zoe to the floor, smashed the gallery's windows and sent a fireball thundering out into the street. Display cases were splintered. Flying debris skipped off walls. Ash rained on people as if a volcano had erupted. Alarms started clanging. Several ceiling panels sagged and fell. One crashed onto Tyler as he shielded the Vice President.

The shock waves of the blast were now just an echo. Dust settled. Smoke swirled. People began to groan.

Lying on the floor, Lydia slowly opened her eyes. The gallery was rapidly becoming a cacophony of shouts. All around, people scrambled toward exits. Agents pulled the fallen ceiling panel off Tyler and rushed Vice President Baker out of the gallery.

Rolling up onto all fours, Lydia prepared to flee. She then saw the pistol lying beside her foot. Nearby, Zoe lay groaning.

Lydia grabbed for the gun.

A hand yanked Lydia to her feet. She jerked around. It was Tyler. She scratched viciously at his bleeding face.

Tyler spun Lydia around, kicked her behind the knees, and shoved her to the floor, where he pinned her with a knee.

Teague motioned for an agent to help Zoe while he and his men surrounded Tyler and Lydia. Tyler rose unsteadily to his feet and Teague's agents took Lydia into custody.

"You're hurt. Sit down," Teague said.

Tyler waved away the suggestion and stepped in front of Lydia.

"Where's Qaderi?" he demanded.

Lydia looked defiantly away as Teague's agents snapped handcuffed on her wrists.

Tyler grabbed Lydia by the chin. "He tried to kill you!"

"You're bleeding. Sit down," said Teague, touching Tyler on the arm.

Tyler shrugged off the suggestion.

"By all rights, you should be dead," he said to Lydia, wiping blood from his eyes. "He sent you in here with a bomb. Tell us where he is."

Indecision began to cloud Lydia's eyes but she did not reply.

"If you don't help us find him," said Tyler, "guess who he's going to come looking for once he hears you failed."

"Tyler, you're bleeding. You need to sit down," said Zoe.

"You're the one person who can identify him," Tyler said to Lydia. "The one person who can *testify* that he put you up to this. Now for the last time, tell us where he is! Before it's too late."

Lydia started to reply then looked away.

"Get her out of here," said Teague.

A pair of agents took Lydia by the arms.

"All right!" said Lydia.

 Teague signaled the agents to wait.

"Youssef said I was to hand you the phone," explained Lydia, looking at Tyler.

"So Vice President Baker wasn't the target?" asked Teague.

Lydia shook her head. "This was about Tyler. But I swear I didn't know the cell phone was a bomb. I thought he was going to tell you to go to Fisherman's Wharf, that if you didn't follow his instructions, he'd kill Sharifa."

"*Sharifa?* Is she all right?"

"She's alive. That's all I know."

"What about Qaderi? Where's he?"

"Somewhere in the city. In a rental car. A white BMW."

Teague motioned for one of his agents to follow that up.

"What's he planning next?" asked Teague. "Does it involve tonight's speech at the convention center?"

"Not that I know of."

"Where did he tell you to meet him when this was over?"

"At the airport."

Adino pushed his way to the front of the spectators. "She's Jafar's aide. Qamat tried to *kill* us!"

"I knew nothing of this!" cried Jafar.

"We all could have died," said Tyler, losing his balance and stumbling into Teague.

"You need to sit down," said Teague, helping Tyler to a chair. He nodded to his agents and they took Lydia away.

"I'm fine. Just a little dizzy."

"Why would Qamat wish to kill you?" asked Adino.

"It wasn't Qamat," said Tyler, standing. "She was working with Abu Nazer."

"Are you sure?" asked Jafar.

"Positive. Abu Nazer forced Dr. Mostafa to carve a replica of the Ishmael tablet, which was supposed to be destroyed in an accident so that he could collect the insurance money. I ruined his scheme."

"So the tablet—"

"Is a fake," affirmed Tyler. He wobbled slightly then steadied himself.

"My God, it's true," said Adino.

"Yes, your God. But what about theirs?" asked the stocky Chaim Halevy.

Adino looked quizzically at the Israeli Prime Minister.

"The Temple Mount, your tunnel, the explosives."

Adino's eyes widened.

"We found it, Adino. It is closed."

"I knew it!" screamed Wassim Jafar, appealing theatrically to the surrounding media with an expression of horror before jabbing an accusatory finger at Adino. "And I swear *vengeance* for this vicious assault!"

Halevy turned to Jafar.

"Golda Meir had a great love for the Arab people, so I will say to you what she once said to your countrymen: I can forgive you killing our children; I cannot forgive you for making us kill yours. Lives were saved today, not taken. So perhaps appreciation, not vengeance, would be a more appropriate response against an atrocity that was prevented."

While several people applauded, Jafar looked around at the media cameras now pointed at him. Forcing a smile, he nodded his agreement. Halevy looked again at Adino.

"As for you, I have nothing more to say other than your passport has been revoked, and American Immigration is waiting outside."

Tyler suddenly toppled backward. He collided with several people and crashed over a chair.

Zoe pushed everyone back. "Get back! Get me a doctor!" she

311

shouted, falling to her knees beside Tyler and rolling him onto his side. She checked his pulse then looked around. "Where's a *doctor?* For God's sake, *hurry!*"

Three minutes later, a team of paramedics wheeled Tyler into the elevator. An oxygen mask covered his face.

"They said he'd be all right," said Teague.

"Yeah, he looked just great…"

"I think you should get checked out as well."

"Did you notice how fast he moved?" asked Zoe. "He tackled Vice President Baker before the Secret Service had a chance to react."

"Speaking of which," said Teague, "that phone bomb would have killed a lot of people, including Baker, if it weren't for you. You saved lives today, Gustaves. Well done." He clasped Zoe on the shoulder and she flinched. "What's wrong? Are you hurt?" he asked.

"It's nothing. I'm fine," she replied.

Teague touched Zoe's shoulder again and she recoiled.

"You are hurt!" Teague said, motioning for a paramedic.

A medic came over but Zoe waved him away.

"I said I'm fine," she repeated.

"I want it looked at," said Teague.

"And I told you, I'm *fine!*"

"Have you made it your personal ambition to argue with everything I say?"

"I'm not arguing. I just don't need medical attention. Yes, my shoulder is bruised, but that's all it is. A bruise. People get them I get them. They're part of the job."

"Then go back to your hotel room and rest."

"We've still got work to do."

"This isn't a request, Gustaves. You've done enough for today."

Zoe bit her lip.

"By the way," said Teague, "I'll be requesting an award of valor for what you did today."

Zoe did not respond.

"I can see that impresses you," said Teague.

"Sir, I don't mean to appear ungrateful, but this isn't over – not by a long shot. Abu Nazer would not have put his entire plan in the hands of a drone. Yes, he was hoping she'd get lucky. But she didn't.

He'll try something else."

"And we're on top of it. We now know what Abu Nazer looks like and we'll be watching for him."

"We were watching for him this time and look what happened."

"The attempt was thwarted. You thwarted it!"

"We got lucky, that's all. What about next time? We don't know where he is or what he'll try next. Or who he'll use. Remember Tariq? Where the hell is he?"

"Not your concern. You've done enough."

"Sir, Abu Nazer's still out there."

"And we've got it covered. There's no way he'll get into that convention center."

"That isn't his focus. Tyler is. And he was just wheeled out of here on a stretcher!"

"Which is something Abu Nazer wouldn't know."

"All the more reason to let me stay on. I know Abu Nazer by sight."

Teague signaled one of his agents.

"Yes, sir?" the agent asked.

"Ben, I want you to take Ms. Gustaves either to the hospital or to her hotel, whichever she prefers. And if by chance she manages to talk you into driving her to the convention center, you'll both be scrubbing toilets for a year. Is that understood?"

Ben swallowed and nodded.

"You can't do this!" shouted Zoe.

"Do you really want to test me on this?"

Zoe stormed to the elevator in a huff. Ben hurried to keep up. When the elevator doors dinged open downstairs, Zoe stepped out, grabbed Ben, and pulled him aside.

"We need to keep walking," said Ben.

"Ben, wait – we need to talk."

"We need to *walk*. Come on!"

"He can't see us. What's the big deal?"

"Scrubbing toilets! That's the big deal. Now, come on!"

With a growl of disgust, Zoe followed Ben outside.

"I'm parked over here," Ben said, pointing to a silver sedan.

"Something about this keeps bothering me," said Zoe.

"What do you mean?"

"Why bother filing a report saying Qaderi's tablet had been destroyed? Why not tell the police the truth – that it was a fake and that it was on its way over with Faisal?"

Ben took out his car keys and punched a button, sounding an electronic chirp.

"It's as if Tyler *wanted* the claim to be approved so that Abu Nazer would think his scam had succeeded," said Zoe.

"Hotel or hospital?" asked Ben.

"Then – pow! – his claim gets yanked away once Faisal delivers the tablet and the truth's discovered."

"Hotel or hospital?" asked Ben again. He removed his suit jacket and the lightweight Kevlar vest he had been wearing beneath it. He opened his car door and tossed the vest in the back seat before putting his jacket back on.

"None of this makes any *sense,*" muttered Zoe. She opened her door but stood thinking, one arm on top of the doorframe. "Tyler's up to something. But what?"

"We need to go," said Ben. He glanced nervously at the upstairs windows to see if Teague was watching.

"Tyler's no dummy," said Zoe. "He'd know the denial of that claim would send Abu Nazer into orbit. That he'd drop everything to hunt him down."

"We really need to be going."

Lost in thought, Zoe did not reply.

"Zoe, get in the car!"

"Son of a bitch, that's *it!*" Zoe exclaimed, slamming her hand on the roof of the car. "That's *exactly* what Tyler wanted to happen! He knew he wouldn't be able to find Abu Nazer. So he made sure Abu Nazer would find *him!*"

Zoe pulled out her cell phone and touched one of the speed dial buttons. "It's me," she said once the connection was made.

"Way to go!" said Tony. "I hear you saved the Vice President's life."

"Remember that recording I sent you for analysis?"

"Dude, I'm sorry I didn't get back with you sooner. It's just with everything that's been going on…"

"Did you analyze it or not?"

"Of course. I just didn't get around to sending you the results."

"He was telling the truth, wasn't he?" asked Zoe.

"How did you know?"

But Zoe had already slammed shut her phone. "Get in and drive!" she shouted, jumping into the car.

"Hotel or hospital?" asked Ben.

"Ben! Get in and *drive.*"

CHAPTER 60

While thunderous applause welcomed President Fitzgerald to the podium at the convention center, Tyler inserted a plastic card into the slot and unlocked his hotel room door.

"Thanks, I'll take it from here," he said to the paramedics.

"You sure you're okay?" one of them asked.

"I walked all the way up here, didn't I? If you'd have let me, I'd have raced you to the top of the stairs – and won!"

The paramedics laughed.

"Seriously," said Tyler, "I'm fine. A decent night's sleep and I'm good as gold."

"Your call. Take care."

"I will. Thanks again."

The paramedics headed down the hall.

Tyler stepped inside his hotel room and closed the door, where he leaned wearily against the wall. He switched on the bathroom light and examined his face in the mirror. His head was throbbing but the cuts had quit weeping. His whole face was a grim reminder of how close it had been.

Meanwhile, against a backdrop of thunderous applause filling the main auditorium of the convention center, agent Ron Matthews showed his ID to the Secret Service agent at the door. Matthews was average in about every way: height, weight, dress – even the laptop that he carried. Nothing fancy. Nothing outstanding. Nothing worth noticing.

Average.

"Can you direct me to Vice President Baker?" he asked, glancing past the agents to where the President was addressing the crowd.

"One moment," the agent replied, handing Matthews' ID to Tony, who was standing nearby with a scanner.

Tony touched the data strip to the scanner's sensor and handed it back.

While he waited for clearance, Matthews reviewed his plan. Step one: Pass through security. Step two: Locate Baker, open his laptop, and enter an access code that would activate a timer and automatically place a call to his cell phone. Step three: Excuse himself to take the call. Step four: After the C4 inside the laptop exploded and killed Baker, drop his diver's watch on the floor. Although it kept amazingly good time, its main function was to emit a seven-minute electromagnetic pulse that would jam all communications within a hundred meters. Step five: Amidst all the chaos and smoke, leave by the nearest exit. Step six: Flaming margaritas in Mexico.

Tony looked at the small display window on his scanner. Next to Matthews' name was a confirmation number. Tony entered the number into his laptop, which was connected to the Agency's mainframe by means of a secure intranet channel. Seconds ticked by while the mainframe compared the number to the list of agents supplied earlier by Teague.

A password flashed on the screen.

"Your clearance code is 'Sequoia,'" Tony told Matthews.

Sequoia. *The warning code.*

Nightingale Six was immediately surrounded by eight Federal agents and within seconds he had been disarmed, handcuffed, and escorted from the convention center, where he was stripped and searched. His laptop was scanned and placed in an explosives bin, his other belongings bagged and transferred to an FBI forensics team. Matthews was then given an orange jump suit for the long ride to Leavenworth.

Tony took out his phone and called Teague.

"We got one," he said.

"Abu Nazer?" asked Teague from a wing of the stage.

"One of his drones. With a laptop full of C4."

"Keep looking. He's still on the loose."

Back in the hotel, Tyler washed his face, then went to check out the mini-bar. He entered the bedroom, hit the light switch and jolted to a stop.

Across the room in a chair was Sharifa.

"Sharifa! Thank God, you're—"

Tyler stopped when he felt the cold steel of a gun barrel touch the back of his head.

"Go right on in," commanded Qaderi, pushing Tyler to the center of the room.

"Sharifa! Did he hurt you? Are you all right?"

Qaderi spun Tyler around and jammed the pistol up under his chin. "Keep your mouth shut unless I tell you to speak! Hands in the air."

With a darting glance toward the bedside table, Tyler slowly raised his hands.

Seeing the quick eye movement, Qaderi kept Tyler in his sights, reversed his way over to the nightstand and opened the drawer. Inside it was a pistol.

Qaderi stuck the weapon in his belt. "The amateur thinks with his eyes."

"What do you want?" asked Tyler.

Qaderi feigned surprise. "What do I *want?*" His expression hardened as he slammed shut the drawer. "How about a hundred million *dollars!*"

"Blame the CIA. They're the ones who capitalized on your flaws."

"There were no flaws!" shouted Qaderi. "Everything was perfect!"

"I gotta hand it to you, that was pretty clever stirring up controversy with that *Jerusalem Post* ad. With everybody wanting to get their hands on your tablet, you more than doubled its value."

"Who told you that?" demanded Qaderi.

"Then you got stupid by taking hostages."

Qaderi took three angry strides and planted the tip of the silencer against Tyler's forehead. "You left me no choice!"

"You could have walked free."

"Do you seriously think I was going to fall for an offer of immunity?"

"I told them you wouldn't, but the funny thing is, they were telling the truth. I wanted to shoot you. But, no, they wouldn't let me."

"Who are you, Tyler? No journalist I know can handle a rifle like that."

"It's not too late. Let Sharifa go and there's a good chance they'll let you walk. Especially if you help them catch Nightingale."

"Who are you?" repeated Qaderi.

"I'll talk to them. Convince them to—"

Qaderi smashed Tyler across the face with his pistol. The blow sent him sprawling backward.

"I said, who *are* you?" Qaderi demanded as Tyler hit the credenza and fell hard to the floor. The skin near his eye was peeled back and bleeding.

Tyler looked up and saw the blurred figure of Qaderi standing over him. He struggled up into a sitting position only to have Qaderi crack the gun across his forehead, ripping open a fresh wound and slamming him to the floor.

"Who *are* you, Tyler?"

Tyler groaned and tried to sit up. Blood streamed down his face. Qaderi reared back to hit him again.

"That's enough!" commanded Sharifa.

"He's stalling!" Youssef replied.

Sharifa rose out of the chair and walked over to where Tyler was lying on the floor. Tyler peered up at her, perplexed. He looked back and forth between Sharifa and Qaderi.

Youssef let out a laugh. "Have you finally figured it out then? All this time, you were after the wrong person. She's Abu Nazer. Not me."

"You talk too much!" snapped Sharifa.

"What difference does it make?" said Qaderi.

Sharifa grabbed Youssef's pistol and knelt beside Tyler.

"*You?*" Tyler whispered. "But…*why?*"

"Times are changing, I had to change with them. That's why we needed new identities. That's also why we needed you to document Youssef as the owner of the tablet and I as his assistant. The airplane carrying the tablet would have gone down over the Atlantic, allowing us a hundred million dollars in insurance money. The CIA would have had the body of Tariq Yassin, whom they would have assumed was Abu Nazer. Everybody would have been happy." She clicked her tongue. "If only you'd left well enough alone. If only you'd minded your own business and done what you were supposed to do."

Tyler looked away in disgust.

Sharifa yanked his face back toward her. "Don't you dare look away from me like that!"

"You took me to meet your parents."

"They weren't my parents! That little act was strictly for your benefit. You kept asking about them, so I found an old *zabbaline* couple willing to play the part for a few hundred dollars. Naturally, I couldn't risk letting the truth get out, so after we left, I had Majli kill them."

"*Majli?*"

Sharifa tilted her head back and laughed.

"And the woman at the gallery?" asked Tyler. "The one with the cell phone bomb?"

"Lydia was one of several young militants whose services – and passports – I've used over the years. Her passport was especially useful after my failed attempt to kill Vice President Baker. One of my few misses. Ever. But, like I said, times are changing. Digital imprints, data chips, facial recognition software… All the more reason to get out of the game. All Youssef and I needed was enough retirement money."

"Shoot him and let's go," growled Qaderi.

"So I meant nothing to you?" asked Tyler.

"You'll get over it. At least I hope you do, in the short time you have left."

"Hurry up!" said Youssef.

Sharifa stared down at Tyler's bruised and beaten face. At his blond hair matted with blood.

"Come on!" said Youssef.

"You're right, it's time," Sharifa said. She stood and smiled sadly at Tyler, then suddenly swung the pistol toward Youssef.

He jerked as the muffled, nine-millimeter bullet slammed him against the dresser. With a gargled gasp, he slid to the floor and left a smear of blood on the wall.

Sharifa knelt again beside Tyler. "Sorry, but the CIA needs to think you and Abu Nazer killed one another," she said. "That was always the plan if things didn't work out with Tariq." She sighed reflectively. "I suppose you think me calloused. Youssef did, after all, provide me with a fabulous lifestyle. And, of course, the perfect cover. No one – not even you – suspected the lowly secretary." She shook her head with what seemed like genuine disappointment. "You and I, we could have been lovers."

"Said Abu Nazer to her piece of chocolate."

Sharifa laughed. "Oh, come now, don't tell me you actually believed that?" Her mirth then faded into a hardened sneer. "So, before we say our good-byes, I need a few answers. Tell me how you and Zoe Gustaves managed to hack into my Swiss account. Tell me how you discovered the tablet was a fake and convinced Faisal to confess. Tell me how you – a celebrity journalist – managed to kill Majli and a dozen terrorists. Who are you, Tyler?"

Tyler coughed but said nothing.

"Tell me!" Sharifa demanded, jamming the gun up under his chin. "You handled that rifle like a *professional!*"

Tyler's eyes drooped closed.

"Fine. Have it your way," she said.

She stood and took aim.

"Planned it…with Tariq," whispered Tyler.

The statement was like heroin to an addict.

Sharifa knelt and grabbed Tyler by the hair. "What did you say?" She wrenched his head back and pressed the gun up under his chin again.

Some unintelligible garble emerged from Tyler's throat.

"Tell me!" she shouted. "Where is he?"

Bubbles of saliva appeared on his lips. "Water," he said hoarsely, slumping to the side.

"No!" Sharifa shouted. She slapped him in the face several times, attempting to rouse him.

Tyler's cell phone rang, and as Sharifa glanced instinctively toward the noise, she unwittingly shifted the gun.

Tyler grabbed her wrist and jerked it to the side.

The gun fired, shattering a mirror.

"*You bastard!*" Sharifa screamed, wrestling Tyler for control of the weapon while his cell phone continued to ring. She hammered a fist into Tyler's face and sent a fresh spray of blood into the air. She grabbed the gun with both hands, yanked it violently one way then the other. They fell onto their sides, wrestling and grunting. Tyler would not let go.

But Tyler was also bleeding and weak. One eye was swollen shut.

Sharifa twisted, pulled Tyler's arms up over her shoulder and slammed her head back – a head butt to the face.

Tyler tucked his chin and deflected the blow.

Sharifa wrenched the gun forward, extending Tyler's reach while jerking and twisting.

His grip was loosening!

Tyler knew he could not hold on. And so, with his remaining strength, he propelled himself forward in a crawling motion. Up over Sharifa's head he went, bending her wrists – and the pistol – in toward her stomach.

The weapon kicked slightly as it fired.

With a horrified gasp, Sharifa let go as a fiery pain spread through her. A dot of blood appeared on her clothes.

Rolling free, a winded Tyler climbed unsteadily to his feet.

Gasping and moaning, Sharifa pushed herself up into a sitting position and leaned back against the credenza. She tried desperately to catch her breath.

"Should... have killed you... when I had... the chance!" she said between breaths.

"I should have known who you were the moment you lied about having had a tattoo."

Sharifa stared quizzically up at Tyler.

"That scar on your back's from a bullet. And I did notice the scar on your chest. Barely noticeable, to be sure, but it's there. I just didn't put it together."

"Put what together?"

"The gunfight, eight years ago, north of Gaza."

Sharifa stared dumbfounded at Tyler. "Only one person in the world could know about that," she said.

"*Enta mish aref ana meen?*" Tyler responded in Arabic.

Sharifa's mouth dropped open as she struggled to understand what she had just heard. "Don't you know who I am?" she said, translating the Arabic into English.

"*Akshav atta yodea mi ani?*" Tyler then asked in Hebrew.

Her confusion became incredulity.

"Yes, Sharifa, I'm Aaron – the man you thought you killed that night on the beach. I've already done what you tried doing by abandoning my old identity and creating a new one."

"But…*how?*"

"I didn't die, that's how. After our shootout, Ismail Yassin found me washed up in the surf. He took me in and kept me hidden until I recovered. That's how I met Tariq. That's also how I met Louise Kappelmann, and with her help, I made my way to America, where she helped me create my new identity."

"Louise Kappelmann?"

"It wasn't difficult for someone with a degree in computer science and expertise in stolen identities. She told me if you give people a good reason to believe in you, they will. So I settled in Austin, made friends and took photos, while Louise did my writing. Which she was happy to do because she needed to remain anonymous. Once I became established, I contacted Tariq and we began searching for you.

As a cover, Tariq worked his way into *Qamat,* believing we could find you via the underground network, since you were one of those who offered your services for hire. Knowing Senator Ashford had been freezing your assets and tightening the noose to find you, I came up with the idea of carving a replica of the Ishmael tablet to use in an insurance scam. Tariq sent word through the underground and you sent Majli to meet with him in Mecca, where he handed over the remainder of everything he had found – adding that one of my celebrity interviews would increase the tablet's value and create the perfect opportunity for a new identity. Which, of course, paved the way for you to accept my offer of an interview. Initially, I wanted to kill you. But over the years, I found I'd changed. So I decided to involve the CIA and let them take care of things. Unfortunately, they had a leak."

"So the offer of an interview was your way of tracking me down?"

"Like a homing device," said Tyler, laying his pistol on the credenza and kneeling to examine Sharifa's wound. "Once Youssef made his announcement, I knew I'd found my man. Or so I thought. The interview was also a way to get inside your house so that I could access your financial records... to prove who you were and bring down Nightingale."

"How do you know about Nightingale?"

"Back in the days when I was Aaron, they tried to recruit me."

"And the bus? The dud explosives?"

"Modeling clay."

"You and Tariq... I never would have guessed."

"Nor did I, that you were Abu Nazer."

"Falling in love with your enemy!" laughed Sharifa. "Aaron would never have committed such an error."

"Love isn't something you know much about when you've been taught only to kill. In the years since, I've been trying to make up for that."

Sharifa groaned and started to cough.

"Save it. The wound isn't fatal. I'll clean it and call the police."

Tyler stood and turned toward the bathroom, then suddenly stopped and steadied himself with a hand on the wall. His head was throbbing. He couldn't think. He glanced back and saw the pistol on the credenza.

"Do you think I could do it, too?" she asked.

"Do what?" he asked, picking up the gun.

"Start a new life."

"You can't be serious."

"You did it."

"How can you even think about asking me that?"

"Because I was a fool not to have listened to my heart."

"Don't start! I fell for it once. Never again."

"You have every right to be angry," Sharifa said penitently. "I used you. But you used me, too!"

"Save it."

"What we had was real, Tyler. You know that as well as I do. In spite of everything else that happened, what we had was *real.*"

Tyler shook his head. "It was a lie. Everything was a lie."

"Not everything."

With a snort of disgust, Tyler looked away.

"Look, you say you're not good at love because you were taught to kill," Sharifa said. "Well, I'm not good at it, either. But I know I'd like to try. That is, if you'll give me the chance."

"You are a real piece of work, you know that? Just a minute ago you mocked me for believing I was your piece of chocolate. I believed you! And you laughed."

"I was angry!"

"At what?"

"At you! For doing what I longed to do but didn't know how. But you did it, Tyler. You changed."

Tyler chuckled bitterly and shook his head.

"All I'm asking is that you give me the same chance. For God's sake, don't give up. Not now. Not after what we've been through."

Tyler did not respond.

"Please!"

"I need to clean that wound," he said.

"At least think about it. That is all that I ask." She gasped and grabbed her side.

"Don't move," said Tyler.

Sharifa watched Tyler disappear into the bathroom, and as soon as she heard water running in the sink, she scooted over to Youssef's body, pulled the pistol out of his belt and scooted back to where she had been sitting. Very quietly, she cocked the weapon.

Downstairs in the lobby, Zoe raced into the foyer. She had been trying to phone Tyler but got no answer.

The desk clerk was working quietly at her computer when Zoe ran up to her.

"May I help you?" asked the clerk.

"I need to speak with the manager," said Zoe, out of breath.

"May I ask what this concerns?"

"One of your guests. Dr. Rutherford Tyler."

"We don't release information on guests."

Zoe flashed her ID. "I need to know if Dr. Tyler is in his room."

"Like I said, we don't release that kind of information. It's against hotel policy."

"Then let me speak with your manager."

"He's on break."

"Call him! This is urgent."

"He doesn't like to be interrupted."

"Well, that's very unfortunate," said Zoe, taking out her cell phone, "because it means I have to call for a command post to be set up in your lobby so that we can tell your guests about a potential terrorist threat in your hotel. And, of course, the fact that you're refusing to cooperate will be sent to Homeland Security for a full investigation."

Three minutes later, the manager was leading Zoe down the carpeted corridor. Wringing his hands, he took nervous little steps. His eyes darted between Zoe and the pistol she was carrying.

"Room seven-sixteen, here we are," he said.

He straightened his suit jacket and prepared to knock.

Zoe yanked him away from the door and held a finger to her lips.

In the bathroom, Tyler held the hot washcloth to his forehead. Youssef's blows had been savage. He was exhausted.

Tyler's elbow slipped on the counter and he jerked up. He was falling asleep! He ran the washcloth under the hot water again and the sink swirled red. He laid the washcloth aside and grabbed a clean hand towel and ran it under the hot water.

Maybe she did deserve a second chance. A second chance like he had been given.

He turned off the tap and wrung out the towel.

Sharifa lifted the pistol and took aim.

Zoe pounded her fist on the door. "Tyler! Are you all right?"

"Zoe?" he replied.

"Are you all right?"

"We're fine. What's going on?"

Zoe stiffened. *We?*

"Sharifa – she's Abu Nazer!" Zoe shouted. "I'm coming in!"

Zoe inserted the keycard in the slot.

The door cracked open.

Sharifa fired once, twice, three times.

The bullets tore through the panel and slammed into Zoe's chest.

Zoe tried to cry out – to warn Tyler again – but she had no voice, no strength. Her legs buckled and she dropped to the floor.

Tyler dove low through the bathroom door. He was looking right. His weapon was raised. He saw Sharifa's rage as she followed him with her gun. He felt Sharifa's bullets slice the air near his head.

He fired once before hitting the floor. Sharifa jerked as the bullet struck her forehead. Tyler lay there breathing hard. He watched the hatred in Sharifa's eyes gloss over as she slumped back against the credenza with a final sigh.

Panting, Tyler rolled onto his side but couldn't sit up.

Out in the hallway, Zoe struggled for the breath that had been knocked out of her as a result of three bullets hitting Ben's Kevlar vest, which she was wearing.

"Call the police," she told the white-faced manager in a croaking voice.

The manager nodded as she climbed unsteadily to her feet and ran back down the hall.

Zoe began pounding frantically on the door. He jammed the keycard in and out of the slot. "Come on, you piece of shit…"

"I'm okay!" Tyler called out.

Suddenly, the door flew open and Zoe rushed in, her gun trained on Sharifa until she saw Sharifa's vacant eyes staring up at the ceiling. Holstering her gun, Zoe looked down and gasped when she saw the bloody mess that was Tyler's face.

"Dammit, Tyler, you stubborn, pigheaded *jackass…*"

"Glad to see you, too."

Half crying, half laughing, Zoe helped Tyler to his feet and over to the bed. She ran into the bathroom, grabbed one of the hot towels and ran back to Tyler.

By this time, a small crowd had gathered outside the door.

"Federal officer! Go back to your rooms!" Zoe shouted. She walked over and kicked the door shut, then returned to begin gently cleaning Tyler's face.

Lying on the floor nearby, Qaderi slowly opened his eyes. The vague shapes that were Zoe and Tyler came into focus.

Zoe's back was to him and Tyler's vision was obscured because of where Zoe was standing. As far as he could tell, Sharifa's bullet had gone right through him – upper chest, right side, missing the vital organs and arteries. In other words, he would live.

Two people stood in his way of his getting out of here before the police arrived. And they were talking, not paying attention.

Moving slowly so as not to make any noise, Youssef pulled the leg of his slacks up and quietly withdrew the small revolver from his ankle holster.

The agent first. Then Tyler.

"How did you know who she was?" asked Tyler.

"Analysis on a recording of Qaderi's voice," answered Zoe, dabbing his face with the hot cloth. "He was telling the truth when he said Sharifa had been the one who hired Majli. Add that to your little scheme of getting Abu Nazer to come looking for you..."

"How in the world did you figure that out?"

"Let's just say I know better than most how conniving you can be."

"Said one pigheaded jackass to another."

Zoe laughed then fell silent as she continued to clean Tyler's wounds.

Youssef softly pulled back the hammer of his pistol.

Click.

Zoe recognized the sound and spun right, her hand grabbing her SIG and sweeping outward and around as she bent to the side, as if dodging a baseball coming straight for her face.

Aiming for Zoe's head, Qaderi fired a split second before Zoe pulled the trigger.

Qaderi's bullet missed.

Zoe's did not.

Qaderi stiffened as the bullet tore through his heart. With a gasp he toppled sideways to the floor.

Her pistol at the ready, Zoe kicked the revolver away then knelt and felt the side of his neck. Holstering her gun, she rose to her feet and stared at him for a moment before looking over at Sharifa. When she looked down at Tyler, he looked away.

"I'm sorry. I know she was special to you."

"Don't be. The whole thing was a lie."

"Even so…" said Zoe. She picked up the damp towel and placed it on Tyler's eye.

"At least it's over. The lies are over."

"Not completely," Zoe replied.

"Not completely? What do you mean?"

Zoe paused. "I know who you are."

CHAPTER 61

Dressed in an ill-fitting, rumpled gray suit more than twenty years old, Ariel Cohen walked slowly along the jetway. Even at this early morning hour, the airport was busy. People rushed by him impatiently.

The call from a Ms. Gustaves at the CIA had come as a complete surprise. She had asked if he would come to Washington and give testimony about Aaron. Ariel questioned why he, an old man, would be sought for testimony on a dead man whose identity no one knew. Zoe had patiently informed him that she was aware of his past relationship with Aaron. When Ariel inquired how she had managed to find that out, she simply replied that she had.

Zoe announced that Aaron's identity may well have been discovered.

Stunned was an inadequate description of how Ariel felt. He remembered asking Zoe why his testimony would be needed if Aaron's identity were already known.

"Because you're the only person who can tell us for certain whether or not we're right."

So here he was, in America, for the very first time.

"Mr. Cohen?" asked the smiling young woman with unruly brown hair.

"Yes, I am Ariel Cohen."

"Zoe Gustaves. It's an honor to meet you." She offered her hand and Ariel shook it. "I appreciate you doing this," she said, pointing the way toward the baggage claim area.

"It is a strange thing that you ask," Ariel replied.

"I know."

He glanced over at Zoe, who smiled but did not elaborate.

They rode to Washington in Zoe's government sedan mostly without conversation, with Ariel observing the affluent suburban sprawl blanketing the countryside. The mirrored office buildings and trendy shopping centers lining the freeway eventually gave way to inner city tenement housing and featureless apartment blocks. Groups of youths in oversized jeans and baggy shirts shuffled aimlessly along the sidewalks.

"This won't be a formal hearing," Zoe explained as they reached the first in a series of stoplights, "so you won't be cross-examined, per se."

"Per se? What does this mean?"

"It means you might be asked to clarify a statement or provide additional information, but no lawyer is going to grill you like you're a pork chop."

Ariel looked sharply at Zoe.

"Sorry, I should have said steak. Point is, the lawyers won't be asking too many questions."

"With whom will I be meeting?" asked Ariel.

"Dan Eskridge, from the State Department, plus officials from the FBI and CIA."

"FBI and CIA?"

The light turned green and Zoe hit the accelerator.

"According to both the State Department and the FBI, Aaron is still classified as an assassin, whereabouts unknown. There's still a reward on his head. As you know, he was *thought* to have been killed, but because his body was never found, he's still classified as 'whereabouts unknown.'"

Twenty minutes later, Zoe parked her car in an underground garage. After checking in and receiving visitor's badges, she and Ariel took the elevator up to the third floor. Turning right, they proceeded down a hallway to the conference room.

The paneled room could easily hold a hundred people but today contained only fourteen. Zoe ushered Ariel over to one of the cushioned chairs positioned around a long oval table. Ariel smiled his thanks and Zoe started to sit beside him.

She stopped when she saw her mother, Congresswoman Diane Gustaves, seated at the far end of the table.

Her jaw tightening, Zoe stared hard at her mother, who was dressed in a red power suit and had streaked blondish hair. Diane made brief, impassive eye contact before glancing again at the folder in front of her.

Teague discreetly cleared his throat and Zoe sat.

"Mr. Cohen, my name is Jackson Teague," said Teague, "and I'm the acting Director of Operations for the Central Intelligence Agency. I presume Ms. Gustaves has told you this is not a formal hearing?"

Ariel nodded.

"That being said, I would like to advise you that an official transcript will still be made of these proceedings. Do you have any questions?"

"No."

Teague nodded and looked to his right. "Mr. Eskridge, the meeting is yours."

After introducing himself, Eskridge asked a number of background questions about Ariel, his family, and his trade as a printer. He was asked to elaborate on – Eskridge purposely did not use the word "explain," as Mr. Cohen was under no obligation to explain anything – his association with Rubin Yehuda, and whether or not he – Ariel – maintained an affiliation with the *gibburim*. Ariel said he did not, and went on to detail his long but stormy friendship with Yehuda, including their philosophical differences.

Eskridge then asked about Ariel's relationship with Aaron.

Ariel responded by recalling how Aaron had once sought him out to print his legendary *Aleph* cards, adding that although he and Aaron had talked numerous times by phone, they had never met.

"Is it your clear and unequivocal statement that you have never knowingly met Aaron face to face?" asked Eskridge.

"That is correct."

"Are you certain?" Eskridge inquired, leaning forward, elbows on the table.

"If I give you a clear and unequivocal statement, then I am certain."

"I mean no disrespect, Mr. Cohen, but we're here to ascertain the identity of an assassin who's still officially wanted by the State Department and the FBI. So we need to fully understand the depth of, and limits to, your relationship."

"I understand."

"Would it be fair to say you knew the sound of Aaron's voice?"

"Aaron had an unmistakable voice."

"One which you would recognize – or did, at one time?"

"Yes."

Eskridge looked at the sheet of paper in front of him. "I have before me Ms. Gustaves' statement regarding her knowledge of certain facts ascertained from her own exhaustive research on Aaron, along with the profile she has compiled. Ms. Gustaves is an analyst with the CIA whose specialty is composite profiles, so she comes to us with a high level of qualification and experience. It's her conclusion that Aaron was killed approximately eight years ago in Gaza. However, Israeli Intelligence tells us there are rumors that Aaron may still be alive. Hence, I need to ask you once again – do you think, with a relatively high degree of certainty, that you would recognize Aaron's voice if you heard it?"

"I am certain that I would. His voice was unmistakable."

"Then I need you to tell me if the voice you are about to hear is one you recognize."

Eskridge nodded to a young woman sitting to his right. She touched a control button and Adino's voice was heard making an inflammatory statement about Israel's right to drive the Arabs out of Jerusalem. After nearly a full minute of the diatribe, the recording was clicked off.

Eskridge looked directly at Ariel. "Do you recognize that voice?" he asked.

"Yes, I do."

"Was it the voice of Aaron?"

"No, it was not."

"Please be certain, Mr. Cohen. Two different informants tell us that he drops hints about being Aaron, although he does not openly make such a claim."

"Then allow me to be unequivocal. That voice does not belong to Aaron."

Eskridge was unable to hide his embarrassment. "Thank you, Mr. Cohen." He looked at the others around the table. "Are there any additional questions?"

The others shook their heads.

Eskridge looked back at Ariel.

"Thank you, Mr. Cohen, that will be all. Your willingness to help put this matter to rest is greatly appreciated." Eskridge scanned the other faces around the table. "If there is no further discussion, I hereby declare as dead the assassin known as Aaron. Pursuant to that, I likewise declare the State Department reward for his apprehension officially canceled."

With an expression of bewilderment over the deliberation of something so obvious, Ariel rose to leave.

Just then, Congresswoman Gustaves looked at Tyler. "Dr. Tyler, I'd like your clarification on a point."

After a quick glance at Ariel, who was turning to leave, Tyler leaned forward with the hope that Ariel would make it out of the room before he was required to speak.

"You stated earlier that you knew your personal assistant, Val Johnson, was in fact Louise Kappelmann. Is that true?"

Tyler nodded just as Ariel paused at the mention of Louise Kappelmann's name.

"What was your reason for withholding this information from tax authorities, the CIA, and other law enforcement agencies?"

Ariel turned and looked inquisitively at Tyler.

Tyler glanced at Ariel, then back at Diane Gustaves, knowing that he had no choice but to answer.

"To my knowledge, Ms. Johnson had broken no laws," he explained. "She chose to use an anagram of her initials as her first name, followed by her maiden name. I'm aware of no laws against that – especially since she had a valid Social Security number to support what is a common practice among many women."

Ariel stared open-mouthed at Tyler.

"But you knowingly withheld that information from Agent Gustaves," said the congresswoman.

"Ms. Gustaves phoned me about something entirely different," explained Tyler.

"Which was?"

"Information about a *Qamat* supporter in London," Zoe interjected. "I was purposely vague when I telephoned Dr. Tyler, and not knowing my actual agenda, he had no reason to volunteer what could be viewed as irrelevant information. I do not regard his actions to be an obstruction in any way."

"Are you defending Dr. Tyler's actions?"

"I'm merely clarifying what occurred."

"With my full support," added Teague.

"Are you implying that I did something illegal?" asked Tyler.

Under the scrutinizing gazes of everyone at the table, Congresswoman

Gustaves saw that she was beginning to look pedantic and petty.

"Not at all, Dr. Tyler," she replied, closing the folder in front of her. "You have answered our questions clearly and honestly." She then noticed Ariel's stunned expression. "Mr. Cohen, are you all right?"

At the mention of Ariel's name, Zoe whirled around and saw the look on his face. Jumping from her chair, she rushed to his side. "Mr. Cohen has had a long flight," she explained. "I'll take him for some coffee."

She gently touched Ariel on the elbow and Ariel looked at her with confusion. Zoe smiled, took him by the arm and ushered him out of the room.

Once the door had eased shut behind them, Tyler leaned back and closed his eyes. Meanwhile, Eskridge made a few closing remarks before saying what an honor it had been to serve the people of America.

Out in the hallway, Zoe and Ariel were sipping vending machine coffee when Tyler emerged from the conference room.

"Hello, Ari," Tyler said quietly.

Ariel dropped his styrofoam cup, splattering coffee across the linoleum as he rushed to grab Tyler in an emotional embrace. "It is you!" he cried.

"Yes, old friend, it is I."

"Let's get out of here," said Zoe.

An hour later, they were driving past farms and silos and open fields.

"So you were there, at Ma'alot?" asked Ariel.

"I was five years old when the massacre occurred," said Tyler. "My sister was the first to be killed. My mother died protecting me. I still have nightmares about seeing them murdered before my eyes."

"And your father?"

"Killed by Egyptian soldiers the year before. So Ma'alot not only left me homeless, but completely lost. For years I struggled to find meaning in what had happened."

"And did you?"

"I never understood why Arabs hated us so much. So I decided I would hate them back, and not just hate them, but become better at it. I went to live in a kibbutz, where that hatred was channeled into retribution against anyone who attacked Israel. An eye for an eye and always without mercy. I was an expert marksman by the time I went into the military. No one knew that I was Aaron, and while many considered me a hero, in the end I was just a killer...not much different than all the rest. Until, that is, you and I began speaking over the phone. You were the first person to talk of mercy and peace. But I didn't really understand those concepts until an old Arab – Ismail Yassin – rescued me off the beach. You two changed my life, although when it comes right down to it, I guess I'm not that different. Abu Nazer died by my hand."

"In self defense," Zoe pointed out.

"Killing's still killing," said Tyler.

"No, my friend, it is not," replied Ariel. "To fight when required is one thing. To provoke a fight is another."

"With Abu Nazer, it was kill or be killed," said Zoe. "You did what you had to do."

Tyler shrugged.

"So the fact that I knew your voice," said Ariel, "was this the reason you would not take my calls in Austin?"

Tyler smiled and laid a hand on Ariel's shoulder. Ariel chuckled and placed his hand on top of Tyler's. Tyler then looked over at Zoe. "Mind telling me how you figured things out?"

"Call it an accumulation of positive and negative spaces."

"What does this mean?" asked Ariel.

"Don't ask," said Tyler with a chuckle. He turned back to Zoe. "You laid your career on the line back there, convincing Eskridge and the others that Aaron was dead. Why'd you do that?"

"I'll let you know when I figure it out."

"Well, I owe you," said Tyler.

Zoe smiled and nodded.

After a pleasant drive along the gravel roads of rural Virginia, Zoe returned Tyler and Ariel to the underground parking garage. Awkwardly, she hugged Tyler then looked at Ariel.

"May I take you to your hotel?" she asked.

"I'll take him," said Tyler.

Zoe looked inquisitively at Ariel and he nodded.

"Then I'll say my goodbyes," said Zoe, shaking hands with Ariel. "Thank you again."

Ariel nodded and watched Zoe get into her car and drive away.

"How long will you be here?" asked Tyler, leading the way to his car.

"I return to Israel tomorrow."

"Any chance you can stay?"

Ariel smiled, but shook his head.

"I'd like you to come back for a visit," said Tyler. "To Austin. My treat, of course."

"It's not easy for an old man to travel."

Tyler paused by the driver's door to his rental sedan. He looked across the top of the car at Ariel's weathered skin, deep lines, and pale blue eyes. "My family's gone; you're all that I've got."

Ariel stared into Tyler's eyes for several moments. He saw the kindness, the regret, the shadows of loneliness and buried pain.

"It would not be so difficult, I suppose."

"Springtime is best," said Tyler.

Ariel smiled. "Then springtime it is."

CHAPTER 62

Tyler finished reading an article in the latest issue of *Time* magazine. It was by Louise Johnson Kappelmann and of course was brilliant. After nearly eight years of ghosting and editing his material, Val was free to use her own name.

Tyler was seated in the late afternoon sun at one of the Hula Hut's outdoor tables. The sleeves of his faded blue chambray shirt were rolled up and he had an empty beer bottle in one hand as he gazed pensively out over Lake Austin. It was hard to believe it was really over.

But it was. And Abu Nazer was dead.

Val, of course, was still feeling guilty for what she had written when he was in Cairo and she had just called again to apologize.

"I lost faith in you, Tyler," she said. "I said things I shouldn't have said."

"If I'd have been in your shoes, I'd have said the same things."

"That's bullshit and you know it. But thanks."

In an odd way, it was comforting to know he had made Val so angry. That meant he *had* changed. That he was no longer Aaron. That the difference was obvious.

But was he really that different? Because when it came right down to it, his instincts with a gun were as honed as ever. And he had used them to kill a woman that he loved.

Or thought he did, anyway.

Tyler still couldn't quite accept the fact that Sharifa had been Abu Nazer. Harder still to swallow was the fact that she had played him like a fool. Which made him wonder if he would ever be able to trust another woman.

How can you trust anyone when your own life is a lie?

At least Val was finally free.

Tyler thought back to when it all began, when Val said she could create a new identity for him. After all, no one had ever seen Aaron's face.

"It'll be a fresh start for both of us," she had said.

"It'll never work," Tyler had replied.

"America is full of good people. If you give them a reason to believe in you, they will."

And while it had been money earned from his retaliatory strikes that had supported them, it had been Val who made "Rutherford Tyler" truly come to life. It had been she who taught him to take photos. It had been she who spent endless months editing inferior text into publishable prose. It had been she who turned the repentant assassin into a reputable journalist.

Could he keep living the lie?

He had to. There was no other choice.

And yet he wondered how long it would take for another old adversary – or a new one – to come calling. He looked despondently down into the water. As usual, the ducks were demanding handouts. Glancing toward the bar, he caught Mary Lou's eye, raised his bottle and made an eating motion that translated into "chips".

Tyler's cell phone suddenly rang.

"Not again," he mumbled irritably after checking the caller ID. He put the phone to his ear. "What now?"

"Sorry to bother you," said Val.

"Quit apologizing! How many times do I have to tell you?"

"Tyler, Zoe Gustaves is on the other line and says she needs to talk to you. I didn't know if you wanted me to give her your number."

Tyler rubbed his forehead. "Val, I'm sorry."

"Forget it," she replied.

"I shouldn't have yelled at you," he said.

"You're under a lot of pressure. I know. I've been there myself."

Tyler sighed and closed his eyes. A long moment of silence ticked by.

"Tyler?" Val asked. "Are you all right?"

"I don't know how to make the pain go away. It's like somebody reached inside and ripped everything out before running over me with a truck. I know what you're going to say: time heals all wounds. I just wish it would hurry up."

"I hate to break this to you, Tyler, but time does not heal wounds. The hole in my heart is as dark and empty today as it was when Sack was killed. Only love can break a heart. Only love can mend it again."

"That sounds like something out of one of your women's magazines."

"Worse," she said. "Gene Pitney. For whatever it's worth, my advice to you is this: Be open to love. It'll come knocking."

"How can it if I have to keep hiding the truth about who I am?"

338

"Who you *were*, Tyler, and there's a difference. But truth be told, who you were has made you who you are. It's molded you – given you a new set of values. And one day the right woman will come along and fall in love with the whole package. Not just the semi-pretty wrapping."

Tyler wanted to smile, but couldn't.

"If truth be told," he said, "I don't know the first thing about love. I was trained as a killer."

"We're not talking brain surgery here. Just don't shut yourself off."

"You did."

"My choice. Stephen was one-of-a-kind, so I'm more content living with his memory than I would be with another man."

"Why can't I do the same thing?"

"She tried to *kill* you, Tyler! Everything she said and did was a lie."

"Shutting myself off seems safest."

"You never were the kind of guy who played it safe. Now, what do I tell – Oops, never mind. The line's quit blinking."

"Did she say where she was calling from?" he asked.

"No. And caller ID withheld the number."

A snort of disappointment was Tyler's response.

"Look, I was about to head on home," said Val, "but if you'd like I can hang around for a while. In case she calls back."

"Don't worry about it," said Tyler.

They said their goodbyes and Tyler closed his phone just as Mary Lou approached with his order.

"Here you go," she said, placing it in front of him.

"Thanks."

She stood there for a moment then said, "How you doing, hon?"

"I'll be fine."

Mary Lou patted him on the shoulder and returned to the bar.

"I'm worried about him," she said to the other waitress. "He just sits there, all glum and silent."

"Looks like he just needs time to think."

Mary Lou nodded and went to wipe down some tables.

"Hey there, handsome, remember me?" a perky voice asked. Tammy peeked over Tyler's shoulder before stepping into full view, her posture erect, her breasts on full display in a tight Western shirt. "You didn't tell me who you really were, *Dr. Rutherford Tyler,* journalist to the stars! Mind if I sit down?" She pulled out a barstool and sat.

"Look, uh…what was your name?"

"Tammy. And we got some *serious* reacquaintin' to do."

"Yeah, well, I'm really not in the mood."

Tammy wagged her finger at Tyler. "You're not trickin' me again, ya li'l stinker!"

"Honest. I'm not in the mood."

"I can't believe you told me you were a mechanic." She feigned a clueless expression.

"I really don't want any company right now, okay?"

Tammy looked toward the bar. "Where is that waitress?"

"Will you please just get the hell out of here and leave me *alone?*"

Tammy stared at Tyler with disbelief, then jumped up and stormed away.

Tyler was staring absently down into the water again when a hand tapped him on the shoulder.

"This seat taken?" a voice asked.

Tyler looked up and saw Zoe. She was dressed in jeans and boots, with a mint-green spaghetti-strap tank top layered over a pink one. On the back of one shoulder was a small tattoo of *chikara,* the Japanese character for power.

"Zoe!" he said, brightening. "Val told me that you called. I thought you were back in D.C."

Folding her arms, Zoe remained standing in place.

"Of course it's not taken," said Tyler, jumping up and pulling out the other barstool for her.

They sat down and Tyler leaned forward. "What are you doing here?" he asked. "How did you know where I was?"

Zoe shrugged and looked toward the bar.

"Don't tell me my phone's still bugged?"

"Sorry, that information's classified," Zoe replied. She raised a hand and signaled Mary Lou.

Tyler chuckled and shook his head.

Mary Lou hurried toward the table with an inquisitive smile. When she neared the table, Zoe looked up and Mary Lou became instantly deadpan.

"I'll have what he's drinking," said Zoe.

"You got it."

On her way back to the bar, Mary Lou turned and gave Tyler a thumbs-up.

Tyler waved her away and leaned forward again. "Come on, Zoe, what are you doing here?"

"Does my being here pose a problem?"

"Don't be silly. I'm just surprised to see you, that's all."

"That gun case of yours has sure stirred up a hornet's nest," Zoe said. "Brad Henschel was getting pretty vocal about it, so Teague had General Ramsey call his C-O and shut him up. There are a few people who want to talk to you about it, though."

"I'm sure there are."

"Who made it for you, anyway?"

"A couple of old friends."

"Care to elaborate?"

"Not really."

"Well, since we're on a roll here, let me ask you this: Who the hell is Toy Soldier?"

Tyler smiled. "Tariq Yassin. Another old friend."

"You clever bastard! So Tariq sent us intel on himself!"

"We created the Toy Soldier identity to protect him from Nightingale so that he could keep you guys in the loop."

"Smart thinking."

They sat in silence while Mary Lou served Zoe's beer. Tyler smiled his thanks, clinked his bottle against Zoe's and then joined her in a long, slow swallow.

"No zoot suit today?" he asked.

"Taking some time off from work," she replied.

Tyler cocked his head and glanced down. "Are those Hyer boots you got on?"

"Finest cowboy boots ever made," said Zoe, holding one up for Tyler to see. "Olathe, Kansas. My dad's family came from Kansas and these belonged to his mom."

"Well, you're looking good," he said.

"You're getting there," she replied.

He laughed and took a swallow of beer. "So why are you here?" he asked.

Zoe gazed out over the water for a long moment. In the late afternoon sun, it appeared to be flecked with gold. "You saved my ass by stealing that tablet," she finally said.

"I'm the one who got you into that mess. I never should have allowed you to go it alone."

"I didn't exactly ask your permission."

"I should have known you'd pull something like that."

"Are you saying I'm predictable?"

"Believe me, you're anything but predictable."

Zoe smiled. "Well, I owe you for what you did," she said. "And I guess I didn't want to say thanks over the phone or with some stupid card."

"Forget it," Tyler replied. He extended his bottle and Zoe clinked hers to his.

They took a drink.

"Of course, I did save your ass, too," she said. "So maybe it's a good thing I showed up since you owe me."

"What do you mean, I owe you?"

"That's what you told me over in Virginia and Ariel Cohen will back me up. And I'm not telling you to forget it, either. I'm not that dumb."

Tyler stared at Zoe in disbelief. "You set me up," he said, "going first like that and thanking me for saving your ass. You knew I'd tell you to forget it!"

Zoe shrugged and tossed some crumbs to the ducks.

"You played me!" Tyler declared.

"Kind of like the way you played me in the Cairo airport? Stringing me along like you didn't know who I was."

Tyler slumped back and smiled sheepishly. "So you remember that?" he asked.

"You better believe I remember! And, buddy, I plan to collect!"

Tyler shook his head. "Just what did you have in mind?" he asked.

"Why don't we start with those drinks you mentioned?"

"All right," he said, "drinks it is. What then?"

Zoe tossed some more crumbs to the ducks. "I'll let you know," she said. "Fair warning, though: I'm stubborn, I've got a short temper and a very long memory."

"Gee. I never would have guessed."

"You know," she said, looking at the label on the bottle, "I kind of like having you indebted to me like this. Not that I'm all that used to fraternizing with unsavory characters such as yourself. But, hey, if you like Stony Lonesome, I guess you're not all that bad."

Tyler jaw dropped. "Stony *Lonesome?* How in the world do you know about *that?"*

Zoe shrugged.

And for the first time since his return, Tyler laughed.

EPILOGUE

Five hundred and twenty miles above the earth, the F-12 weather satellite moves in a sun-synchronous orbit. Images obtained by its three digital instruments are downlinked to Thule Air Force Base, Greenland before being transmitted by way of a communications satellite to Offnut Air Force Base, Nebraska. Sensors operating in the visible light spectrum during the dark half of the lunar cycle can detect city lights, cruise ships, gas flares, even campfires.

F-12 is now above the Sinai Peninsula, and the cameras are making their usual sweeps back and forth. Traveling at the speed of light, the images reach an Air Force computer, where they are viewed on a series of twelve monitors by Dr. Molly Ziviani and her team of scientists.

"We got some cruise ships out on the Med," she said. "A few coastal lights. Then nothing but black as we head inland over the peninsula."

Molly and the others continued to watch the monitors. Interference lines occasionally distorted the field.

"Not much action out there tonight," remarked technician Ed Morton. He typed a few commands and a new set of images appeared on the monitors.

"Except there," said Lieutenant Gary Kidman, pointing to a white dot on the screen. "There shouldn't be anything out in that part of the desert."

"Let's see what it is," said Molly. "Hit it, Ed."

Ed moved an adjustable rectangle over the dot and entered some commands. The rectangle was enlarged and filled one of the screens. The speck became larger but fuzzier. Ed entered some additional commands. The program enhanced the image and it became clear again.

"More," said Molly.

Ed repeated the procedure several more times.

"That's as far as we can go," he finally said.

"What have we got?" asked Molly.

"Campfire, by the looks of it," said Ed.

"What are the coordinates?" asked Molly.

Ed glanced at the indicators on the bar at the bottom of the screen. "34-30," he replied.

"That's the middle of nowhere," Molly said, staring at the screen. "Sorry, guys, looks like a dud. Probably some nomads roasting a snake."

Far below, a family of Bedouins crouched around their fire. The sky above was a tapestry of timelessness. Familiar. Majestic.

Mulazim, his hair now wiry and gray, sat on the worn stone bench he had built so many years ago. As he looked up at the sky, the cool desert winds scrubbed his leathery face. The bright speck that was F-12 streaked off to the south and disappeared. Looking back at the fire, he watched a log tumble into the embers. The resulting flurry of sparks was carried away by the wind.

"Grandfather," a child called out. "Tell us again the story of Ishmael."

"Yes!" cried several others.

Mulazim cackled a toothless laugh as more than a dozen children gathered around. In the darkness away from the fire, their mothers and fathers went about nightly duties in the encampment of tents.

"Tell us how you hunted down the thieves!" a young, fiery-eyed girl of ten called out as she squatted near his feet. "Tell us how you found them and slit their throats." She grinned and ran a finger across her own neck.

Mulazim issued a token rebuke before beginning his story. "Long ago, when I was a lad, I came into the desert with an Englishman. He was tall and strong. A good man, and a Christian."

When the word 'Christian' was mentioned, several of the children muttered insults.

This time the rebuke was genuine, and the children cowered in silence.

"Clayton was his name, and he taught me to read and write," Mulazim continued. "He made me his First Officer and each day we searched this mountain."

"What did you find, Grandfather?" the girl called out.

"We found the sacred tablet of Ishmael, our great forefather," he said.

"What did it say?" a small boy called out.

"No!" shouted the girl. "Tell us about the thieves!"

Sitting in reflective silence, Mulazim allowed his gaze to descend into the embers. He thought about Clayton's death and how he came back to this mountain to bury what remained of his mentor and friend.

"Grandfather!" the children called out. "You are dreaming again!"

Mulazim blinked and laughed. "Yes, yes, so many dreams. They run and I cannot keep up with them."

"The *thieves,* Grandfather!"

"Yes, yes, the thieves. Well, I rose early the last morning and journeyed by camel to Suez, where I gave Clayton's journal to the captain of a steamship. Then I wait for Clayton to arrive."

"What happened?" the girl shouted, scooting nearer with excitement.

"A week later, I see the old Bedouin. He and the others ride into Suez but Clayton is not with them. But I see Clayton's camel, his canteen and his boots, and I know then these men, they have killed him. One of them even carried his gun."

"He had a *gun?*"

"Yes, but I had this."

With a quick movement, Mulazim whipped his dagger high into the air and the children all cheered.

"What did you do?" the girl said eagerly, knowing too well what he had done since she had heard the story countless times.

Mulazim narrowed his eyes and looked menacingly at each of the children while the desert wind swirled ominously about them. He suddenly shrieked, as he always did, and the children jumped, as they always did. He then ran a finger across his throat.

The children leaped to their feet, screaming and dancing.

"But—" he called out, waiting for them to grow silent as they gathered again at his feet to the chuckles and nods of their parents "—it was because they first tried to kill me. They came at night, all three of them, to my tent."

A hush fell over the small audience and Mulazim threw his dagger into the sand, where it stuck by the point of the blade. He then leaned forward and spoke. His voice was animated and husky. "The night was dark, the wind like a demon," he said, lifting his hands and allowing the folds of his *jellaba* to flap in the stiff breeze. He stared at them wildly. "And they were men, and I was but a boy." He paused for drama. "They come when it is late, when they think I am asleep. But I hear them whispering. So I sneak out back of tent, holding knife in teeth." He picked up his dagger and grinned. "In those days I had teeth."

The children all giggled.

"Moving like a shadow, I creep around outside of tent just as they plunge their knives into my blanket. But I am not there, and I listen to them arguing about what to do. So I crouch and wait with my dagger. Soon, the first one, he look out and – swish! – with my dagger I make him a dead man. Then come the next, and – swish! – I make him the same!"

"And the third, Grandfather!" screamed the girl. "What about the third?"

Now on his feet, the aged and stooped Mulazim circled the fire slowly and theatrically with the aid of his staff. He told how the third man sliced his way out the rear of the tent. "His dagger was long and sharp and he was like a giant to me. He say we make a deal, that we work together and make money selling tablet to English. He say I should put down my dagger, that I can trust him, that he my friend."

"What did you *do?*"

Mulazim nodded solemnly and returned to the rock bench on which he had been sitting. "I put down my dagger," he said.

"*No*, Grandfather, what did you *do?*" the children called out in protest.

Mulazim cackled again.

"I *pretend* to lay down my dagger," he said to squeals of excitement, "and old Bedouin, he lunge at me when I bend down. But I not stupid like he think, and I *leap* to side and raise dagger like this—" Mulazim raised his outstretched arm, his hand gripping the dagger, its tip angled toward the sky. "The evil Bedouin, he stumble when I leap to side, and dagger go – *ugh!* – through his neck!"

The children jumped up, cheering, then joining hands as they began dancing wildly around the fire. Mulazim watched them relish what seemed to him like an ancient victory as he remembered with fondness his time with Clayton. He recalled creeping later that night into the tent of the three thieves, and what he found.

"To bed, all of you, it is late!" Mulazim's granddaughter, Hadia, called out, waving her arms and driving the children away to their tents. Several scampered up to kiss Mulazim good night before darting off.

The fiery-eyed young girl, who was Mulazim's favorite, was the last to kiss and hug him, after which she skipped off into the darkness.

"You fill their head with such stories!" said Hadia.

Mulazim shrugged. Another flurry of sparks hissed away into the darkness as a log tumbled deeper to its death.

"It is said people have actually been killed over this legend," Hadia continued. She squatted near her grandfather's feet and rested her arms on his knee. "People think it is real. The *children* think it is real. That it really exists."

The smile faded from Mulazim's face.

"You should tell them the truth," said Hadia.

"What would you have me say?"

"That the tablet of Ishmael is a story you made up to entertain them. Like a movie from America."

"I have never seen a movie from America."

"Grandfather, that is not the point! What matters is that the children think this story is real. That it actually happened."

"Is that so bad?" asked Mulazim, still watching the fire.

"Yes, when it concerns something so dangerous."

Mulazim said nothing and Hadia stood.

"At least think about what I have said," she said.

"I will," he promised.

With a wan smile, Hadia leaned down and kissed Mulazim on the cheek.

"Besides," she said, "we have been coming to this mountain for years and never once have I seen this tablet. If it were real, you would have told me."

An understanding smile was Mulazim's response.

"Good night, Grandfather," she said.

"Good night, my dear," he replied.

Once he was alone, Mulazim gazed again up into the vast starry night. Then, with a contented sigh, he stood and looked down at the bench on which he had been sitting.

It was little more than a pile of mortared rocks, the seat worn smooth from decades of sitting.

But it was, in one important way, much more than a pile of mortared rocks.

With a reflective smile, Mulazim leaned down and reverently brushed his hand across the smooth black stone. There were, of course, no inscriptions on this side.

But there were on the other.

After another glance up into the Sinai's wonderful, wide desert sky, Mulazim hobbled off toward his tent.